*To my close friend Rebecca, who was the
first person to ever read this;
my mother, Anna who hates fiction;
and my late father, Louis, who encouraged me to write*

PROLOGUE

My whole body is shaking like an earthquake and my breathing is rapid and shallow. I feel like all of the air is being sucked out of my lungs and that I'm going to pass out. My whole body is paralysed yet alert with fear. My scalp prickles with numbness and my heart is beating so hard that I'm scared that I'm going to die. I can't think clearly but all I know is that everything is a lie.

It's funny how you think that you know someone, but you realise that you don't really know them at all. That you have no idea about the thoughts that run through their complex mind each and every day. Nor the secrets that they hide beneath their smile; buried deep inside like a shipwreck that has been firmly lodged underneath the ocean for centuries. Undiscovered until now.

It's often the people closest to us that keep the most secrets and who hurt us the most. Once you open Pandora's box of secrets, there's no going back. It's amazing how like a weapon, when you detonate it, a secret has the power to cause destruction in an instant.

I feel like the princess trapped inside of Clara's fairy-tale snow globe; cocooned inside a secure little world only for the globe to smash into a thousand little pieces. The walls of your world shatter, suddenly exposing you to the big scary reality like an animal being released back into the wild. A reality that I didn't know existed. Maybe on some level I knew, but I buried it at the back of the graveyard of my mind. The problem is that ghosts will always find a way to come back to haunt you.

PART ONE

CHAPTER ONE

THURSDAY 24TH MAY

THURSDAY 24TH MAY

The clouds hang like dirty drawn curtains in the dismal grey sky as the rain crashes down like an army ready to attack. That's typical British weather for you. Even in the midst of summer, the season changes like the flick of a switch. As soon as I've got enough money saved, I'm going to book a holiday somewhere with beautiful warm weather like California or Australia. A million miles away from my mundane existence here in London.

It's always been my biggest dream to travel the world. Whenever Elizabeth was in one of her erratic moods, I'd hide under the fusty stained duvet with Snoop, Henry and my old globe. We'd play this game where we'd close our eyes, spin the globe and then take turns reaching out our fingers to point at a random country. Well Henry and I would do this; Snoop would just watch, but he was still very much part of our game. I'd pretend that myself, Snoop and Henry were there in the country that the finger landed on. I'd imagine all of the things that we'd see and all of the adventures that we'd go on.

The realisation that I have so much work to do snaps me out of my thoughts and back into reality. I don't have time to think let alone breathe. I'm working crazy hours and my boss Julio is putting extra pressure on everyone with the opening for the new exhibition. The Waldenburg Gallery is one of the most lucrative gallery chains that there are with chains in New York, Zurich and Milan. Some of the art there sells for millions, though I can't understand why people would want to buy some of it. It's mostly modern art. Some of the pieces there make a mockery of art. However, working here is a good way to get my foot in the door. I hope that the long hours and the measly pay will potentially lead to other opportunities and possibilities. The Waldenburg Gallery can open a lot of doors.

My phone buzzes for the seventh time. I know that it's Elizabeth. I've told her so many times not to call me at work, but she doesn't listen. Sometimes I don't know if she does it on purpose just to annoy me. Elizabeth is like a child sometimes. I reject her call and put my phone on the *do not disturb* mode. I'll deal with Elizabeth tonight, even if I'll pay for it later. If Julio catches me even glancing at my phone, he'll go berserk, especially as the exhibition is right around the corner. Julio is like a hurricane crossed with the Incredible Hulk when he's stressed.

The gallery is so quiet at this time, but I've got to be chained to the desk in case any very important clients ring or come. There also tend to be a lot of last-minute changes, which makes the situation even more stressful. There's still a lot to be done, even though the opening of the new exhibition is not until tomorrow evening. I'm dreading it. I'll be working all the way from eight in the morning until midnight. I've got to be there for the opening, serving canapes and champagne and making small talk.

I hate these openings; they're full of stuffy millionaires with more money than manners or sense for that matter. The men come in their custom-made suits from Emporio Armani and Tom Ford. Women with swollen inflated lips like trout fish and fake breasts like blown-up balloons, wearing outfits that probably cost twice as much as my monthly salary, hang off their arms like limpets.

These people treat me like I'm beneath them because I'm nobody important. To them I'm nothing more than just a gallery assistant and receptionist, even though Felicity does pretty much the same thing. But because she's one of them, it's ok.

Felicity is an intern straight out of university. She managed to skip the recruitment process because her father is one of the sponsors of the gallery. Felicity is one of those posh and rich Surrey girls who grew up having her own horse and living in a huge manor in the country. She also went to one of the top boarding schools in England where only those of aristocratic background are accepted. Also secured for Felicity was a place at Edinburgh to study art history.

Felicity is extremely entitled. For her this opening is an excuse to schmooze and climb the social ladder. She also uses any opening as an excuse to buy herself a new designer dress. Julio says that we need to dress smart yet elegant, but not too casual for the opening. I'm still secretly panicking about what to wear. Julio certainly doesn't hold back on critiquing somebody's fashion sense or lack of. I can tell that he looks down on my Primark rags. Unlike Felicity, I don't have unlimited funds or much time to go shopping. Maybe Magda will let me borrow one of her dresses though they probably won't look good on me.

Magda likes to wear short and sexy dresses that show off her amazing body. If I had a body like Magda, I would show it off too. Magda is your typical Eastern European beauty. Genetically gifted with model height, long legs and good bone structure. I would hate Magda is she wasn't so nice. I can't help feeling like an ugly dwarf next to her. Elizabeth always said that I was never genetically gifted. She always tells me that I should ask these clients at the gallery whether they know a good surgeon.

"I don't know where you get your flat chest from darling; it's certainly not from me. There's nothing wrong with a little help; all the girls do it," Elizabeth would say. As if I have the money for a boob job or any sort of plastic surgery.

We haven't even had time for lunch today as Julio is going crazy. He's only allowed Felicity to leave to go to Starbucks to bring everyone extra strong coffee. I'm surprised that Julio hasn't had a heart attack from all the coffee that he drinks. Every time I see him, there's practically a cup of coffee in his hand. He kind of reminds me of those dolls I had when I was little. The ones with a handbag or something fused or sewn onto their hand. If Julio was a doll, a coffee cup would be his ultimate accessory. Julio doesn't allow us to drink coffee in the gallery, but he constantly breaks his own rule. He thinks because he's the manager, that he can do whatever he pleases.

All of a sudden, things start to get busy and my inbox is inundated with emails from clients asking whether there's vegan and gluten-free catering to what's the most expensive piece of artwork at the exhibition. I don't drink coffee, but maybe I should have taken up Julio's offer. Today we're allowed to have coffees on us in the gallery. I'm so exhausted that I succumb to the offer of a strong Americano. I wince at the pungent and bitter liquid but I force myself to drink it like a child being made to drink disgusting medicine. However, my mind feels sharper afterwards and I'm ready to tackle my heavy workload. I also have a meeting scheduled with a client this afternoon to show around the gallery. It's usually Julio's job but because he's so busy he's left me in charge of all of his appointments. It'll probably be some stuffy and arrogant middle-aged creep with a blatant hair transplant and nothing better to spend his millions on than crap art.

Nevertheless, I feel flattered to be left in charge of this appointment. I just hope that I don't screw it up. I would have thought that Julio would have left Felicity in charge. In fact, Felicity has barely been doing anything whilst I've been working like crazy. She's just been sitting there sending

WhatsApp voice messages to her posh friend with a ridiculous name like Tiggy and scrolling through Instagram when Julio isn't around. I see the panic in her eyes when she hears Julio's shrilling voice and the furious thud of this of his footsteps. She hurriedly shoves her phone behind the desk and tries to look like she's working. Felicity might not care about this job but I do. The last thing I want to do is lose my job and be forced to go back home. Well it's not really home. It's never really felt like home. I don't ever want to go back. It's hard enough to get a job in London, especially a job where you can afford to have your own place. All I've ever wanted was to have my own place.

I'm deliberating getting another strong coffee and Felicity is midway through her voice message to Tiggy when we both hear the door swing open. It must be my client.

"Hello I'm here to see Julio Hernandez," a clipped, deep and calm man's voice says with an American accent. I look up from my computer screen and at take a proper look at my client. I feel my heart miss a beat. The man standing in front of me takes my breath away. He's one of the most gorgeous men I've ever seen in the flesh. Even though many of the clients are attractive, you can tell that they've paid for it with hair transplants, age defying treatments, personal trainers and expensive suits.

This man is different from the usual clients. He's younger for a start; maybe in his early or mid-thirties. Nothing about him seems false or unnatural. He is tall, around six foot two or three, and well built. I can see his muscles straining through his suit. His hair is jet black; as black as a dark night sky and his eyes are a cloudy grey moss colour like a murky sea. His facial features as so perfect and manly and his lips throbbing to be kissed.

The words struggle to form in my mouth and my cheeks flush red. I feel like such an idiot. Just get over it, I tell myself in my head. Get a grip Iris; you're acting like you've never seen a gorgeous guy before. He's probably married or has a girlfriend. Or he's gay. As if he'd be interested in you. Even if he is single and heterosexual, Felicity is most likely his type. Look at her and look at you.

"Um unfortunately Julio is extremely busy today and has asked me to take over his appointments. If you'd rather meet with Julio, I can reschedule for another date," I say. I'm surprised that I can even get the words out of my mouth let alone string a coherent sentence together.

"That won't be necessary, I'd be delighted for you to show me around," he smiles. His smile is intoxicating. His teeth are strong and gleaming like marble. They're natural unlike many of the men with their whitened teeth. I feel my cheeks burn and I suddenly feel stupid. The sheer gorgeousness of this man is enough to make Felicity forget that her iPhone even exists. I can tell that she is enthralled by him; how can anyone not be? He's the type of gorgeous that has everybody in his proximity gawping helplessly.

"Perhaps I could show you around sir. Iris don't you have that other meeting?" Felicity says bossily as though she was my boss. I know that she's desperate to have him all to herself and I don't blame her. I wish I could stand up for myself more and not allow everybody to walk all over me. I might as well allow Felicity to take him, after all she's probably his type. How could she not be? I'm definitely not his type. I'm the dowdy wallflower who blends into the background just as easily as wallpaper. I want to kick myself. This is not a date; this is a client of the gallery! Act professional for goodness sake!

"I'm Felicity Harrington-Astor," Felicity says confidently, stepping in front of me and completely blocking me from his view. She holds out her hand for him to shake but he doesn't take it. Even our snootiest and most elitist clients always follow the handshake etiquette apart from devout Muslim and Orthodox Jewish clients who are forbidden by religion to shake hands with the opposite sex. Perhaps he's an Orthodox Jew; he certainly has a Semitic look about him. However, I don't think he is as he doesn't have a kippah on his head like our Orthodox clients.

"I think I'd like Iris to show me around," he says coldly and I think I nearly faint. I must have heard wrong, but Felicity hasn't. She's persistent about showing him around.

"But Iris you're busy at the moment, aren't you?" Felicity says in a superior manner, as though she's my boss.

"I'm sure that Iris can spare a few minutes from her busy schedule, can't you Iris?"

I can see the rage on Felicity's face. I feel smug but intrigued that this gorgeous man wants me over the tall model-like blonde bombshell that Felicity is. Perhaps he's gay and doesn't want to give her the wrong impression. That's probably what it is.

"I'm Eric Irving," he says, sticking out his hand to shake mine. His hand is large, firm and strong. I place my small dainty cold hand in his big warm one and my body feels as though electricity is running through my veins at the mere touch of his skin. I mentally tell myself to stop it and act normal and professionally.

"I'm Iris Shaw," I say.

"It's a pleasure to meet you Iris, please show me to the gallery," Eric says. His eyes linger on mine for a few seconds and again I feel the electricity. I realise that our hands are still touching. I pull back my hand and lead him through to the gallery. I can see Felicity seething out of the corner of my eye. I know that she's never really liked me but now she must positively hate me. I know that Felicity is recently single after dumping her equally posh boyfriend Giles or Jeremy after he cheated on her on a wild lad's holiday in Kos. Since becoming single, she's been on countless dates from the stories that she regales Tiggy with.

Felicity is lucky that she gets to go on dates. I don't have time for dating and even if I did, I'm completely useless at it. I completely clam up and never know what to say or what questions to ask. I must come across as a complete bore. I never have interesting stories or witty anecdotes to share. I don't watch the latest TV shows or have exciting plans to talk about. I'm not confident and flirty and sexy. I don't know how to be. People say that you should be yourself on a date but that's probably the worst advise anyone could give especially if you're me. If I were a good actress, I'd be anyone but me.

As I lead Eric into the gallery, I feel his eyes glance me up and down. I tell myself to stop imagining things.

"So, this is one of our latest pieces and the one that a lot of clients are bidding for," I say, showing Eric one of our newest pieces of modern art, which consists of a painted grey canvas with splodges of red.

"Do you like it Iris?" he asks me. None of the clients have ever asked me for my personal opinions about any of the paintings. My opinion has never mattered.

"Well...," I start. My personal opinion on most of the pieces in this gallery is that they're complete rubbish and a two-year-old could do better blindfolded, however I can't say that to the clients. I have to promote the art and make the clients want to buy it.

I struggle to find the words to portray this joke of a painting in a politically correct way. "It's not something that I would personally go for, but I can understand why it's so popular. I guess it has a lot of hidden depths that really speak to people. The artist bases his art on communism and I think he's trying to portray the bleakness of it and the red symbolises communism."

Eric bursts into peels of laughter. I can see the glint of joviality reflected in his eyes.

"I know that you're trying to say that it's a piece of shit. Don't worry, I completely agree. What kind of art do you like then Iris?" I like the way that he says my name; the fact that he even calls me by my name. A majority of the clients always forget my name or don't even bother asking for it in the first place.

"I like real art; art that really speaks to people and isn't pretentious. Art that captivates you and tells you a story. I love artists that know how to use colour," I say.

"Do you paint?" he asks.

"Yes." I love to paint; it's one of my favourite things in the world. In my spare time when I'm not working or sleeping, I paint.

"Do you display any of your works here?"

"Of course not! None of the customers here would be interested in my artwork."

I asked Julio ages ago if I could display any of my art, but he said it's not the type of art that the clients here are looking for.

"Dahling you're a great artist, but clients here aren't looking for paintings of pretty landscapes and cute animals. They want something more unique, more edgy," Julio said. Despite the blow, being called a "great artist" by Julio is like being told you're a great singer by Simon Cowell.

"Why don't you show me your art?" Eric says.

"It's not that good," I mutter shyly.

"It's got to be better than this crap," he laughs. I find myself laughing too. He looks at me intensely with those captivating eyes and I think my stomach must be a bird cage set free of a dozen birds. I could gaze at him all day.

"Why don't you show me your favourite piece of artwork here?" Eric asks.

Out of all of the paintings my current favourite has to be *A Night In Paris* by an artist called Betty Sanger.

"Her style reminds me of a cross between Van Gogh and Chagall. I just love the use of colour and the tenderness. It's so dream-like but real at the same time," I say.

"It's a beautiful piece. You clearly have good taste."

We stand in silence for a few moments; I feel his eyes burn on me. Our blissful silence is interrupted by Julio's shrill voice.

"Iris I need you to help out in the exhibition hall," Julio says abruptly. "Hello you must be Eric Irving; I'm Julio Hernandez, manager." I can tell that Julio is just as mesmerised by Eric as I am.

"I'll take over Iris," Julio says sharply.

"Thank you very much Iris for showing me around, you've been absolutely marvellous," Eric beams. I can't help glowing inside. I've never been praised so openly by a client before.

"It was a pleasure to meet you," I say.

"Likewise." I meet his eyes for the final time and I feel the spark pass between our eyes like strong currents. Even when I turn back and walk towards the exhibition hall, I feel his eyes burning into me like a flame.

CHAPTER TWO

When I get home at ten in the evening, I'm ready to drop. I don't know how I'm going to have enough energy to last until tomorrow evening. The exhibition will probably go on until about midnight. I still haven't chosen what to wear for it. My mind keeps wandering back to Eric and our encounter. Knowing me, I'm probably misreading all the signals anyway. Elizabeth always said I had a wild imagination. I still can't help hoping that he'll be there tomorrow.

I rifle through my wardrobe for something apt to wear tomorrow. I don't have that many clothes. I don't really go out very much so I have no outfits suitable for bars and clubs or nice events and occasions. In my spare time I usually just wear jeans and plain tops, most of which are covered in flecks of paint. I spend most of my time painting so it wouldn't make sense to wear nice clothes only to get paint on them. The only other clothes that I have are work clothes; smart blouses, plain black skirts and warm cardigans. I try on the only two dresses that I own, which are both formal work dresses. Both are plain and shapeless.

I tell myself to stop being so stupid and making an effort for a guy who probably isn't into me. For all I know he might not even come to the exhibition tomorrow night, but I know that it's a very important event and that all of the art dealers will be there. I really hope that I see Eric there tomorrow night but I don't want him to think that I look frumpy and unstylish.

I knock on Magda's door, hoping that she might be able to hear me through the Polish rap music that is blaring through the loud speakers. Magda loves nothing better than turning up her music on full blast and dancing around to it. I try knocking even louder but she doesn't hear me, so I just walk in. I know that Magda doesn't mind; she's not one of those people who gets really uptight about privacy. Magda's the type of person who leaves the bathroom door open whilst she's shaving her legs or doing a wee.

Magda beams at me and pulls me to dance with her. I wish that I was as confident and as vibrant as Magda. Magda would probably be the flatmate from hell for most people. She listens to loud music during unsociable hours; she's really loud and she's really messy, but I don't mind. I can't stand quiet for too long; it makes me feel even lonelier and it makes it especially harder to switch off the dark thoughts that swim around in my mind like sharks ready to attack.

I think the fact that Magda and I are so different is the reason that we get along so well. I wouldn't want to be friends with someone as dull as myself. I've never really had any real friends. Well never any proper long-term friends. Magda is the first and only real friend that I have. She's been there for me in my darkest moments.

"Magda can I borrow one of your dresses for the gallery opening tomorrow?" I shout over the music.

She turns the music down. "Sure, I thought that you'd never ask."

Magda always tries to lend me her things, but I always say no. Magda loves clothes and is always buying so much stuff that it doesn't even fit in her wardrobes and cupboards. She often leaves the clothes that she's bought in their original bags. She's always going through her wardrobe and getting rid of things that she doesn't want anymore. She always says that there's a dress or top that doesn't look good on her, but would totally suit me.

Everything looks ridiculously amazing on Magda; no wonder she buys so many clothes. Although Magda and I are close in dress size; she has the perfect figure equipped with boobs, a bum and hips. I'm just straight up and down like a boy. Some of her clothes hang off me and make me look shapeless and child-like because I've got no curves to fill them out.

"You never usually like to dress up, what's going on?" Magda laughs. This is indeed very out of character for me. So many times Magda has begged me to come on nights out with her. On the rare occasions that I would go, Magda would spend hours getting ready whilst I'd pull on jeans and a top. Magda, outraged that I couldn't go out like that, would try to unsuccessfully cajole me into a makeover. Even with a full makeover, I'm an ugly duckling next to Magda.

"I just want to look nice for tomorrow evening; you never know who I might meet and what opportunities it might hold, so it's important that I try to look my best."

"There's a guy isn't there?"

"What? No, of course not," I protest.

"I can see it in your eyes and you usually never make this much effort"

"It's not effort really, I just want to look nice. Maybe it's time I started taking care of my appearance a bit more."

"That's what I keep telling you! You're so beautiful Irenka, but it's like you want to hide your beauty." Magda likes to call me Irenka because she says I'm like her sister, so I should have a Polish name.

"I'm not beautiful Magda, please stop it."

"You stop it, you know I'm not just saying it. I'm Polish and if you were ugly, you'd know about it." We both laugh.

Magda finds me a beautiful smart black knee-length dress with a small V-neck opening. Although it's a bit loose on me, it has a belt around the middle and when pulled tightly the dress doesn't look so loose. I actually look sophisticated. Magda gives me a wolf whistle.

I thank Magda for the dress and head straight to bed as I'm so exhausted. I pull out my phone and see five missed calls from Elizabeth. I sigh. I'm completely and utterly exhausted but I'd better ring her or else I'll never hear the end of it. Most people would say that I should just cut Elizabeth out of my life, but it's not that easy. Apart from me and her cats she has no one. I wonder what the rant of the day is going to be about. Before I used to allow Elizabeth's moods to bring me down, but now I try and find humour in it. I bet you ten pounds that she's going to have a rant about how she wishes that she had aborted me and how I'm the worst daughter in the world for abandoning her. Twenty pounds that she's broken up with Rick again and wants to kill herself.

"Darling!" a cheerful voice trills through the phone. Lucky for me she's in one of her good moods today. I'd rather deal with her on a good day than a bad one.

"I've been trying to get hold of you all day darling, but I know that you're so busy with work. You career girls; you work up to your ears and then cry bitterly when all of your eggs shrivel up. I know you say that you don't want children Iris darling, but I would love to be a grandmother. Can't you think about me for once? Anyway, Gilly at my church club has a new baby granddaughter and she is just the most adorable little thing. If you saw her Iris you would want to get knocked up immediately, I promise you," Elizabeth prattles incessantly.

This is rich coming from the woman who wishes that she had me aborted.

"A baby isn't the latest must have accessory. Anyway, what church club are you on about? You're not even religious mum!"

"Darling you know how much it infuriates me when you call me mum; it makes me feel so old. Anyway, I listened to what you said about going out and trying to make some friends. See I do listen to you darling. They're ever so nice at the church and the vicar isn't bad looking either; shame that he's married." I snort to myself. Married men have never put Elizabeth off before.

"What's so funny darling?" she demands.

"Oh nothing, I was just about to sneeze," I lie. "So you and Rick are over for good I take it."

"Of course not darling; he just said that we need to take a break. He said that he wants me to prove to him that I can stop drinking and start taking my meds. I've joined an AA group down at the church and I'm taking my medication again; isn't that wonderful?"

"Hmm," I say doubtfully. This is not the first time that Elizabeth has promised that.

"This time it's for real darling; I've realised that I need to change."

"It's a shame that you couldn't realise that when you had kids," I say cuttingly.

"Oh darling let's not go there. You know how hard it was for me being a single mother and I didn't have anybody." With Elizabeth there are always excuses.

"Fine, well I hope that you want to change because of you, not because of Rick. Rick is hardly an angel himself."

Rick along with Elizabeth's other ex-boyfriends, is a useless waste of space. He's a misogynistic lout who believes that a woman's place is in the kitchen. He's got a drinking problem himself and an even bigger gambling problem.

"You're so judgemental darling; you don't even know him." What Elizabeth does with her life is none of my business. I don't particularly care for Rick nor do I particularly want to get to know him. It's just frustrating when Elizabeth rings me after they've had another blazing row because he's been talking to other women online or because he's gone off for days without letting her know where he is. Whenever they go through a bad patch, he's the worst man in the world and she can't stand the sight of him, but when they go through a good patch, all is forgiven.

"Whatever, as long as he makes you happy." I don't bother to argue with Elizabeth.

"You need to find yourself a boyfriend darling. You know that I worry about you. I keep telling you that you should put yourself out there more."

Elizabeth is the last person who I would take dating advise from. In her opinion the only way to get a man's interest is to dress like a hooker and act like one, which I have no interest in doing. I'd rather be single than end up with the type of men that Elizabeth attracts. Men who only care about one thing. I'm careful to avoid those kinds of men.

I've never been lucky with guys. When I was at school, all of the boys fancied Elizabeth, not me. Elizabeth was always like the hot big sister. Whenever I go out with Magda, all the guys drool over her like dogs. I don't ever really get asked out. Magda says that I need to be more confident and all the guys will want me just like that. It's hard to feel confident when Magda looks like a model from the pages of a magazine.

I tell Elizabeth that I'm exhausted and need to go to bed, hanging up before she can keep me on the phone for any longer. I collapse into my bed and fall into a deep dreamless sleep.

FRIDAY 25TH MAY

Waking up is usually always pure torture, but this morning I feel energised and excited. Excited that I might see Eric tonight. Even though I tell myself to stop being so ridiculous, I can't help but feel happy. The sun streams through my window as I pull back the thin beige curtains and the birds singing outside gives me a warm peaceful feeling inside. For once I don't even put my alarm on snooze. Instead, I shower and from the back of my wardrobe, I pull out the make-up kit that Elizabeth got me last Christmas. I dab some smoky grey eyeshadow on my eyelids and successfully manage not to poke myself in the eye with the mascara wand. I even add a bit of plum coloured lip-gloss on my lips and dusty rose blush on my cheeks. I hope that I haven't overdone it with the make-up. I don't usually wear make-up very often so I'm not very skilled at applying it.

When I come into work, I get an email from Julio asking me to come into the office. My heart is pounding. Maybe I'm going to get fired. Julio never usually calls me into his office. Maybe I've done something wrong. All of a sudden, my mouth feels dry and my palms are clammy. I rack my brains trying to think of anything that I could have done to get myself fired. Or maybe I'm just not a good fit here or one of the clients complained about me. My legs wobble from beneath me as I nervously knock on the door. Julio summons me in and gestures for me to sit opposite him.

"Iris do you know why I've called you here?" Julio asks.

"No." My heart is in my mouth at this point. Perhaps I'm in trouble for something. Perhaps I was being unprofessional around Eric.

"As you know Gabriella is going on maternity leave soon and I will need someone to take her place as assistant manager."

He's probably going to tell me that Felicity got the job. I know that Felicity has had her beady eye on the assistant manager role. I didn't even bother to apply as I knew that she'd probably get it. Nepotism gets you places, especially in this industry.

"I know that you've chosen Felicity, but thanks for giving me the heads up. I'll make sure to congratulate her."

Julio looks at me as though I'm crazy and wrinkles his nose like there's a bad smell in the room.
"Felicity? Are you serious? The girl is completely and utterly useless. If her father wasn't one of our sponsors, I'd have her fired straight away. I've called you here because I want you to take the role as assistant manager. I see the hard work you put into keeping this gallery running and your dedication. You're so efficient and you get everything done. I feel like I can rely on you. Also, I've had positive feedback from clients".

Positive feedback from Eric, my inner voice tells me.

"You want me to be assistant manager?" I repeat.

"I don't know why you're so surprised. I'm hoping that you'll say yes. This is a really big thing. You'll be getting paid more and you'll be more involved with the clients and the artists. They'll even be opportunities to travel and work more closely with international branches."

I can't believe this. I never even expected to get the assistant manager role so this is a huge shock, but a good one. I know that Felicity will be fuming, but I don't care. I'm so happy that I could cry for joy. Julio has never given me any praise or indication that I'm good at my job. All Julio ever does is rush around in a blind panic, snapping at everyone and demanding that we don't just sit there.

"Yes of course I'll take the job," I say.

"Fantastic! I wish there were more people like you here. By the way are you wearing that dress to the exhibition tonight?"

I look down at my dress and start to panic. Perhaps it's not smart or stylish enough.

"Er yes."

"It's fabulous darling, I love it! You look great in it; it really suits you. You look different today. I'm sure that Eric won't be able to keep his eyes off you tonight."

"Eric is coming tonight?"

"Of course he is; this is a very big night. God he is such a gorgeous man; if only he were gay," Julio sighs sadly.

"How do you know? He could be gay."

"Dahling as a gay man, you just know when a man is gay and when he's not. Eric is definitely not gay. Anyway, off to work now. There's still a lot to do but before you do that, get yourself a coffee and a pastry on me; you could do with something to eat." He reaches into his wallet and hands me a ten-pound note.

"Really Julio, you don't have to."

"I insist, it's a congratulations present from me. Now get out of here!" Julio says sharply, but he's smiling. I have the urge to throw my arms around him and give him a massive hug, but Julio doesn't strike me as a hugger. The confirmation that Eric isn't gay lifts my spirits further. *Just because he's not gay, doesn't mean that he's into you*, the voice in my head tells me. He's probably married or has a steady girlfriend. He was just being friendly. I don't stand a chance.

***

Felicity is in a foul mood after finding out that I got the promotion, though she tries to act like she isn't bothered. As stuck-up and unpleasant as Felicity is, I can't help but feel a bit bad for her.

"I know that you really wanted the job. I'm really sorry that you didn't get it. I'm sure that they'll be other opportunities."

"I don't really care; I'll find something far better anyway. It's only an assistant manager job anyway; you'll practically be doing the same thing as you do now anyway, just longer hours and only for five and a half grand extra. It's not like you have what it takes to get much further than being an assistant manager," Felicity retorts superciliously. I ignore her cruel jibes and get ready to tackle my heavy workload but Felicity continues her bitter tirade.

"Is that make-up that you're wearing?" she sneers. "Trying to impress Eric? He'll soon realise that you're just a nobody and that you don't belong in his world. I'm more his ilk. Look at me and look at you in your cheap dress. Is that from Primark?"

"Are you done yet?" I say nonchalantly. "Unlike you, I actually do my job and I suggest that you do yours. Since I'll be assistant manager, I'll be in charge of making sure that you actually work, not sit around on Instagram all day."

Felicity's mouth falls wide open, but nothing comes out of it. Felicity thinks that I'm meek and quiet, but not anymore. I have a new found confidence. Felicity doesn't say anything else and for the rest of the day she actually does some actual work. The hours fly by as I'm so busy but as the opening approaches, my stomach lurches and I get butterflies in my stomach at the thought of seeing Eric.

I can't remember the last time I had the butterfly type of feelings for a guy since my teenage crush; a boy in the year above me in school called Toby. All of the girls fancied him.

He only dated the pretty, popular and confident girls with big boobs and blonde hair. He never even as much as glanced in my direction.

My first and only boyfriend was a guy called Dan at university. That was years ago. We dated for about two months but he broke up with me because he said that he felt that he wasn't ready for a relationship. I was pretty gutted as I had lost my virginity to him and he told me that he really liked me. Looking back, I don't think that I really had very strong feelings for him. I think that the only reason I dated him was because he was the first guy who showed any real interest in me.

Dan and Eric are worlds apart! Dan was attractive in that arty and creative Indie lead singer kind of way; skinny with floppy hair and T-Shirts with the names and images of famous rock bands printed on them. Eric is the guy that everybody desires. One look is enough to have everybody hooked. Eric is out of this world. He's like the movie star that every woman fantasizes about; a million miles away from reality. Maybe Felicity was right, maybe it's all in my head that he has any iota of interest in me. Felicity is the kind of girl that he belongs with.

I wish that I was blonde and blue-eyed like Felicity or dark haired and tanned like Magda; both tall, pretty and slender with curves in the right places. I'm an average five foot four inches with the figure of a boy. Even if I gained weight, I still wouldn't have any shape or curves. My hair is dark brown, but I'm too pale to be exotic looking. My lips are thin, my muddy brown eyes too small and my nose slightly crooked. I hardly sound like a pin-up. Even Dan said that I wasn't his usual type, which was blonde, busty and curvy.
However, I feel a new found confidence that I never felt before. Despite what Felicity says, I feel good in my "cheap" dress and make up. I redo my make-up and spray myself with a fruity scent that I found from a gift set that Magda gave me for

Christmas, which I never opened until I found it at the back of my wardrobe, stuffed together with Elizabeth's make-up set.

***

It's ten to nine and my feet are killing me. I've probably done at least ten thousand steps in the past hour, walking around offering guests champagne and canapés, which they greedily guzzle. It's even harder making my way through the hordes of people that congregate in the gallery. I sharply keep my eyes out for Eric, but even amongst the crowd of people I don't spot him. My good mood suddenly plummets. Perhaps he isn't coming after all. Perhaps I needlessly built up all of this excitement and misread the signals. He most probably only just likes me in a professional capacity. I suddenly feel so stupid and pathetic. I feel like I've been stood up for a date. I have the sudden urge to go to the bathroom and cry.

"Cheer up darling, have some champagne," Maurice says cheerfully. Maurice Greenberg is one of our most regular clients and probably one of the perviest. He's in his sixties or seventies, but that doesn't stop him from eyeing up girls more than half his age. He's clearly not fussy when it comes to women. He likes them fat or thin, tall or short. Maurice himself is fat, short and bald.

"Oy Iris you're looking very fine tonight, did you get all dressed up for me?" Maurice chortles, laughing at his own lame joke.

"Hello Maurice, I hope that you're enjoying the exhibition," I say, trying to deter him from anymore smutty talk.

"Oh absolutely, but I'm enjoying it even better now that I've seen you." I can feel his small and squinty grey eyes scan my body. I try to quickly think of a way to politely get away.

"It's great to see you Maurice, but there's something that I've remembered that I need to do."

"I don't want to hold you up darling, but if you ever want to go for dinner, do give me a call," Maurice says.

"Will do," I lie and rush off before he can try to lure me back into conversation.

The more that I feel the minutes slipping away, the more anxious I get when I can't spot Eric. It's almost half past nine and I'm losing hope. I tell myself not to let myself get caught up over some guy that I don't even know and could have any woman he wants. I'm not sixteen anymore. I'm twenty-three and need to stop acting like a teenager with a crush. This is so out of character for me. Whatever I tell myself, I can't get rid of that anxious feeling. When nobody's looking, I sneak back into the kitchen and sneak a glass of prosecco. I rarely drink, especially not at work, but I need something to ease my nerves.

"Somebody's thirsty!" I hear a familiar voice say.

The shock makes me drop my glass. It shatters into a dozen pieces all over the floor.

"Shit!" I curse.

"Here let me help you."

It really is him. He's here and he's even more gorgeous than when I last saw him if that's even possible. My heart is beating as though there's a heavy rock concert going on inside of my chest. He crouches down on the floor beneath me and starts scooping up the fragments of glass with a dustpan and brush. The sheer proximity of him takes my breath away. I long to take his smooth clean-shaven face in my hands and bury my head in his aftershave scented chest. He smells heavenly and his shirt is so ivory and crisp, reminding me of the story in religious studies at school, where Jesus wore the whitest clothes. Not that I'm religious or anything, but for some reason it just reminded me of that. I have the urge to put my hand underneath that pristinely white shirt and run my hands over his stomach. I wonder what his stomach looks like. I can't imagine it being anything other than toned, hard and buff; not far off of one that belongs to a male fitness model.

"I didn't mean to scare you," he says.

"It's fine, though what were you doing in here?" I want to kick myself for sounding so accusatory. Non-staff aren't really supposed to be in here.

"I saw you come in here and I just wanted to talk to you. Anything wrong with that?"

"No not at all." My heart is really hammering at full speed.

"You look gorgeous." Did Eric really just call me gorgeous? Nobody has ever called me gorgeous before.

"You should really believe in yourself more Iris; you're beautiful." I've never been called beautiful before. Not even by Elizabeth and supposedly every mother tells her daughter that she's beautiful.

We're standing right in front of one another; there's barely an inch between us. I want to take the moment and kiss him. It sounds crazy, especially as I barely know him. I don't want to ruin the moment plus just because he complimented me doesn't mean that he's single or available. Also, what if I'm a bad kisser? I haven't kissed anyone in God knows how long.

"I think I should head back; I've been gone a while." I don't want Julio to notice that I've been skiving and change his mind about my promotion. I panic at the thought. I'm breaking all of the rules; drinking on the job and bordering on behaving unprofessionally towards a client.

"I don't want to get you in trouble. I've also got to speak to these wretched investors and agents and of course the artist himself. His work looks like a pile of shit, but apparently he's the next big thing." We both snigger.

The artist whose works we're exhibiting is a Finnish interior designer whose work is based on the soul and the environmental crisis. It's all pretentious rubbish. His works consist of photographs of people meditating and interior designs comprises of mirrors and nude sculptures made of rubbish. It is pretty awful and devoid of any meaning, but I have to pretend that his work is akin to Michelangelo. I'm sure that Michelangelo would be appalled at would people would consider "art."

I can't take my eyes off of Eric the whole night. I can sense him watch me as well out of the corner of those intense gold-green eyes. I see him standing with a group of people. Although his stance appears to be intimidating, it also denotes confidence and ease. The group of people that he's standing with appear to be enthralled with him and it's not hard to see why. From the expressions on their faces, they drink in every word that he's saying. Whenever he laughs, they laugh, as though he's told the most hilarious joke that they've ever heard.

I'm so distracted by Eric that I almost spill the drinks on a woman's dress. Luckily, I manage to grab the champagne flutes just in time. The woman scowls at me and tells me to watch where I'm going. I mutter a quick apology, but I'm too happy to care. I can see the women, both young and old, eyeing up Eric and waiting for their chance to make a beeline. However, despite the attention, Eric doesn't seem phased or even interested by their presence.

My feet are killing me and I'm dying to sit down. I have floaters in my eyes from the intense strobe lights and my head starts to hurt from the mixture of bizarre alternative music and the chatter of voices that fill the room. As I take a seat for a minute, a woman with large artificial lips like a goldfish and equally large artificial breasts poking out from her expensive looking gold sequined dress, takes a seat next to me. It's hard to tell how old she is from the combination of make-up and surgery. She could be older or she could be younger than me.

"Wow isn't he gorgeous?" the woman says in an accent that sounds like it could be Russian. It's clear that she means Eric. I nod in agreement.

"Do you know if he's single?" the woman asks. I shake my head.

"Look he's coming over, oh my God!" the woman squeals clutching my arm with her perfectly manicured gold nails; as though we're best friends.

"Hi there, I'm Valeria Malekovich," the woman says, extending her arm out towards Eric.

"Eric Irving, nice to meet you," Eric says casually, shaking her hand, but not really making eye contact with her.

"Are you an art dealer as well? Do you know my father Nikolai Malekovich?"

"The name rings a bell yes."

Valeria makes eyes at me that indicate that it's my cue to leave. I take the cue. Eric is obviously more suited to this beautiful and wealthy Russian princess.

"So would you like to grab a drink afterwards?" Valeria says, fluttering her long, obviously false eyelashes at Eric.

"I'm sorry, but I'm afraid I can't. Do excuse me, I must go," Eric says, leaving Valeria and heading towards me. I see the aghast and furious expression on Valeria's face. It's probably the most natural expression that her face has allowed her to make. She's just as gobsmacked as I am as Eric rushes in my direction towards me.

"Iris I'm about to head back, but I wanted to ask you if you'd like to have dinner with me sometime?" Eric asks.

"You mean you don't want to have dinner with the Russian Princess?"

Eric laughs. "Come on you must be kidding. I've dated enough rich princesses to know that they're a complete nightmare. Girls like Valeria are high-maintenance, spoilt daddy's princesses who expect everybody to treat them like royalty. I like girls like you; modest, natural and unspoilt."

"So, you don't have a wife or a girlfriend?" I ask boldly.

"I wouldn't be asking you for dinner if I did. You are funny Iris," Eric laughs. I can't believe that a man like Eric could be single. It seems inconceivable. Men like Eric aren't single. Unless they're players of course. Eric doesn't seem like the type who's a player. He rejected Felicity and the Russian Princess. Surely if he were a player, he'd be all over every woman in the room and lap up their attention. How can a man like Eric who is so good-looking, funny, charming and definitely not a player, be single?

"So will you come to dinner with me?"

"Yes of course."

"Brilliant. I'll book a table at The Vine. If you message me your address, I'll get a car to come pick you up." Eric hands me his gold-plated business card. I've never been to a restaurant like The Vine before; only celebrities and very wealthy people go to places like that. I've never been anywhere remotely posh or classy. This doesn't feel real in any way. Things like getting asked out by gorgeous wealthy men only happen in movies like *Pretty Woman* and *Fifty Shades of Grey*. Things like this don't happen in real life to ordinary girls like me, do they?

CHAPTER THREE

"I can't believe that you're going on a date with this guy!" Magda squeals. "Not only is he gorgeous, he's ridiculously rich too."

Magda and I are sitting in the lounge, eating brunch with the TV on in the background. I tell her about my upcoming date with Eric and she wants to know everything. We look him up online (Magda's idea). There's not an awful lot of information, but there are enough articles to know that Eric's net worth is around five-hundred million dollars and that he comes from a wealthy family. His father, Eric Irving II is also in the art business. According to Forbes, the Irving Family is one of the richest and most prominent families in America. There are a few headshots of Eric on Google Images. He looks like an actor or a model in those shots, rather than a prominent businessman.

"Wow you're so lucky Irenka! I'm so so jealous!" Magda shrieks.

"But you've got Arek," I point out. Arek is Magda's boyfriend. They've been together on and off for about two years. Magda always moans that he's possessive, drinks too much and doesn't approve of her modelling. There are times when they have blazing rows, but other times they seem completely loved up. Arek is a bit rough around the edges, but I know that he's crazy about Magda. Even though Arek shares the big double room with Magda, he's hardly ever around. He's either working or going out drinking with his mates and his brother, which Magda doesn't like.

"I'd definitely swap him for your Eric. Eric doesn't happen to have a super-hot single brother, does he?" Magda laughs. "Anyway, I'm really happy for you Irenka, you really deserve this! I just hope that your luck rubs off on me. Now let's get you dressed up for this date! I think we should go shopping!"

Shopping is one of Magda's favourite activities. I'm usually not a fan of shopping, but I have to admit that even I'm excited. I want to look my best for tonight. After rummaging through my wardrobe, I can't find anything that isn't too casual or too smart for a date. It's arranged that I'm meeting Eric at 8pm for dinner at The Vine.

Magda and I finish the rest of our toast and eggs, get ready and get the tube down to Oxford Street. We spend hours going in and out of various stores and trying on different things. We find a beautiful maroon Bardot-style dress in the sale at Topshop. It's skin tight and sexy. It's surprisingly very flattering. I've come to realise that tight-fitted dresses suit my body shape and add some curves. Magda also persuades me to buy a push-up bra, which I feel a bit dubious about but when I try it on it transforms my B-cup chest into a D, so I buy it. I realise that I don't have any heels so I buy a pair of not too high simple red velvet heels that go with my dress. I also buy some pretty new tops, skinny jeans and a leather skirt from Primark. I've never brought so many clothes before, but I feel invigorated. I feel a new sense of confidence that I never felt before.

Elizabeth would faint if she saw me especially as I've always rejected her offers of girly mother-daughter shopping trips. Shopping trips with Elizabeth are a nightmare. She constantly criticises my choices to the point that I don't bother trying anything on. The whole focus turns to Elizabeth as she parades around trying on countless items, whilst asking me if she looks fat. Elizabeth knows that she isn't fat; she only does it because she's fishing for compliments. It's exhausting having a mother who thinks that the world constantly revolves around her.

***

Magda and I are both exhausted when we get back home, but in a good way. I really enjoyed the shopping trip with Magda. Magda is great with fashion and knowing what suits somebody. I never knew that different clothes could make me feel so confident. I promise Magda that I'll throw out my baggy t-shirts, old jeans and sensible skirts and blouses.

I only have time for a quick rest before I have to start getting ready for my date. I can't remember the last time that I went on a date or a date worth getting excited about for that matter. I remember an awful date that I had with a guy whom I met on a dating app. It was all Magda's idea to sign up for it. I was only on the app for two weeks before I decided to delete it. One of the guys that I met on the app looked completely different from his pictures and if that wasn't bad enough, the conversation was non-existent. Beyond small talk, there was nothing else to talk about. We kept glancing at our phones and made intermittent comments about tea and coffee and what a sunny day it was. After we finished our drinks, we made our excuses to leave. I never heard from him again, not that I particularly wanted to anyway.

The second date that I went on from the dating app was also disheartening. Although the second date was more attractive and talkative, it didn't go anywhere. I thought that things went well, especially when at the end of the date he kissed me and said that he wanted to see me again. He never contacted me after that. I sent him a message the next day but he never responded. I decided to delete the app, especially as I had read more horrible dating stories from the people using them. That must have been last year.

I suddenly sense a rise of panic welling up inside of me like a volcano. What if this date goes badly as well? What if we have nothing to talk about and Eric finds me boring? What if it doesn't go anywhere and I get all excited for nothing? I think about cancelling the date, but Magda tells me not to be ridiculous or she'll go on the date with Eric herself.

"If he turns out to be an idiot or if you're not compatible then it's a sign from God that it wasn't meant to be. My mother says that every frog you kiss is another frog closer to finding the right one."

Magda does my make-up for me. I never really made much effort with make-up despite Elizabeth always buying me make-up sets. I guess I didn't want to be like Elizabeth so I tried so hard to be different. I was always the sensible adult whilst Elizabeth was the careless and reckless teenager who would go out on wild nights out and dates, only to return the next morning. I was used to being the "mum". Even Henry used to call me mum.

Being the "mum", I never really had the chance to be a teenager and do teenage things. Someone had to be the responsible one. Instead of experimenting with make-up and going out with friends and boys, I would stay up late, working out how to pay all of the bills so that our electricity wouldn't get cut off and that we didn't get evicted. I had to stay home and make food for Henry; help him with his homework and put him to bed. Elizabeth seldom did these things.

I feel that I'm not used to having fun and doing nice things for myself, because I've had to be the sensible one for so long. Maybe it's time to let my hair down and focus on me. I want this to be a new era of my life. When I look in the mirror, I look more confident and mature. I don't look young and naive. I'm usually mistaken for a sixteen-year-old but now I look my age. I look like a real woman. Magda has painted my lips a bold scarlet and my eyeliner rimmed eyes look a radiant golden hazel. My cheeks look full with the port wine blush and my skin smooth and beige from the foundation. I like this look. Magda also puts my hair up in an elaborate twisty plait.

"Oh wow! Irenka you look so gorgeous, what a laska! Eric is going to faint when he sees you." Arek pokes his head around the door and nearly drops his beer.

"Wow Irenka you look so beautiful!" he gasps. For the first time I feel almost as beautiful as Magda.

At seven-thirty on the dot, the chauffeur that Eric sent arrives. The driver leads me over to a gleaming Mercedes and opens the door for me. Magda and Arek stand there with their mouths hanging wide open. I can hear them both swearing in Polish. Magda hugs me tight and wishes me luck. I need it more than ever.

"I really hope that he's the one for you Irenka! I mean his chauffeur drives a Mercedes and he's taking you to The Vine! This is like real life Pretty Woman." We both laugh. I'm so nervous. I'm so worried that this is too good to be true.

In the car my palms are clammy with sweat and my stomach is in knots. The chauffeur is courteous and makes polite small talk, but we soon lapse into an awkward silence. I wonder if he does this all the time; chauffeuring different women to go on dates with Eric. I try to sink back into the plush leather and relax but I can't sit still. I can't help but wonder if I'm making a mistake going on this date. Before I have the chance to change my mind, the chauffeur pulls up outside of The Vine. It looks so grand yet modern with the large gleaming panelled glass offering a glimpse into the large space filled with polished marble tables and velvet vermilion red armchairs.

When I step inside, it's even grander than it looks on the outside. The pearl and gold marble pillars and floor twinkle underneath the light of the chandeliers like stars. Rich ruby and canary gold embroidered rugs bearing the initial *V* bedeck the floor. Soft jazz music fills the room, adding to the elegant and refined ambience of the place. I've never been anywhere like this before.

The restaurant is busy but not crowded. Fashionable, well-groomed and wealthy-looking people sit at the tables and by the bar. The people blend into the sumptuous background as though they were in a painting. This isn't a place for ordinary people like me. Across the room, I spy a plastic-looking woman in a tight black and gold designer dress with a tiny chihuahua perched on her lap. Opposite her sits a much older man with receding grey hair and a paunch visible underneath his suit. I wonder if they're on a date or perhaps it's more innocent. Maybe they're father and daughter or uncle and niece. I'm roused from my thoughts by an impeccable and pretty hostess. She's wearing a crisp white shirt, a red skirt and jacket with a gold embossed V on the pocket.

"Do you have a reservation?" she asks politely but sharply in an accent that sounds like it could be Polish or Russian. She looks me up and down like I'm not the kind of person who belongs here. Can she tell that my clothes and jewellery aren't expensive?

"Um I'm supposed to be meeting Eric Irving III here," I say uncomfortably. The hostess suddenly gives me a wide smile.

"Ah of course, please follow me."

I follow the hostess to the back of the restaurant to a more private looking area. There he is scrolling through his phone with one hand and sipping a drink with the other. He looks up from his phone and suddenly slides it into his pocket. He gets up from his seat to greet me.
"Wow you look absolutely stunning Iris," Eric says kissing my cheek. I want to lean into his muscular body and inhale his

divine cologne. I feel the butterflies erupt again in my stomach when I look at him. He really looks like he belongs on the set of a Bond movie. In fact, he looks like he could be the next James Bond. In a true gentleman style, he pulls my chair back for me.

The hostess is still there hovering over us. She eyes me with her cold grey eyes; the evident glint of jealousy reflected in them. However, her demeanour remains professional and she politely asks us to let her know if there's anything that we need. She hands us both red leather menus and leaves us to it.

I nervously scan through the menu and panic at the prices. The cheapest starter on the menu is twelve pounds! The most expensive food items on the menu are lobster and caviar. I feel anxious over what to order. Apart from being exorbitantly priced, most of the foods have fancy French names and contain things that I've never heard of. I don't want to feel stupid and ask what they are so I decide that I'll settle with the goat's cheese salad which is also one of the cheapest main courses. The alcoholic drinks are also far too expensive so I also decide that I'll stick with a Diet Coke.

"What will you have Iris?" Eric asks.

"I think I'll just have the goats cheese salad and a Diet Coke."

"Don't be silly Iris, you can't just have that. You can have anything you want and however much you want; it's my treat. I can afford this."

"I really appreciate it but you don't have to. I can pay for mine."

"You'll do no such thing. This is my treat. Forget about the prices, just pick whatever you want."

"I'm not really sure what to have." I really do have no clue; the menu seems so alien to me. I feel like an alien from another planet.

"Why don't I order for us? I know the best dishes here."

Internally I breathe a sigh of relief. Sometimes life is so much easier when others make decisions for you.

Eric orders steak tartare for the starters and duck for the main course. He also asks for a bottle of red wine of which the name sounds very expensive. For all I know it could be a bottle of red wine from Tesco and I wouldn't be able to tell the difference. The wine tastes bitter and stale, but I drink it anyway as I know that it's probably worth a lot of money and plus, I don't want Eric to think that I'm uncultured and inexperienced.

"So tell me more about yourself Iris," Eric says.

"Um what would you like to know?" I'm really awful when it comes to talking about myself. I never really have anything interesting to say.

"Anything, what do you like to do?"

"I like to paint."

"You were meant to show me your paintings," Eric says earnestly as though I were a pupil that forgot to hand in their homework.

I apprehensively take out my phone and open my portfolio that I have stored in my albums. I love to paint anything; landscapes, cities, beaches, animals, people. I worry that he won't think that my art is any good. I hold my breath whilst he scrolls through the album. I'm worried that Eric will think my paintings are uninspiring and unoriginal. Eric thumbs through the album as though he's an examiner grading my work.

"Did you really do this? Your paintings are incredible!" Eric says. "I especially love the painting of the wild horses and the one of Times Square. The scenes really come to life and your use of colour is exquisite. You really have a lot of talent and I'm not just saying that. You have a unique flair that can't be learnt.

I can put you in touch with some agents. I really think that you could make a career with your paintings."

All that I've wanted more than anything is to sell my paintings and be a full-time artist. I made an account for my paintings on a business website but I got very little interest. Now I feel like I've been praised by Michelangelo himself! I can't believe that Eric thinks that I'm talented and that I could make a career out of my paintings.

"Do you paint?" I ask.

"Unfortunately not. I don't have any artistic talent, but it doesn't mean that I don't appreciate good art like yours. My family have been in the art business for years; that's how my great-grandfather made his fortune. He came from nothing. He was born to a poverty-stricken family in Poland. He managed to sneak onto a ship to New York. He had less than two dollars in his pocket and he ended up making millions."

"Wow that's incredible. So are you from New York?"

"No, I was raised in a small town in New Hampshire. My parents owned a big house there, but they decided to move to Florida so they signed it over to me. I thought about selling it but it's where I grew up and the house has been in my family for generations. My great-grandfather purchased it. I don't live there full-time though. I have a place in New York where I stay, but I travel a lot. Anyway, what about your family Iris?"

I feel too embarrassed to talk about my family. My family is the polar opposite to his. I don't have any wealth that runs in my family nor do I have a normal family with normal parents. Elizabeth is definitely not what you would describe as "normal". Elizabeth has never even been able to hold a proper job.

"Well I just have a small family really. It's just me, my mother and my brother."

"What about your dad?"

"Look I don't really want to talk about my family ok." I don't intend for it to come out so harshly and abruptly. I want to kick myself.

"Hey I'm sorry, I really didn't mean to upset you. It's fine if you don't want to talk about it but if you ever do, I'm here for you." He reaches across the table and takes my hand. A warm glow spreads throughout my body. His hand feels so strong and manly yet so soft.
"When I met you, I was surprised that you didn't have a boyfriend. I thought how can a beautiful girl like you be single," he continues.

"If only I were that lucky. I thought that Felicity would be more your type. She's practically every guy's type."

"Who's Felicity?"

"The other girl who was with me when we met; the one who wanted to show you around."

"Oh yes, I remember now. I know the type; one of those shallow and self-absorbed poor little rich girls. I don't find that kind of woman attractive."

"I'm surprised that you don't have a girlfriend or a wife. Unless maybe you do," I say bluntly. I want to kick myself again. Why do I let whatever comes into my mind come out of my mouth? Why am I being so confrontational all of a sudden? However, I'm pleasantly relieved when Eric laughs and doesn't seem at all offended.

"I've not been very lucky in love myself. I always seem to find the wrong woman; women who care more about my money and status than they do about me. I'll be honest and I hope that this won't put you off but I was married before. I've been divorced for almost two years now. I was married for two," Eric says solemnly. I can see the sadness in those deep olive eyes.

"What happened? Why didn't it work out?"

"She passed away."

"Oh my gosh I'm so sorry". This news comes as a shock to me; I did not expect that. So Eric is a widower.

"Don't be. Before she died, we were going through the process of getting a divorce. It was a very volatile marriage." Eric pauses. "She was very volatile. I tried everything that I could to make her happy but it wasn't enough."

"I'm sorry to hear that."

"It was very difficult but I've moved forward. I'm very saddened by her death of course, but I don't mourn the relationship itself."

"How did she die?"

"She committed suicide. She couldn't accept that I wanted a divorce. She threatened suicide many times but I didn't think that she would actually do it. I thought that it was a tactic to manipulate me into staying in the marriage. I feel extremely guilty but I couldn't stay in that marriage any longer; it was very toxic. She was an extremely toxic person. Despite asking for a divorce I promised that I would get her help and give her whatever financial support that she needed."

"That sounds tough, but you mustn't blame yourself."

"My therapist says the same thing. The guilt really ate away at me but I'm learning to deal with it. It's not only the guilt of her death and not being there to stop her but the guilt that I didn't want to be with her. I tried so hard to help her and to make our marriage work but she didn't want to be helped. She blamed everything on me and didn't want to take any responsibility for her actions. There's only so much that you can do. She had some very deep issues. In the end I had to put my health and my sanity first. I just couldn't do it anymore. It took a huge toll on me. As tragic as her death was, I've moved on. I just know that this time I'll pick the right woman."

His eyes linger on mine and we gaze into one another's eyes. Our gaze is broken when the food arrives. I take a small helping of the starter. I'm not too keen on the steak tartare but Eric seems to relish it. The steak tartare doesn't exactly activate my appetite. Eric picks up on this.

"You don't seem to eat very much. Is the steak tartare not to your liking? Perhaps you'd like something else."

"No it's delicious," I lie. I scoop more onto my plate and pick another piece of bread.

"I like a woman with a good appetite. You have a lovely figure but you could do with some feeding up. What do you like to eat?"

"I'm not really too fussy. I guess I like the usual foods that everyone likes; pizza, pasta, chocolate."

"They do a really good pasta dish here. Do you like cheese?"

"I love cheese." I really do. Thinking about it starts to make me hungry. Eric orders the pasta with gorgonzola and it really is delicious, though very filling. Although the portion looks small, the size is deceiving. It's like one of those conundrums where you have to guess the size of something and it ends up being surprisingly bigger or smaller than you expected.

The wine starts to get to my head and I'm feeling giddy and excited. The fact that he's been married before doesn't put me off. His ex-wife sounds like she was completely crazy. That wasn't Eric's fault; he tried so hard to help her and make it work. He seems like such a giving, kind and generous person. *I* want to be the right woman for him. I give myself a mental thump. I sound crazy! I barely know Eric and here I am hoping that I'm the one for him. Get a grip girl! For all I know there probably won't even be a second date.

I *really* hope that there's a second date. I'm having the best evening. I've never had such an incredible time on a date before; not even in my wildest fantasies! The conversation flows and I can feel the intense chemistry between us. Maybe I'm a bit drunk or I'm imagining it.

I love how intelligent and experienced Eric is. He tells me about all of the places that he's travelled to. He went backpacking all around Asia for a year and spent many summers travelling around Europe. He worked in China and South America teaching English when he was in his early twenties. He told me how his father wasn't too happy about that and wanted him to get a "proper job", especially as he had so many connections and opportunities in the art world. Eric also went to Harvard like his father and grandfather had done and studied Business and Economics.

He tells me about the famous people that he's met and mentioned that he dated a famous supermodel but found her to be incredibly boring and shallow. Eric knows so much about politics, current affairs and general knowledge; far more than I know. I don't think that I've ever met anybody as fascinating and brilliant as Eric before.

I feel so bland and uncivilised in comparison. I don't have any anecdotes of travels, meeting interesting people or funny stories. Although I did well at school and got straight A's, I didn't go to a top university. Also, a lot of people don't think an art degree is a real degree. I love reading, especially things to do with literature, history, geography and art, but I wouldn't say that I'm really knowledgeable. I'm certainly not an intellectual. Not like Eric.

I feel so envious of all of Eric's travels. I've never been anywhere apart from France and even that was awful as Elizabeth spent the whole time drinking. Elizabeth is one of those embarrassing Francophiles that tries to act all French. She's always banging on about how wonderful and classy the French are and how they're not all uptight about sex like the English.

Some summers if Elizabeth could afford it, we'd go to Normandy. She would rent this crumbling and dilapidated cottage which she would call rustic and *charmant* for dirt cheap from a man called Jean-Claude. Henry and I would have to amuse ourselves whilst Elizabeth fucked Jean-Claude and the other local men.

"French men are such wonderful lovers," Elizabeth would tell me even though I wasn't quite old enough to know much about sex. Sometimes she seemed to forget that I was merely a child.

I want to travel but at the moment I can't afford it and I'm still saving up. I've missed out on a lot, including having a father. I've never even met my father. He remains an elusive mystery. According to Elizabeth he was an Italian she had a holiday romance with in Rome. He was already married with kids.

As a child I used to ask Elizabeth endless questions about my father but she never gave me the answers that I needed so I gave up. All I knew was that his name was Marco, but Elizabeth couldn't remember his surname nor did she even have a picture of him. Sometimes I wonder if Elizabeth was making it up because it made a more exotic story. I often wonder if Elizabeth even knew who my father was.

I feel like part of me is missing; like one of those dark mysteries where you never find the truth no matter how hard you keep on searching. Even if my father didn't want me, I'd still want to know who he is, even just to know who I am. These are things you don't really tell someone when you're on a date. Maybe I should open up to Eric; I mean he told me about his ex-wife. He didn't have to do that. However, I don't want to put him off with my baggage, especially not on the first date.

"I wish I was as exciting and interesting as you," I sigh sadly.

"Don't be ridiculous Iris; you're one of the most intriguing and alluring women that I've ever met. You're far more interesting than the poor little rich girls and superficial supermodels in my circles that I've dated. You're different. There's something about you."

I feel a happy glow spread within me like a fireplace gently heating me up. It could just be the wine that I'm drinking. I usually don't drink much so it doesn't take much to hit me. I don't know how I've managed two glasses of such strong red wine. As Eric is about to order another bottle, I refuse.

"I like a woman who knows her limits when it comes to drinking. I think maybe I'll just settle for a Brandy. Would you like anything else to drink, perhaps a cocktail?"

I don't want Eric to think that I'm an alcoholic so I just settle for a glass of water. I really shouldn't drink anymore alcohol; I don't want to act like Elizabeth does when she drinks. I don't want to become like Elizabeth full stop!

The rest of the food comes and it's truly exquisite. The duck is crispy and the potatoes are so tender. The dark chocolate caramel cake is gooey and thick. I can't remember the last time that I had such an appetising meal nor do I remember the last time that I felt so stuffed. I usually don't have much time to eat and when I do, either I'm too tired to want to eat much or I get full quickly. The years of indoctrination from Elizabeth about men liking thin women have probably on some subconscious level contributed to my lack of appetite. Or maybe because growing up, there wasn't much food around so I had to get used to eating little.

I feel really full but this time it feels pleasant and comforting. I don't even care if I look bloated. I don't want the night to end, but as in life, all good things must come to an end. I try to persuade Eric to let me pay my half, even though the bill almost comes to four hundred pounds, but Eric won't hear of it. Like a gentleman he helps me into my coat and orders another car to take me home.

"I've had a really lovely evening. Thank you," I say.

"It's my pleasure. I'd love to see you again Iris." We gaze at one another hungrily; his lips aching to be kissed. For a brief moment our lips touch only to be disturbed by the buzzing of Eric's phone, which is a message from the driver, indicating that he has arrived.

"Get home safe Iris," Eric says. He pulls me close to him. The closeness of his body to mine is enough to set my endorphins off. My heart is racing and I want him more than I've ever wanted any man. He kisses me and the fireworks set off inside of my brain. His lips are firm but soft. It's just a brief kiss but it's enough to make me excited.

Once I'm inside the car, I keep smiling like a fool. I feel like I'm in a fairy tale and I don't ever want it to end.

CHAPTER FOUR

SUNDAY 27TH MAY

After my date with Eric I'm on a high. It's like Eric is my drug. I can't remember the last time that I felt this good. That evening it takes me a while to fall asleep. Eric is all that I can think about. It's the best night that I've ever had in my whole entire life. I just worry that I'll wake up and find out that this has all been a dream.

The next morning Magda practically gives me the Spanish Inquisition about my date with Eric. I'm all too happy to recall my glorious date with Eric.

"Oh my God he is like a fairy tale prince; he sounds so perfect. It seems like he's really into you. I haven't seen you this happy since I've known you; your eyes are glowing when you talk about him," Magda gushes, taking my hand.

"What if he doesn't feel the same way about me?" I suddenly panic.

"Don't be so ridiculous Irenka; he sounds completely smitten with you."

"He hasn't messaged me since last night."

"It's still early and men are not the best at communicating."

I'm not the kind of girl who sits around waiting for a guy to text but I worry that maybe Eric isn't into me after all. I know that I could just message him but I don't want to come across as desperate. Elizabeth always instilled into me that I should never message a guy first (though Elizabeth always breaks this rule when she doesn't hear back from a guy- she'll send dozens of frantic and angry drunken messages and calls). I know that it's such an archaic and outdate principle and I consider myself a feminist in every sense, but I'm scared. I'm scared that he won't message me back. I'm scared that he doesn't feel the same way and that it was all in my head. I'm so scared that he'll slip away from me like a vanishing magic trick.

Eric is all I can think about the whole day. I try not to check my phone but I can't help it. I try to busy my mind by doing some painting and watching trash TV with Magda but Eric is constantly in the back of my mind. Every time I see that there's no message waiting for me from Eric, a little piece inside of me withers away each time. Like petals slowly falling away one by one. Maybe this was all too good to be true.

The next day Eric doesn't message me either. I'm in such a foul mood that even Felicity is taken aback. I never snap at anyone and try to always be polite and pleasant, even to Felicity although it isn't reciprocated. I snap at Felicity to put her phone away and I don't greet the clients in my usual polite and pleasant manner.

My helplessness turns to anger. I'm sure that there was a spark between us, I can't have imagined it. Why couldn't he message me out of courtesy? He said he wanted to see me again. Why would he say that? Then I feel angry at myself for letting myself get so hung up on a guy that I don't even know and for being as naive and crazy as Elizabeth. Elizabeth always gets hung up on some guy that she barely knows or that is no good for her.

I always promised myself that I wouldn't be like Elizabeth. That I wouldn't cheapen myself to get a man's approval and that I wouldn't get caught up on the first guy who shows me a bit of attention. I promised myself that I wouldn't allow men to define my self-worth.

I still feel low nevertheless. I don't have any appetite. The thought of eating my sandwich makes me sick, so I end up giving it to a homeless man in the street. It feels like a dream; one of those really good dreams which feel so real. Then you wake up and the crushing tidal wave of reality hits you. Maybe this was all one big dream; a dream that I confused with reality. Maybe I'm going crazy like Elizabeth. The fact that bipolar disorder could be genetic fills me with dread. Maybe I'm already showing signs.

I tell myself not to be stupid. Even in the depths of her mania Elizabeth didn't hallucinate and conjure up pretend men. She had delusions of grandeur that they loved her and wanted her even though they clearly didn't. Maybe like Elizabeth, I've got delusions of grandeur. Maybe I misread all of the signs. Felicity was right; what would someone like Eric see in me. We come from completely different worlds. Maybe he realised that on the date. Maybe he didn't feel any chemistry.

I feel so stupid for letting myself get swept up by all of this and for not knowing my place. I don't belong in his world. Things like this happen in movies and in books but rarely in real life. I belong in my dull little world with no friends apart from Magda, not much money, no love life and a stressful job that barely covers the bills. I don't care about Eric's money or status; it's just that he made me feel different. He made me feel alive for once in my life. I could feel that there was something between us; I could sense it, but obviously I was wrong. Wrong, wrong, wrong.

I dread going back to work after my lunch break when all I want to do is curl up in bed and cry. I try not to look at my phone as I know that there will be no message awaiting me from Eric. I feel so defeated and gutted that I don't even notice the courier talking to me.

"Hello ma'am are you Iris Shaw?

"Yes I am."

"There's a delivery for you."

"There must be a mistake; I didn't order anything."

"There's no mistake, unless you aren't Iris Shaw."

"I am."

"Well these are for you," the delivery man says, thrusting a huge bouquet of red roses into my arms. I've never received flowers from anyone before in my life. These are not your usual shop brought flowers. The roses are so lively and lush; the petals such deep vivid scarlet shades of red. There's a note attached to the bouquet.

I had the most wonderful evening. You are truly incredible. How about drinks on Thursday at 7pm at the rooftop bar at the Cavendish Hotel?

Love Eric x

I feel so happy that I could scream it from the rooftops. Eric is into me and he wants to see me again! I message Magda immediately and send her a photo of the bouquet. I am utterly and completely on cloud nine.

"Who are those beautiful flowers from Iris?" Julio says.

"Eric," I blush.

"You are one lucky girl Iris. I'm so jealous. Why can't I meet my Mr Right?"

I can't help feeling a little smug, especially as Felicity gives me a lock that could kill. Her icy blue eyes are like daggers. I can sense the jealousy seething inside of her like a volcano ready to erupt.

"I wouldn't get too excited if I were you; I've heard some rather unsavoury things about Eric. A friend of a friend of mine knows a few things that would put you off," Felicity says snidely, after Julio walks away.

"Look I don't care what you say Felicity, it's clear that you're just bitter and jealous. I don't need any negativity."

"As if I'm bitter and jealous," Felicity snorts. "From what my friend has told me, I'd run a mile from him."

"If you're trying to put me off him, it's not working."

"It's all true, you can ask my friend and find out for yourself."

"No thanks, I've got better things to do with my time."

I know that Felicity is making things up because she's irate and green with envy that Eric didn't go after her. However, I'm too jubilant to let Felicity and her pathetic little lies get to me. I just want Thursday to come around as quickly as possible. Every fibre in my body yearns for Eric. He consumes all of my thoughts. I've never felt like this about anybody ever and it's the most amazing feeling.

Apart from Magda I have nobody else to share my happiness with. I feel a tinge of sadness that I don't have the kind of relationship where I feel comfortable sharing things with Elizabeth. Growing up I felt that I was never able to share anything with her because everything was always about her. If I tell her about Eric, she'll only end up giving me unsolicited advice and fill my mind with further negativity and doubts. My mind has been so preoccupied with Eric that I haven't even responded to her messages. I'm so excited for Thursday that the world could explode and I wouldn't even notice.

THURSDAY 31ST MAY

After work I get ready for my date with Eric. I don't have enough time to go home and get ready so I get ready in the toilets of the nearest pub. I pull on the silk silver top that Magda lent me and my new black jeans and black ankle boots.

I give my hair a brush and outline my eyes with eyeliner and smear silver eyeshadow on my eyelids, topped off with mascara. I'm getting the hang of all of this make-up stuff. Magda showed me some good make up techniques and I've started watching make-up tutorials online. I never thought that I'd be so into make-up and clothes. I'm even quite enjoying doing make-up and dressing up. I was always bookish and boring Iris, but now here I am wearing make-up and sexy clothes. I even get wolf whistles from the men when I walk through the pub. I've never gotten wolf whistles before in my life. It feels kind of good.

Again. I start to worry if I'm too under or overdressed, especially for a place like the Cavendish. The Cavendish Hotel is only a ten-minute walk from the gallery. I still have some time to kill so I sit in Starbucks and read some of my new book; a non-fiction book about artists that shaped the world. Elizabeth always told me that I read far too many books and that men don't like women that are smarter than them.

"It's all about looks darling, not books. Men aren't interested about what's in your mind," she'd say as though it were a mantra.

I try to shake the bad thoughts from my mind. I've let Elizabeth bring me down and make me feel low about myself for long enough, now it's time to let go and emancipate myself from her mental taunts. I feel more confident than I ever have and I want it to stay that way.

***

I arrive at the Cavendish five minutes before seven and head to the rooftop bar where Eric is already waiting for me. The Cavendish is so grand and chic with its polished marble floors and black and white furniture. The bar is made out of white gold marble and the selection of spirits and wines are kept in gleaming glass cabinets. Outside, the rooftop is comfortably heated with special outdoor heaters even though it's a balmy evening with a slight breeze. An array of chromatic and exotic plants have been carefully arranged on the terrace.

Eric looks as gorgeous as ever. The butterflies start dancing around in my belly like little ballerinas. He's wearing a shirt which is slightly unbuttoned. The sleeves are pulled up, revealing his tanned muscular forearms. As usual, he gets up and greets me with a kiss on the cheek.

"You look absolutely beautiful," he says. "I've ordered some champagne but they do very good cocktails here."

I browse the long cocktail menu and choose a drink called Tropical Twist which consists of mango and pineapple juice, rum and gin. It's such a perfect evening. I can't believe that I'm here with Eric. He starts off asking me about my week and then in turn telling me about his week, which has been extremely busy and how he wishes that he could have seen me much sooner, but his work commitments made that very difficult.

"I just kept thinking about you the whole time, wishing that I could see you," Eric says, taking my hand. "I had such a wonderful time on Saturday."

"Me too."

"I hope that this doesn't sound too forward and I'd never forgive myself if I scared you away, but I've never felt this way about anybody before, not even my ex-wife."

"I'm glad that you said that because I feel exactly the same way about you."

"I'm so relieved. The last thing I wanted was to come across too strong. I know that it's still early days, but I could see myself marrying you one day Iris. I don't want you to think that I've got any ulterior motives or am trying to get you into bed. I'm an honest guy and I say what I feel, but I don't want to scare you away either."

"You haven't at all."

"I'm a gentleman and I'm not into the whole being a jerk thing. Maybe that's why I've never been lucky with women. Many women think that all men are assholes, but I've met far too many women who are only interested in my wealth and status and aren't interested in getting to know the real me. You're different Iris. You don't care about money and superficial things.'

"I think that you're a great person and I'm really enjoying getting to know you. You're different from other guys too. Most of the guys I know are jerks."

"I would never behave like a jerk. I want to treat you like a princess because you deserve to be treated like one."

"I don't want you to spend lots of money on me. I can pay for things as well."

"I want to spend money on you. I want to spoil you."

"Ok I'll try reverse psychology. I want you to spend loads of money on me and buy me everything that I ask for."

Eric laughs. "You make me laugh Iris. You're funny. I like a woman who has a good sense of humour."

If this is what heaven feels like, I'm sure that I'm already there. The evening is filled with laughter and tenderness. I feel like I'm in a romantic film. I've never really believed in love and finding a guy who treats you like a queen. The men that Elizabeth always attracted treated her like shit and I thought that's what all relationships were like. Maybe that's why I always shied away from relationships and subconsciously shut myself off to men. Eric is different though. I feel that I can put my guard down around him. I don't have to protect myself like a wild animal protecting itself from prey. Maybe it's the alcohol talking, but I'm so happy.

"I could sense the last time that you weren't into the red wine. I thought that you'd like the champagne and cocktails here."

I love how Eric is so thoughtful. I've never drunk so much in my life but I don't care. I've never really been into drinking. Once Magda persuaded me to drink a shot of vodka and that was bad enough. It was so strong that I ended up spitting it straight out. I've always stayed away from alcohol because I was scared of getting drunk and making a fool out of myself like Elizabeth. However, with Eric I feel comfortable enough to drink and let go of my fears. There's no way in hell that I would allow myself to make a fool out of myself and fuck everything up.

I order another cocktail, this time a White Russian. We also order food to share; fresh oysters, polenta fries and a selection of breads and cheeses. I feel more and more relaxed around Eric. As the evening goes on, it starts to get colder. Eric sees me shivering and suggests that we go inside. He puts his arm around me and leads me inside.

We sit side by side on one of the couches. Eric puts his arm around me again and holds me close to him. I feel my body internally respond to his closeness. I want to kiss him and rip his shirt off. I feel the urge to have sex with Eric right now. I've never felt such a strong urge like this before. I love the feeling but at the same time I panic.

I've only ever slept with two people. Dan and a guy at art college who I had a one-night stand with shortly after breaking up with Dan. I regretted it so much. I wanted to feel wanted and loved, but it was exactly the opposite. Needless to say, I have so little experience. That must have been about four years ago. What if I'm truly terrible and inexperienced that it puts him off? Elizabeth always told me that in order to keep a man, you have to be good in bed.

I remember when I was only fourteen years old, she waltzed into my room one night drunk and tossed a packet of condoms at me. "You should get started soon darling. Always remember to have safe sex; you don't want a mistake. Mind you I had two," she laughed. I stuffed the packet of condoms in the back of my drawer. By the time that I was sexually active, they had long expired.

At the back of my mind, part of me worries that what if Eric does only want one thing? I want it to be special and actually mean something. As much as I want to, I don't want it to be a rushed, spur of the moment thing. I don't want to lose Eric.

"Eric?"

"Yes, Iris baby?" he says, tenderly stroking my hand.

"You don't mind if we wait until we get to know one another better to have sex?"

"Did you think that I brought you to a hotel so we could have sex? I know that you're not that kind of girl Iris. I'm happy to wait as long as you'd like and whenever you feel comfortable. Like I said, I'm a gentleman. In the meantime, I hope it's ok to kiss you."

"I'd like that," I say. Eric pulls my face towards his and kisses me gently on the lips. The butterflies are doing somersaults in my stomach and my body completely surrenders. Eric's kiss is gentle and passionate. His lips are warm and soft and his breath fresh with the taste of peppermint and champagne. In this moment I can't think of anything else. It's like time has stopped and everything has ceased to matter or exist. All I can focus on is the kiss and how perfect everything is.

CHAPTER FIVE

SATURDAY 30TH JUNE

I feel as though I've been reborn. Reborn into a wonderful new world where every sense is sharper and stronger. The lens through which I saw the world before was bleary and tinged with grey. Now it's like seeing through a high-resolution camera where everything is crystal clear and vibrant. Before everything was just white noise in the background. Now I hear every sound as sharp as a bell and as melodic as birds singing. Everything used to taste bland and flavourless. Now I can taste flavours that I hadn't tasted in so long; flavours so rich and palatable. Before everything was odourless. Now everything smells of roses and perfumes. I feel like the sun is constantly shining down on me with its luminous and candescent rays.

"Wow I can't believe how happy you are and how great you look," Magda comments. We're sprawled out on towels in the fields of the local park, basking in the glorious June sun. Magda is already as brown as mahogany, whilst I've slathered myself in factor 30, hoping for even the lightest shade of tan. It's nice just relaxing on a Sunday afternoon and making the most of the British weather when it's at its best.

I feel the best that I ever have done in my life. This whole month has been a sublime wave of ecstasy. Even though it's only been a month, I'm in love. I want to sing and shout it out. I want to world to know. Even Elizabeth suspected something the last time that we spoke.

"What's happening to you darling? It's not like you to ignore my calls and messages like this. You sound different. You sound happy. Have you found yourself a man?"

"No."

"Don't lie to me darling, a mother can pick up on these things. We're like police dogs; we can sense everything."

"Well if you must know, I have met someone and he's amazing."

"At long last darling; I was starting to think that you were a lesbian. Not that it matters darling, you know that I love the gays, but all I've ever wanted is for you to settle down and find yourself a nice man. Oh darling, I'm so happy for you. You must tell me everything. What does he look like, what does he do, what's his name? I'm simply dying to know."

"It's still early days, so I don't want to say too much just yet."

"You never tell me anything darling. At least tell me his name."

I regret even saying anything to Elizabeth as she keeps bombarding me with messages pleading with me to tell her about Eric and to send her a picture. I don't want to share Eric with her. I want to keep him to myself. I don't want Eric to meet her either, but I know that if things progress, which I hope that they will, he'll have to meet her eventually.

Every time I see Eric, I find myself falling a little more in love with him. Eric makes me feel like royalty. Last week he took me to the opera. I had never been to the opera before but it was one of the most incredible experiences. The voices were so mellifluous and erupting with passion. The fact that it was in Italian made it seem even more passionate and alluring. Afterwards Eric took me for dinner at this charming little Italian restaurant that does the best authentic Italian pizza; thin and crispy with succulent mozzarella and Parma ham. Eric also presented me with a rectangular gold box tied with a royal red ribbon.

"I really can't accept this. You've been so good to me already.

Are you sure that I can't give you money for the opera tickets or even the meal?"

"I don't want to hear of it. Like I said, you deserve to be treated like a queen and you deserve only the best. I won't take no for an answer."

I opened the box to find a beautiful diamond necklace. I'd never seen real diamonds in reality. My mouth dropped in awe as the diamonds coruscated in the light and revealed a plethora of rainbow colours. It must have been extremely expensive.

"I really can't accept that, it's too much."

"Iris, I'm not going to take no for an answer. Unless you don't like it, I can change it for something else."

"What don't be ridiculous; how could I not like it?"

"Well in that case you have no excuse but to accept my gift."

When I showed Magda the necklace, her mouth fell wide open.

"Kurwa! That must have cost a couple of thousand. It's so beautiful. Eric must really, I mean *really* like you. Arek would never buy anything like this for me. Please can I try it on?"

Magda seemed far more thrilled with the necklace than me, gazing at it and touching it like a child with a new toy at Christmas. She took endless selfies of herself wearing the necklace. I would feel so uncomfortable wearing something so extortionate and fragile. I would have let Magda keep the necklace, but obviously that would be ungrateful and rude to Eric. I carefully placed the necklace back on the red satin cushion of its box and put it in my drawer, like an ancient and precious artefact from a museum that must not be touched. I don't want gifts like this; it's far too much. I want to get something for Eric but I don't have enough money to buy anything that would be in Eric's league. Even something worth fifty pounds is expensive to me, but for Eric fifty pounds is probably like small change.

"I don't need these expensive gifts," I tell Magda.

"If you don't want them, then maybe I should date Eric," Magda laughs. "I definitely wouldn't say no."

I know that Magda is impressed with material things, but for me, that's not important. Eric and I have a special connection. I feel so comfortable around Eric. I feel like I can be myself and for once being myself is a good thing. I don't have to wish that I was more confident, more compelling or more attractive. Being the way that I am is good enough for Eric. I even opened up to him about my life. About my childhood, about my fears and about my hang-ups.

I felt like Eric really understood. He tenderly stroked my hand as though it were a delicate flower. I could see the deep understanding in those entrancing dark olive eyes.

"Oh baby, you've been through so much. You have so much maturity and strength. You have nothing to be ashamed of. Probably more people than you realise have dysfunctional families and there are definitely far more people that have grown up without a father. The way that you coped with everything is incredible. You don't have to worry about becoming like your mother because you're not like her. You're like you."

That moment was my confirmation that Eric is definitely the one. I hadn't opened up to anyone like this before, not even Magda. Even with Magda it took me ages to open up to her. When I first moved in, I was so reserved that I barely said anything apart from "good morning", "hi" and "bye". I didn't really have friends and I definitely didn't know how to make them.

Most people would have given up bothering with me, but Magda didn't give up easily. She would always ask me if I wanted to join her and Arek in the sitting room or if I fancied a coffee. I would politely decline her invitations. I thought what would somebody as magnetic and vivacious as Magda have in common with someone like me? She already had a myriad of friends.

Our friendship began after about two months of living together when one day Magda just asked me bluntly. "Iris why don't you ever want to hang out? Do you not like me? Did I do something wrong? If I have, I'd rather you said it to my face."

"Of course I like you Magda. Why on earth would you think that you've done anything wrong?"

"It's just that you never really want to talk to me. Maybe my English isn't good enough, that's why."

"Don't be daft Magda, your English is great. It's not you, it's me. I'm not really good at talking to people."

"Well you're talking to me."

"You're so exciting, interesting and beautiful; why would you want to talk to someone as dull and boring as me?"

"That's rubbish Iris! How can you say that? You paint so beautifully and you read so many books. That's much more interesting than my other friends. Sorry, you left your door open one day and I saw your paintings. They're incredible. I couldn't help but have a look. I didn't take or touch anything I swear! I hope you're not upset with me. It was ages ago."

"Of course not. Oh Magda, I'm so sorry that I was so rude and made you feel that way."

"Well you can make it up to me. How about we grab a coffee from the Starbucks across the street? My friend Kasia works there; she can get us free drinks. The golden caramel macchiato is the best," Magda winks.

This time I gladly accepted Magda's invite and from that day on we were inseparable.

***

"So when am I meeting this wonderful Eric?" Magda asks me. She lifts herself up from the towel to take another sip of beer whilst I reapply my sun cream.

"Hopefully soon."
"It seems pretty serious. If you do get serious then I hope you're not going to move to America and leave me here."

"We haven't spoken much about it but Eric says he's pretty flexible when it comes to where to live. He says he can work pretty much anywhere in the world and he was looking into buying some real estate in London. He says he really likes London, more than New York. Oh gosh I'm really going to miss him this week."

Eric is going away to New York for a week for some business meetings. I know it's only a week, but whenever we're apart, I pine for him. I worry that he'll forget about me when he's away or that he'll meet somebody else. I share my fears with Magda.

"Relax! He's not going to meet anyone else! The man is clearly crazy about you. Isn't it obvious?"

"I guess, after all it is only a week, but I'm scared that something will go wrong; that it's too good to be true."

"There's no point wasting time worrying Irenka; just focus on the here and now. Just enjoy what you have now. You never know what the future holds; sometimes things work out, sometimes they don't. Everything happens for a reason. Anyway, the most important question is, have you and Eric had sex yet?"

"We're taking things slow; there's no need to rush anything.

We're still getting to know each other."

"Wow he really sounds like a gentleman! I bet that he'll be really good in bed. You'll have to tell me everything."

"Magda!" I gasp, but I can't help giggling. "I'm sure that it'll be great as Eric and I have such an amazing connection."

I can't wait for Eric and I to be intimate. I know that it'll be worth the wait. Each time I get more and more tempted but I want to know that the connection is real and that the relationship is going somewhere. I want the time to be right and not rush into things and end up getting hurt. I definitely want to do it soon though as I'm feeling more and more ready.

When I get back from the park with Magda, there's a box and a bunch of peonies waiting outside of our flat. There's a note attached that says:

Every moment that we're not together I pine for you. Hopefully this week can go by as quickly as possible so I can see you again. Enjoy the chocolates. Love E x.

"That is so romantic. I wish that Arek could be this romantic," Magda pouts, pinching one of the chocolates from the box.

"Hey don't take my chocolates," I laugh. I don't really mind though. It is a bit annoying sometimes when Magda pinches stuff without asking but I know it's because we're like sisters. Magda would never get fussy if I borrowed her stuff or pinched her chocolates. I had housemates before who were so stingy. One of them had a right strop when I borrowed a small drop of their milk. Magda is one of the most generous and open people that I know. Her *mi casa es tu casa* attitude is one of the things I love about her. I've never felt so at home living with somebody else before.

I open the box to find a variety of fastidiously decorated chocolates with intricate designs including gold leaves and pearly pink hearts. On the box I see the chocolatier brand printed in elegant and swirly gold writing. It's from one of the most expensive chocolatiers in London. Even a small box of their chocolates can cost up to ten pounds, so I can't imagine how much these must have cost. The chocolates look almost too good to eat.

I try one white chocolate praline and it tastes incredible. According to the little leaflet there's chocolates with nougat, fudge, marzipan, truffle, tiramisu, crème brûlée and caramel. If I'm not careful, I could gladly devour them all in one go. The other day I noticed that my trousers were a little snug. Dating Eric means that I'm pretty well fed. I don't mind gaining a few extra pounds, but I don't want to overdo it either. I take one more chocolate and put the box in the kitchen cupboard so I'm not too tempted.

I slump down on the sofa and watch more reality TV with Magda. I rarely watch TV. I prefer to read, but lately I've gotten into the habit of watching too much TV with Magda. She's obsessed with the latest reality TV programme which everyone is raving about called *Holiday Romance*, where people go away on an exotic island to find love. Most of the people are on the show just for fame, but it's a good laugh. Magda and I have a laugh at all the plastic wannabe girls with fake lips and boobs and the gym obsessed guys with bodies of Greek Gods but personalities of planks of wood.

I can't help thinking about and missing Eric. I feel like a stupid teenage girl with a crush. Even I'm surprised by how strong my feelings are. I know that it's good to have some space and it's not healthy to be together all the time, but I can't stop thinking about Eric. A text from Eric flashes on my phone and even that makes me grin like a fool.

MISSING YOU ALREADY XX

SATURDAY 7TH JULY

Today is the day that I'm finally reunited with Eric. It's only been a week, but it feels like it's been much longer. I'm meeting Eric at the rooftop of the Plaza. Eric said that he has a big surprise for me. It's probably a gift that he brought me when he was away. I hope it's not another ridiculously expensive and imposing gift. I don't know whether I can accept any more gifts like that. However, I put on the diamond necklace that Eric bought me to show that I'm grateful. The necklace truly is beautiful. The diamonds scintillate whenever they catch the light, like beacons.

I wear my new midnight blue velvet dress and black heels from H&M. I'm really enjoying dressing up and doing girly things. Growing up with and mothering a younger brother meant that I did a lot of "boy stuff". I miss Henry and feel guilty that we haven't spoken in ages. He's seventeen now and lives with his dad Seamus in Limerick in Ireland. Seamus was a pretty rubbish dad to Henry, visiting only when he could be bothered or when he was sober enough for that matter. After I moved away to university, Henry didn't want to stay by himself with Elizabeth and asked Seamus if he could live with him. Apparently, Seamus doesn't drink as much as he used to and is trying to make up for being a lousy father. Henry is lucky that he at least knows who his father is.

I pick up the framed picture of Henry and me years ago with Snoop, our beloved cocker spaniel who had to be put down. I feel a huge surge of sadness. I didn't realise how much I missed Henry. I really wish that I could see him. The last time that I saw him was months ago when we went to see Elizabeth for Christmas. It was another awful Christmas. Elizabeth got far too drunk as usual. The more she drank, the bitter and angrier she became, accusing us both of abandoning her and wailing that she regretted ever having us. Henry swore that he would never return to that shit hole and left as soon as the trains began running after Christmas.

Henry and I used to tell each other everything. I really want to tell him about Eric and I want him to tell me about his life. I want to know how he's doing at school, what girl he likes and if he's happy living with Seamus. The only glimpse of Henry's life I get is on Facebook and even then, he doesn't post much apart from the odd photo with friends. I blame myself for not being a better big sister and being in touch with him more. I find Henry's WhatsApp and send him a message.

Hi Little Bro, long time no speak. I know we haven't spoken for ages; just to say I really miss you. Let's chat on the phone soon, got loads to tell you. Lots and lots of love, your Big Sis x

Knowing Henry, he'll probably take forever to reply. I focus on getting ready for tonight. I try a new smoky eye make-up technique and spray myself with my new wildflower and jasmine scented perfume. After I finish getting ready, Magda and I muck around taking pictures and selfies until the chauffeur arrives at eight thirty to pick me up and take me to the Plaza.

As I walk through the Plaza, I drink in the luxury and sumptuousness; the colossal crystal chandelier hangs from the ceiling like the moon and the royal carmine red and medallion gold tapestry carpet makes you feel like royalty. The concierge, a friendly and polite middle-aged man in an elegant uniform, escorts me up to the roof terrace.

"Have a wonderful evening madam," he smiles.

The rooftop is filled with dozens of ruby red roses and irises; deep violet and lavender coloured irises. There are rose petals sprinkled all over the floor and table. There's a man playing the violin. The tune so soft yet melancholic fills the warm and musty July air. The sun is setting; shades of candy floss pink, mauve, baby blue and gold permeate through the sky. I think about how I'd love to paint the sky with all its glory and splendour.

Eric stands by the table. He's wearing a light blue shirt, which is slightly buttoned down; beige chinos and shiny onyx Italian leather dress shoes. His jet-black hair is slightly tousled and he looks more tanned. I feel a swell of affection and warmth; the butterflies start again like an orchestra. I didn't realise how much I missed him until now. It feels like he's a soldier who has returned home from war. I run into his arms. I lean into his hard-toned chest and breathe in his potent and heady aftershave.

"I missed you," I breathe.

"I missed you too baby," Eric says. "You look so beautiful, as always."

"Why are there so many flowers?"

"Do you like them? I hired out the whole roof top just for us."

"I love the flowers, how thoughtful of you to get irises; what a wonderful surprise."

"You're just as beautiful and as delicate as the flower that you were named after. However, this isn't the main part of the surprise."

I don't mention that Elizabeth named me Iris after the Greek goddess, not after the flower. Many people don't know that so it's an easy mistake to make. It's not like it matters; it's the thought that counts. I'm so deeply touched by Eric's thoughtfulness that it makes my heart burst with love.

"Another surprise? Oh Eric this is far too much. Seeing you is the best surprise of all. I don't need anything else but you."

"But I want to make you happy and spoil you. I really do hope

THE MAN THAT I MARRIED

that you'll like this surprise though. Let's sit down first though and have something to eat."

I follow Eric to the table where a brightly lit candle and ice bucket of champagne are waiting. A waiter brings us a selection of bread and a platter of sea food. I'm too excited to see Eric to eat. I ask him about his trip and he says it was all boring work-related stuff. I tell him about my week and how I'm enjoying my new position at work even though it's a bit stressful.

Things at work have been pretty good. Julio seems happy with me. The perks of being Julio's assistant manager means that I get to deal with more important clients and take part in business meetings. I'm also in charge of organising events. I enjoy it much more than sitting at the reception desk all day and answering calls and emails. Julio even mentioned that there may be a trip to Paris coming up and he'd like me to assist him. I know that Felicity is boiling with jealousy and resentment. She still can't get over the fact that I got the promotion and that Eric wants me, not her.

As I talk, Eric nods; drinking in every word carefully. I love how when he listens, he gives me his full attention like what I'm saying is really important. The waiter brings out the main course which consists of coq au van and dauphinoise potatoes. We sit in silence for a while, but I don't mind as the silence doesn't feel awkward or strained. Just gazing at Eric is a pleasure itself.

"Thank you so much for bringing me here Eric, it's such a special evening."

"I'm so glad that you like it Iris. I really hope that you'll like this next surprise. I'm so worried that you won't, so sorry if I've been a bit quiet."

"I'm sure that whatever it is, I'll love it. What is it?"

"Patience dear Iris, you'll find out after dessert," Eric smiles.

The waiter clears our plates and brings us crème brûlée for dessert. It's delicious but I'm feeling far too full. Eric guzzles the champagne rather quickly. He seems nervous. Surprises aren't meant to make people nervous, are they?

Once we've finished our dessert, Eric takes me by the hand and leads me over to the edge of the rooftop overlooking the whole of London. The whole view is incredible and breath-taking. I take out my phone and take a picture of the awe-inspiring panorama. I feel a bit like a tourist in my own city, but I don't care. The mesmerizing landmarks beam proudly and stand tall in the soft violet and powder blue sky. Big Ben, The London Eye and The Shard accompany us in the background. It's like the set of a romantic film; a film where Eric and I are the leading stars. Eric still holds my hand and my heart is beating really fast.

"Iris," Eric begins. "These past few weeks that we've been together have been incredible. I've really fallen for you fast and hard. You're beautiful, smart, kind, funny and talented. You're everything that any man could ever want in a woman. From the moment I saw you, I fell for you. I know it sounds corny, but I've never felt this connection with any woman before in my life. I love how you don't care about my wealth and my status and that you truly like me for who I am. I feel that I can be myself around you, which with most people I can never be. I think...no I don't think, I know that I love you."

"I love you too Eric."

He then gets down on one knee and takes a small red velvet box out from the pocket of his jacket. "I know that we've only known one another for six weeks; but I feel like I've known you forever. I completely understand if you say no and you may think I'm crazy, but Iris Shaw, will you make me the happiest man on earth? Will you marry me?"

"Oh my God yes, yes of course!" I gasp. I feel dizzyingly stupefied with happiness and surprise. This is beyond my wildest dreams. I secretly pinch myself to make sure that it's real.

"Oh boy I'm so relieved that you said yes. I was so worried that you'd say no. Oh Iris, I'm so so happy!" Eric places the ring on my finger. It's absolutely exquisite. In the centre there's a big diamond stone accentuated with small tiny white sapphires on a white gold band. I don't even want to imagine how much it must have cost, but I'm too happy to want to think about it.

With his strong arms, Eric lifts me into the air and we share a passionate kiss. The man with the violin appears again and plays classical pieces such as The Flower Duet by Leo Delibes and Por Una Cabeza by Carlos Gardel. The waiter offers his congratulations and opens another bottle of champagne.

"Here is our best vintage champagne to celebrate this wonderful news," the waiter says, handing us our flutes filled with champagne. "Perhaps you'd like me to take a picture as well." Eric hands the waiter his iPhone 11 Pro and we pose for the camera.

"Here's to my beautiful wife to be," Eric says, raising his glass in a toast.

"To my wonderful husband to be," I say. The joy that I'm currently feeling is indescribable. I'm so happy that I want to shout it from the rooftop for the whole of London to hear.

CHAPTER SIX

I'm so ecstatic that I don't even know what to do with myself. My body is fully awake with adrenaline. If someone had told me that one day, I was going to marry the man of my dreams, I would never have believed them. I'm still so scared that this is all one big dream and when I wake up, I'll go back to being dull old Iris Shaw who leads a mundane existence and who nobody notices.

The minute the chauffeur drops me back at the flat, I race to Magda's room to tell her the news. I'm surprised to find her asleep at midnight, especially on a Saturday night. Usually, she's either out or at least chilling out in her room, drinking and playing music. I feel bad for waking her, but I really want to tell her the good news.

"Magda! Magda!" I hiss, shaking her awake. Arek is snoring away heavily next to her like a lumberjack. Not even the sound of a pneumatic drill would be enough to rouse Arek from sleep.

"What the fuck?" Magda murmurs. "Iris? What's going on? I've got to be up early for a modelling job tomorrow."

"Magda I'm engaged!"

"What?"

"Eric proposed this evening."

"Isn't it a bit too soon? You barely know him." I feel a stab of disappointment that Magda isn't happy for me.

"You could at least pretend to be happy for me."

"I am but I just think it's too soon. Look I really need to get some sleep, we'll talk about it tomorrow ok?"

I feel really deflated by Magda's ambivalence, but I try not to let it get me down. I still can't stop starring at my beautiful ring and the pictures of Eric and I from this evening. I can't believe that this is my fiancé. I fall asleep looking at the pictures. I have the most peaceful and restful sleep that I've had in a long time. I wake up feeling rejuvenated and refreshed. I fix myself a healthy breakfast of eggs and fruit. I'm so full of energy that I even go for a run around the local park; something I barely ever do. I've got so much energy that I need to burn it off.

When I get back, I take a long shower and then message Elizabeth the picture from last night of Eric and me, plus one of my engagement ring. Elizabeth calls me immediately.

"Darling I can't believe that you're engaged! What a gorgeous man; you both look so good together. Please tell me more about this hunk of yours," Elizabeth says excitedly. She sounds sober for a change and I don't think that's she's ever told me that I look good.

"I'm so glad that you decided to listen to me darling. I told you that if you make more effort with your appearance then you'd get yourself a man," she continues.

"Eric is really great," I say ignoring her remark. "He's kind, funny and intelligent and treats me like a queen."

"That's wonderful darling; how long have you known him?"

"About six weeks."

"Darling don't you think getting engaged after six weeks is a bit too soon?"

"That's rich coming from the woman who goes gaga about a man she hardly knows," I snap.

"There's no need to be so cruel darling. I know that I haven't exactly set the best example, but I don't want you to make the same mistakes as me."

"Wow I didn't realise how profound you are."

"Really Iris, you can be very hurtful sometimes."

"And you've never been hurtful to me?"

"Are you really trying to start an argument?"

"No, but I don't understand why you aren't happy for me. You of all people."

"Don't say it like that darling, you know that I do care about you. Of course I'm happy for you, but I'm just saying that it's all a bit too soon. Anybody would agree with me. I'll even ask Frieda."

"Whose Frieda?"

"My therapist darling. If you had bothered to read my messages, you'd know that. I didn't realise how fantastic therapy is. Frieda has been an absolute godsend."

"I hope that you don't talk about me to her."

"Of course I do darling. I know that I haven't been the best mother in the world, but Frieda says that I need to forgive myself and move on. Frieda's also made me completely re-evaluate my life and my relationships. She says that my relationships sound like they were very intense and that I always go for the wrong men because I crave approval."

"Did you really need a therapist to tell you that?"

"Oh don't be so negative Iris. If you ever bothered to come and see me perhaps we could go and see Frieda together. She says that you and I should have a session together."

"No thanks."

"I wish that you could be a bit more supportive darling. If you hadn't been so busy ignoring me, you'd also know that I've been sober for almost nine weeks now and I've started taking my meds again. I want to better my life darling and stop falling into the same bad habits. I can't sit and home and drink and cry my life away. I'd even like to go back to university and study psychology. You know that I was very bright; I was studying French and Italian at university, but then I fell pregnant with you. The sacrifices I made for you."

The idea of Elizabeth studying psychology is far too ludicrous to imagine. I try my best to suppress my laughter.

"Well I hope that your new found sobriety lasts," I snort.

"You could sound a little more positive, but Frieda said that a hostile reaction is normal. I've made some lovely friends at the church too and I've joined a pottery class at the community centre. You told me to go out and do things. See I do listen to you darling. I've also been on a few dates with this lovely man Kevin. He's divorced. His ex-wife left him for the Polish builder that was doing their extension. Kevin's not really my usual type but he's ever so lovely. He treats me like a queen. Frieda says that I should change my type. I dumped Rick after I found out that he was seeing other women. Perhaps I can bring Kevin to the wedding. That's if I'm invited."

"Yes, you are invited."

"Well brilliant darling. Let me know if I can help with wedding plans. Anyhow must go; I'm going to the cinema with Kevin soon. We're going to see this charming French film."

"Goodbye Elizabeth and please don't talk about me to your therapist."

ONE WEEK LATER

Eric wants us to get married as soon as possible. He says that it'll be more romantic and he's so desperate for me to become his wife already. He's already set the date for Saturday August 11th. We're going to get married in a beautiful stately home in Sussex. Eric showed me the photos and it looks so royal and lavish. It must have cost thousands. I told Eric that we don't need to get married somewhere so grand and that we could hire a hall somewhere, but Eric wouldn't hear of it.

"Come on Iris, as if I'm going to let you have the wedding of your dreams in some old and stuffy community centre hall where old people play bingo."

We're keeping the wedding fairly small; just close friends and family. I'm inviting Elizabeth and Kevin, Magda and Arek, and Henry and Seamus. Eric is inviting his parents and two close friends.

"I don't understand why we have to hire such a big space for such a small wedding," I say to Eric whilst we're in the car on the way to the bridal dress shop.

"The Havensbrook Estate is such a beautiful place Iris; it's perfect. You'll love it. Just because we're having a small wedding doesn't mean that it can't be a big affair. I want you to feel like a princess on your wedding day. I want you to have a wedding to remember."

"I don't care where we get married. Wherever we get married, it'll be a special day that I'll never forget. We don't need to spend lots of money and make a big fuss to have a special and memorable day. As long as I'm marrying you that's all that matters."

"Come on Iris, every woman wants a fuss on their wedding day."

"You know that I don't like a fuss."

"Don't be so sulky Iris; I'm trying to make you happy."

"I am happy. All I'm saying is that I don't need a lot to make me happy."

"I know, but like I keep on saying, I want to spoil you so you better get used to it."

I don't discuss the matter any further. Maybe I am being really ungrateful. I sound like such a brat. Most women would jump at the chance to get married somewhere so resplendent and feel like a princess on their wedding day.

The car stops outside of the bridal dress shop in Regent Street. It looks very fancy from the outside and is one of those places where you can't just walk in; you need to ring a bell and confirm your appointment. A snooty woman opens the door, eyeing me up and down with her heavily made up eyes. She gives Eric a warm smile but frowns at me.

"I'm Sam, nice to meet you. What kind of dress are you looking for?" she says in a false, over the top friendly way.

"I'm not really sure, not anything over the top. Maybe something simple."

"Why don't you try a few dresses from this rack?" Sam says indicating to the rack on the other side with her long perfectly manicured nails.

"Would you like anything to drink while you wait sir?"

"No thank you, I'm all good. Please call me Eric."

I choose two dresses that appeal the most to me; a pretty but plain ivory silk dress with a V-neck and a demure and simple lace one. I look at the price tag and feel really uncomfortable trying on the dresses. I like the simple lace dress best but Eric shakes his head.

"If I'm being honest Iris, it's far too plain and simple. It doesn't make you stand out."

"But I really like it and plus I don't really want to stand out," I protest.

"I want you to look and feel like a princess. If you really like it then we'll go with it but at least try some other dresses on."

"Ok fine."

"I have some really nice dresses that I think would really suit you," Sam says. She fetches some more fancy and puffy dresses adorned with jewels, ribbons, bead and feathers. I try on a sleeveless dress with a jewelled bodice and big flouncy skirt with a large bow at the back. It's nice but I don't really feel that it's my style. I try another dress with a V-neck satin bodice and big tulle skirt decorated with gems. It is beautiful, but I feel it's a bit too much.

"Wow you look gorgeous Iris. It really suits you," Eric says.

"Yes it definitely flatters your shape," Sam agrees in unison. "It's gorgeous but it's not really my style."

"You look like a goddess in this dress, but it's your choice. If you'd rather go with the plain one, then we'll get it."

"Maybe you're right, maybe I should go for this one." I don't want to disappoint Eric. After all it's a stunning dress. It's certainly the kind of dress that Magda would die for. Maybe it's time that I start to stand out anyway. I've been plain and dull Iris for far too long.

Sam also recommends a glittery tiara that will go with the dress and a pair of white satin heels with jewels. We get them as well upon Eric's insistence. Sam smiles her fake and sickly-sweet smile and tells me that I'm one lucky girl. It's clear that she'd kill to have a man like Eric who would spoil and lavish her. I should be really lucky to have Eric. No, I *am* lucky! I'm the luckiest woman in the world!

Although I feel so elated, a part of me wishes that Magda could have come dress shopping with me. I wanted Magda to come initially, but Eric insisted that it'd be more special if just me and him chose the dress together.

"Since you can't do these kinds of things with your mother, I want to be your anchor and support system. It can't have been easy growing up with a bi-polar, alcoholic mother. Iris you poor thing. I want to be the family that you never had."

I feel so touched by Eric's devotion to me. He's right; we can form our own family. The family that I never had. I never used to want children, but being with Eric has changed that. I know that he'd make a brilliant father and I'd be a different mother than Elizabeth. Hopefully a much better one. Part of my fear of having kids was that I'd inherit bipolar and be a bad mother as well.

"Iris baby, you need to stop worrying. I told you that you're nothing like your mother and you're not going to inherit her illness. I know that you'll be a fantastic mother; you're so caring and so full of love."

Eric saying that made me feel so much better. I can't help thinking about what we'd be like as parents. I know that I want children with Eric, but not for a few more years. I still feel that I'm too young. I want to enjoy quality time with Eric and build a decent career before a baby comes along. I'm curious about meeting Eric's parents. I wonder what they're like and if they're as wonderful as the son that they raised. Eric hasn't really spoken much about them. It must mean that they're pretty normal and nice people. I can't imagine them not being nice and normal. I'm really looking forward to meeting them.

As the wedding draws closer, I feel nervous but excited. I feel lucky that I don't have to organise anything as wedding planning seems really stressful anyway.

"I want you to sit back and relax; I've got it all under control. I know how stressful planning weddings can be and I don't want you to be stressed. I've hired the best wedding planner in London. Leave everything to her, she's an expert and will plan the dream wedding," Eric said.

I feel a bit overwhelmed by how fast this is all happening, but in the past, it was normal for people to get married within a few weeks of knowing one another or even after a few meetings. Even now, in some religious communities and cultures it's the norm. I read an article in Cosmopolitan about a woman who met her husband on a drunken night in Vegas and they got married the very same night. Once they were sober, they wanted to get a divorce but they decided to give things a chance and ten years later they're happily married. Anyway, I know that Eric is the one and that I'm making the right decision. Magda is desperate to meet Eric, so later this evening he's coming round to the flat.

"I can't believe that I'm meeting your husband to be," Magda says. "Finally I get to meet this Mr Wonderful."

Magda goes fully out with the Polish hospitality. She gets out a selection of Polish ham and cheeses, and bread and biscuits. She even baked an apple charlotte cake for the occasion. Magda's apple charlotte cake is to die for. I really hope that Magda likes Eric, but I'm sure that she will. I can't wait for my best friend to meet my fiancé.

Magda treats Eric like he's already family. She greets him warmly with three kisses on each cheek, Polish style and offers him a drink. I open a bottle of white wine for us all to share.

"I finally get to meet Iris's prince charming," Magda beams. "Iris has told me so much about you."

"Likewise Magda, it's good to finally meet you," Eric says stiffly. He seems nervous, but it's probably because he wants to create a good impression. I've told him all about Magda and how important she is to me.

"Please help yourself to the food."

"I'm alright thank you; I ate something before I came." I can see the disappointment on Magda's face so I tuck into her spread even though I'm not hungry, just to make her feel appreciated. Magda, like many Polish people gets offended when people turn down food. I did warn Eric not to eat beforehand as Magda was going to make a lot of food, but he probably just forgot.

"You must eat something. You should try some of the apple cake; Iris loves it."

Eric ignores her and changes the subject. "Your English is very good Magda; how long have you lived in England?"

"For seven years now. I'm hoping to study here at university. I just need to pass some exams, which I'm hoping to do soon."

"Magda is super brainy; she wants to study science," I boast like a proud mother.

"I can't wait for the wedding. I can't believe that it's only in two weeks. Iris told me the story of how you proposed. Oh my God it was so romantic."

"I wanted it to be as special as possible," Eric says flatly. He's being very reserved this evening and not saying much, which isn't like him, but I'm not worried. Like I said, it must be the nerves of meeting my bestest friend who is practically like family. He knows how important Magda is to me. Though I wish he could have at least tried a bit of the spread as Magda put so much effort and heart into it.

"So where will you guys move after the wedding? I'm going to miss Iris so much when she moves out. I hope you'll visit me a lot Iris and won't forget about me after you're married."

"Don't be daft Magda, of course I won't forget about you. Anyway, Eric and I aren't sure about where we're going to live yet."

"What? You're getting married and you don't know where you're going to live?" Magda says abruptly.

I can see that Eric looks irritated. "It's still early days and there's no pressure. Anyway, I've got my parent's home in America," Eric says matter-of-factly.

"I thought that we were going to live in London? You said that you can work anywhere in the world."

"I'm just saying that it could be an option Iris. Of course we'll live wherever makes you happy."

"Where are you guys going on your honeymoon?"

"I want to keep it a surprise," Eric says.

"But what if Iris doesn't like the place?"

I can see in Eric's eyes that he's starting to get peeved with Magda's constant questioning the way a cat gets annoyed after too much petting.

"I'm sure that Iris will like it; it's an absolute dream."

"Just to let you know that Iris isn't really the beach kind of girl. Not like me. I could spend all day lying on the beach whilst Iris is all into the culture and museums. We went on a long weekend away to Brighton and we spent the whole time apart. I spent all day at the beach and Iris went sightseeing. Not that there's much to see in Brighton," Magda laughs.

"The Pavilion was really interesting, you would have liked it," I protest playfully.

"Who spends a hot day indoors in a museum especially as we hardly have any sun in England."

"Not you!" I respond. Magda and I burst out laughing whilst Eric sits there looking very uncomfortable. I don't want him to be upset. I wish that Magda hadn't told him that I prefer cities to beaches. I don't care where Eric takes me, as long as we're together.

"I don't really mind where we go babe; I like beaches too of course," I say to Eric.

"It's Iris's dream to go to Rome."

"I've been to Rome; it's another tourist clap-trap," Eric says.

"Magda, do you want to see a picture of my wedding dress? Eric and I went dress shopping today," I say, trying to change the subject. I show Magda the picture that I took on my phone.

"It's nice but I thought you said that you wanted something a bit more simple. I didn't think that you were into big dresses and diamonds."

"Well Eric persuaded me to go with this one. The more that I look at it, the more that I feel it's perfect. I mean it is my wedding day, why not go all out?"

Magda doesn't seem convinced. I can tell that she's ready to retaliate. I really want it to be a nice meeting without any unpleasantries. If Magda doesn't like or agree with something, she certainly doesn't hold back. I really don't want Magda to have a go at Eric especially as he's so good to me. He probably feels nervous enough as it is already. Luckily Magda bites her tongue, though the conversation is a bit awkward and stilted. Eric leaves shortly after, saying that he has to be up early for a conference call.

"It was nice to meet you Magda, see you at the wedding," Eric says formally as though Magda were one of his business clients.

"Yes, it was nice to meet you too," Magda says, but I can tell by her lacklustre tone that she doesn't mean it.

"There's something strange about him," Magda says after he leaves.

"You didn't have to grill him like that."

"I'm sorry but he comes across as a control freak Iris and how well do you really know one another? He doesn't know much about you. They say that men hardly get any say in the wedding, but I don't think that you've had a say in anything. I know for a fact that you would never choose a dress like that. You hate those kinds of dresses."

"It's just a dress Magda and I have changed a lot these past few weeks. I've been wearing stuff that I don't usually wear."

"Yes, but this is different. I know there's certain things that you would never wear. I know that you're not into the whole princessy fairy tale wedding bullshit. I mean for fucks sake you don't even know where you're going to be living!"

"It's not an urgent thing. There's no rush to do anything."

"I just don't think that you should rush into getting married; you barely know each other."

"Just give Eric a chance, you were so keen on him when he was giving me gifts and taking me to nice places."

"Yes he sounds perfect on paper, but there's something odd about him. Yes he's as good-looking as fuck, but there's something about him that I can't put my finger on. Have you guys even slept together yet?"

"No; Eric thinks it'll be more special if we wait until our wedding night, which is in two weeks anyway. Anyway, what's that got to do with anything?"

"You're getting married and you haven't even had sex?"

"Yeah, loads of people save themselves for marriage."

"Well I know that you're not the devout Catholic type saving herself for marriage and he doesn't seem like the type either."

"Maybe he's just being respectful and a gentleman."

"Look I love you like a sister Irenka, but I don't want you to get hurt. I don't understand why there's this rush to get married."

"Well I think it's romantic."

"I just think that you need to be more realistic Iris. I'm not sure if I've got a good feeling about this."

"I know it's love between me and Eric and we know how we feel about one another."

"Look it's your life, but just be careful is all I'm saying."

"I appreciate it, but you've got nothing to worry about. I'm certain that Eric is the one and I can't wait to marry him."

CHAPTER SEVEN

SATURDAY 11TH AUGUST

Today is the day of my wedding. I'm feeling a bit dizzy from the little sleep that I had the night before but at the same time I feel energized. A mixture of nerves and excitement burst through my body like fireworks. I feel even more psyched after two strong black coffees. I had the strangest sleep. I kept drifting in and out of light sleep which made me feel like I was neither awake nor asleep. I eventually fell into restless dreamful sleep.

The dreams were really strange and vivid. In the dream I was walking down the aisle and there was a man there who said that he was Eric and sounded like Eric but didn't look like him. He was wearing a really scary mask. When I looked closer, I realised that it wasn't a mask but his face. I ran away from him, running as fast as I could until I realised that I was falling through the sky. Falling from this really tall building. I saw Eric; the real, normal looking Eric through one of the windows. I shouted his name and banged on the window, but he ignored me even though he saw me. Then I kept on falling.

I woke up with a jolt and my pyjamas soaked in sweat. I had a long shower to wash away the sweat and to wake myself up. The dream really shocked me. It just felt so real and scary, but I told myself that it was just a stupid dream. Dreams are supposed to be random and weird. I usually don't dream very much. Apart from this dream, I can't remember the last dream that I had. I don't even know why I'm overthinking this. I read that scary dreams are normal, especially during big life events. The point is that I'm happy and I'm marrying the man that I love.

***

I feel a bit carsick on the way to the venue, but I'm too excited to let it affect me. Just as long as I don't puke all over my expensive dress. This feels so surreal; me about to get married. It still feels like a dream itself. A really good dream. No matter how many times I pinch myself, I still can't get over it. I need to start believing in myself. I never used to believe in luck, but now I feel that the universe has turned my bad fortune around and dealt me a lucky hand. An extremely lucky hand. Maybe the saying, *"good things come to those who wait,"* is really true. I need to stop doubting my happiness and embrace it.

As the driver pulls into the Havensbrook Estate, I really feel the nerves kick in. The Havensbrook Estate is resplendent with its acres of perfectly manicured verdant lawns and mammoth ivory brick mansion home with large gleaming French windows, romantic Juliet balconies and stone pillars. It's practically a palace! All of the guests are waiting for us in the elegant bar. The wooden floors are pristinely polished and the round refined glass coffee tables glisten without a single smear or speck of dirt. Comfortable beige leather armchairs are placed around the tables and long drapes hang by the open windows, showing off the exquisite view. It feels like being on a film set for a period drama. Eric generously paid for all the guests' travel and overnight stay at the Havensbrook Estate which is also a hotel.

"Darling!" Elizabeth cries, wrapping her arms around me tightly. Elizabeth looks good; she's wearing a navy flowery dress which shows off her figure and her chestnut curls bounce around her shoulders. She looks really healthy. I see Henry and throw my arms around him. He's grown so much since I last saw him; he must be around six foot two or three now. He still has such a baby face. He'll always be my baby brother.

"I've missed you so much sis," Henry says, holding me tightly.

"I can't believe that you're getting married; I hope that he's good enough for you."

"He is, I swear."

"Iris ye look beautiful, come en give ye old uncle Seamus a hug," Seamus says, clumsily reaching out to hug me. He definitely seems more sober than the last time I saw him.

"I remember ya when ye were a small girl, you were so sweet. My God how you've grown. There's always a place for ye to stay with us, we miss ye."

It feels strange seeing Seamus after so long. He hasn't changed much apart from a few grey hairs. He has the Irish charm about him, which Elizabeth certainly fell for. When I was little, I adored Seamus. Well, when he wasn't in a drunken stupor. He would make me laugh and buy me treats. He wasn't like a father figure, but more like a fun uncle. At least he treated me like I existed unlike most of Elizabeth's boyfriends who wanted me and Henry out of the way. However, most of the time him and Elizabeth would have huge blazing drunken rows and he'd go off for days and weeks without contacting her. When him and Elizabeth got on, he was too drunk to behave like a responsible adult.

I'm pleasantly shocked and surprised when Elizabeth introduces me to Kevin, her new boyfriend. Kevin is the polar opposite of her usual type, but that can only be a good thing. For a start, Kevin isn't very tall; he's a little bit shorter than Elizabeth in her heels, and his hair is thinning on top. However, he seems kind and intelligent, which is the most important thing.

"It's so lovely to meet you Iris, your mother has told me so much about you," Kevin says warmly. He's very well-spoken and eloquent. As I get chatting to him, I find out that he's a chartered accountant and runs a walking and bird-watching society. Kevin seems like the quiet and gentle type; worlds away from Elizabeth's cocky, sleazy and loud exes. He's definitely what Elizabeth needs. He seems smitten with her and doesn't seem to mind her brazen and crazy personality.

"So how did you two meet?" I ask.

"You like to tell this story darling," Kevin chuckles, putting his arm around her waist. It's clear to see that he's perfectly happy for her to take the lead.

"It's such an unusual story and the last place that I'd ever expect to meet anybody. We met at the hospital."

"Hospital?" I'm puzzled. What was Elizabeth doing in hospital?

"Yes darling, if you had bothered to show any interest in my life or had read my messages, you'd have known about my scare."

"What scare?" I'm truly baffled now.

"A few months ago, I found a lump in my breast. Darling you must remember to check your tits, even if you haven't got much in that department. You clearly didn't take after me in the breast department. I always hoped that you'd be a double D like me."

"Wait you had a scare? You should have told me."

"I didn't think that you would care darling; you'd probably wish that I was dead."
"How can you say that?" As much as Elizabeth irritates me, I would never wish her dead.

"When I found that lump, I was so scared that I was going to die. Death was all that I could think about. So, I scheduled an appointment with the doctor and he wanted to do a biopsy. On the day of the biopsy, I was so scared. I was crying so loudly and shaking. Kevin saw me and came over to me, asking if I was alright. I told him how scared I was and he really made me feel better. He told me that he had a scare when he found a lump in his testicles a few years ago, but it turned out to be nothing. Kevin was so kind to me; he asked if I wanted to go for a coffee afterwards.

Kevin rang me every day to see how I was doing and if I needed to talk. I ended up telling him my life story. He was what kept me going that whole terrifying week, waiting for the results. He went with me to the doctor to find out about my results. I could have jumped for joy when the doctor said that it wasn't cancer, but fat necrosis, a benign and harmless breast lump. The doctor said that it tends to go away on its own."

"Oh Elizabeth, I'm so glad that you're ok. You really should have told me."

"Don't worry about it darling. It was a real turning point for me. The prospect of potentially facing death really made me re-evaluate my life. I decided to get back on the right path with my life and be a better person. I didn't want my children to hate me anymore. Kevin really helped me with that," Elizabeth smiles, beaming adoringly at Kevin.

Elizabeth really seems genuinely happy. I find myself feeling a swell of affection for her. Maybe she really is trying this time. Maybe this was the wake-up call that she needed.

"Oh Elizabeth, I don't hate you," I say, hugging her. She hugs me tightly and strokes my hair with her manicured navy painted nails. It almost feels like we have a real mother and daughter relationship.

"I'm just so glad that I'm here darling; I thought you were joking when you said that you were getting married here. Your Eric must be loaded; you lucky girl. Not only have you got yourself a hunk, but a millionaire! This Eric is a catch! Oh darling I'm so pleased for you; my only daughter marrying a rich and handsome businessman. Doesn't that sound wonderful? You should have seen the look on that snob Pamela's face when I told her. She's this terrible snob at the church darling; thinks that she's better than everybody else."

"Well I don't care about Eric's money and status; he's an amazing person and that's what matters the most," I retort.

"Of course darling, but every woman wants a rich and good-looking man to sweep them off of their feet. Nobody apart from celebrities and royalty gets married at the Havensbrook Estate. That lady on the telly; the fat blonde one that does that discussion show whose name I can never remember got married here. She's one of the richest women on TV; they did a big spread on her wedding in *Hello* magazine," Elizabeth prattles. "Anyway, where is your wonderful husband-to-be? I can't wait to meet my son-in-law to-be."

***

I spot Magda and Arek sitting outside smoking. Magda kisses me coolly on the cheek and doesn't say much, which is unlike her. Since the meeting with Eric, things have been a bit frosty between Magda and I. Before we used to talk all the time, but for the last two weeks we haven't spoken much. Eric says that it's obvious that Magda is jealous of me and that he could see it clearly when he met her. Maybe Eric is right, maybe Magda is jealous. Maybe she wishes that she could have Eric. I don't want to think that Magda is jealous; she's my best friend. We're practically like sisters.

Magda looks so gorgeous in her dark purple dress, which compliments her dark hair. Arek looks handsome as well in his light-grey suit.

"Are you sure you want to do this Irenka?" Magda asks. "Arek has his car; we can make a run for it now."

"Are you crazy Magda? Why are you trying to talk me out of

marrying Eric?"

"Because you barely know each other."

"Look Eric and I really love one another; I know that he's the one. I'm just really sad that you can't be happy for me, especially as today is my wedding day."

"I just want to know that you're making the right choice and that you're not rushing into anything."

"I am making the right choice. It all feels so right. I'm going to marry Eric and I'm hundred percent sure."

"OK Irenka; if you're sure that this is what you want, I'll support you." I reach out and hug Magda. She hugs me back firmly, like she's a mother hen protecting her baby chick. I don't want to argue with Magda. I know that she worries about me and wants the best for me. I think she's scared of losing me as we've always been so close. She's not going to lose me. She doesn't have to worry about that.

***

Once Eric arrives with his parents, the registrar moves us to the Grand Meeting Room for the ceremony. As neither Eric or I are religious we decided on a non-religious ceremony. The Grand Meeting Room is absolutely huge; much bigger than mine and Magda's apartment put together. Crystal chandeliers hang from the high ceilings and the cream carpets are embellished with a carefully intricate gold leaf design.

We still have a few minutes before the ceremony starts so Eric introduces me to his parents, Eric Senior and Genevieve. Eric Senior, like his son is tall and imposing. Despite his age he's still handsome in an older man kind of way. He still has a full head of grey hair which is neatly parted and a stern expression on his face. He looks like the kind of man that could run for president. He must be very patriotic as I spot a pin of the

American flag on his expensive jacket.

"Nice to meet you," he says expressionlessly, shaking my hand as though I were a business client, not his daughter-in-law to be. Something about Eric Senior scares me a bit.

"Nice to meet you Iris," Genevieve says dryly with no hint of warmth in her voice. Her only embrace is a formal barely-there peck on the cheek.

Genevieve, who is around my height, is a very elegant woman, yet very conservative in her ash grey tailored tweed dress suit and sensible thick heels. Her blonde hair is coiffed in an unflattering old-fashioned way. Although she has delicate features that make her pretty, her expression is blank and vacant. Genevieve looks like she could be the runner-up for president's wife. I feel guilty for judging my new in-laws so unfavourably, but there's something about them that makes me feel uncomfortable. They just seem so stiff and cold. They don't seem very excited to meet me, but maybe they're nervous. After all, they've only just met me. Maybe they'll be more open and embracing once I get to know them.

Elizabeth's reaction couldn't be more different to that of my in-laws to be. She rushes up to Eric and throws her arms around him as though he were the prodigal son.

"You must be Eric! I can't believe that I'm meeting my son in-law! Oh, isn't he gorgeous? Iris you didn't tell me that he was such a hunk!" Eric's parent's look at Elizabeth with disdain, as though she had two heads. Eric seems just as uncomfortable, as though Elizabeth were his own mother embarrassing him in front of his friends.

"We're going to be family; one big happy family! Just tell these two to actually visit me and involve me in their lives!" Elizabeth natters loudly, embracing Eric Senior and Genevieve; both of them as stiff as planks of wood. They certainly don't look as though they want to be part of my family. When I ask Eric where his friends are, he said that they couldn't come.

"Unfortunately, Tripp has something really urgent that came up this week at work and Brett has a really bad infection, so the doctor advised him against travelling or going anywhere."

"Oh no that's such a shame; we could still postpone the wedding and wait until they're better and available."

"No there's no need, if they can't make it, they can't make it. It's not the end of the world," Eric says flippantly.

"But they're your closest friends and this is your wedding day," I protest.

"Look it's no big deal, as long as you're here, that's all the matters. You look so beautiful by the way; I can't take my eyes off of you."

"You look ridiculously handsome, as usual." Eric looks irresistible in his navy Armani suit. He's had his hair styled and slicked back, which makes him look like an old classic Hollywood movie star. He arranged for me to have my hair and make-up done by one of the top make-up artists and hairstylists. They spent two hours doing my hair and make-up, which frankly I could have done myself or with Magda's help as Magda is really good with hair and make-up, but Eric insisted that I be pampered for my special day. I usually never have my hair up, but the hairstylist said that it would look good with the dress, so she did my hair in a special plaited bun.

"Oh Iris, you look so so beautiful," Elizabeth cries. "See I've always told you that when you wear make-up and do your hair nicely you can be so pretty. Oh your dress is so gorgeous; I wish that you had let me come and pick it out with you. I wish we could have more mother and daughter bonding time." I almost feel bad that I didn't bring Elizabeth wedding dress shopping with me, but I knew that it'd be a nightmare as she'd criticize all of my choices and try to persuade me to wear something that I don't like.

The registrar, a tall and graceful woman in her sixties, tells the guests to take their seats as the ceremony is about to start. It's a nice ceremony with a group of musicians playing Pachbel's Canon in D Major. Elizabeth starts sobbing and noisily blows her nose with her tissue, garnering dirty looks from Eric Senior and Genevieve.

"Sorry this is just so emotional; I can't believe my only daughter is getting married. I never thought I'd see this day. Sorry I'll be quiet now."

The registrar ignores her and proceeds with the service. "We are here today to celebrate the union of Eric Theodore Irving III and Iris Katherine Shaw," the registrar says. She continues to talk briefly about the sanctity of marriage and how love conquers all. When the registrar then proceeds to the main part, my heart is flapping away inside my chest like a broken bird. I can't believe that this is really happening. All of a sudden, I feel sweaty and light-headed.

"Eric, do you promise to love, care for and stay faithful to Iris?"

"I do," Eric smiles. Seeing the affection and warmth in his face makes my body light up. It reinforces the fact that I'm making the right choice.

"Iris, do you promise to love, care for and stay faithful to Eric?"

"I do."

"I now pronounce you husband and wife. You may now kiss the bride." Eric kisses me fervently on the lips, as though I were Sleeping Beauty. I will savour this moment for ever. I feel like the heroine in a movie, kissing her hero. Eric takes my hand is his and we make our way to the dining room for the celebrations.

The dining hall is even grander than the Grand Meeting Room. Instead of lots of tables; there's one large rectangular table to seat all of the guests, like at a banquet. The noise, the fuss and the talking make me feel even giddier. All I want to do is grab a few moments to myself. I excuse myself to go to the toilet and sit there processing the fact that I'm married. This is my wedding day, but why do I feel like this isn't real? I feel like I'm on drugs; everything feels so far away and intangible. Should I be feeling like this? Is it normal to feel this way on your wedding day? I feel like I'm in a bubble, like I can't feel anything. I give myself ten minutes to breathe and let it all sink in. I want to splash some water on my face to wake myself up, but I don't want to ruin my expensively made-up face.

"Are you ok baby? You were in the toilets a while?" Eric whispers when I make my way back to the dining room. We start with a delicious salmon starter, which is ornately displayed on the plate like a piece of art. There's also baskets of different types of bread, olives and feta stuffed pimento cherry peppers to go around on the table. There's also plenty of champagne to go around for everybody as well as bottles of red wine and chardonnay. Eating seems to help and stops my head from spinning. I haven't eaten since eight o'clock this morning and it's now three in the afternoon, which is probably why I felt so weak and light-headed.

I try to make conversation with my new in-laws but it's like getting blood out of a stone. Both Eric Senior and Genevieve are extremely reserved and beyond the mundane polite small talk of work and British weather, they're not interested in getting to know their new daughter in-law. Maybe they preferred their previous daughter-in-law. I feel so insecure. On the other hand, Elizabeth can't stop bombarding Eric with questions and treating him as if he were already her own son.

When the main course comes (leg of lamb with creamy

mashed potato and vegetables), I swap and sit next to Henry. I've barely spoken to my little brother who I haven't seen in months. It feels so good to see him; I've missed him so much. I act all big sister-like, asking him about school, grades and girls, as well as nagging him not to drink too much, which is rich coming from me. I'm on my second glass of champagne and it's only the second course.

I'm so proud and impressed when Henry says that he doesn't drink and doesn't ever want to either after growing up with two alcoholic parents. I'm so happy to see that Henry has a strong head on his shoulders. He's doing really well at school and gets the top grades. He's hoping to study Biochemistry at university. Henry was always super into science. I remember the time when I got him a science kit for his seventh birthday. He was so delighted. You couldn't tear him away from it.

Henry also tells me about this girl that he really likes called Niamh, but he's not sure if she likes him as all the girls are crazy about the most popular boy in their class, Connor. I don't get how any girl wouldn't want to date my little brother. Maybe I'm biased, but he's kind, smart and mature. He's also got this adorable British-Irish accent. I'm also happy to hear that Seamus isn't drinking as much and finally he seems to be stepping up in his role as a father.

"It's a shame that he couldn't step up earlier," I say.

"He's really trying to make it up to me. He knows he was a shitty father and that he let alcohol ruin everything. I can't believe that Elizabeth is actually sober for a change and on her meds. I wonder if it's for good or if she'll be back on the bandwagon anytime soon. Mind you Kevin seems pretty decent. I would never put the two of them together in a million years, but they seem good together. I even promised Elizabeth that I'd come down for Christmas if she kept up with her sobriety. Kevin said that he'd keep an eye on her."

Elizabeth does indeed look happy. Her face is radiant and rosy and she can't stop laughing whilst Kevin looks adoringly into her eyes. They really do seem crazy about each other. They're constantly touching and laughing compared to Eric Senior and Genevieve who sit there rigidly as though they were mannequins. True to her word, Elizabeth is sticking to the alcohol free champagne. Sober Elizabeth is still a pain, but nowhere near as much of a pain as Drunk Elizabeth. Drunk Elizabeth gets over-emotional, angry and nasty.

"I can't believe you're married sis," Henry says.

"I know, I still don't believe it myself. What do you think of Eric?"

"I don't really know the guy to be fair. As long as he treats you right and you're happy that's the main thing. His folks seem pretty strange to me and I find it a bit weird that none of his mates or other family are here."

"Eric's friends couldn't make it unfortunately, but not everyone needs to have loads of mates. I mean I've only got Magda. Plus, we don't have a big family either." I notice that Henry's eyes light up whenever I mention Magda. I think that he's got a crush on her.

"I know, but I still find it a bit strange. There's just something a bit off if you know what I mean. I guess it just surprised me the way that you got married so quickly; it took me by complete surprise as it's not something that I would imagine that you'd ever do."

"When you know it's the right person, then it feels right. People get married after a few weeks all the time and what about arranged marriages? The bride and groom have never even met and it's perfectly acceptable. It's not like I don't know Eric; I feel like I've known him all my life. You'll understand when you find the one." I feel so patronising saying it.

"Maybe," Henry shrugs, but I can tell that he's not convinced. "You just don't seem that happy."

"What do you mean? Of course I'm happy."

"I don't know, it seems like you're just going through the motions. You seem like a deer in the headlights."

"Of course it's overwhelming, it's my wedding day. It's normal to feel a bit overwhelmed on your wedding day."

"I guess I wouldn't know. Anyway, I just want to be sure that you're happy."

"I am happy; happier than you'll ever know."

"Steady with the drinking though; I swear this is like your third glass and we're not even onto dessert yet."

***

My head is spinning and I'm unsteady of my feet, but I can't stop dancing. I've had God knows how much to drink, but I'm so happy. I finally asked the DJ to put on some better music to dance to; I was getting really fed up with all of the slow, steady and sombre songs. I could see that everyone was starting to get bored. I requested the DJ to play Valerie by Amy Winehouse, which is mine and Magda's favourite song. We started dancing together and singing along to it like two demented cats. We then asked the DJ to play some more upbeat music including cheesy pop and R&B hits.

"Now this is what I call a party," Magda smiles, dancing to Beyoncé. I dance with everyone, including Seamus who is surprisingly a good dancer.

"I'm like Michael Flatley, aren't I?" Seamus laughs. I start oddly feeling as though Seamus is really my uncle. He even gave me a hundred pounds as a wedding gift, which is really generous of him. Him and Elizabeth seem to get along too, which is good for Henry's sake. Elizabeth is usually bitter and full of scorn about her exes. Henry seems much happier as well; even happier when he's dancing with Magda. Arek doesn't seem to mind and offers me a dance. He's a man of few words, but I know that he's a good guy and he loves Magda like crazy.

I'm having such a good time that I don't even notice that Eric isn't there. I go off to find Eric but I can't find him anywhere. I give up and ask the receptionist if they know where he is.

"He's gone upstairs to check into the honeymoon suite. Congratulations," the receptionist says sweetly. I ask her for the room number of the honeymoon suite and rush upstairs to find Eric. I knock firmly on the door. Eric opens it. His shirt is unbuttoned and his hair is sticking out.

"Eric why didn't you tell me where you were going?" I ask frantically.

"I don't have to inform you of my whereabouts just because we're married," Eric replies coldly.
"What's going on babe?" All of a sudden, I feel stone cold sober, like someone has slapped me really hard across the face. My heart is in my mouth. Eric seems angry.

"You go downstairs and keep on making a fool out of yourself."

"Eric, what are you talking about?"

"Dancing like a slut in a nightclub and listening to such vulgar music. You really made a great impression to my parents. Well done," Eric says cuttingly.

My head is spinning. Why is Eric acting like this? I'm speechless.

"My parents think that you're a classless drunken hussy. It was truly embarrassing to watch you. That's why I left because I couldn't bear to watch my wife behave like that. I thought that you were demure and classy."

"I am Eric; I was just having fun. That's what people do on their wedding day; they dance and drink and they have fun."

"Well it didn't look like fun to me. You made a complete fool out of me and my parents. I don't want my wife behaving like this."

"I'm sorry Eric if you felt that way. Let me make it up to you. Let's enjoy our wedding night; just the two of us. We can finally consummate our marriage," I say with a grin. I'm hornier than I realise. I'm willing to forget Eric's tirade and finally have the sex of my life. I know that the moment will be worth the wait and will be filled with passion. I've been fantasizing about the moment when we finally get intimate.

"I'm not the mood," Eric says despondently.

"Please Eric," I beg.

"Look I just want to go to bed; it's been a long day and I'm tired.

"You sure I can't change your mind?" I ask devilishly, unzipping my wedding dress to reveal my new sexy pearly lace underwear.

"I'm tired Iris. You can go back and enjoy yourself. I just want to go to sleep," Eric says dispassionately, as if I were nobody.

I stand there in the middle of our beautiful and luxurious honeymoon suite and burst into tears.

CHAPTER EIGHT

I toss and turn for most of the night. It feels like I've been punched in the stomach. This doesn't feel real. It's like my mind can't rationalise what's happened. Did I really behave so inappropriately? Maybe I did drink too much and make a fool out of myself. Everything was so perfect up until now. I wanted it to be the perfect wedding night. I'd fantasized about this moment. Everything was ready specially for this moment; the rose petals scattered on the silk spread as well as a huge bouquet to congratulate us on our wedding day. Also, a box of chocolates and a bottle of champagne await us. The room is so spacious with plush rose-pink carpets, all white furniture and Egyptian cotton sheets so comfortable that in other circumstances they'd have me out like a light. There's a gorgeous view of the estate from the wide bay windows.

Eric snores away next to me whilst I lie there staring at the ceiling. This is the first time that Eric and I have shared a bed together. It feels like there's a stranger lying next to me and not the man that I've just married. Everything in my mind becomes so fuzzy and eventually I fall into a light sleep which I keep awakening from. I have strange dreams that don't make any sense. When I wake up, I feel like I haven't slept at all. My head is pounding and I can't focus. I wake up to a tray being placed next to me. The tray is abundant with crispy golden pastries, pots of jam and fruit.

"Good morning my beautiful wife," Eric says softly. "I also ordered some cooked breakfast and tea, coffee and fresh orange juice. Eat up darling."

"I'm not really hungry," I say. My stomach is churning and I feel nauseous.

"I wanted to apologize for last night darling, I think that I overreacted. My parents just really got under my skin. They're just so conservative and so disapproving of everything. They want me to marry some WASPY rich girl who has important parents. but I've never wanted that. They have to get used to the fact that you're my wife. I shouldn't have taken my frustrations out on you."

I feel a sense of relief wash over me. I'm the one who overreacted. I should know how difficult and demanding parents can be. I really should have been more understanding. All couples argue and say hurtful things to one another. I shouldn't be so naive and over-sensitive.

"Why don't we skip breakfast and have sex on our wedding morning?" I say provocatively. "We missed out on our wedding night and now is the perfect time to catch up.

"I would love to baby, but I promised my parents that I'd have breakfast with them." I feel the surge of disappointment wash over my body like a tidal wave.

"I thought that we were going to have breakfast together and you could always meet your parents a little later."

"I know but I promised them darling and I've got to go down soon. You just sit pretty and eat your breakfast. If there's anything else that you fancy just call reception," Eric says, giving me a kiss on the forehead as though I were a child.

"Don't be upset baby, we've got the whole honeymoon to spend together and fuck. Our flight is this evening. I promise that you'll love where we're going. It's a big surprise."

Eric goes to the bathroom to get dressed.
"Babe why don't you get undressed in here, after all we are husband and wife and I'd like to meet your friend downstairs,"

I say flirtatiously.

"Sorry babe it's always been a habit of mine. I always get dressed in the bathroom."

Once Eric has gotten dressed, he gives me a dry peck on the lips and leaves to have breakfast with his parents. I sit under the silk sheets with a selection of breakfast fit for a king surrounding me, but I can't face any of it. I've completely lost my appetite.

***

I meet with everybody for brunch before they all go home and Eric and I leave for our honeymoon. The boys excluding Eric are happily bonding over the football on the big TV, so I spend some quality girl time with Magda and Elizabeth.

"I can't believe you left so early! We had a great night and danced till like two. You really missed out; Kevin and Seamus had a dance-off. It was hilarious!" Magda chats animatedly.

"What? Kevin doesn't strike me as the kind of guy that would be bold enough to do a dance-off," I say. I wish that I had been there to see it.

"Kevin is just full of surprises darling, though he isn't the best dancer. Of course, I won't tell him that. I'll just sign us up for dance lessons," Elizabeth laughs. Magda is laughing too. I suddenly feel left out. It's like Magda and Elizabeth have their own private joke that they won't let me in on.

"We all had such a laugh! It's a shame that you missed it Iris. Where did you go?" Magda asks. I can see the concern in her eyes.

"They were probably having some hanky panky Magda darling; that's what the wedding night is for," Elizabeth says.

"Elizabeth!" I hiss.

"What darling it's nothing to be ashamed of. We're all adults here."

"It's so cool that you can talk to your mum about sex. My mother, bless her, is far too conservative and Catholic to talk about sex," Magda says.

"See how lucky you are darling to have such a liberal mother. I do everything wrong in Iris's eyes."

I roll my eyes; I really don't have the patience for Elizabeth's pity party.

"So how was it Iris? Is he good in bed?" Magda giggles.

"Look I'm not going to talk about my sex life with both of you, especially my mother!" I snap.

"There's no need to be defensive darling. Why are you in a mood?" Elizabeth says. "Was he not good in bed? These things take time darling, though mind you Kevin completely took me by surprise in that department. He's such a kind and considerate lover," Elizabeth swoons.

I almost choke on my water. "Elizabeth, I really don't want to know about your and Kevin's sex life."

"Oh darling don't be such a prude. What do you think that Kevin and I get up to? Knitting and watching EastEnders on telly? Sorry I'm not a prude and sexless middle-aged old matron. Did you and Eric have an argument? Why isn't he here?"

"He's spending time with his parents before he leaves."

"Why don't they join us? His parents act like they've got a poker lodged up their asses. What's wrong with them? They didn't want to talk to anybody yesterday. Are we not good enough for them?"

"Maybe they're not the talkative type," I say though my sentiments echo Elizabeth's.

"They just seem really strange; it's like they didn't want to talk to anyone. It's like they didn't seem very happy about the wedding. I don't think you're going to have an easy time with your new in-laws," Magda says. "I certainly wouldn't want them as my in-laws."

"Maybe they're just one of those people that take time to get to know."

"They don't seem like much fun darling. Anyway, you'll be in London and they'll be in America, so thankfully you won't have to see them much," Elizabeth remarks. "Oh, look at this food, it's incredible. Why are you hardly eating? If you're worried about putting on weight, it's a special occasion darling and you can always diet when you're back from your honeymoon. Mind you darling, you don't need to lose any weight. You're looking very thin; thinner than usual. I hope you're not developing an eating disorder."

For the past two or three weeks I seem to have lost the bit of weight that I gained. I think it was probably from all the nerves and excitement of the wedding. When I'm nervous or excited, I seem to move around more and eat less.

"I'm fine," I sigh.

"So, do you know where you're going for your honeymoon yet?" Magda asks.

"No, Eric wants it to be a big surprise."

"Oh how exciting darling! Eric really does spoil you," Elizabeth chats excitedly, clapping her hands like a little girl.

"You have to take loads of pictures," Magda adds.

"You are happy aren't you darling?" Elizabeth asks.

"Of course I am, why wouldn't I be?"

"I don't know darling; you don't seem completely happy."

"I am but I'm just tired."

My head is still fuzzy and I'm so exhausted. Whilst everybody piles their plates high at the special wedding buffet, I can barely manage a slice of bread. There's a selection of succulent salmon, crispy bacon, roasted new potatoes, egg fried rice, tuna pasta, chicken legs and an array of aromatic sauces. The desserts are even more impressive. There are white and pink cupcakes with little marzipan brides and grooms and ones with swirly writing spelling Eric and Iris inside of a heart. There's also left-over wedding cake. Eric had a special three tier cake made all in white icing with Eric and Iris written around each tier in pink icing.

Everybody around me is having a good time. Magda tries to pull me in for selfies. I politely oblige but I don't feel like smiling. When everyone asks me why I'm not eating, I lie that I'm still stuffed from the huge breakfast. Why am I not happy? I've just married the man of my dreams; I'm in this luxurious estate that many brides would kill for and I'm about to go on a surprise honeymoon. Everything is fine between Eric and I now; last night was a big misunderstanding. Then why do I feel that there's this big distance between us that was never there before?

CHAPTER NINE

I'm so exhausted that I sleep for almost the whole flight. Eric has gotten us seats in business class and we're given five-star service. The flight attendant offers us champagne and snacks and constantly asks if there's anything that she can do to make us feel more comfortable. I haven't flown by plane much, but I do know that this is world's away from economy class. The seat is so comfortable that I sink into it. It's going to be a long flight so I might as well get as much rest as I can. Eric still won't tell me where we're going.

"You'll love it baby, I promise. We're going to have the best time," Eric says, stroking my hair. "Try to get some rest as it's going to be a long flight."

I wake up after a few hours feeling even more groggy and confused. Eric is asleep next to me, his MacBook Pro still open on his lap. I feel the sudden urge to look through it. I move the touchpad but the login in box pops up on the screen. I give myself a mental shake. What am I doing sneaking up on my husband? Why am I trying to look through his computer like a paranoid psycho? This is my husband and I trust him. Of course I trust him. I wouldn't have married him if I didn't.

I check out the in-flight entertainment but I don't feel like watching any of the films. I just end up reading my book; the latest best seller about human psychology that I brought at WHSmith. I also picked up another book, a silly holiday romance novel to get me in the mood of the honeymoon. My mind still feels too tired to read so I just end up closing my eyes and nodding off again until the flight attendant gently wakes me to ask if I want to have my meal. My stomach is rumbling like crazy. I realise that I've barely eaten. I devour my chicken club sandwich and fries and go back to sleep until I'm awoken by the announcement that the plane is going to land soon.

"Ladies and gentlemen, this is your captain speaking. We'll be making our landing in The Dominican Republic in around fifteen minutes. Please ensure that all electronic devices are switched off and that you have your seatbelt on," the captain announces.

I stare out of the window and see stretches of crystal-clear blue water. It looks truly incredibly.

"I know that you'll love The Dominican Republic baby," Eric says clutching my hand.

"Eric, The Dominican Republic is like paradise!" I grin. I can't stop smiling now.

"It really is. It's the perfect Honeymoon destination. I thought why not do it again?"

"What do you mean do it again?"

"I went to The Dominican Republic on my honeymoon with my ex-wife," Eric says casually. In that exact moment I feel my good mood vanish like a cloud of fog.

***

"You came here with your ex-wife??" I shout. I'm absolutely livid.

"Come on Iris it's no big deal. Why are you making a big thing out of this?" Eric says composedly.

"This is a big thing! Why would you bring me to the place where you went with your ex-wife on your honeymoon?"

"What so I'm not allowed to like The Dominican Republic just because I came here with my ex-wife? Do you know how ridiculous you sound?"

"Me ridiculous? I thought a honeymoon was meant to be somewhere special; not somewhere that you've already been with an ex!"

"It's just a place Iris! You're acting jealous and crazy."

"You could have at least chosen somewhere else for a honeymoon! Somewhere that you didn't go with your ex-wife!"

"You're completely overreacting! You're acting like my ex-wife is here! I wanted us to have an amazing time together in a beautiful place where most people would die to go, but if you're going to ruin it so then be it. I wanted to enjoy myself but if you're going to throw a hissy fit, we can go back home."

"What home? We can't even decide where we're going to live!"

"I came here to have a nice time and I'll have a nice time with or without you!" Eric says frostily, slamming the door behind him and leaving me all by myself in the luxurious honeymoon suite. Maybe Eric is right, maybe I'm making a big fuss about nothing. I mean The Dominican Republic is such an incredible place, why wouldn't anyone want to come back here? Maybe Eric really does want to make me happy but I'm the one being ungrateful and starting an argument over nothing. It's not like he's still with his ex-wife. She's history. She's not even alive!

Being here feels like being in heaven. The sand is so white and pure, like tiny diamonds and the water is as clear as the sky; mesmerising shades of aquamarine, turquoise and teal. I've never seen anything like it in my life. Eric booked us the most expensive honeymoon suite with direct access to the beach. It's like the beach is the back garden.

The suite is so lavish, like a palace. The marble floors scintillate like jewels and the rugs are snow white and plush like animal fur. Vivid abstract paintings hang from the wall and there's a huge king-sized bed in the middle of the huge room with rose petals scattered all over the silk sheets. The bathroom is massive with a big Jacuzzi and large step in shower with multiple settings and features. I've never stayed anywhere like this in my whole entire life. This is the kind of place where only celebrities stay. We even have our own pool outside!

Eric is right. I'm being so petty and ridiculous. It's like heaven here and I'm making such a fuss like a spoilt and bratty child. I really should make it up to Eric. I want to have the time of my life. I take a long soothing shower and mess around with the settings on the shower which is really fun. I wrap myself in the fluffy white towels and select my racy red lace underwear. I'm going to surprise Eric. I went underwear shopping a week before the wedding and chose some sexy pieces. Hopefully Eric will cheer up when he sees me and we can have hot passionate sex.

Eric will probably be back soon. Whilst I wait, I read my book. An hour passes and he's still not back so I send him a message. I wait patiently, hoping that he'll reply soon. Three hours go by and he still hasn't replied. I start to get anxious so I ring him. It goes straight to voicemail. I throw the phone down on the bed in frustration. A moment later the phone starts to ring. Annoyance hits me when I see Magda's WhatsApp photo flash up on the screen. I reject the call. I really don't feel in the mood to talk to Magda.

I start wondering if perhaps Eric really has booked a flight back home. He wouldn't leave me stranded here would he? I start crying. Maybe he really has left me here. It's been four hours since he went off and I'm frantic. I try to call a couple more times but it keeps going to voicemail. I check the string of WhatsApp messages that I sent him but it still shows two grey ticks for all of the messages. Maybe he's been hurt. My anger turns to worry. The worst-case scenarios spring to mind.

What if he's been hurt, kidnapped, stabbed or drowned? Tears are streaming down my face like the power shower setting which feels like a massive rainfall. I'm hysterical now. It's approaching five hours since he left and I'm frantic. I call the reception desk to ask if they've seen him but they haven't. They're very kind and tell me that if there's anything I need to just call.

I curl up in a foetal position on the large bed. I wish that I hadn't had a go at him. It's all my fault. Now the sky is starting to turn dark and the fear hits me even harder. There's still no response from Eric. The ticks are still grey and there's no missed calls from him. I'm here alone in this beautiful paradise, but it's starting to feel like hell. Hot tears are constantly streaming down my face. I feel as lost, alone and abandoned as an infant that's been left by its mother.

After a while I can't lie still any longer. The adrenaline is pumping through my veins. I start pacing the room like a lunatic. It's getting really dark outside now and I'm really scared. Perhaps I should call the police. Though a person needs to go missing for twenty-four hours before you can report them as missing. I ring the reception again but they still haven't seen him anywhere. They ask if I want to come downstairs for dinner. Apparently, they've got a delicious curry on the menu, but I don't fancy it. I feel too anxious to eat.

I consider looking for Eric myself. I put my shoes on and head out to the beach. I call Eric's name desperately like an owner searching for their cat. I'm scared to venture out too far in case I get lost. I walk down the beach calling Eric's name. There's nobody out there apart from me. I see some lights in the distance. It looks like it could be a bar or a restaurant, so I walk that way.

My heart begins to thud as I see a group of men approaching. They eye me up like a lion eyeing up a piece of meat. They wolf whistle and say "hey there pretty lady," but I ignore them and keep on walking quickly. Luckily, they don't try to persist or follow me. Just in case, I keep on walking as fast as I can until I reach the well-lit place. I feel so much safer now.

It's a bar/restaurant with plenty of people. I feel hugely relieved but worried about where I am. It feels like I've walked for hours, though I'm pretty sure that it can't have been for more than forty-five minutes. The straps from my sandals are rubbing and I'm starving. I could get something to eat and go back to the resort.

A wave of extreme frustration overcomes me when I realise that I didn't take my bag with me which contains my purse. I only took the key card to the suite. I haven't eaten all day and my stomach is growling with hunger like a fierce lion. The thought of walking back fills me with dread and exhaustion. It's dark and I won't be able to see where I'm going or recognise the resort where we're staying. I don't even know how far away I am. It feels like I've been walking for miles. I'm so stupid not to have taken my bag or even my phone. Maybe Eric finally answered my messages or what if he hasn't? What if something awful has happened to him? The welling panic building inside of me threatens to swallow me up.

I ask the bar staff if they've seen a man of Eric's description but they shake their heads. My body shakes with panic and tears are racing down my face. I end up revealing everything to one of the barmen. He's very consoling and orders me a taxi back to the resort.

"Don't worry miss, I'm sure that he'll turn up. Please take a taxi home; you don't want to be wandering around by yourself at night."

In the taxi back to the resort I'm still sobbing my eyes out. How can he do this to me? Where is he? What if he doesn't come back? The bleakest scenarios run through my mind. What if he's not back? What do I do? Maybe I'm overreacting. My whole body feels like jelly. The taxi stops outside of the resort and I run to the suite to get my wallet to pay the driver.

"God Iris where on earth have you been?" Eric's voice fills the room the moment that my key card swipes open the door.

A mixture of relief and anger floods me. "I could ask the same of you! I called you so many times but you didn't answer. I was worried sick!"

"I couldn't get any reception and only got your calls and messages now."

"Where were you!?"

"For goodness sake Iris, I just went for a run to cool down and then I stopped at a bar on the way and had a few drinks. They had the soccer on, so I watched that."

"Couldn't you have gotten WIFI?"

"For God's sake Iris, I don't need to be glued to my phone twenty-four seven. Also, we both needed time to cool down."

"You could have at least replied to my messages. I was so worried."

"You surely didn't think that I would just leave you?"

"Well that's what it felt like. Look I need to pay the taxi driver."

"Don't worry, I'll ring reception and ask them to pay the fare from my card," Eric says, picking up the phone to call the reception desk.

I'm so relieved that Eric is ok that I want to cry with joy but I feel angry too. What was so hard about dropping me a message to let me know where he was and when he'd be back? Surely he could have gotten reception on his phone. Eric has the best iPhone on the market with superior connection and reception.

Plus, it's not exactly the middle of nowhere out here.

After Eric is done speaking on the phone, he wraps his arms around me, but I'm rigid.

"Come on don't sulk baby."

"I was so worried about you!"

"Come on you can't be serious; this is one of the safest parts of the island. What could possibly happen to me?"

"I don't know. Anyway, I don't want us to argue anymore, this is our honeymoon."

"I didn't start any argument; it was *you* who started it," Eric says accusingly.

"So it's my fault?"

"Come on I thought you said that you don't want to argue, now you're looking for a new fight."

"I'm not! Anyway, why don't we do what couples do after they argue?" I hint cheekily.

"What's that?"

"Have make up sex of course," I say, pressing my lips against his and reaching my hands to unbuckle his belt.

"Wow you really are quite the little minx aren't you?" Eric laughs, removing my hands from his trousers.

"Does it turn you on?" I whisper breathily.

"It just surprises me that's all. You're so delicate and docile, that I didn't think that you'd be like this."

"Isn't that what guys like? A lady in the street and a freak between the sheets?"

"I'm just not used to that. I have very particular sexual needs

Iris."

My heart starts thumping like someone is continuously punching me and I feel sick. Is he saying that I'm not enough?

"What kind of needs? Things like role-play? Role-play sounds like fun."

Eric shakes his head. "I'm not talking about role-play. I'm a kinky sort of guy; vanilla sex doesn't do it for me."

"Do you mean you like stuff like BDSM? I don't feel ok with being hurt."

Eric looks shocked and hurt. "I would never do anything to hurt you baby, how could you even think that?"

"Ok well what sort of stuff are you into?"

"I want to ease you into it slowly Iris. I don't think that you'll be ready for it quite yet."

"Ready for what?"

"Let's just take it slowly first. I would love to see you naked."

I allow Eric to pull off my yellow sundress and unhook my bra. My heart begins pumping again, this time with excitement. I help him to unbutton his shirt, revealing his toned and tanned torso. I run my hand over his hard stomach. He lifts me up and throws me down onto the bed. I'm so aroused. We kiss frantically. I feel like I'm doing a sex scene in a movie. I get even more excited and aroused as Eric pulls down his trousers. I can't wait to see his huge manhood. I've fantasized about this moment for so long. I've fantasized about his big hard dick thrusting away inside of me, back and forth.

I groan with pleasure as Eric sucks on my nipple. He pulls off my panties and tosses them across the room. Every time I reach to feel his dick, he brushes my hands away. Why doesn't he want to show me his marvellous manhood? I can't see it through his thick pants.

"No need to be so inpatient," Eric hisses.

"But I want to see your huge cock," I giggle.

"For goodness sake Iris, stop ruining the moment." Maybe I am taking things a bit too fast, but I'm so excited. I want him to enter me so bad. He runs his hand over my vagina, but yet he gets touchy about me touching his cock. I try to tug down his pants. Eric sighs and finally pulls down his pants. I expect to see a hard, gleaming cock, ready for me, but I try hard not to mask my disappointment. His penis is completely flaccid and tiny; about two inches. I know that size doesn't matter but I feel so deflated that I can't turn him on.

"Are you nervous? Or is it me?" I ask.

"Look I told you that vanilla sex doesn't turn me on. You know what, I'm not in the mood," Eric says huffily, heaving himself off of me. He reaches for his pyjamas.

"What's wrong? Is it me?" I cry frantically.

"Maybe, I don't know."

"What can I do? Maybe we didn't do enough foreplay. Come back to bed and we can just cuddle and do other stuff."

"You don't seem to get it Iris, normal sex doesn't do it for me."

"What does do it for you?"

"Look I'm really tired Iris, let's talk about this another time," Eric sighs irritably, pulling on his pyjama bottoms.

"No let's talk about it now."

"For God's sake Iris, you just don't drop things do you?"

"Why are you mad at me? Why can't we talk about things and try to make them better?"

"Look I don't want to talk about things now. Let's just go to sleep," Eric snaps, turning the light out.

The tears cascade down my face like Niagara Falls. Why doesn't my own husband want to have sex with me? This is our honeymoon. We should be having hot steamy sex. Maybe he's not attracted to me. That makes me cry even harder. What kind of things turn him on? If he's really into all of that Christian Grey stuff, I'll try it. It can't be that bad can it? Maybe I'll grow to like it too. Maybe he has sexual problems and is embarrassed. Perhaps he uses not being turned on by vanilla sex as an excuse. I mean loads of men and couples have sexual problems, don't they? They say sexual dysfunction is really common in men. Maybe we can see a doctor and get help. Eric is my husband and I'll do anything to make this marriage work.

CHAPTER TEN

Far from feeling rested on my honeymoon, I feel more exhausted than ever. I didn't sleep very well at all. I kept drifting in and out of sleep. During the periods that I slept, I kept having strange and fragmented dreams that I couldn't remember properly when I woke up. It almost felt like I was being choked. I'd wake up gasping for air; Eric fast asleep next to me as though nothing in the world mattered.

I fell asleep again and had another strange dream. This dream I remembered because it was so vivid and clear. At first it started off as a nice dream. Eric and I were on a romantic moonlit walk by the lake in the park. There were swans swimming peacefully in the lake and the lights from the nearby buildings shone brightly. The light from the radiant moon reflected onto the lake, twinkling magnificently like glitter. Everything was so perfect and so still. One minute we were kissing and holding hands, then the next Eric wasn't there anymore.

I shouted his name but he wasn't there. I looked around but I couldn't see him anywhere. Suddenly everything became dark. The beautiful lake turned into a murky and tempestuous sea and the beautiful pearly swans turned into ugly and menacing vultures, squawking manically and flapping their heavy grey wings. I was no longer in the park, but in a dark forest, surrounded by gnarling trees. I screamed and screamed to the top of my lungs but nobody could hear me. I was all alone in the dark and dire forest.

Suddenly, I saw him. I called his name but he didn't turn around. I tried to run after him and catch up with him but he kept walking until I couldn't see him anymore. Then the ground began to swallow me up. It pulled me down, down, down into the dark depths of the earth.

I woke up drenched in sweat. I didn't feel like going back to sleep; I was too shaken from the nightmare. Instead, thoughts swirled around in my mind like a hurricane on full blast. I tried to push out the negative thoughts but I couldn't get rid of them. I couldn't stop thinking about what happened last night. Maybe Eric doesn't find me attractive? Maybe there's something wrong with me. Maybe we need to go to a doctor. Sexual problems are common, right? We wouldn't be the first couple. Sex isn't everything and it certainly isn't what makes a stable relationship. But I crave sex. I crave it more than ever. Shouldn't newlyweds be at it like rabbits? I felt more confused than ever. Gradually all my thoughts became a blur and I fell into a light but dreamless sleep.

When I wake up properly, it's around half eight in the morning. Eric is nowhere to be seen but there's breakfast on the table. There are separate baskets filled with pastries, fruit and bread plus a selection of cheeses, cold meats, jams and butter. It looks delicious but I'm not hungry. Instead I make myself a black coffee and nibble at a piece of bread.

Eric comes back half an hour later. He's in sports gear and looks very sweaty. He kisses me on the cheek.

"Hey gorgeous, did you sleep well?" Eric says cheerily.

"Yes, really well," I lie.

"Look I'm really sorry about last night babe, I was just so tired. I feel so ashamed that I couldn't fuck you."

"Don't feel ashamed, these things happen to men all the time. There's nothing to be ashamed about," I say, reaching out for his hand.

"God I'm so lucky to have you Iris; you're so wonderful and

so understanding. I feel like I haven't been myself. My ex-wife made me feel very insecure and I think that that's a big part of the reason why I'm like this "

"Why, what did she do?"

"She liked to emasculate me; she constantly told me that I wasn't big enough and that I didn't satisfy her enough."

"That's awful, I would never do that or make you feel like that."

"I know baby, that's why you're different and I love you for it. My ex-wife liked to dominate me; she was very into BDSM and that sort of thing. Normal sex wasn't enough for her. I wasn't enough for her."

My heart breaks when I see the sadness in Eric's eyes; they look like lost puppy dog eyes. Seeing him so vulnerable really hurts me. I get up from the table and throw my arms around him as though he's my child.

"Oh Eric baby. I don't understand how anyone could do that. Your ex-wife really sounded as though she had serious issues."

"She really did. I think that's why I've been having problems. I feel so embarrassed about last night."

"Don't be, these things happen. Have you spoken about this with your therapist?"

"I don't feel comfortable confiding these kinds of things to my therapist."

"I'm sure that your therapist won't judge you. We could even go to therapy together."

"For goodness sake we don't need therapy for this."

"Then how are we going to sort this out? Honestly your therapist isn't going to judge you or think that there's something wrong with you. If anything, this is probably quite a common issue."

"Look I'll talk about it with my therapist if it really means that much to you."

"I think it'll help. You've got nothing to be ashamed of."

"I do feel ashamed; ashamed that I let my wife use me as her sex slave and belittle me. It's like normal vanilla sex doesn't turn me on anymore. At first her kinky sexual quirks didn't turn me on but she'd get even angrier if I couldn't get it up so in the end my body just responded. I wanted to make her happy. That's the problem with me; I like to please people too much. I was so upset that I couldn't please you last night. It killed me," Eric says poignantly, touching my cheek.

"We'll get through this together, I swear."

"God I'm so lucky that I married a woman as wonderful as you Iris."
"So, what shall we do today? I looked as some of the leaflets on the local attractions and there seems like loads of really amazing things to do and explore. There are so many parks and beaches to visit. We could also book some tours. I'd love to swim with dolphins and see the monkeys. There's also horseback riding. That sounds so romantic doesn't it? We could also go to this really cool bar that does karaoke in the evenings. That sounds like fun. There's also a really nice market."

"Babe I'm really sorry but I've got so much work today. I keep being pestered with calls and emails."

"But we're on our honeymoon! Can't work wait until we get back?"

"It really can't babe, I'm so sorry. Please don't be mad at me. That's just the nature of my work; I'm working on a really big deal at the moment."

"But nobody works on their honeymoon. Don't the people that you work with understand that you're on your honeymoon?"

"I'm afraid it doesn't work like that baby. Look, I promise it'll only be for a few hours. Perhaps in the evening we can go for dinner and then to that karaoke bar."

"Whatever!" I sigh.

"Please baby I don't want you to be upset with me. Go and have an amazing time. Here, take my card. Spend it as you like," Eric says, handing me a credit card.

"Eric, I have my own money and my own credit card, I don't need yours."

"I want to spoil you. You know that most women would just gladly take the card and spend it."

"You know I'm not like that."

"Please Iris, I earn enough money not to care about it."

"If you earn enough money, I don't understand why you have to work so much."

"If you want to be successful you have to work hard baby."

"I know that, but still we're meant to be spending time together."

"And we've got lots of time still to spend together. Look I'll try and get as much work as I can done so we can spend more time together, ok?"

"Fine," I sigh. "But I really don't want the card. I just want to go to the beach."

I lie back on the sun lounger and allow the radiant sun to spread its warm glow around my body. I've slathered my body in sunscreen so that I don't get burnt. I probably won't get too much of a tan, but I don't care. I just enjoy the feel of the sun on my body and the cool breeze of the sea. I take in the lush surroundings and relish them. I've never been anywhere as heavenly as this before. The sand is so white and soft and the water is so clear like an aquamarine crystal. This definitely beats Brighton and even the South of France. The Dominican Republic is really like what you see in those beach screensavers and holiday brochures. No, it's even better. It's better than anyone could ever imagine.

The beach is so still and so peaceful, like the night. Well it is a private beach, but it makes a difference from being on a crowded beach filled with holiday makers arguing over sun loungers; large men and women parading around showing off their protruding bellies and angry sunburn, and kids running around screaming. It's nice to have peace and quiet. I get a Piña Colada from the bar on the beach and lie back in relaxation. I read a bit of my book and then go in the water.

The water is cool, but not too cold. It feels like being in a giant bath filled with clear and clean water. I lie back and let the small waves wash over me. Holidays like this are one in a lifetime for most people. I've never been on a holiday like this before. As breath-taking and luscious as the beach is, it's not somewhere where I would want to spend the whole day every day. Magda would happily spend the whole week at the beach, but I want to see things and explore. Plus going to the beach everyday loses its novelty.

After two hours at the beach, I decide to take a little walk and explore the local village. It's very quiet and sleepy around here; a bit like a ghost town. There are mainly just luxurious villas, resorts, restaurants and building complexes in the area with a few local shops, bars and restaurants scattered around. As luxurious and dream-like as it is here, I find the silence and the stillness jarring. I crave the buzz of a city and vibrant and lively atmosphere. Here it's almost too quiet. Perhaps tomorrow I can book a tour or take a bus to one of the bigger towns.

I head back to the beach and order lunch at the beach bar. The bar is empty; a stark contrast from its welcoming and vivacious vibe. Cheerful reggae music plays in the background and a chromatic mural of a sunset fills the walls. There are straw umbrellas and the seats and tables are carved from wood. Jars of shells and garlands of colourful fake flowers fill the room.

I order another cocktail and a chicken club sandwich with fries. I'm hungrier than I realise. The food and the alcohol take my mind off the mind-numbing loneliness that I'm feeling. I feel a stab of disappointment when I check my phone and don't see any messages from Eric. I can't understand why he can't just leave his work for when he gets home. We're meant to be spending our honeymoon together.

The only company I have is Josiah, the man who works at the bar. He's friendly and chatty and asks me lots of questions about London. He asks me if I'm travelling by myself.

"Why are you by yourself? If I were your husband, I wouldn't let a beautiful woman like you out of my sight," Josiah says.

I feel even sadder when he says that, especially when another couple walks into the bar. They seem so loved up; holding hands and laughing as if they had no other care in the world. I envy them. Maybe I'm just being stupid and petty. Eric loves me, I know that he does. I mean we are going to spend time together. Maybe it isn't healthy to spend too much time together anyway.

I see an incoming call from Magda pop up on my screen. I should be excited to talk to her and tell her about my wonderful, envy-inducing holiday and the amazing time that I'm having. I am having a good time though aren't I? I mean this is only my second day here. However, I don't feel like speaking to Magda. I don't feel like talking. I don't want to have to try to pretend that everything is ok.

***

After lunch I head back to the suite for a nap. I've barely done much yet I feel so exhausted. There's a note from Eric saying that he's gone to work in the resort bar and that we should have dinner together later. I fall into a dreamless sleep for what feels like hours. I wake up to see Eric standing next to me.

"Hey Sleeping Beauty, did you sleep well?" Eric says stroking my hair.

"God what time is it?"

"It's half five."

"God I've slept for nearly three hours."

"Let's go for dinner babe; I've booked us a really nice seafood restaurant." I don't bother to tell Eric that I'm not really a huge fan of seafood. I'm just grateful that we're finally spending time together. I get dressed up for the event. I wash my hair and put on my make-up and new baby blue jeans dress. Eric tells me that I look beautiful and we walk hand in hand to the restaurant. Now I'm finally starting to feel that this is what a honeymoon should be like. For the first time since we've arrived, I'm actually smiling.

The restaurant is overlooking the beach. The sun is starting to set and it's so romantic. Eric picks a yellow flower from one of the bouquets and puts it in my hair, telling me that I look so gorgeous, like the goddess of sunshine. His hands reach out for mine and he tells me how much he missed me today and that he was so distracted from his work because he kept thinking about me.

We drink good wine and eat lobster and king prawns, which

I'm not too keen on. Even though I try to peel the shell as best as I can, bits of the shell get stuck. Whenever I chew, I keep coming across little pieces of shell, which really puts me off. I'm not really that hungry anyway. Well not hungry for food. All I want is to have hot sex with my new husband. I want us to tear one another's clothes off. I think that the wine is really getting to my head. Drinking is the only thing that takes away the layer of unease and doubt that constantly plagues me. I scold myself again for being so dramatic and ridiculous. It's clear to see that my new husband adores me and would do anything for me. Nothing or nobody is perfect.

Eric keeps reaching for my hand and brushes the hair away from my face. God, he looks so gorgeous tonight. I feel so lucky. After dinner, we go back to the bar at the resort for more drinks. A friendly American couple from Texas, also on their honeymoon, starts chatting to us.

The husband looks about twenty years older than the woman. He's freckled with white hair and stands out in his loud red Hawaiian shirt. The wife looks like the kind of woman who could be on one of those Real Housewives programmes; bleached blonde with bum and breast implants. They ask us if we want to join them for drinks. Eric and I politely accept. The prospect of talking to other people makes me feel less alone. I've never really been much of a people person, but all of a sudden I feel the urge to talk to people. Maybe I'm lonelier than I realised.

"How long y'all staying here?" the woman, who introduces herself as Tammy, asks.

"Ten days," Eric replies.

"Us too! It's like paradise here, but it ain't half quiet round here."

"Well sugar cup this is a honeymoon resort and most people

don't come on their honeymoon to socialize if you know what I mean," her husband, Bob, laughs. "Of course, I'm too old to be at it all the time."

"Oh Bobby, don't embarrass our new friends," Tammy scolds, but she's smiling.

"That's why you married me darlin'. So how did you two lovebirds meet?"

"We met at a gallery," I blush.

"It's nice to find a couple that actually met in person. All these kids meet online these days," Bob says. "How long have you kids been together?"

"Our wedding was kind of a whirlwind one. We've been together for about over two months, nearly three," I explain.

"It was a whirlwind wedding with my first ex-wife. I married her after six weeks. Boy was I young and stupid. It was a common-law marriage. We got divorced after about a year. We were just kids and didn't know a thing about marriage. We didn't really know one another as well as we thought either.

Now I'm not saying that'll be the case for you kids; when you know someone's the one, you know. That's how I knew my Tammy was the one. I didn't get that feeling with my ex-wives. I know this time will be third time lucky." Bob reaches over and plants a big smooch on Tammy's lips.

They're not a couple that you would necessarily put together; older man in his late fifties with a bit of a paunch and thin plastic model blonde who looks to be in her late thirties, but somehow, they exude chemistry. They're constantly touching one another and laughing. I wonder if Eric and I exude chemistry.

Eric has been rather quiet, not really saying much. I wonder what Tammy and Bob think of us. The conversation changes from love to jobs. Bob works in the oil industry and Tammy owns her own clothing store. Bob and Eric talk mundanely about the stock market and business, whilst I chat to Tammy about more "girly" things.

"He's a looker your guy. You're real lucky," Tammy says, twirling one of her sandy platinum curls around her ultra-long, pink manicured nails. Tammy has the sort of nails that make you wonder how you can conduct daily activities. By the looks of it, it doesn't seem that Tammy does much.

"Yeah I am lucky," I agree.

"I'm a lucky girl to have Bobby; he's a real sweet guy and he makes me laugh. People think I'm with him for the money, but I have my own successful business that I started all on my own. Bobby and I were friends for years and it just kinda happened ya know? I wasn't into him at first but he kept growing on me and well here we are."

"I don't want to sound nosy, but is it normal to have problems so early on in the marriage?" I look around to see if Eric has heard, but he's engaged in conversation with Bob a few feet away. I can't believe that I just said what I did out loud. I must be really drunk. Why am I sharing my marital problems with a complete stranger? Maybe these "problems" aren't really problems and are all in my mind.

"What kinda problems hon?" Tammy asks.

"It doesn't matter. It's no big deal anyway. Eric is great."

"Every couple has problems; it just depends on the problems. My ex-husband kept cheatin' on me; swore each time he'd never cheat again. I believed him but he kept on doin' it. I decided enough was enough and I deserve way better. Does Bob drive me crazy? Sure. His snoring drives me insane and he's obsessed with baseball and soccer, but he makes me happy. The question you gotta ask yourself is if they make you happy."

"Sure I'm happy," I say. "You can't be happy all the time though right?"

"Of course not, but if they make you more sad than happy, then that ain't right. Will you have another drink hunny? You seem so young. How old are you, twenty? My baby girl is twenty-one."

"Twenty-three; twenty-four in October."

"You're still a baby. Don't worry. I know that marriage seems scary, but you'll figure it out."

I'm about to order another drink when Eric taps me on the shoulder. The tap is so sharp that I almost drop my empty glass.

"I think we'd better get back," Eric says sharply.

"Aw come on you guys; it's not even nine yet. Bob and I want to check out this really cool bar round here where they do karaoke and if they like your singing, you get free drinks. Sounds fun!" Tammy says enthusiastically.

"Wow what a fantastic idea!" Bob grins. "Hey honey why don't we do the Sonny and Cher duet?"

"Oh my God, love it!" Tammy squeals.

"You should join us," Bob says animatedly. He puts his arms around Tammy and pulls her in for a kiss.

"I think I'll call it a night," Eric says coolly. "You join them though if you like Iris."

Part of me really does want to join them. Tammy and Bob seem like a laugh and it could be fun, but I don't want to let Eric down. Maybe we can finally have some time to ourselves, which is all I've been craving. Perhaps Eric wants us to spend the evening together, just the two of us. I tell Bob and Tammy that I'll join Eric. I feel really rude, especially as they both seem so nice, open and fun. I feel slightly sad as I see them walk away, holding hands and pausing every few moments to kiss. I can hear the laughter and the ease between them.

Eric is in a rubbish mood. He barely talks to me. I reach for his hand, but he doesn't take it. He doesn't even make eye contact with me. He just scrolls through his phone.

"Why are you being like this? I thought that we were having a good night," I say. My heart is in my mouth and this wave of uneasiness washes over me. Did I do something wrong?

"I'm just tired. I really wish that you hadn't insisted that we hang out with those god-awful people," Eric says exasperatedly.

"Bob and Tammy were really lovely. They seem like a lot of fun," I protest.

"Brash and classless dullards are what they seem like to me," Eric says agitatedly.

"That's a bit harsh, you don't know them."

"Neither do you Iris; you're so sweet and naïve. Trust me I'm a good judge of character. I don't want us to hang around with people like that. God that Tammy woman is so vulgar and plastic; I wouldn't want you to be around someone like that."

I don't agree with Eric, but I don't want to fall out over somebody that I don't even know. Maybe Eric is right. Maybe he's a far better judge of character than I am. I've never exactly been good at reading people.

"Let's go to bed my beautiful wife," Eric says tenderly and pulls me in for a kiss. I was right, Eric did want us to spend quality time together. We don't have any issues. I was just making a big deal out of nothing. I hope that I'm not turning into a drama queen like Elizabeth. She makes the smallest thing into something huge.

We lie down onto the bed. Eric pulls down my dress and slides his hand underneath my bra, squeezing and massaging my nipple. I can feel my body respond to Eric's touch and I'm getting excited. I don't want to allow myself to get overexcited and put too much pressure on Eric.

"We'll take this slow baby, OK?" I whisper.

Eric unbuttons his shirt and I run my hands over his beautifully sculpted lean chest. He obviously works out a lot. I suddenly feel self-conscious. Although I'm thin, I'm not toned. I've never been into exercise. I get a stitch even running for the bus. At school I was hopeless at PE at got picked last for the teams. Magda once made me come along with her to a Boot Camp class at the gym. I hated every minute of it. It was pure torture. I could barely manage two press ups. The instructor went easy on me though, getting me to do the easier exercises and less reps than everyone else, but I still felt so stupid.

Eric has the body like a male stripper; six pack and rock-hard abs. I feel so lucky to have a husband that looks this amazing. I run my hands over his large muscular biceps. I feel so euphoric that I could orgasm just touching his body alone. I want Eric to run his hands all over my body, but he keeps playing with my nipple. It feels like we're two teenagers hooking-up; not even reaching third base. This feels so tame, but I want to please Eric. If it means taking it slow, I'll take it slow. I want him to rip my underwear off impatiently and relish my body; his hard dick pressed against me, showing me how much he wants me. I want him to lick me and kiss me frantically, like he can't get enough of me.

Eric pulls down my pants and sticks his fingers in me, moving them around inside of me. At first it feels good, but then he starts moving his fingers more roughly.

"Ow! That really hurts!" I wince.

"Come on Iris, I barely touched you. You're so sensitive," Eric says, removing his fingers from me.

"I'm sorry."

"It's ok baby. I need to go to the bathroom anyway."

Eric takes a long time in the bathroom. I start to get a bit impatient but I don't want to rush him. I know that I need to be patient with him so I wait. When Eric finally emerges, he takes off his trousers and lies back on the bed.

"I'm ready. I'm hard. Let's do this," Eric says, pulling down his pants to reveal his erection. His erection is obviously larger than when flaccid, but not as big as I expected it to be. I tell myself to stop caring about size. I'm hardly well-endowed in the breast department. So what if he's slightly below average? Big isn't necessarily better. I'm still so horny. I want him to penetrate me.

Eric enters me with ease and I can't believe that I'm finally having sex with my husband. The moment I've been waiting so long for. However, it doesn't feel as passionate and romantic as I expected it to be. It seems as though Eric is just going through the motions. He doesn't make eye contact with me. Maybe he's nervous as well, especially after what his bitch ex-wife put him through.

I try to lie back and just enjoy the sensation but something just seems out of sync. It just feels so robotic and mechanical.

"Baby talk dirty to me," I say. Maybe talking dirty will heat things up.

"Iris please!" Eric snaps sternly. Obviously dirty talk isn't his thing. I just want him to feel like he's enjoying this moment too. After a minute or so, it's over. Eric ejaculates and that's it.

I don't know what I expected. At least I finally had sex with my husband even if it was slightly awkward. I remember Elizabeth once telling me that first time sex isn't always all that it's cracked up to be and it takes time to get good at it. I cringed when she said it at the time, but maybe she's right. I'm being so stupid with my ridiculous expectations. We have the whole of our marriage to get better at sex. I mean we're still getting to know one another.

I want to kiss and cuddle my husband. I want his large protective arms around me. I stroke his bicep and kiss his shoulder but he doesn't respond. I hear light muffled snores. He's already fallen asleep. I can't help but feel disappointed. My husband is right here next to me, but I can't help but feel that he's a million miles away.

CHAPTER ELEVEN

TUESDAY 14TH AUGUST

"Thank God you're ok! I've tried to call you like a thousand times!" Magda bellows through the phone.

"I'm sorry Magda, the WIFI connection here isn't great," I lie.

"You had me worried sick. So how is it? It looks like paradise from all the photos that you've sent."

"I'm having a really good time; such a good time that I've barely glanced at my phone." I feel guilty for not messaging Magda.

"How are things with Eric?"

"Things are really great between us."

It's not exactly a lie. Eric has been really loving and attentive. It makes me feel that he really does love me and care about me. So what the sex wasn't what I thought it would be; maybe we're both a bit inexperienced. We have the whole of our marriage to work on it. I'm hardly the best judge as I haven't got that much experience. Eric was in such a good mood this morning. He brought me breakfast in bed and we had a cuddle. It was perfect. Today we're going on a boat trip.

"So how are things in the bedroom?" Magda asks brazenly.

"Magda that's personal!"

"Hello, I am your best friend and sister. You can talk to me."

"It was good," I say.

"Just good?"

"It wasn't as mind-blowing as I thought it'd be, but I mean what do I know? Maybe my expectations were too high."

"This is why you should sleep with someone before you marry them and I'm saying this as a Catholic."

"I'm glad I waited and not everything should be about sex. I didn't marry Eric for sex. Look I don't want to talk about my sex life."

"Ok ok, anyway tell me what it's like here."

I tell Magda about how divine it is here and it's like a dream come true, but there's not really much else to say. I haven't really been up to much, but on the other hand it is only my third day here. I've booked to go on some of the tours organised by the resort. I've booked a tour to go to one of the main towns and I've also booked a tour to swim with dolphins and see monkeys. I'll be going alone as Eric isn't keen on going.

"I've already been before babe; I don't need to go again. You know that I'm not into all that tourist rubbish," Eric says flippantly. "I don't even know if I want to go on this boat trip and ecological reserve tour; I've got so much work to do."

"But it's about spending time together! I didn't come here to spend the honeymoon by myself," I whine.

"I know baby, but I've got so much work to catch up on here. Anyway, we don't have to spend every single moment of every day together."

I can feel the tears forming in my eyes. This is our honeymoon and we're meant to be spending time together.

"I know you're disappointed baby, but we don't have to do everything together. I'm not keen on animals and there's nothing special about the main town".

"That's not the point. The point is spending time together.

What's the point of even going on a honeymoon if all you're going to do is work? Even Julio who is super demanding hasn't given me any work to do whilst I'm away."

Julio has been acting like I'm his best friend. He rarely gets pally with anybody. He wanted to know everything about Eric and our dates. He's been acting like I'm dating, well marrying a celebrity. Julio got super excited when I told him that we were getting married.

"Oh my God it's like something from a movie. You are so lucky Iris! Eric sounds so perfect and so romantic. Why can't I find a rich and gorgeous man to sweep me off my feet? Does Eric happen to have any gay friends?"

I thought about even inviting Julio to the wedding, but Eric said he didn't want there to be too many people. I guess it's not like Julio and I have ever been close. Julio can be a tough boss, but lately he's been so nice. I never used to ask for much holiday. Whenever Felicity would ask for holiday, she'd moan that he's so unfair. Having said that, Felicity would always ask for holiday during the busiest times. I was a bit worried that Julio would say no to me having holiday, especially with such short notice, but surprisingly he agreed. It's probably a good time, as after any big opening, things are usually quiet for a while.

"Come on babe, your job is completely different to mine; you're not a big shot in the art world. No one relies on you," Eric says condescendingly.

His words sting. I may not be anything special but my job is important and I'm good at it. Eric notices that I'm upset.

"I didn't mean it like that baby. You work so hard for practically nothing. You don't have to work anymore. You can do whatever you want baby; you can paint all day and sell your art."

"But I like working. I would love to be an artist, but I want to make it on my own. I don't want to make it just because my husband is a rich and important person in the art world."

"That's how most people make it babe. It's not what you know, but who you know. Most of the big names in the art world at the moment are rich trust fund kids who can't paint for shit, but daddy has the money and the connections."

"That's not how I want to make it and that's not how it should be. As much as I love painting, I need to and I *want* to make money. Sitting around painting all day and hoping that someone will show interest won't help me. I want to earn my own money and be independent."

Eric laughs. "You're quite the feminist, aren't you? Most women in your position would be thrilled not to have to work and spend their days doing what they love. It's not like you wouldn't be working. You'd make money from your art. All I'm saying is that I can give you a helping hand and connect you to the right people."

"I appreciate it Eric, really I do, but for the time being I want to continue with my work. I recently got promoted and who knows what other opportunities it might lead to."

"Come on, it's hardly a big promotion. You've just been promoted to do more dirty work. Trust me I'm in the art world and your job won't lead to much. You told me how stressful and tiring you find it and that you have to do overtime."

"I mean whose job isn't stressful? I only do overtime if we've got something big coming up, but I don't mind. I'm good at what I do."

"I know you are baby, but I don't want you to be stressed."

"I don't want you to be stressed either. I mean we're here on our honeymoon. Please babe, can't you just put work aside for one afternoon?"

Eric sighs. "OK, but I've really got a lot to sort out. I've got a conference call at three so I'll have to take that."

"OK fine, but can't you at least go on one of the other tours with me?"

"Look, you know that it's not my thing. However, if it means that much to you, I'll plan some really special things for us to do together that we can both enjoy."

"Thank you for making the effort baby," I smile and kiss him on the lips. Relationships are all about compromise. I think Eric is a bit of a workaholic; maybe spending some more time together doing things will make him realise that life isn't all about work. Then it dawns on me that perhaps Eric isn't used to spending time with a woman. It was obviously different with his ex-wife as he probably wanted to escape from her craziness.

Eric and I walk hand and hand to the harbour. There's man holding up a sign for the boat trip. Eric pays the money and we step up onto the boat. We're joined by a Japanese couple who nod at us and smile, but are perfectly intent on babbling away just to each other. The man in charge of the boat tells us to wait five more minutes and then we'll get going. Eric is looking at his phone, whilst I take pictures of the stunning scenery. I'm so startled by a loud voice that I almost drop my phone into the water.

"Howdy neighbours!" Tammy squeals as if we we're close friends. I can see the annoyance on Eric's face.

"Fancy seeing you two here!" Bob chuckles.

"Y'all should have come last night; we had a great time!"

"They all loved Tammy's Dolly Parton rendition. In fact, they liked it so much that they sent us a big jug of this curacao cocktail for free. We'd have gladly shared it with y'all; there was more than plenty to go around. Boy we're still hanging. I don't know what they put in that stuff, but boy was it strong," Bob natters loudly. Tammy starts singing Dolly Parton's *Nine To Five*. Tammy is actually a good singer and Bob has a proud look on his face.

"Isn't she a good singer?" Bob grins, patting her bottom. "She's got a good ass too."

"Oh Bobby stop, there's people here," Tammy says, but she's laughing as well. Eric looks embarrassed.

"I'm sorry I'll turn it down a notch. Sorry I'm not usually this embarrassing. I'm just so happy that I'm married to the love of my life that I can't stop braggin' about it. What did you lovebirds get up to last night, anything fun?"

"We just had a quiet evening; we were tired," I say.

"Such youngsters like you two, tired? I'm fifty-six and I feel like I'm seventeen! Well Tammy keeps me young," Bob chortles.

"Ain't this boat trip exciting? It got good reviews on Trip Advisor so we thought why not?" Tammy chimes in.

"I love boat trips. They're so romantic, like Titanic. Hey honey muffin why don't we take a picture doing the Titanic pose?" Bob suggests.

"What a great idea!" Tammy hollers like an excited child. They both ask the boat owner to take a picture of them doing the Titanic pose before we depart. He obliges especially when they offer him a tip.

"God those people get on my nerves," Eric whispers grumpily. "I wish I had decided not to come."

"Don't be so silly, they're just having fun," I say.

140

I wish that Eric and I had gone to the karaoke bar with Bob and Tammy last night; it seemed like it would have been a laugh. Magda and I would always enjoy doing karaoke. Sometimes we'd go to the local pub for karaoke every Thursday. At first, I was far too shy to get up there on stage. I was worried that I'd make a fool out of myself. Magda seemed so confident and natural up there on stage. She would pressure me to go up and got the other pub-goers to egg me on. Once I got stuck into the song, all of my fears vanished. It wasn't as bad as I thought. There were people who were far worse than me and truly sucked, but nobody made fun of them. Everyone was just having a good time regardless of whether or not you could sing. Karaoke is a good exercise for shyness. I smile at the fond memories.

"Maybe we could try the karaoke bar," I say to Eric.

"It's not really my thing if I'm being honest. I'm not into making a fool out of myself. I didn't think that it'd be your thing either."

"It's just a bit of fun, but never mind." I feel a bit disappointed but I can't expect us to have everything in common. Maybe karaoke is just mine and Magda's thing; it doesn't have to be Eric's thing. Eric likes sports and I don't, yet he doesn't expect me to see the games with him. The boat starts moving and we're off. I feel really excited and get my camera ready to take lots of pictures.

The boat tour is incredible! It's not like anything I've ever seen. It takes my breath away. Our tour guide points out the different part of the island and the sea life that can be found. We even get a glimpse of dolphins. On the boat tour we also see the other beaches along the coast, which are breathtakingly sublime. Real tropical beaches with palm trees, golden sand and a fantastic blend of azure, teal and sky-blue waters. I'm in absolute awe. I can't stop taking pictures. However, not even the photos reflect the beauty. The tour guide tells us that on one of the beaches, one of the scenes of a James Bond film was filmed.

I feel disappointed that Eric doesn't seem interested. He's annoyed that there isn't any WIFI on the boat and keeps trying to change the setting on his phone to get better signal. I wish that he could switch of and enjoy the majestic beauty that the Dominican Republic has to offer.

Eric doesn't seem interested in the tour of the ecological reserve either. I'm mesmerised by the lush vegetation and the jewel-like cerulean and emerald waters of the lagoon. I'm glad that I brought my bikini as we get a chance to go out into the water. This is even better than the private beach at the resort. The lagoon is clearer than bath water. It's absolutely magical. I beg Eric to come in with me.

"Babe I think I'll just sit here and watch you; I don't really feel like getting wet," Eric says disinterestedly.

"Come on babe it'll be fun! Look how beautiful it is here!"

"I haven't got my trunks. You go and have a swim; I'll watch you."

"I'm sure you can borrow some. The tour guide mentioned that they have some spare towels and things."

"Babe, honestly I'm good, we can take a dip together later on. Watching your gorgeous body is good enough for me."

I'm glad that at least Eric appreciates my body. I want him to come in the water with me and splash around like the other couples. Tammy and Bob and the Japanese couple have also joined us for the tour of the ecological reserve.

The Japanese couple are laughing and taking endless selfies together whilst Tammy and Bob are messing around, splashing each other. Bob lifts Tammy up and throws her in the water. Tammy has an incredible figure. Her expensive red bikini shows off her super toned stomach and legs, large breasts and full bum. I suddenly feel self-conscious. I wish I was as sexy and as curvy as Tammy; maybe Eric would want to have sex with me more.

I give myself a mental slap and tell myself to stop being so ridiculous. Eric doesn't fancy Tammy; he said that plastic women aren't his type. Eric would have married someone like Tammy if he really wanted to, not me. Eric obviously isn't shallow like other guys and Tammy obviously isn't shallow. Bob certainly doesn't look like he works out much. Whilst he's not fat and is fairly well built, he's got a bit of a beer gut. Whilst Tammy has a golden-brown tan, Bob looks a bit like a lobster. Before he gets into the water, Tammy slathers his back with sunscreen.

I relish being in the pellucid cool water. I feel like I'm in heaven. I take plenty of pictures and get the couples to take some of me and in turn I take some of them. I pester Eric for a picture of us both together. He's not keen, but reluctantly poses for a picture with me, which Tammy takes. I want to take another picture, as Eric is frowning in the one that Tammy took, but I don't want to make Eric irate. He's glued to his phone now that he's gotten better signal. He doesn't even look up at me. I feel a deep pang of sadness. Why can't Eric put down his phone for five minutes and join me? Why is he being so distant, like he'd rather be somewhere else?

I'm sad once the trip is over. It's been such an incredible experience. I can't wait to send all of the pictures to Magda. I'll send some pictures to Elizabeth and Henry as well. Elizabeth calls me this evening. Apart from the call, she hasn't once bombarded me with any of her usual messages during the trip so far. Maybe now she appreciates my personal space more that

I'm married. I'm glad that she has Kevin to keep her in check as well.

"Well darling how is it? Oh how I wish I was there; it looks like absolute paradise from all of your lovely pictures. Darling you are really living the life. What a catch you've found yourself in that Eric; boy does he spoil you. It was really a beautiful wedding and you looked absolutely beautiful. I just hope that you're happy darling because that's what matters most at the end of the day," Elizabeth jabbers. It's not like Elizabeth to be so concerned about my happiness, but I don't pass any comment.

"Of course I'm happy. I'm having the best time," I say.

"You must be in seventh heaven. When you're both back you *must* come and stay. Don't worry darling I'll be on my best behaviour. I've even gotten into cooking. Kevin *loves* my cooking; he says that I should be the next Nigella Lawson."

The idea of Elizabeth turning into Nigella Lawson is quite laughable. Elizabeth could barely even make toast! I was the one who did all of the cooking and all of the food shopping for that matter. Elizabeth would have been happy for us to live off of convenience food, but I was fed up of having baked beans, oven chips and fish fingers all the time. So I went to the library and borrowed some cookery books and that's how I learnt to cook. I was only about seven or eight, but even at that age I was a lot older mentally than my peers. Most kids that age wouldn't be trusted to be near a hot stove or oven, but life taught me to grow up fast and as a result I was sensible and advanced for my age.

"Where are you going to live darling?" Elizabeth continues.

"We're not sure; Eric wants to buy something in London so we'll be looking as soon as we get back. Eric thinks that we could split out time between London and America."

"Well he can afford to do that darling; just as long as you

don't move to America for good. I couldn't bear the thought of you abandoning me like Henry. I've really tried hard as a mother, no one quite appreciates how hard it is. Wait till you have children of your own Iris. I can't wait to become a grandmother."

"Well I don't plan to have kids just yet, so you'll have to wait."

"Quite right darling; enjoy married life first. When you have kids, they get in the way of everything. I'd be happy to babysit. In fact, I was thinking that I could move back nearer to London to be closer to you. Kevin's son lives in London as well so he'd be happy to be closer to him as well."

"But you like living in Cornwall," I say. I really don't want Elizabeth to move close by; even in small doses she's a pain. Part of me feels mean for pushing her away when she's trying, but she does drive me mad.

"Don't be silly darling; I can always come up here for the summers. Kevin wants to keep his cottage and rent it out if we move to London. By the way, Kevin thinks you're a lovely girl. Oh, and I absolutely *adored* your lovely friend Magda; what a fabulous girl. You *must* invite her to come down as well; she can stay in Henry's old room. Anyway darling, I must go, Kevin's picking me up soon. We're going salsa dancing. I'm so excited! Bye darling, kisses to Eric."

"Good chat with your mother?" Eric asks when I walk back into the room.

"It wasn't too bad; Elizabeth is slightly more tolerable these days. She asked us where we're going to live and I think we should discuss it," I say.

Eric takes his eyes away from his MacBook. "I don't know why you're stressing about it babe. I thought that the plan is to live in New Hampshire?"

An unpleasant feeling rises in my chest. "I thought that we were going to live in London or at least split our time between both London and New Hampshire."

"We can do that babe, but I thought that you said that you wanted to get away from your mother."

"Moving to New Hampshire is a bit drastic. I don't hate her enough to get as far away as possible from her."

"Why don't we live in New Hampshire for a few months and see how you find it. I think you'll love it there; it's a much quieter and slower pace of life. You love nature."

"I do, but I'd prefer to stay in the city. What about my job?"

"Come on Iris, I told you that you wouldn't have to work and if you're that intent on getting a job, you can find a new one."

"Why don't we at least stay in New York? They'll be far more job opportunities there; maybe I could even transfer to the Waldenburg Gallery in New York."

"New York is no place to raise a family," Eric says.

"But I'm not ready to have kids yet. Maybe in a couple years, but not now. Anyway, we could stay in New York for a few months or a year, but I'm not sure that I want to live in America for good. What about Elizabeth and Henry? What about Magda?"

"You said that your mother drives you crazy plus she's got this new boyfriend; she won't need you as much. Henry lives in Ireland; you said that you don't see him much anyway and as for Magda, you'll find new friends. She's not your only friend. Personally, if you ask me, I'm not all that keen on Magda."

"She's my best friend! We're practically like sisters. How can anyone not like Magda?"

"I just don't think she's a good influence that's all. She's a bit all in your face. She's too loud and drinks too much."

"She doesn't drink too much and we get on because we're so different!" I protest.

"Look she's your friend and I respect that, but you need to stop being so naïve Iris. You don't get see people the way that I do. Magda is clearly jealous of you and jealous of what we have. Surely you don't want to be friends with someone who is really toxic."

"Magda isn't toxic. How can you think that about her? She just worries about me," I say defensively.

"Look you clearly know her better than I do, but I'm just telling you my opinion. Anyway, you can't just have one friend. Magda and you aren't going to be close forever. People drift apart and go their separate ways. Anyway, Magda strikes me as a fair-weather kind of friend. I know some really nice women in New Hampshire that you could make friends with. See how I think about you?"

"I know and I appreciate that." Maybe Eric is right, maybe it's naïve of me to think that Magda and me will be BFFs for life. I hope that we will always be best friends, but maybe it's not realistic to think that. Maybe I do need some new friends.

"I know what's best for you Iris, trust me."

"I know you do babe. I just want us to be on the same page like about kids. Maybe I'll be ready in five, ten years, but not now."

"Iris I'm almost thirty-six; I can't wait around like you! I don't want to be an old dad. I'm at the age where I'm ready to start a family. You don't want to wait too long either; so many women have fertility issues and regret not having kids earlier. Women in the past had kids way younger than you and they were ready.'

"Please don't put pressure on me."

"I'm not putting any pressure on you, but you need to be realistic. If you're worried about raising a child don't worry; I'll hire nannies so you won't have to lift a finger."

"It's not that; having a child is a big responsibility."

"Don't worry, I'll help you baby. You have nothing to worry about when you're with me," Eric says, stroking my cheek tenderly.

"OK but do we have to live in New Hampshire? I do want to go back to London."

"Why don't you give it a chance for a few months and if you don't like it, we'll find somewhere in London ok? You'll love New Hampshire; I promise. In the meantime, we can look at properties in London as well. You need to trust me on this babe. I'm just so excited that I'm getting to spend my life with such an incredible woman. I can't wait for the adventure in front of us and it's going to be a big one."

Eric is right. This is a fresh start; a fresh start for a new adventure. If it means making sacrifices, I'll do it for the man I love.

CHAPTER TWELVE

SATURDAY 18TH AUGUST

The supposedly soothing sound of waterfalls and chirping birds fill the muggy room and the sensual massage should feel like utter bliss. However, the sounds of nature irritate me. The room feels too hot and the masseuse presses too hard, making me feel even more tense. I should stop being so unappreciative. Eric has organised for us to spend a lovely afternoon together at the spa in the resort. I'm glad that we're finally spending some quality time together. Now it finally feels like we're on a proper honeymoon, spending time together as a couple.

Being in the Dominican Republic has been an incredible experience even if I have had to experience most of it by myself. Well, I wasn't completely by myself as Tammy and Bob were signed up on a lot of the same tours as me. It felt a bit awkward when they asked me where Eric was and why I was by myself. I told them that he was working and that he wasn't into these kinds of tours, which is true. I think that they felt a bit sorry for me as they constantly invited me to join them. It was really nice of them I guess. I ended up really enjoying their company, though I felt sad that Eric wasn't there.

Swimming with dolphins was an incredible experience. I've always loved dolphins so being up close with them was a dream come true. Bob got really excited about the dolphins and treated them like they were big dogs. Tammy was a bit apprehensive at first especially as the dolphins got overexcited but she soon warmed to them. Also, when we went to the Monkeyland, Tammy shrieked when a little monkey jumped on her shoulder. "He ain't gonna hurt you baby; he's tiny. Even the animals can't get enough of you; I've got competition. You stay away from my gal, you got that?" Bob joked, talking to the monkey. It made Tammy laugh and she stopped being scared. It was sweet the way that Tammy and Bob always walked hand-in-hand and were so tactile with one another. It made me pine for Eric even more.

I told myself not to be so maudlin; that Eric and I don't have to do everything together. We're still getting to know each other so maybe it's not a good thing to rush into spending too much time together. We've still spent time together. We've had dinner every night and we had a romantic walk by the beach together. Now Eric has organised this lovely spa treat.

After the massage, Eric and I head for the sauna where we drink champagne. It's just the two of us. We're wearing close to nothing and Eric's body looks incredible. I run my hands up his gym honed biceps and then over his hairless rock-hard chest. I want to fuck him right now, right here. I try to reach my hand below his towel, but he bats my hand-away.

"What if somebody comes in?" he hisses.

"So? Who cares? Plus, it's just us here and there are two other sauna huts."

"Well, people can still come in, especially when you least expect it. I'm not into public indecency."

"Relax; you care too much about what other people think. Even if anybody sees us, it'll just be another couple who probably came to do the same thing. Kids aren't allowed in here, so there's nothing to worry about."

"Well maybe you should care more about what people think of you," Eric says scathingly.

I can't help but feel hurt. Earlier Eric was in such a great mood but now it's like a grey cloud has suddenly appeared in the previously sunny sky. I do find his vagary a bit disconcerting, but maybe it's my fault. Maybe I am being inappropriate. Having sex in a public place is hardly classy. Eric is right; someone walking in on us might be awkward and unpleasant.

I try to make it up to Eric and tell him about swimming with the dolphins, but he doesn't seem interested. I tell him about the funny incident with Tammy and the monkey in Monkeyland but he doesn't laugh.

"I'm sorry babe, are you upset with me?" I ask.

"No of course not. I've just got a million and one things on my mind. I'll have to get back and do some work soon," Eric replies.

"Can't you forget about work for once?"

"No, I can't Iris; I've got a really big deal coming up and I'm under a lot of pressure!"

"Do you want to talk about it?"

"No, I don't! Look, I didn't mean to snap at you, but it's nothing that you could possibly understand."

"I could try."

"It's all boring business stuff. It would bore you to tears. Look babe, I've got a conference call soon. I won't be able to join you for dinner. Order what you want; everything will be charged to my card. Once I get all this out of the way, I'm all yours. I promise," Eric says, kissing me on the lips.

***

The room is spinning and I can't even stand properly without being unsteady on my feet.

"I think you need some water hon and some air," Tammy shouts over the music.

She's probably right; I've had way too much to drink. The cocktails were lethal. I don't know what was in them but they're bloody strong. I'm starting to see double and my head feels fuzzy. Tammy and Bob support me on each side and guide me outside to the fresh beach air where my drunkenness really hits me.

"You ok honey?" Tammy asks. "Bob's gone to get you some water. Do you want me to call Eric for you?"

I shake my head. Suddenly tears are escaping from my eyes.

"Oh honey, what's wrong?" Tammy asks, putting her arm around me.

"Maybe Eric doesn't love me or find me attractive."

"Now why would you think such a thing?"

"We haven't spent much time together and Eric always seems to be too busy."

"Have you talked to him about it?"

"I've tried, but he said that he's busy with work."

"You need to try talking to him again hon; make him realise how much spending time together means to you. Marriage takes work hon and plenty of communication. As long as you love one another and are committed to making it work, everything will fall into place. You're young and you've both got a lot to learn and figure out. Trust me, it takes time."

I suddenly feel so much better. Maybe Tammy is right. After all no marriage is easy. Tammy, Bob and I head back to the resort. Luckily, it's only a few meters away so I can manage the walk. I've sobered up a little after drinking some water. Bob also bought some fries, which help to soak up the alcohol a little. They're both really lovely. I went down to have dinner alone this evening in the resort restaurant, when Bob and Tammy

THE MAN THAT I MARRIED

saw me and waved me over. They invited me to join them. I didn't want to intrude but they insisted that we have dinner together. Afterwards, we decided to go to one of the bars near the resort.

Tammy and Bob walk me to my suite, which is really kind of them. They both hug me and Tammy tells me to call her if I ever want to talk. I open the door to the suite to find a myriad of red and pink heart-shaped candles lined around the room as well as dozens of red roses scattered on the bed and on the floor.

"Goodness Iris, where have you been? I've been worried!" Eric says, the worry in his voice evident.

"I messaged you to tell you that I went to a bar with Tammy and Bob," I respond.

"I was going to go out looking for you! I even planned a romantic surprise for you to make up for earlier."

"Aww Eric," I gasp. I'm really touched. How could I even think that Eric didn't care about me or love me?

"I see that you would have rather spent your evening getting drunk and hanging out with those ridiculous buffoons," Eric says derisively.

"I thought that you were working and I like Tammy and Bob; they're good people. If I had known that you were planning this, I wouldn't have gone out with them. I just want us to spend more time together."

"That's why I planned this. I know I've been working a lot and I feel really bad. I've booked for us to go on a luxury yacht tomorrow; just the two of us."

"Oh Eric, you've made me really happy. I love you so much. I just want us to be open and honest with one another from now on and talk about our problems."

"We don't have any problems Iris. It's you who invents these problems. You know that I love you and want to make you happy."

"All couples have problems Eric."
"Just because those trashy Texans have problems, doesn't mean that we do. I hope that you didn't go blabbing to them about our imagined problems."

"Of course not," I lie. "Eric, you do find me attractive, don't you?"

"Don't be so ridiculous Iris; how could I not? You're absolutely gorgeous. Like I said to you, I need time after everything that my ex-wife put me through. I'm not used to being with a normal and loving woman. It's hard to ignore years of abuse and being told that you're not good enough or enough of a man."

"You need to get those thoughts out of your head because they're not true. You are enough and I love you. I want to help you heal." Seeing Eric so vulnerable and broken breaks my heart.

"I know that you will baby; I already am healing."

Eric puts his strong arms around my waist and pulls me in close towards him.

"Have I told you how amazing you are?" Eric says. He leans in and kisses me passionately. All of my worries and fears about my marriage suddenly evaporate. I imagine all of my worries being cast away into the beautiful blue ocean and swept away by the vigorous and mighty waves.

There is nothing wrong with my marriage.

PART TWO

CHAPTER THIRTEEN

TUESDAY 4TH SEPTEMBER

"What do you think of your new home babe?" Eric asks, caressing the small of my waist.

I'm overwhelmed by this huge, imposing brick Victorian-style mansion standing before me. On one hand it's so grand and impressive, but on the other hand it's intimidating and eerie-looking. I expected Eric's home to be more modern. The mansion seems so silent, sombre and still, as though it hasn't been lived in for years. The roof is grey and the railings, windows and shutters are painted a dull, faded white. It reminds me a bit of a Scooby Doo mansion; haunted and creepy with secrets hiding behind the peeling walls.

I know that I should feel lucky that I get to live in a huge place like this, but I can't help but feel a longing for the flat that I shared with Magda in Kennington. The flat might not have been that big, but it was filled with character and laughter. It was all the space that I needed. I give myself a mental shake. Why am I complaining? Why am I acting like such a princess? Most people can only dream of living in a mansion or about even having somewhere to live! It's not like I would live at the flat in Kennington forever. Magda and I would eventually move on. Now I have a *real* home that I can call my own. A home that will be so different from the home that I grew up in. A proper home filled with wonderful new memories and love.

"It's beautiful; I love it," I say pliantly.

"I knew that you'd love it baby," Eric beams. He unexpectedly picks me up in his strong arms.

"What are you doing baby?" I giggle.

"I'm carrying my new bride over the threshold as a welcome to her new home."

"Aw Eric." I'm really touched by his sweet and thoughtful gesture Any doubts that I've had about Eric and our relationship have vanished completely. When we got back from The Dominican Republic, Eric treated me to endless dinners and surprises. I wanted to spend my last few days with Magda in the flat, but Eric arranged for us to stay at the Ritz.

"I want my wife to live like a queen," Eric said.

Moving out of the flat that I shared with Magda was really difficult and emotional. Eric arranged to have all of my things sent over to the house in New Hampshire.

"It's not like you have many things anyway baby, but it'll take a week to deliver everything, plus I've got some deals to close in London."

Not only was saying goodbye to Magda and the flat hard; leaving my job was surprisingly tough too. Even Julio seemed sad to see me leave.

"How am I going to find anyone as good as you Iris? You're the most dedicated and hardworking girl I know. I should have known that this would happen. Marrying a man like Eric means you never have to work again. You've got the life one can only dream of dahling. Well I guess the job will go to Felicity now. God help me; I'm going to have ten times as much work to do," Julio sighs.

I feel down and rather crestfallen in my last two weeks in London. Magda is very unhappy about me leaving.

"I thought you wanted to stay in London," Magda said.

"I do. We're only moving to New Hampshire for a few months,

whilst we find property in London."

"Surely it doesn't take that long to find property in London, especially if you're as rich as Eric," Magda says coldly.

"It's not as simple as that. Also, Eric needs to sort out some stuff in New Hampshire as well. His parents signed the house over to him so he has to take on all of the responsibilities that come with it," I say.

"Do you get any say in this Irenka?"

"Of course I do. I wouldn't move to New Hampshire if I didn't want to. I can't live here forever; we'd have to go our own way at some point."

"I know that, but you said that you wanted to stay in London."

"Don't worry, I'll come back to London. We'll find somewhere to live here as well. I think that moving to America for a bit will be a good opportunity. Eric says that I'll love New Hampshire."

"It seems like you're moving to the middle of nowhere. You always said that you were fed up of living in Cornwall and that you much prefer the city."

It's true. I've always wanted to live in London or in any city. I couldn't stand the loneliness and desolateness of Cornwall. I was used to moving around in my childhood and that was lonely enough; starting over in a new place where we didn't know anyone. Whenever any of Elizabeth's relationships ended, we always ended up moving for a "fresh start". Our moves were far from a fresh start. Elizabeth would continue drinking and dating bad men whilst I was left to take care of Henry and myself. We moved all over. We moved to Manchester, London, Bristol and even Wales.

Elizabeth finally decided to settle for the past few years in Cornwall. Elizabeth liked to be by the sea. She thought it was terribly romantic. Whilst Cornwall is beautiful and inspired a lot of my paintings, I felt so alone there. I felt so alone in this little town where everyone knew everyone. We were just the strange new family. Henry and I were the strange children with the man-eating, alcoholic mother. At least in the city nobody cared about us and we were diversely surrounded by people with problems, just like us. At the school that I attended in London, I was just one of many problem kids. There were kids who came from single parent homes; had parents that were druggies; parents who were alcoholics; or were in foster care. Weirdly it made me feel less alone.

I feel Magda and myself drifting further and further apart. Each time we saw one another I could feel the tension in the air like a bad smell. Magda made her disapproval of Eric and the way that she felt I had changed clear. In turn, her objection only made me more defensive of mine and Eric's relationship. We weren't as at ease with one another as we were before. We didn't laugh the way that we did before. It's like anything that we had previously shared in common evaporated into thin air. Maybe Magda really is jealous about mine and Eric's relationship. I didn't want to think that my best friend could be jealous of me. Maybe she feels left out that I'm moving on with my life. She has no real reason to dislike Eric. I didn't tell her about our problems. I had only told her how wonderful everything was.

"If everything's so wonderful then why don't you tell me anything?" Magda asked sharply.

"Because there's nothing to tell."

"Bullshit, you used to tell me everything. It's like Eric has taken over your mind. You would never just quit your job, especially after getting a promotion. I know how excited you were to get that promotion. You've always wanted a career! You always said that you don't get women who just stay at home. You've never cared for expensive things, now you're letting

Eric turn you into some sort of trophy wife. You used to tell me everything. Now all of a sudden, it's like it's none of my business."

"Are you jealous Magda?"

"Oh Irenka, how could you think that I'm jealous? Yes, I like nice things and it'd be nice to have money, but doesn't everyone think that? You really don't know me if you think that I only care about money and want a rich man. I'm happy with my life. If I wanted a rich man that bad, I'd find one. I was happy for you when you first got with Eric, but I feel there's something not right about him. All of a sudden he's making you quit your job and move to some place in the middle of nowhere in a completely different country away from your friends and family."

"Eric didn't make me do anything. Marriage is about compromise and that's what Eric and I are doing."

Magda shakes her head. "You've changed Irenka."

"People change when they get married," I say.

"Not like this."

***

Inside, the mansion is vast and grand with ivory and ebony marble floors. The staircase is curved like an arc with two sets of stairs and a beautiful, but fragile chandelier hanging in between. There's a gleaming glass table standing on an impressive ornate gold and black rug. The glass table is filled with an abundance of white lilies in a ceramic oriental patterned vase. Grey sofas are placed opposite the table. Elaborate swirly black balustrading adorns the stairs. Portraits of people who look like they belong from several generations ago; frozen in time, cover the white walls above the stairs. This place is so grandiose and palatial, but it doesn't feel homely. It feels like I'm in a stately home or in one of those grand estates in period dramas. Despite its vastness, it has a claustrophobic feel to it.

I'm thrilled with my new home. Really I am, however, it's a lot to take in. I've never lived anywhere like this before. It's a lot of space for just two people, even for an average sized family. I've never set foot inside a home like this other than a stately home which nobody even really lives in. It's like a castle. I feel like a fairy tale princess. Every girl dreams about living in a castle and marrying their prince. I'm living the fairy-tale life.

A short overweight Hispanic looking woman in her fifties wearing a blue maid's uniform greets us.
"Hello Señor Eric," the maid greets him formally.

"Guadalupe this is my wife, Iris," Eric says.

"Hello Señora Iris; it is nice to meet you. If you need me, you call," Guadalupe says flatly in a strong accent.

"Guadalupe has been with my family for many years. Her late husband Hector was our gardener and handyman," Eric explains. Guadalupe makes the sign of the cross at the mention of her late husband.

"Are you hungry? I make food, no?" Guadalupe asks.

"I could do with something to eat," Eric says. "What would you like to eat Iris?"

"I'm really not that hungry," I mutter. My appetite has been a bit up and down. Stress and big life events tend to make me lose my appetite. Moving to a new home in a different country is a big thing.

"Come on Iris, you're looking a bit thin. You could do with a good meal. Guadalupe will you prepare some sandwiches? Also did you do all of the shopping that I requested for my return?"

"Si Señor Eric," Guadalupe nods. "I call you when food ready."

The kitchen is probably the most capacious kitchen that I've even seen in my life; probably more than the size of mine and Magda's flat put together. There's an expanse of white marble floors, tinged with gold and silver. The kitchen island looks like a small isle stranded in the middle of a large ocean. There's a long dark mahogany table with matching chairs, big enough to seat twenty people. The immaculately polished French windows are longer than the table itself, offering a view of the New Hampshire countryside. Miles of trees in shades of carmine, fire, canary gold and forest green; and grey and steel blue river fill the landscape. It's utterly breath-taking, but it feels like I'm so far away. Maybe being in nature will do me good. I can even paint this remarkable landscape. Maybe I'll really come to love it here and won't want to leave. After all, everything is a matter of getting used to.

Guadalupe brings out plates of carefully cut thick sandwiches filled with tuna and cucumber, egg cress salad, salmon and cream cheese and chicken liver pâte. Guadalupe also brings out a wooden box containing a whole selection of different kind of teas; many that I've never even heard of. She also offers to make me coffee from the special state of the art coffee machine. I feel like I'm at afternoon tea.

"I hope you like it here baby," Eric says. He reaches out and touches my hand. "Anything you need, just let Guadalupe know. I want you to feel at home here. I want you to feel like it's yours. I appreciate so much that you agreed to move here. I know it's a big deal. This evening I've invited some people I know for dinner, so that you can make some new friends. I've invited an old school friend of mine, Tripp Barrett and his wife Tiffany. They're very nice people. I'm sure that Tiffany can introduce you to her circle. I hope you don't mind."

"Of course not; it'll be nice to meet them," I say. I feel really tired and jetlagged after the long flight, but I'm sure it'll be fine after I've had a nap. It's not even midday yet and I've got the whole day to rest and relax.

After we've had our sandwiches and tea, Eric takes me for a tour around the rest of the mansion. I'm still so overwhelmed by the size of the place. Everything is so orderly and infinite, like a show home. On the ground floor there are two humongous sitting rooms with one of them containing a bar. There's also a games room, a state-of-the-art gym and a wine cellar that holds Eric's large wine collection. Eric then takes me for a tour upstairs. He tells me that the house has ten bedrooms.

As I go up the stairs, I stare at all of the portraits that hang on the wall. The people in the portraits look lifeless; their expressions serious and austere. I get chills looking at them. The portraits remind me of those creepy self-portraits in galleries that always make me feel a bit uneasy. Eric explains that the portraits are all of his family starting from his great-great grandfather and their wives and children. There's a recent painted portrait of Eric's parents together; both looking stiff, severe and overly conservative. There's also a portrait of Eric. The artist has taken great care to capture every inch of his handsomeness. Eric's dark hunter green eyes burn into me, as though they're watching me.

I wonder if Eric will have a self-portrait of me painted. I wonder if he had one of his ex-wife painted but then had it taken down. All of these portraits on the wall make me feel perturbed, like I'm in some ancient museum where the people behind the history are long dead but their presence still lingers in a way that is bothersome and unsettling. I've never been a particularly spiritual person, but I get this strange chill that makes me feel slightly unnerved. I'm being ridiculous; they're just portraits after all and they're portraits of Eric's family. Every family history is important.

Eric takes me to our bedroom, which is at least six times larger than my old room at the flat. There's a king-sized bed in the middle of the room, covered with the purest soft pearl white Egyptian cotton covers and plump pillows that look so comfortable that you're out like a light once your head hits them. The carpets match the colour of the bedcovers and right opposite the king-sized bed there's a huge wide-screen television. Eric shows me the walk-in wardrobe, which is even bigger than my old room. All of my new clothes are there hanging, already fresh and ironed.

During the remaining two weeks left in London, Eric sent me on a shopping spree to Harrods. I remember when I once went to Harrods with Magda long before I met Eric. We tried on the clothes (well mostly Magda did) and took pictures. Our eyes practically popped out when we saw the ludicrous price tags. Magda and I would remark on how you could find something so similar in Primark. It was a really fun day. I miss all the things that Magda and I would do. I feel a pang of sadness. I really miss Magda. I even miss the flat and Arek.

Although Magda and I parted on good terms, I feel like something between us changed. I wanted her to come to Harrods with me and pick out outfits, but I knew that she'd only voice her disapproval about Eric. Plus, Eric hired a personal shopper to come with me to pick out some outfits.

"I really don't need such expensive clothes," I argued.

"Iris I can't have you walking around like a beggar. You're my wife and being my wife comes with certain standards. My world is a different world. People care about what you wear and how you look. I want you and I need you to fit in. Money for me is no object," Eric said.

I didn't bother arguing with Eric even though I felt uncomfortable allowing him to buy me such expensive clothes. I felt uncomfortable wearing a piece of clothing that cost more than somebody's monthly income. It made me feel sick. However, I let Lucy, the personal shopper and stylist do her job and help me pick out some outfits. It was a long and tedious day. We spent practically the whole day in Harrods selecting outfits. Well mostly Lucy selected them for me. I wished more than ever that Magda was there with me. At least I'd be fun and we'd have a laugh.

Lucy was all prim and proper and posh. If I wasn't with Eric, she would be the kind of person that would look her plastic nose down on me. She only sucked up to me because it was her job to. She treated me as though I was some kind of celebrity and I hated that.

"Your husband said that there's no budget, so we can go fully out. What a lucky girl you are having a husband who spoils you like this," Lucy said.

I know that I'm lucky and that any other girl would be thrilled, but I didn't want all of this money spent on me. I know that Eric wants to make me happy and I know that he wants to spoil me, but sometimes it feels too much. I don't like spending other people's money. I miss spending my own money.

I can't believe how ungrateful I sound. Eric treats me like a princess and all I do is moan. He spoils me and he brings me here to live in his beautiful palace. It's time that I start enjoying my new life instead of feeling guilty. I lie back on the bed and am engulfed by a huge wave of comfort and softness. The view from the large bay windows is stupendous. Two navy armchairs sit by the bay windows and stylish art deco paintings and ornaments embellish the room. Two large vases of white lilies are placed on either side of the television. There's also a large rhapis palm plant in the corner; it's leaves luscious and deep velvety emerald.

This room is magnificent, like a luxury hotel suite. It's minimalist, but homely at the same time. I am so lucky. So so lucky. I sink back onto the bed and close my eyes. I feel like I'm in a beautiful dream. I curl up underneath the sheets and I'm in heaven. The mattress is like a comforting mother, embracing me with her loving arms. Even my bed in my old flat wasn't that comfortable. The bed was small and creaky; the mattress long needed to be replaced and the duvet was lumpy.

"You have a nap babe, I've got some work to do," Eric says, stroking my hair. He kisses the top of my head. I feel so loved and so peaceful.

"You look like an angel," Eric comments. His voice is like falling asleep to a lullaby. Soon enough I'm drifting off into a blissful sleep, only to be awoken by a crying noise. I dismiss it. I'm probably imagining it. It's normal to hear noises as you fall asleep.

I close my eyes again, ready to drift off again, only to be awoken by the crying again. I feel too awake for it to be a figment of my imagination. It sounds like a baby's cry. It's odd as there's only three people in the house. Eric, Guadalupe and myself. There's no neighbours and the house is too huge to be able to hear noises. Maybe I really am hallucinating, but it doesn't feel like I'm imagining it. It doesn't sound like it's coming from my head. It sounds like it's coming from outside of my room. There's no mistake that it definitely sounds like a baby is crying.

I wonder who it could be. Maybe it's Guadalupe's grandchild that's come to visit. Eric says that she has two children and a grandchild. I close my eyes and try to go to sleep but the crying is so loud and piercing that I can't sleep despite the comfort of the bed. I get up and decide to see what the commotion is all about.

I walk out of the room and Guadalupe and Eric are right there. Guadalupe is holding a chubby blonde-haired screaming toddler who is red in the face from all of the screaming and crying, whilst Eric coos over it. It's so sweet how he treats Guadalupe like she's part of the family and makes a fuss over her grandchild. The sight of the screaming child definitely doesn't get my maternal juices flowing. I feel irritated by its screaming. I just wish that it could stop so that I could go back to sleep.

"Who's this?" I yawn.

"I'm sorry that she woke you baby. Oh Clara you woke poor Iris," Eric says gently, taking the baby from Guadalupe and rocks her in his arms.

"She's lovely Guadalupe," I lie, although I don't think there's anything lovely about a wailing infant. Guadalupe seems a little confused.

"Your granddaughter?" I say, pointing at Guadalupe.

"Ah no no Señora Iris; no my granddaughter."

"Then whose is she?" I say loudly over the screaming. Maybe the guests that Eric invited have decided to come now. Maybe that's their baby, but I don't see them anywhere.

"Shh young lady, listen to daddy," Eric says softly to the infant. Did he just say *daddy* or am I imagining things? Did I mishear?

"Let's wipe those tears away little one and say hello to your new mommy," Eric says.

CHAPTER FOURTEEN

I feel sick. My head is spinning like a cyclone and for a few seconds I'm seeing stars in front of my eyes. I hold onto the balustrade to keep myself from falling. Eric has a child! A child that he didn't tell me about! Once the dizziness and stars fade, I rush to the built-in bathroom of our bedroom and throw up.

"Iris, Iris, are you alright?" Eric says, his tone full of concern.

"You have a child and you lied to me!" I seethe.

"Please Iris, let me explain."

"What's there to explain?"

"Please Iris," Eric pleads. "Just look at me!"

"I don't want to look at you! I want to go home!" I sob frantically. Tears are streaming down my face like a downpour of rain.

"This is your home Iris and I was going to tell you about Clara."

"How can you lie to me like this?"

"This is exactly why I didn't tell you before! A majority of single women without kids don't want to date a man who has kids."

"The fact that you have a daughter wouldn't have bothered me. It's the fact that you lied about it!"

"Would you really have dated me if I had told you? This is exactly what I was scared of. The moment that I saw you, I knew that you were the one for me. You were so different from all of the other women that I've dated. You're funny, smart and beautiful. I was so scared that once I told you that I had a kid you wouldn't be interested and not only do I have a child, but her mother isn't around. That's a lot for women without children to handle. All I've wanted is to find love and find a mother for Clara," Eric says poignantly.

"So this is why you married me? So that you could have a new mother for your daughter?"

"Yes I wanted a mother figure for Clara, but that's not why I married you. I married you because I fell in love with you."

"Eric I can't be a mother. I'm too young and I'm not maternal. I don't want to come into this little girl's life only to try and be the mother that I'm not. I'm not prepared to be a mother and I can't give her the love and care that she needs."

"Iris you'd be excellent, trust me. The way that you took on the mothering role when your own mother couldn't step up to the mark and raised your brother is so incredible. You're perfect mother material without even realising it. Clara would be so lucky to have you. That poor little girl has been left without a mother. I know that this sounds cruel, but in a way, I think that maybe it's a blessing in disguise that Juliana, my ex-wife, isn't around. She was a terrible mother."
"Eric you're asking me for too much."

"I know it's a lot and this is why I was scared of telling you. Please don't leave me Iris," Eric implores.

I can see the tears forming in those beautiful green eyes of his and for a moment my heart melts. I'm so confused. This changes everything. The idea of having my own kids is scary enough, but raising somebody else's is an even bigger thing. Practically raising Henry, I should have been prepared for motherhood, but that was different.

Raising Henry made me miss out on my own childhood. Seamus was equally useless and when he left Elizabeth, she completely wasn't able to function. She'd just stay in bed and drink. From the age of seven I was the one left changing Henry's nappies, feeding him and giving him a bath. I had to step up or else we'd be sent to care. As much as I couldn't stand Elizabeth, I knew that we'd be worse off in care. Plus, she was still my mother and I loved her and didn't want her to get in trouble. I cherished all of the good times.

When Elizabeth was in one of her manic phases, she could be so much fun and sometimes it was a brief glimpse into what having a normal mother was like. Elizabeth would take us on fun days out to the beach or the funfair. Once she took me to the Ritz for afternoon tea so that we could pretend that we were wealthy and sophisticated. And there was that time when we went on a shopping spree in London and Elizabeth let me buy all of the toys that I wanted, even though she couldn't afford it. She ended up having large unpaid credit card debts, which wasn't without repercussions. We'd end up having our electricity cut off and angry landlords would chuck us out onto the streets. We'd then have to live in some horrible grotty hostel or B&B for a while until Elizabeth would find a new boyfriend and we'd move in with him.

I just don't know if I can take on the responsibility of looking after somebody else's child. I just want to enjoy married life and being free without any big responsibilities. I'm not ready. I'm only twenty-three. I understand why Eric was scared to tell me, but I'm so livid that he lied about having a child. What else has he been lying about?

"Iris please, don't leave me. I'm so sorry that I didn't tell you about Clara. I know that it's a lot to take in right now, but it doesn't have to change things. You don't have to do anything for Clara. You don't have to change her diapers, feed her, bathe her and watch over her; that's what Guadalupe is for. On Guadalupe's days off, her cousin Conchita takes over with caring for Clara."

"Eric it's not about that," I sigh.

"It's all new and it's all fresh but you'll love Clara too. I want her to have someone as wonderful as you as her mother. Please don't walk away from me. From us."

"I'm not going to leave Eric, but this is a lot to take on board. I'm not ready to be a mother."

"Nobody is ever prepared to be a mother. Do you think that I was prepared to be a father? I was scared shitless, but once I held Clara in my arms, the fear went away. Maybe if you got pregnant, the fear of motherhood would go away."

"Eric the last thing that I want is to get pregnant."

"I want another child Iris and it'd be so nice for Clara to have a little brother or sister."

"I can't believe you're asking me this! You expect me to just be ok with this whole situation."

All I want to do right now is to walk away. I want so badly to go back to my flat in Kennington. I want to curl up in my bed; my bed at home in the flat, and cry. The man that I married is a liar and he lied to me about such a big thing. Would I have wanted to be with Eric if he had told me earlier on that he had a child? I don't know. I love Eric and we have such a deep connection. Clara didn't get in the way of that.

Maybe I'm the one who is being selfish. It's not poor Clara's fault that she doesn't have a mother. Maybe Eric is right; she needs a mother figure but I don't know if I can be her mother or be the mother that she needs. This is such a complicated situation. Maybe I'm the one who's being so unreasonable. I ask myself the question if I would still want to be with Eric if he had told me earlier on that he had a child; on the first or second date. Our connection was so strong and so deep, I don't think it would have mattered to me that he had a child.

"I know that it's not going to happen overnight and it'll take a while to bond with Clara and get used to her. You'll soon see what a joy she is and she'll love you. Don't give up on our marriage just because of a child. It's not her fault; it's my fault that I lied."

Eric is right, it's not Clara's fault. Maybe mothering Clara would help me to find my maternal instincts and prepare me for when Eric and I have our own child. I still don't feel ready for a child yet. I'm on the pill and have enough supply for a few months before I have to renew my prescription. I don't know why Eric sees the rush. God I'm still so mad at him, but at the same time I understand why he lied. This situation isn't ideal but I'll have to get used to it. I don't want to give up on my marriage. I love Eric and I meant my vows. After all marriage isn't easy and comes with many challenges. I'm not going to let a child be the end of our relationship. A child who hasn't done anything wrong. Eric is right, maybe I can do this. I was practically like a mother to Henry.

"I'm still so furious that you lied to me."

"I know baby, I'm so so sorry. I only lied because I was so scared of losing you. Just so you know, Clara doesn't change anything between us. It doesn't have to change you. Like I said, Guadalupe is there to do all of the childcare so you don't have to lift a finger."

"Isn't it a lot for Guadalupe to take on looking after Clara full-time?"

"Of course not! Guadalupe loves Clara and hates to be apart from her. I always tell Guadalupe if it's too much that I can hire somebody else to share the childcare, but she won't hear of it. She only lets Conchita take over."

I feel like saying, isn't Guadalupe already the mother figure that Clara needs? However, I don't say anything. I don't want

Eric to feel like I'm not making an effort in getting to know Clara. At least Eric isn't forcing me into becoming a full-on mother. The shock is beginning to pass and I'm starting to feel a bit more rational. Maybe this could turn out to be a good thing. Maybe in time I'll bond with Clara and feel that she really is my daughter.

"I know that this is a big shock and a huge surprise thrown onto you baby and I love you for not walking away from me. I know that many women would, but you're not any woman Iris. That's why I know that you'd be the perfect role model and mother figure that Clara needs. You're such a strong and amazing woman, that deep down I knew that not only would you make a great wife, but a great mother. I really hope that you can forgive me for lying. I never wanted to hurt you."
"I know, but please don't ever lie to me again! And whilst we're on the subject please be honest if there's anything else that you've not been honest about."

"That's it baby; there's nothing else that I could possibly hide from you. Not telling you about Clara wasn't technically a lie; you never asked me if I had children. I just didn't tell you. I just wish that I had told you earlier. I was the one who was stupid for thinking that you'd be shallow enough to care about me having a child. You're the woman of my dreams Iris and I swear on Clara's life there's nothing else that I'm hiding from you or not telling the truth about."

"OK good. If this marriage is to work then we need to be open and honest with one another about everything. Don't ever lie to me again."

"I swear to God that I'll never lie to you again."

CHAPTER FIFTEEN

I'm getting ready for the dinner with Eric's friends. I'm so tired emotionally and physically that I'm not sure whether I'm really in the mood, but I don't want to bail and cancel last minute. It would be rude to do that. I really hope that I like Tripp and Tiffany. It'll be nice to make some new friends. Moving to New Hampshire and discovering that Eric has a child has been a huge shock to the system. I just wish that Eric had told me earlier about Clara. The idea that I've suddenly got a step-daughter; a new daughter, is really overwhelming. I just hope that I'll grow to love Clara as much as I love Eric. Why wouldn't I love her?

After Clara stopped her tantrum and calmed down, I went to see her in her nursery. Clara's nursery is like one of those old-fashioned Victorian nurseries with a rocking horse and an ivory cream white table with a pink china teapot and dainty little teacups. Encircled around the table, sat on little matching ivory cream chairs are an array of Steiff teddies and animals. In the corner, there's a huge stuffed giraffe. The furniture is all white and the wallpaper is baby pink. There's a shelf lined with ornaments including an ornate ballerina figurine and a big snow globe accommodating a glittery frost blue fairy tale castle and a gold haired princess in a flowing rose pink dress. The nursery also contains a lavish white crib with a sparkly ballerina pink canopy. The nursery is the embodiment of a little girl's dream.

I find Clara cuddled up in Guadalupe's arms in the rocking chair. Guadalupe sings something to her in Spanish. I take a proper look at the little girl. She has sandy gold coloured curls and big bright bold cornflower blue eyes. She's a beautiful little girl, though very serious looking. She's wearing a pink gingham frock with white lace up shoes. She looks like a doll. I almost feel a little creeped out especially as Clara studies me intensely with those big blue eyes of hers, covered with thick lashes. I've never felt so intimidated by a two-year-old before.

I scan her face for traces of Eric, but I'm not good at telling who babies or toddlers look like. She definitely hasn't inherited Eric's dark looks. I wonder what her mother looked like. What Juliana looked like. Was Juliana fair and blonde like her daughter? I don't know why I'm so curious about Clara's mother; about the mother that she'll never get to meet. I wonder if she even remembers her mother. Whether she has some faint glimmers of memories hidden deep down in her brain.

Clara looks annoyed that I've interrupted her and Guadalupe. I try to smile and look friendly so that I don't scare her. I try to talk to her; my voice high-pitched and expressive, without trying to be too over the top. I don't really have much experience of talking to two-year-olds. Clara doesn't look at me and burrows herself into Guadalupe's chest like a little cat.

"She is shy," Guadalupe says. "Look mi amor it is Señora Iris, your new mama." But Clara refuses to look.

"We show your new mama your toys," Guadalupe says gently.

Clara shakes her head forcefully and says, "no!"

"Mi amor, that is no nice," Guadalupe says.

"No! No! No!" Clara wails and I walk out of the nursery before she has another full-blown tantrum. Bonding with my new daughter is going to be a lot harder than I thought. I'm filled with trepidation and more anxiety about bonding with Clara. When Eric asks me how things went, I burst into tears.

Eric laughs. "She's a stubborn little thing, take no notice of her.

She had a meltdown with me earlier, hence all that screaming that woke you. It's just the terrible two's; she'll eventually grow out of it. Give her time to get used to you. I know that in time she'll grow to love you. Trust me."

I think of what to wear for the dinner this evening. The walk-in wardrobe is filled with my new clothes from Harrods. I wonder what Tiffany will wear. Will she wear a fancy dress or smart casual? In the end I choose a smart knee-length navy dress and smart matching navy heels. I apply my make-up (new make-up which I also got from Harrods with a private tutorial on how to apply it properly) and brush my newly styled hair (Eric had me go to one of the best hairdressers in London). I spray myself with expensive perfume as a finishing touch. I really feel like a wife of somebody famous and prominent. I look at myself in the mirror and I almost don't recognise myself.

All of a sudden all I want to do is ring Elizabeth. She was in hysterics as predicted when I told her that I was moving to New Hampshire for a few months. She accused me of abandoning her yet again, though luckily Kevin managed to get her to calm down eventually. Even Elizabeth has refrained from her usual barrage of messages and bitter diatribe. For once I find myself oddly missing it. What would Elizabeth do if her husband told her that he had a child? A child that he kept hidden from her? I think that it would be the least of her problems. Married men with kids have never put Elizabeth off. Elizabeth has stayed with men who have lied to her and cheated on her. It's not like Eric has cheated on me. OK he lied, but I understand why.

Would Elizabeth be glad that she has a new granddaughter? Elizabeth loves babies. Maybe I could ask for her advice. I still have some time before Tripp and Tiffany arrive so I ring Elizabeth. Surprisingly she doesn't pick up. Since she's been with Kevin, she's been less needy. Elizabeth has never been unavailable. I want to talk to Magda too. I can't tell her about Clara. She wouldn't understand and she'd try to convince me that I should leave Eric. Magda and I used to message each other all the time, but now we barely say anything to one another. Maybe we don't have much in common after all. Maybe Eric really is right and has better insight into our friendship than me. Perhaps this dinner will be a good opportunity to make friends with Tiffany.

Tiffany and Tripp arrive at eight o'clock promptly. Tripp is tall, muscular and handsome in the popular high school jock sort of way. He looks like he could be an Abercrombie and Fitch model. He has dark wavy blonde hair and hazel eyes. Tiffany also matches Tripp's level of attractiveness. She is tall, blonde, graceful and athletic. She looks stylish but conservative in her light teal dress, pearl necklace and smart kitten heels. Both Tripp and Tiffany seem so serious and aloof. Tiffany gives me a cold peck on the cheek and Tripp shakes my hand as though we were doing business together.

First, we sit in the lounge and have drinks. Eric opens a vintage bottle of wine.

"Let's make a toast to my beautiful wife and our recent nuptials," Eric smiles, looking lovingly at me with those big green eyes of his.

"Yes to your wedding and to Iris," Tripp says, raising his glass. "I'm so sorry that we couldn't be there."

I wonder why Eric didn't mention Tripp and Tiffany at all. Eric hasn't really mentioned any of his friends.

"So how do you know Eric?" I ask.

"Our families know one another and we run in the same circles. My older brother Colton was friends with David," Tripp says. Eric shoots Tripp a dirty look.

"Who's David?" I ask.

"He's just a mutual friend of ours in our circle; well was a friend. We don't talk anymore," Eric says a little too tersely.

"That's a shame; I guess people lose touch and grow apart," I say although I feel that there's more to the story than meets the eye. I wonder who this David is, but then again maybe I'm reading into things too much. Instead I try to focus on getting to know Tiffany.

Tiffany is reserved and says little. Apart from general small talk it seems that we have little in common and little to talk about. Tiffany is a rich WASPY girl with all of the privileges that being a WASP brings. She went to an Ivy League university and she works for her dad who has his own investment company.

I feel like Tiffany looks down on me because I don't come from a well-respected and wealthy family. Tiffany asks me a bit about England but looses interest when I tell her about the places that I grew up in and it transpires that I'm not from a well-to-do wealthy British family. I ask her how long her and Tripp have been together. They've been married for two years but dated for years. I want to ask whether they have children, but I don't know whether or not it's appropriate to ask. Tiffany doesn't strike me as the type of person who likes to engage in conversation that goes beyond small talk or gossip.

I just want this dinner to be over. For once I'm glad to be distracted with food. Guadalupe has prepared delicious bruschetta with tomato and avocado and olives for the starter. Then there's duck and potatoes with green beans for dinner and lemon mousse for dessert. I wash down my food with the expensive red wine. Tiffany hardly touches her food and pushes it around on her plate like a fussy child. The closer I look at her, the thinner I realise that she is. Thinner than me.

I can see her collar bones protruding and her arms are like matchsticks.

I feel like an outsider. Tiffany, Tripp and Eric converse with such ease; like old friends that have known one another for years. Well, they *are* old friends that have known one another for years. They act as though I'm not there, reminiscing about shared memories and inside jokes. They discuss wealth and common interests that people in the wealthy and WASPY circles share. I feel as though I'm invisible. They all talk animatedly and loudly, leaving little room for me to get a word in edgeways. Eric acts as if I'm not there. It's like I'm a foreigner and Eric is supposed to be my translator, but he's not doing his job.

I feel the jealousy erupt inside of me like a volcano when Tiffany reaches over and cosies up to Eric. She giggles like a schoolgirl with a crush and puts her hand on his thigh as though she owns him. I feel the sudden urge to push her hard and tell her to get away from my husband. It's obvious that she finds Eric attractive. I mean what woman wouldn't? I tell myself to stop being so paranoid. Tiffany and Eric are just good friends, plus Tiffany is married. Her husband is sitting in the same room, at the same table and obviously isn't bothered.

I wish that Eric hadn't invited Tripp and Tiffany round for dinner. I can tell from the way that they occasionally glance at me, that they view me the same way that they view Guadalupe- somebody who is beneath them. They make no effort to include me in the conversation.

I pour myself another glass of red wine to get through the isolation and awkwardness that I feel. I can feel the alcohol numbing my mind and making me care less. I don't care what Tiffany and Tripp think of me. I don't even want to be friends with Tiffany anyway and her stuck-up preppy league. I miss Magda. Magda and I were always at such ease with one another. With Magda there were never any dull moments and we'd always end up in fits of laughter about something. I want to talk to someone. I want to open up. I can't stand this drab dinner. I reach for my third glass of wine. Eric and Tripp are deep in conversation about politics and the country club, whilst Tiffany is scrolling through her phone.

"Do you have kids? I found out today that I have a new daughter," I slur. Tiffany looks up from her phone and gives me a strange look.

"You mean Clara?"

"Did you know Juliana well?" I ask brazenly.

"I can't say that I did," Tiffany says disinterestedly.

"What was she like, Juliana?"

"Look, like I said, I didn't know her very well. She seemed very quiet and shy."

I've tried hard to imagine Juliana in my mind, but I've never imagined her to be somebody timid and diffident. I pictured Juliana to be loud, dominant and temperamental. Eric said that she would often make a scene in public and that he was so embarrassed and ashamed.

"Was Juliana a member of the Women's League?"

"No, she wasn't." Tiffany's sighs, her tone implying that even talking to me is a chore.

"So, what do you do at the Women's League? I'd like to come along. I really need some friends around here." I feel so stupid and desperate, like a teenage girl who wants to be part of the cool girl gang. However, I find myself pining for company. Surely there must be at least someone nice enough to make friends with in the Women's League.

"I'm afraid that we're all super busy organising a fundraiser at the moment, so we don't need an extra hand," Tiffany says patronisingly. It's evident that she doesn't want me to join her precious Women's League.

"Don't worry; I don't want to join your stupid club anyway. I don't need the humiliation of you and your bitchy WASP friends looking your plastic noses down on me and treating me like a charity case," I retort. I feel shocked at myself for voicing my thoughts out loud, but I don't care. The wine has taken any filter that I have away.

Tiffany seems taken aback by my remark. I bet that she wasn't expecting that.

"I'm sorry you feel that way. Anyway, I really should be going. I'd best find Tripp though I just need to use your restroom first," Tiffany says coolly, as though nothing happened. I suddenly realise that Tripp and Eric aren't there. It's funny how I didn't even register their lack of presence.

I stumble around looking for Eric and Tripp. God it's so easy to get lost around here. Eventually I find my way back to the lounge. Eric and Tripp are talking in hushed voices. They don't spot me. I stand against the wall and try to make sense of their conversation. I only hear snippets of their conversation. Why am I eavesdropping?

I'm about to turn away when I hear Eric's voice. This time it's clearer and louder.

"Why the fuck did you have to mention David?"

CHAPTER SIXTEEN

I wake up with a pounding headache. How much did I have to drink last night? It all feels like such a blur; more like a dream. The memories of last night feel so distant and so far away, yet so vivid. I didn't sleep well. I fell in and out of light and unrestful sleep. Long stretches of time went by where I felt like I was awake, but not awake at the same time. My mind was so overactive with thoughts, but yet it felt like I wasn't in control of my thoughts. Eric was snoring right beside me; dead to the world whilst my mind was racing.

I finally fell into a deeper sleep and had a dream. It was another nightmare. I was walking in the woods by the lake, near the house. At first, it was such a beautiful day. The trees were the colour of traffic lights and the lake glistened in the midday sun. All of a sudden, clouds appeared and the sky went grey. I found myself in the lake drowning. I saw Eric standing near the lake. I shouted to him to help me, but he ignored me. I called his name louder but he kept walking away. He walked towards a beautiful blonde woman. I saw her face more clearly and realised that it was Tiffany. Tiffany and Eric held hands, whilst I was left to drown in the lake. Then I noticed that there was someone in the lake next to me. A man. His face was blurry and I couldn't see him properly. "It's ok, I'm David," the man said. I woke up sweating.

I felt so exhausted by the dream that I went back to sleep, though luckily, I didn't have any more nightmares. When I wake up, my head is killing me and my mouth is dry. I chug the glass of water by my bedside and pour myself another glass. It's eight fifteen and I almost panic that I'm late for work only to remember that I don't have a job anymore. I feel a strong sort of

THE MAN THAT I MARRIED

longing for my job that I never felt before.

I miss the buzz and the constant pace of the gallery. With the day stretching mindlessly ahead of me, I feel unfulfilled. I don't even feel like doing any painting, even though Eric set up a special studio especially for me. I love painting but for the first time in my life the desire has gone. Maybe I could ask Eric if I could find work around here. I don't mind what it is, even if it's waitressing at the country club. Anything to occupy my mind.

Eric's side of the bed is empty, so I go to his study to find him. Eric seems in a bad mood. He doesn't greet me warmly. He doesn't even kiss me good morning like he usually does.

"Hey baby, what's up?" I ask.

"How's the hangover? Is this going to become a regular thing with the drinking?" Eric asks furiously, his face contorted with rage.

"Of course not and I didn't drink that much. I just found the dinner last night so awkward. Tiffany doesn't seem to want to be friends with me."

"Well I'm not surprised! You made an absolute fool out of yourself and a fool out of me too. Poor Tiffany was really upset by your behaviour!"

"By my behaviour? I tried really hard but your friends made me feel like a piece of shit at the bottom of their shoe!" I cry.

"Iris you obviously drank too much and are imagining things in your paranoid mind. I really hoped that you would make a good impression, but now I feel embarrassed."

Before I know it, tears are escaping my eyes. "How can you be so cruel? Your friends made me feel like I wasn't worth anything. You don't get what a big adjustment this has been for me. I've moved to a different country for you and out of the blue I find out that you have a daughter and I have to be her new mother figure and you have the audacity to tell me that I've made a fool out of myself," I rage. I run out of the study and back into our bedroom. I collapse onto the bed and cry my eyes out.

Around two hours later, Eric comes into the bedroom and sits on the bed. He strokes my hair, but I jolt away from him.

"Baby I'm sorry about how I acted. I just worry about you. I don't want your drinking to get out of hand. Juliana used to drink too much and it was part of the reason why our relationship fell apart. Because of her, she gave us a bad reputation. People would stop inviting us to events because she would always get too drunk and make a huge scene."

"But Tiffany said that Juliana was quiet and reserved."

"Well obviously Tiffany didn't want to speak poorly of Juliana and it would have been awkward for her to tell you what she was really like. Tiffany's a classy girl." I hate the way that Eric says it, like I'm Eliza Doolittle and Tiffany is a regal lady that I should emulate and strive to be.

"Girls like Tiffany aren't like Magda," Eric continues, his nose wrinkled in disgust mentioning Magda. "I've known Tiffany since forever and she may seem cold and reserved, but once you get to know her, she'll be a friend for life. She's really been so supportive of Tripp, especially at the height of his gambling addiction. It's thanks to me that he got out of debt. His own father was so ashamed that he refused to pay off his gambling debts.

I'm sure that Tiffany will come round even after the way that you spoke to her. I think that the best way of making amends is by apologizing. I already had to apologise for your behaviour. She was very understanding. She understands that this is a big adjustment and culture shock for you."

I feel so furious that Eric can't take my side. Why is he

defending Tiffany?

"Why should I have to apologise to her?"

"Iris, please just apologise for my sake. I really don't want us to be on bad terms especially as Tiffany's family is so influential and they've known my family for so many years. I know that Tiffany seems a bit frosty, but once you get to know her, she's completely different. I just love you and care about you so much. I want the best for you, really I do and I appreciate everything that you're doing. I want you to fit in and be a part of my world."

"It feels like I'm never going to be a part of your world. I'm not from a wealthy and well-connected background. I felt so invisible last night; like I was a nobody."

"Well people are going to start looking down on you if you keep drinking so much and insulting people like that."

I feel so hurt by Eric's comment. I feel like he doesn't understand me.

Eric senses my upset. "Look baby, I'm only giving you constructive criticism. Don't take it so personally. I love you so much baby and I only want what's best for you."

"I love you too, but I wish that you weren't hiding things from me."

"I'm not hiding anything else from you baby. So will you apologise to Tiffany?"

"I'll apologise to Tiffany once you tell me who David is!"

"Come on Iris, I already told you. He's just some guy who was a part of our circle. He was a very messed up person and did a lot of things to hurt people. He created a big scandal everywhere that he went and was a bad influence on Tripp's brother. Thank goodness David's parents disowned him and he moved far away. I just don't like bringing him up; he left a lot of shame in his wake. You need to stop being so paranoid my darling." Eric kisses me on the lips and reaches up my silk royal blue nightdress. He squeezes my breast hard.

"Ouch," I wince.

"Oh come on Iris, it can't hurt that much," Eric sighs.

When we were in London, I felt that our sex life was a bit better, but not much. I just felt like for Eric, he did it perfunctorily, as though sex was a mundane every day activity like brushing your teeth. Before we had intercourse, he'd spend long periods of time in the toilet. I'm starting to worry that I don't turn him on. I told Eric my concerns, but he told me not to be so ridiculous. "It's just a habit of mine," he told me.

"Have you stopped taking the pill?" Eric whispers. I nod although secretly I'm still taking it. I have a supply left for a few more weeks, but I'm a bit anxious about when it runs out. Maybe I can ask Magda to contact my GP back in London and have some more sent over. I don't want to lie to Eric, but I know how keen he is to have another child. I just don't feel ready to have a baby. The idea terrifies me. It's bad enough finding out that I'm a stepmother.

I suddenly feel like such a hypocrite. Eric may have lied to me about having a child, but I'm lying to him about not taking the pill. That doesn't make me any better.

"Good girl," Eric whispers in my ear. "I hope we'll have a son."

We kiss some more. Eric pulls off my nightdress and I unbutton his shirt and belt. I unzip his trousers and reach my hand down his pants only to find that his penis is completely flaccid again.

"What about a blow job?" I offer.

Eric shakes his head and pulls his trousers back up. "I know I keep on disappointing you Iris; I'm sorry. Sex hasn't been the same since Juliana. I told you what kind of sex she was into. All I have in my mind is her telling me that I'm not good enough."

"I'm sorry baby; look let's not put pressure on things. You shouldn't listen to what Juliana said; it's not true. You are good enough."

"Thank you baby for being so supportive and loving. I'm so glad I married you." OK our sex life isn't great and we've had our moments, but I know that my husband loves me and we can work on things. Marriage takes work, doesn't it?

I get dressed and turn my focus to work. "I was thinking, maybe I could get a job around here. Maybe in the country club."

"Iris baby, you don't want to be doing some job that some Mexican gets paid minimum wage to do. Other than that, I don't want you stressing yourself out."

"I just don't want to sit around all day. I want to be active. I want anything to take my mind off of missing home. Also, what about looking for a property in London?"

"Babe you've got your new art studio. I've stocked it up with every kind of paint, brushes, canvases and magazines for inspiration and ideas. Once you get into your painting, time will fly by. I'll look into some properties in London later on. I've got a friend who does real estate in London."

I sit in my new art studio, searching for inspiration. I try to paint the view of the beautiful woods and the lake out the window, but I can't get the colours and the perspective right. The studio is huge, bigger than the art room that we had at school. There's so many different kinds of paints and supplies; acrylic, watercolour, oil paint, pastels and chalk. Usually I'd be so excited to try it all out, but I feel so tired. For the first time in my life, I can't be bothered to paint. After an hour I give up and decide to take a walk.

The air is so fresh and breezy. The sun is still shining, but it's not warm enough to wear just a t-shirt. It's truly stunning; the perfect place to go on a hike. I can imagine that coming here would be the perfect place for a holiday, especially a holiday where you can truly relax and unwind and feel at one with nature. This is the kind of place where people go for the weekend to rest and get away from the stresses of life. It's so tranquil and still here with acres of woods and land; a true distraction from modern life. I should feel so lucky to be somewhere so beautiful and quiet. After all I love nature and animals. As much as I love it here, I'm not used to the quiet and the stillness. I feel like I'm in the wilderness or stuck in the middle of a desert. The nearest town is half an hour away by car and there's no direct trains or buses around here.

Eric said that this is the most ideal place to live in New Hampshire and that Darton has the biggest homes, the most access to nature and has been voted as one of the best places in New Hampshire to raise a family. I can't get used to living away from the constant motion and action of London. I guess I'll have to get used to it here. After all many people want to move away from London because it's too busy, too expensive and not the best place to raise a family. Maybe change is good for me.

I'm back from my walk a little after six, just in time for supper. Guadalupe has made carrot soup with thick chunky bread and salted butter. I ask if Eric is around, but Guadalupe says that he's busy and will be having dinner in his room. I ask Guadalupe if she'd like to join me for dinner. She seems so shocked that I would ask her. She says that she cannot as she must go and give Clara her bath and put her to bed, but if there's anything that I need, to let her know.

All of a sudden, I feel so lonely here, swamped in this

humongous kitchen. All of a sudden, I don't feel so hungry even though the food that Guadalupe has prepared is delicious. Maybe I could start doing some cooking around here; to give Guadalupe a break. She must have her hands full with Clara. I wonder if Clara will ever warm to me. She seems so attached to Guadalupe as though she were her mother.

I clear up my plate and bowl instead of waiting for Guadalupe to clear up after me. I want to be self-sufficient and help around the house. Maybe tomorrow I can do some cooking. The fridge is stocked with so many ingredients that I'm spoilt for choice. There's fresh vegetables and eggs from a nearby organic farm and a huge rack of herbs and spices. There's also a whole array of different meats in the fridge. Maybe I could even make something tasty for Clara like a dessert. Kids like sweet things, don't they?

I search through the multitude of cupboards and find fine Brazilian cocoa powder and a variety of icing flavours and a colour set for decorating cakes. Perhaps I could make cupcakes. As a treat for everyone. Once I eventually find all of the ingredients and items that I need, I get to work. I enjoy the baking; I feel like I'm doing something useful and it takes my mind off of the loneliness. I enjoy icing the cupcakes most of all. I use the pink icing as Clara seems to like pink and make big swirls. I adorn the cupcakes with little white iced hearts. When I'm finished; I put them onto three plates. I take one plate for Guadalupe who looks like she's going to faint with shock. It's like nobody has ever done anything nice for her. She thanks me profusely and tells me that Clara is asleep, but that I can give it to her tomorrow.

I then make my way to Eric's study. I knock on the door, but he doesn't answer, so I walk in. Eric registers my presence and quickly shuts his laptop, as if he has something to hide.

"Please knock in future babe," Eric says.

"I did knock, but you didn't answer. What are you doing?"

"Just working. Is everything ok?"

"I made some cupcakes. I used the ingredients in the kitchen. I hope that's ok."

"It's perfectly fine and that's so sweet of you baby, but I don't eat sugar. I don't want to turn into one of those fat Americans that are the poster picture of American obesity. I'll go to the gym later on."

"But you already went this morning and you never told me that you don't eat sugar."

"I like to keep in good shape baby and you don't have to know about all of my dietary requirements. Why don't you use the gym as well?"

Eric showed me the home gym, which was almost the size of a real gym. It contained a full set of weights, a treadmill, a bike, a rower, an elliptical machine and various other exercise equipment. I've never really liked exercise much but it'd seem like a shame not to use it.

"Yeah sure; we could exercise together."

"Sure babe, if I have time. I like to exercise early, around five or six in the morning. I know you don't like getting up that early. You should use Jen, my personal trainer. I see her two or three times a week. I'll book you with her as well."

"No, it's fine, I'm happy just using the gym."

"I know you're lucky that you're thin now babe, but if you don't start looking after yourself, one day you'll wake up fifty pounds heavier and wonder how you got there. Making cakes won't help either."

I feel really hurt by Eric's remark. I want to burst into tears.

"Hey Iris don't sulk; I'm just looking out for you. Women are always moaning about their weight, especially when they stuff themselves with rubbish."

"I don't moan about my weight and I'm not worried about gaining a few pounds. Having a cupcake once in a while isn't going to make me fat and it won't make you fat either," I sulk.

"Iris baby, don't be like that. You know that I think you're absolutely gorgeous and I want you to stay that way. You know what; why don't we do some exercise of our own? Meet me in the bedroom. I'll join you in ten minutes," Eric says saucily, slapping me on the butt.

I try to feel better. Eric does desire me and care about me. I'm the one who's being oversensitive. On the way to the bedroom, I leave the cupcakes outside of Guadalupe's door. She doesn't seem like the kind of person to be bothered about a few extra calories.

CHAPTER SEVENTEEN

MONDAY 8TH OCTOBER

A month has gone by and I'm still struggling to adjust to my new home. Eric has been distant and busy with work. My artwork has been non-existent. I just can't find any motivation to paint. I just feel so bored and I find myself missing London more than ever. I keep reminding Eric that we should look for property in London, but he always says that he's too busy and that we'll do it soon.

I'm still struggling to fit into the role of a mother. Lately I've been having the same recurring nightmare. In the nightmare I'm in Clara's nursery and all of a sudden, the ground shakes like an earthquake and I hear crying. Suddenly I see a huge baby, three times the size of me in the corner of the room. I realise that I'm the size of a mouse and this baby towers over me like a tiger. It cries and cries and I don't know how to get it to stop. I call Eric, but he's in the other corner with a blonde woman. "Eric, the baby, save me from the baby!" I plead but he ignores me. The earth is shaking and I fall through the cracks in the floor. I keep on falling and then I wake up.

I wake up every time shrouded in sweat. Since I've moved here, I've not been sleeping properly. I keep tossing and turning and when I do fall asleep, I have these nightmares. I tell Eric about my nightmares, but he tells me that I should see a therapist.

"Baby, I'm going to book you for an appointment with Doctor Goldman. It seems to me like you're having problems adjusting. I just want to do everything that I can to help you." I tell Eric that I don't want to see a therapist but he insists.

"Doctor Goldman is a very respected professional; my family and I have used him many times. I often see him myself. Please Iris, I think that you'd benefit from him."

I'm not keen on the idea of seeing this Doctor Goldman but I don't want to argue with Eric. After all, maybe it'll be good to have someone to talk to. Elizabeth has clearly benefitted from seeing a therapist. I've never had therapy before so I don't know what to expect.

My appointment with Dr Goldman is scheduled at three o'clock in his practice. Eric has his private chauffeur take me there. It's very near the town. The driver pulls up outside a large elegant white house with teal blinds and a gravel driveway. It doesn't look like somebody's home but it doesn't look like a practice either. The inside is sterile and hospital-like with plain white walls, plastic chairs in the corner and a reception desk with a glass shield. I tell the receptionist my name and that I'm here to see Doctor Goldman. She smiles and tells me to take a seat. Just as I'm about to open a magazine about home design, I hear my name.

I look up to see a white-haired man in his sixties. He has an attractive and trusting face. He's tall and poised despite his age and he's wearing a smart suit. Perhaps this won't be so bad after all. I follow him to his room which looks like a typical therapist's room. I almost laugh at the long black couch and the bookshelf filled with books about Freud and diagnostic manuals. I almost expect Doctor Goldman to hypnotise me.

"I see that you have some preconceptions about therapy. Don't worry, a lot of people do. The couch is there if you want to feel more comfortable, but you can take a seat in the armchair if you wish," Doctor Goldberg says gently. I indeed take a seat in the armchair opposite him. The couch makes me feel a bit uncomfortable.

"So Iris, your husband Eric rang me and booked an

appointment. How do you feel about that?" It sounds like such a typical therapist thing to say that I can't help but stifle a laugh.

"Laughter is very natural, especially when you're nervous. Don't worry, this is a safe place and what you say in this room stays between us unless it's anything extremely concerning, indicating that you are at risk to yourself and/or others. Then it is my duty to report it, but otherwise, our sessions will be strictly confidential." Doctor Goldman has such a soothing and calm voice. I immediately feel at ease.

At first, I don't know where to start, but then I start opening up about my childhood, Elizabeth and my dreams. Doctor Goldman really listens and digests everything that I say. I even tell him about Eric and how distant he's being. Doctor Goldman reassures me that all relationships take work and effective communication is the most important tool. I also tell him about the shock of finding out about Clara and trying to adjust into the mother role and Clara not warming to me. Doctor Goldman says that forming a bond takes time, even between a biological mother and their new-born.

I also tell him that deep down there's a part of me that still hurts about the fact that Eric lied and didn't tell me earlier. Doctor Goldman tells me that I need to sit down and talk with Eric about my feelings. He also says that it's good that Eric admitted to his fault and apologised and that forgiveness and communication paves the way to learning to trust again.

I feel a bit better after my session with Doctor Goldman. It feels good to talk to somebody. After all I haven't really had anyone to talk to. I've tried to chat to Guadalupe but her English is too poor to have a proper conversation. Apart from basic English, she struggles to understand me. She'll often say "sorry Señora Iris, forgive me but I no understand." She even speaks to Clara in Spanish, though when Eric or I are around she tries her best to speak to her in English. I've tried to interact with Clara and spend time with her but she just won't bond with me. She'll ignore me or throw a tantrum. She doesn't want me to be her new mother and I can't say that I blame her.

"Look who it is mi amor? It is Señora Iris; she is now your mommy," Guadalupe said gently to Clara one morning when I was having breakfast in the kitchen.

"No mommy; Lupe mommy!" Clara screamed, clinging onto Guadalupe. I didn't want to upset Clara even more, so I kept my distance. Maybe Clara can sense that there's something unmaternal about me. Perhaps that's why she rejects me. Eric says that it'll take time for Clara to get used to me and it's natural that she's attached to Guadalupe as she's the person who she spends the most time with. He also said it's normal for toddlers to go through a clingy phase. I still can't help feeling like such a failure. Eric says when we have our own baby, it'll be a true chance for us to bond. I definitely don't think that Clara's going to be wanting a baby brother or sister anytime soon. I think that she'd be more confused.

I feel lonelier than ever in the house. I really wish I had some sort of job. Whilst I'm in town, I might look around. I tell the driver that I want to explore the town and to come back later. Darton is very much a small town; quaint but with not much going on. Even the red brick buildings are old-fashioned. There isn't any hint of modernity anywhere. It feels very much like everything is stuck firmly in the past. The town has all of the ordinary amenities- small supermarkets, hairdressers, boutiques, a small cinema and restaurants but there's not much choice of anything. It's pretty deserted around here.

I know that with most jobs you need to apply online, but that's in London. Here it doesn't seem like there's a lot of job competition going on. I walk into one of the diners and ask if there's any jobs available.

"I'm sorry sweetie, but there's not a lot of job prospects round here, especially with so many businesses folding. You want to try one of the bigger towns. Where are you from sweetie? I certainly ain't never seen you around before," a nice middle-aged waitress with red hair says. I tell her that I'm from London.

"I've always wanted to visit England, but can't afford it. What's a city girl like you doing somewhere like here? There's nothing going on round here."

"My husband is from here, so that's why I moved here."

"Who's your husband, I might know him."

"Eric Irving."

The waitress looks like she's seen a ghost. Her smile is gone and her demeanour is no longer friendly. I suddenly feel chilly. Maybe she's someone who dated Eric before, but she looks like she could be his mother.

"That family is bad news that's for sure. He's got a nerve for sticking around here," the waitress says in a hostile manner.

"What do you mean?" My heart is pounding so heavily in my chest. I feel like I'm going to pass out.

The waitress laughs ironically. "He ain't told you much then? I'd be careful if I were you. I wouldn't want you to end up like those other women."

CHAPTER EIGHTEEN

I can't stop the flurry of disturbing thoughts going through my mind. It can't be true, can it? What girls is she talking about? I feel bile rising in my throat. I'm trying everything that it takes to stay calm, but I'm shaking badly. I try to control my breathing but I feel like a fish out of water, gasping for air.

"I'll get you some water," the waitress says. She goes over to the door and flips the "open" sign so that it says "closed." However, I don't image it would make very much difference as the diner doesn't look like it attracts many customers. A minute later, the waitress is back with some water and a pastry and takes the chair opposite me.

"You look all white. Have something to eat as well; it'll help with the shock."

"Thank you," I mumble, gulping the water desperately as though I were stuck in the middle of the desert. My mouth feels so dry.

"You seem like a nice kid. How long you been married to Eric?" There's pure disgust on her face when she says Eric's name.

"Only about two months. We got married very quickly."

"If I were you, I'd run. Eric and his family are no good."

"Why, what did they do?"

"They've always been a strange family. Filthy rich. It's always the people with so much money that are fucked up. When you got that much money, you can get away with murder. I mean literally."

A chill runs up my spine. "Murder?"

"Well, it weren't proven, but I think that it ain't no coincidence that's for sure. Twenty-five years ago, a woman died; down by the lake near the Irving's estate. They ruled it as a suicide; found a note and everything. I knew Mary and I don't think it was suicide. She wasn't the type to kill herself."

"Sometimes people surprise you. Depression can often be hidden."

"True, but in my bones, I don't feel that it was suicide. She worked for the Irvings; said they were pretty messed up. Then another ten or so years later another girl dies. They say it were drink driving, but it's just a coincidence that David survived and she didn't."

"Who's David?" I ask.

"Eric ain't told you about his own brother?"

"Eric told me that he was an only child. Why didn't he tell me about David? What happened to him?"

"After the accident he just left and never came back. His parents were so ashamed that they moved away as well. Left the house to Eric. The scandal round here was pretty huge. Police said it was an accident; gave David a caution and took away his licence but that was it. I don't think it was just an accident. Poor Christina; she had her whole life ahead of her. She was such a nice girl. She should never have gotten involved with the Irvings."

"Maybe it really was an accident." My head is spinning from taking in all of this information. Why didn't Eric tell me that he has a brother? Why hide it from me? I'm his wife!

"Maybe these tragic events have no reason behind them other than that it was suicide and a car accident."

"There's a lot of suspicion going on about what happened to his ex-wife."

"She committed suicide."

The waitress lets off a shrill laugh. "That's what he'd say."

All of a sudden, I feel angry. Maybe this woman just wants to stir up drama. After all isn't that what people do in small towns; make up gossip because they've got nothing else to do? Eric wouldn't kill his wife. I know Eric and I know that he wouldn't do that.

"Look do you really know Eric and his family?" I snap.

"I only dealt with them briefly. I used to work down at the country club. The people there don't care what a terrible person you are as long as you have money. Eric Senior ain't a nice man, that's for sure."

"Just because he's not nice it doesn't make him suspicious. You don't know him and you don't know Eric. He's nothing like his father."

"The apple don't fall far from the tree. Like his father, he's always thrown his weight around here. Thinks he's better than everybody else. What's strange is that all the women he ends up with end up either dead or missing. Eric dated some other girl from outta town a few years ago; brought her to live here. She was from New York. I think her name was Rivka or something like that. She looked a bit like you actually, but she had this beautiful long golden blonde hair. Seemed like a real nice girl.

I did a bit of research about her and strange thing was that her family reported her missing, but she was here. I went to the police and they said that she was no longer a missing person. Apparently, Rivka wrote a letter to the police, saying the she was safe and didn't want to be found. It made sense as she had some issues with her parents, so the police closed the case, especially as she was an adult."

"What's that got to do with anything?" I snap irately.

"Shortly after, I stopped seeing her. It's like she completely disappeared. It's just strange that she was reported missing, apparently found and then disappeared again. She always looked so scared when I saw her; both her and Juliana."

"It's obvious that this Rivka and Eric must have broken up! What's so suspicious about that?"

"One of the fishermen near the lake saw her running away one night. Everyone knows that there's nowhere to run round here. You can get lost out here for days and die from thirst and hunger. She must have been pretty desperate. Nobody goes out for a run here; especially not at night. Old Bill tried to tell the police what he saw but they didn't believe him cos his sight ain't so good and since his wife died, he's not been too good. He talks to himself, but Old Bill ain't mad. He swears to God what he saw was the truth. I believe him. First it's Rivka and then next I hear is that Juliana is dead. I'm just saying that I don't think it's a coincidence, especially with what happened to Mary and Christina."

"Maybe people are just trying to use the Irvings as scapegoats because they're jealous and want to find somebody to blame."

"Look kid no matter what I say, you ain't gonna believe me. You're under his spell, just like Juliana and Rivka were. I don't blame Juliana for needing therapy. She was a regular at the Darton Mental Health Practice. My sister works as a receptionist there."

"It makes sense that she committed suicide if she had mental health problems. You're just making up gossip because you're bored and have nothing better to do. Look I had better go."

"Believe what you want darl, but just be careful. I've heard some very nasty things about the Irving family. If you change your mind and want to talk, I'll give you my number. I'm Darlene by the way," Darlene says scrawling down her number on a piece of paper.

I storm out of the diner and throw the piece of paper in the nearest bin. It just sounds like malicious gossip. Accidents happen and people commit suicide. These things happen everyday in London. The moment there's a death or an accident, people in these small towns get excited and make up gossip and conspiracy theories. She has no evidence of anything. I know that Eric didn't do anything wrong. Even though I'm not keen on his parents, it doesn't mean that they're guilty of anything. Darlene is probably jealous that they're so wealthy and she has to work as a waitress all her life.

However, I still feel mad that Eric didn't tell me about his brother. I try to push my fury aside. There's probably a logical explanation about why Eric didn't tell me about his brother. Maybe they don't have a relationship anymore and don't see each other. Maybe it's a painful subject but I'm his wife, not some woman that he barely knows.

***

After dinner, I go up to see Eric in his study. It's such a shame that he doesn't come down to have dinner. I said to him that it would be nice for us to have dinner together as a family. Maybe if Clara saw us together, she'd start to feel like we're a family. I suggest to Guadalupe to bring Clara down for meals so that she can slowly get used to me. Clara still won't make eye contact with me. She doesn't like me coming near her or touching her things. Once her teddy bear fell from her highchair and when I went to pick it up for her, she started wailing so loudly that it hurt my ears.

"Mine! Teddy mine!" Clara screamed.

I'm just so glad that I don't have to look after Clara as I'd go crazy. Dealing with a two-year-old doesn't seem like much fun. I've never been a huge fan of babies and small children. Although I looked after Henry, it was different. He was my brother and he was so easy to love. I remember the first time that he smiled at me. He used to love it when I played peek-a-boo with him and told him stories. Henry was always an easy baby and child. He always listened to me and did what he was told.

Maybe I'd be different with my own child. It feels like a horrible thought. Clara needs a mother too, but Guadalupe is the only person that she views as her mother. I don't want to ruin their bond and confuse her further. I really hope that I come to love Clara as though she was my own. I feel guilty that I don't already love her. How can I love her when she rejects me? Nevertheless, emotionally I don't feel ready for motherhood. I want to feel fulfilled with my life. I want to have a career. I want to experience life. I want to travel. I already missed out on so much because I had to mother Henry.

I knock on Eric's door but he doesn't answer. I try to knock a few more times, but no answer. I try to open the door but it's locked. Why does Eric lock his room? I finally hear Eric call, "give me five minutes babe."

Eric joins me later in our bedroom. "Is everything ok babe?"

"Why do you lock your room?"

"Come on Iris, do I need an explanation for everything? I just want some privacy that's all."

"But why do you need to lock the door?"

"You're being silly and unreasonable Iris; it's a normal thing to lock your door."

"I feel like you're hiding something."

"That's ridiculous!"

"Why didn't you tell me that you have a brother?"

Eric's face suddenly becomes contorted with an unpleasant and angry expression. "How did you find out?"

"It doesn't matter. Why did you lie?"

"I know that I should have told you, but my brother isn't part of the family anymore."

"Because of the accident."

Eric's face is red with fury now, as if I'd told him that I was cheating on him. I tell Eric about my encounter with Darlene.

"That stupid old bitch!" Eric fumes. "How dare she? She's always been the town gossip! She's fed up with her own life so she tries to ruin everybody else's. She's pathetic! Don't believe in a word she says."

"But why didn't you tell me about your brother?"

"I'm sorry Iris, but my parents and I no longer speak to him. He caused a huge scandal and cast great shame upon my family. So much shame that my parents decided to move away."

"But it was an accident. David didn't mean to kill Christina. It was a stupid mistake; I'm sure he'll spend his whole life regretting it."

"It's not just that. David has always been very troubled. He was addicted to drugs and stole from my parents to fund his drug habit. My parents always did so much for him, but he threw it back in their faces. Ever since he was a child, he constantly lied and caused trouble. He even killed our cat! My parents were devastated. After an argument with my father, David pulled a knife on my him. It was lucky that I was there. David was always so reckless. A girl died because of his recklessness and David showed no remorse. He just expected my father to sort it all out. My father had enough and decided that he shouldn't be a part of our family anymore."

"Gosh that's so awful, but maybe he's changed. Doesn't everyone deserve a chance? Maybe he could have gotten help. It's it a bit extreme to completely disown him."

"My parents gave David so many chances and so much help. It got to the point where enough was enough."

"Where you ever close to David?"

Eric shakes his head. "Growing up with David was a living nightmare. He hated me and would take pleasure in bullying me. Once he held my head down the toilet. I always feared him. He was only seventeen months younger than me but he was much stronger. I remember the time I built a model aeroplane. It took me forever to build and I was so proud of it. One day I came back home from a friend's house to see that it had been smashed up. I knew it was David. So do you understand why I don't want to talk about him?"

"Oh baby, it must have been so hard but you could have told me. I just wish that we could spend more time together and really open up to one another."

"I know baby, but I've just been so swamped with work. I promise that we'll spend lots of time together. Just to let you know that next month, I'm going to go to New York for three weeks."

"Can't I come?"

"I'm sorry baby but it's going to be all strictly business. You'd be so bored. I also think that it'd be a good idea for you to stay at home so Clara can get used to having you around. It'd give her more stability since I travel so much."

"That's unfair of you to expect that from me. I'm not her mother and she doesn't even like me!"

"Don't be so silly Iris; Clara is two-years-old. How can a two-year-old not like someone? She just needs time to get used to you. I think that it'll be good for you to focus on motherhood, and it'll be good preparation for when we have our own baby."

I feel like someone has slapped me really hard in the face. "Don't I get a say in this? Don't I get any choice? I want a career."

"You can have a career baby. I had one of the rooms specially turned into an art studio for you, but you barely use it. You do nothing all day."

"How can you say that? I want to get a job."

"You also said that you want to be an artist and you have that chance. Start painting and I can help get your art career started."

"You can't just expect me to fall into the role of being a mother. A mother to a child that isn't even mine! A child that you failed to tell me about!"

"Please calm yourself Iris. You know why I didn't tell you about Clara earlier, but if you love me, you'll love Clara. She needs a mother and you'd make a wonderful mother Iris. I know you would. A far better mother than Juliana. I want us to be a proper family," Eric says gently, cupping my face in his hand.

"You can't just spring this on me."

"Iris then when are you ever going to be prepared for motherhood? Nobody is ever truly prepared. It's not like you're going to be alone; you'll have Guadalupe there to help you."

My body goes completely stiff and my lungs feel as though all the air has been sucked out of them. Why am I feeling like

I don't have a say in anything? The same uneasy feeling that I felt earlier when I spoke to Darlene washes over me and threatens to drown me. For the first time I can't help but feel trapped. I've given up so much for Eric and he doesn't get it. I feel that he doesn't even want to try to get how I'm feeling. I burst into tears.

"Hey baby, don't cry. I want what's best for you. I want us to be a proper family. I know that all your life you've craved stability and to have a normal family and now is your chance. Of course it's a lot to take in and it's a big change in your life, but it'll be a positive change. Trust me," Eric says calmly, stroking my cheek.

"I just wish that you didn't have to work so hard so we could spend more time together. You could be around for Clara more."

"I know babe and I'll try to make sure that I'm around more. I just feel under so much pressure since my father retired. I've had to take on so much responsibility and nothing is ever good enough for my father. There's a lot of competition out there with other art dealers and I need to keep up."

"We don't need the money. We can move somewhere smaller. I really miss London. There's nothing keeping us here. Your parents don't live here and you don't have many friends here."

"I know, but this is the place where I grew up. It's my home."

"What about finding somewhere in London?"

"You keep pestering me babe and I said that I'd check out the real estate in London, but at the moment I'm just so crazy busy with work."

"Why don't you sell the business? We could still live comfortably and we could spend more time together as a family."

"I can't sell my father's business! This is a business that's been in my family for generations!"

"You just seem so stressed all the time."

"Iris I appreciate your support, but I'm not going to sell the business. Look I'll take the day off tomorrow and we'll do something special ok? I love you baby," Eric says, putting his arms around my waist and pulling me in for a hug.

"I love you so much, you're the best wife," he whispers in my ear. Somehow, I don't feel soothed and reassured by his loving words. For once I'm beginning to feel that deep down in the pit of my stomach that something isn't right. I feel like I really don't know the man that I married.

CHAPTER NINETEEN

The next morning, I wake up to a bouquet of red roses and a note. The note says: *I love you baby, everyday I count my blessings that I married you. Love Eric x*

I had another sleepless night with the same recurring dream about the baby. The rest of the time that I was awake, I lay there tossing and turning. Am I the one being unreasonable or is Eric being unreasonable? I just can't help but feel trapped here. I tell myself that I'm being stupid and that marriage is about compromise. Maybe Eric is right; I'm not cut out to have my own career. After all Elizabeth would always tell me how useless I was.

Elizabeth has hardly been in touch. Nor have Magda or Henry. Maybe they don't care about me after all. It's not like Elizabeth not to bombard me with a hundred messages a day. Maybe I don't need her after all. Or Magda. If she was a true friend then she'd stick by me. I can't help but miss her though and feel so lonely.

The flowers and the note don't make me feel any better. I can't help but feel so lost and alone. Eric walks into the bedroom holding a tray filled with waffles covered in syrup and scrambled eggs.

"Breakfast in bed for my beautiful wife. I'm going to take the day off and spend it all with you," Eric says cheerily, kissing my neck. I don't feel in the mood.

"What's wrong baby?" he murmurs.

"I just feel so lonely," I cry.

"Hey baby don't cry. What can I do to make you feel better?" Eric says soothingly, pulling me into a hug.

"I just really miss London. I miss Magda and as crazy as it sounds, I even miss Elizabeth in a weird way."

"It's normal to feel a bit homesick, but it'll soon pass, just like any other sickness. I was homesick too when my parents sent me to boarding school. At first, I hated it and wanted to go back home, but I had to be a big boy and cope on my own. In the end I loved boarding school so much that I never wanted to go home for the holidays or weekends. It was also a good respite from David, especially when they kicked him out. You'll get used to it here, after all it's your home."

"You're right, but I can't help but feel lonely. Maybe I could invite Elizabeth and Magda to stay."

"It's up to you but you always said how much your mother drives you crazy. Her coming and staying here would unsettle you and upset you. You always said that you wanted to be far away from her and now she's got her new man, she doesn't need you anymore."

"But she's still my mother and despite everything, I still care about her. She's barely been in touch. Nor has Magda."

"It sounds like your mother realises that now you're married, your priorities are different and she can't walk all over you anymore. She has her new man now and that's probably made her less reliant on you. As for Magda, I could tell when I first met her that she wasn't a true friend."
"I don't have any friends here."

"I'll talk to Tripp and see if Tiffany can get you involved in any events."

"Tiffany hardly wants to be my friend. She can't stand me."

"Nonsense, you just got off on the wrong foot with her, but I'm sure that once you get to know one another you'll be firm friends. She can be a bit of a mean girl, but it's only because she's testing the waters. She's like that with new people. She probably feels threatened because you're so gorgeous, kind and smart. There's also a ladies tennis club at the country club; that would be a good place to start and meet some new people."

The idea of doing something and talking to people makes me feel good, even it they're stuck up WASPs.

"I'll also schedule you for another appointment with Doctor Goldman. It'll do you some good to talk about your feelings. Baby you really don't need to worry about anything."

"Did Juliana and Rivka fit in with your friends?" I ask. I don't know why I'm bringing them up. Although I don't believe what Darlene said, it's been playing on my mind.

"I see that old bitch Darlene has been telling you about my dating history," Eric laughs sardonically.

"What happened between you and Rivka?" I ask.

"Quelle surprise! We broke up! It was years ago. We weren't compatible and we knew that it wouldn't work in the long run. She would only marry somebody Jewish and I made it clear that I wasn't going to convert, so we broke up. She moved back to New York and that's it! No big story. Rivka is ancient history. What crap has Darlene been filling your head with? I have a right mind to go over there and tell her to leave me and my family alone!" Eric rants furiously.

"Eric don't say anything; just ignore her. I won't speak to her again."

"Damn right you won't! I want you to stay away from the old bitch. Nobody around here likes her. She's an old gossip who enjoys inventing stories about people here. You need to stop being so oversensitive and letting people like that get to you."

Eric is right. I am being oversensitive. I trust Eric and I know that he wants the best for me and would never hurt anyone. I'm willing to make the effort and fit in here. I've always wanted love, stability and a proper family. Why am I so intent to ruin that? I should be lucky that I have a husband who loves me and would do anything for me.

"Baby I just thought that I'd let you know that my parents will be coming tomorrow for a couple of days. They want to see how you're settling in and to see their granddaughter."

"Why couldn't you ask me before?"

"Babe I don't need your permission to invite my parents. It's not like you have a busy schedule."

I feel hurt by Eric's sharp words. I don't feel hurt that he invited them, but upset that he didn't discuss it with me.
"Look I didn't mean to be so curt with you baby. I really want you to get to know my parents. I want them to be more involved with Clara's life as well as our future baby's life. I was meaning to ask you if you got your period?"

"It's only been a few weeks since we've been trying. Give it time. What's the rush?"

"You're right baby; I just want to have a baby with you so much because I love you. Don't worry about gaining weight during the pregnancy; I'll hire the best nutritionist and personal trainer. You should be ok as you're still young. Your skin will bounce back."

"I'm not even thinking about that; I don't care about gaining a few pounds. I just don't want to rush this."

"I know baby, but I'm just so impatient with excitement."

"Why don't we do something that will lead to that?" I say

flirtatiously.

"Give me ten minutes baby and let's get down to business."

Whilst Eric is in the bathroom, I open my bedside drawer which contains the box with tablets. I reach for my pill and drink it down with water. I hate lying to Eric, but having a baby is too much at the moment and is the thing furthest from my mind.

SATURDAY 13TH OCTOBER

I wake up feeling sore and groggy with a pounding headache. Doctor Goldman prescribed me some tablets to help with sleeping when I told him about my nightmares. I feel a soreness and aching all over my body. I spot a bruise on my arm, which wasn't there before. I probably bumped my arm and forgot about it. Doctor Goldman says that feeling sore is a normal side effect of the medication and that it will go away. For a brief period in the night, I woke up gasping for breath. I don't remember it very well. A few seconds later I fell asleep again. Everything feels like such a blur. Usually I welcome being able to sleep through the night, but this feels different. It felt as though someone had bashed me over the head with a sack of bricks.

"Did you sleep better after you took those pills?" Eric asks lovingly, bringing me a glass of water.

"I feel like I woke up from anaesthesia. My head really hurts and everything aches. I'm not sure I want to take those pills again."

"My poor baby. They sound like they were pretty strong pills, but your body is probably just adjusting. The side effects should wear off soon."

"I guess that's true," I agree.

"Get dressed baby, my parents will be here soon."

I try my hardest to look presentable for Eric's parents. I already feel nervous about seeing them again as I know that they didn't take to me very well when they first met me. Maybe their visit will be a good chance to get to know one another. I put on a black tweed dress and my set of pearl earrings with a matching pearl necklace. I spray myself with Chanel perfume and perfect my make-up and hair.

I feel so hot underneath my dress and my palms are sweating. Eric holds my hand and tells me that it'll be fine and that once his parents get to know me, they'll love me. Guadalupe has Clara dressed in her finest pearl pink dress with little pink roses on the collar and a matching pink ribbon in her hair.

When Eric's parents finally arrive, the anxiety within me rises like a musical crescendo. Genevieve looks prim and proper in her conservative navy dress and tweed jacket bedecked with a pearl necklace and earrings. Eric Senior looks rigid and unrelaxed in his casual white polo shirt and slim fit slacks.

"Eric," Eric Senior nods, giving his son a squeeze on the shoulder. There's no affection between them nor with Genevieve. She gives Eric a cold peck on the cheek and greets me likewise. Eric Senior just nods and coldly says, "afternoon, Iris." Genevieve however warmly greets her granddaughter. She practically snatches Clara from Guadalupe's arms and makes embarrassing kissy noises at Clara.

Eric's parents have just gotten here, but I already can't wait for them to leave.

CHAPTER TWENTY

We eat dinner together in awkward silence. Guadalupe has made roast beef and new potatoes with vegetables. There's a heavy knot in my stomach and I don't feel like eating. Eric's parents have barely bothered with me. They treat me like I'm invisible. I can see the disapproval radiate from Genevieve's eyes like poison. Eric Senior doesn't think much of me either. They're both just so cold and so disapproving. I drown my sorrows in wine. I move onto my second glass.

"Iris, I don't think that you should be drinking, especially as we're trying for a baby," Eric says sharply. I really wish that he wouldn't keep harping on about having a baby.

"How wonderful," Genevieve says stiffly with a forced smiled. The atmosphere is so tense that you could cut it with a knife. I ignore Eric's advice and drain my second glass. I make an excuse to leave. I can't bear sitting in the same room as Eric's parents with their looks of disdain and covert disapproval. I go to my bedroom and cry. I just feel so lost and so alone. I miss not having anyone to confide in. I ring Magda but the call doesn't go through which is strange. I also try to ring Elizabeth but the phone keeps ringing so I give up and hang up.

I grab another bottle of wine from the cellar and go back upstairs. Why am I drinking more when it's clearly making me feel even more depressed? Maybe I'm looking for the courage to find what is bugging me. I feel like Eric is hiding something from me. I can't get rid of that nagging sensation that something isn't right.

I go to Eric's study. Luckily the door isn't locked. What could he be hiding from me that makes him want to lock his door? The study doesn't look suspicious. The desk is piled with papers and half-drunk cups of coffee. I sift through the papers but there's nothing interesting. It looks like boring business stuff. Why am I being so suspicious of my husband? I trust him. Don't most women feel a bit insecure?

My next move fills me with shame. I open Eric's MacBook Pro. A pretty landscape of a tropical island somewhere pops up with the bar for the password in the middle of the screen. My superego is telling me not to do it, but my id is telling me to do it. The combination of alcohol and paranoia wins. I type in several password combinations. I have absolutely no idea what it could be but I try Clara followed by different numbers and her birthdate. It doesn't work. I try Eric's birthdate and my birthdate but it doesn't work either. I try different combinations but to no avail. Perhaps he keeps his passwords in his drawers.

I really feel like a psycho going through Eric's drawers. What am I expecting to find? I worry that his drawers may be locked but luckily, they all seem open. I rifle through all five of the drawers, one by one. So far, they don't contain anything of use. In three of the drawers there's just folders labelled with things such as "accounts", "portfolio" and "legal documents". I'm not going to go through these folders. In another drawer there's just stationary. I get to the final drawer but it's locked. Why would Eric lock one of his drawers? Is he hiding something? I look around for a key but I can't seem to find one.

Next, I go over to Eric's bookcase. Really what am I hoping to achieve? There are books about art, finance and business. I pick up some of the books to have a look at. As I put one of the books back, I see a picture frame wedged between the books. I pull out the picture frame. A beautiful dark-haired woman looks back at me. She's absolutely beautiful and exotic-looking. She looks Spanish or South American. She has a beautiful smile and her big hazel eyes glow. She looks like a model posing for a picture. I wonder if it's Juliana or more accurately *was* Juliana. It seems like such a tragedy. She doesn't look like a woman with severe problems, but what can you know about somebody by looking at a photograph? I feel so self-conscious. I feel so ugly compared to Juliana. Why does Eric still keep her picture? I keep gazing at the picture until I jump at the sound of Eric's voice and almost drop the picture.

"Iris what the hell are you doing? Are you snooping through my things?"

"No baby, I just wanted to take a look. Was this Juliana? Why do you still have a photo of her?"

Eric snatches the frame out of my hands. "Yes, it was Juliana and I forgot that it was even there. Why are you in my study?"

"I just wanted to take a look at your books. Why are you being so defensive?"

"Don't lie to me Iris. My MacBook is open and I know that it was closed when I left it. I can't put up with this jealousy and mistrust; Juliana put me through so much hell with her insecurity and jealousy. I really can't put up with it again Iris."

"I'm so sorry baby, I do trust you, but why do you lock your drawer and why do you lock your study?"

"Wow you really need to talk to Doctor Goldman about your jealousy and paranoia. You're acting crazy. Since you're acting so suspicious, I locked my door because I was planning something for your birthday and I lock my drawer because that's where I keep special gifts that I don't want anyone to find."

I feel wracked with guilt and embarrassment. How could I not trust Eric? He was planning something nice for me and I act like a crazy woman. Well done Iris, well done, I tell myself. Now Eric thinks I'm one of those crazy jealous women that accuse their husbands of cheating and hiding things.

"I'm sorry baby, really I am," I sob, trying to hug Eric. He doesn't hug me back.

"You really need to work on your trust issues Iris because I can't go through this again. I think that you should also discuss your drinking problem. Now my parents think that I married another crazy and unbalanced alcoholic. The amount that you drink is ridiculous! Are you surprised that Tiffany doesn't want to be around somebody who drinks so much? You're a mess Iris. Look at you! My parents worried about me when I was with Juliana. I don't want them to think that I'm repeating the same mistakes. How can I have a baby with a woman who drinks so much? Will I even be able to trust you around Clara, around our child?"

"I'm sorry baby, I promise I won't drink so much. I'm so sorry that I didn't trust you. I'm so sorry," I wail.

"I think you should go to bed. We'll talk tomorrow."

"Please don't divorce me."

"I'm not going to divorce you, don't be so crazy. I love you, but you need help Iris. I don't want you to end up the same way as your mother."

CHAPTER TWENTY-ONE

The next day Eric gives me the cold shoulder. My actions from last night hit me like a bucket of ice-cold water thrown all over me. Why did I have to act like such a crazy psycho going through my husband's things? What was I hoping to find? No wonder Eric is mad at me. Now his parents are going to have even more cause to dislike me. I don't want them to think I'm crazy like Juliana. I want to prove to them that I'm the right woman for Eric.

I rise from bed around seven since I can't sleep anyway and prepare breakfast. I know that Eric's parents are early risers and will probably have breakfast around half seven. I fry some eggs, bacon, sausages and make a couple of rounds of toast and waffles. I lay the table and pour four glasses of orange juice. When Eric's parents come down, I greet them both with a smile. They don't return the smile. Eric Senior just takes his newspaper out, ready to read and Genevieve just sits there primly.

"Would you like some breakfast?" I ask cheerily.

"We'll just have fruit. Fried food is not good for my cholesterol and Genevieve wants to lose a few pounds," Eric Senior says unappreciatively. I'm shocked by Eric Senior's admission. Genevieve is as thin as a rake. There's nothing of her. If anything, she could do with gaining weight.

"I didn't used much oil and it's only one meal. I can make a salad for lunch."

"No thank you; I'll have Guadalupe prepare our meals. She knows what we like."

I feel like a deflated balloon. Here I am making so much effort and it's not appreciated. I pile some of the food on a plate, ready for Eric and throw the rest away. I don't feel hungry. Eric comes downstairs a few minutes later. He greets his parents and says good morning to me brusquely. He doesn't kiss me and there's no emotion in his voice.

"I made you breakfast."

"No thank you, I don't really have time for a proper sit-down breakfast. I'll get Guadalupe to bring me a coffee and some toast." I muster up all the courage it takes not to cry. I can already feel the tears forming in the corner of my eyes. I'm determined not to cry in front of Eric and his parents. If I cry, it'll show that I've let them get to me. The worst thing I can do is let them win in making me feel like shit. I grab my coffee and tell them that I'm going upstairs. As I walk out of the kitchen, I hear whispering. I pause by the door where they can't see me and try to make sense of their whispering. I can't hear much but then their voices get louder as they think that I've gone upstairs.

"I don't think that girl is right for you darling," I hear Genevieve say.

"I don't understand why you married her. From what you've told me about her background, she doesn't seem very stable. You said that her mother was an alcoholic. She seems to be going the same way. It's like with Juliana," Eric Senior says.

"Look, I spoke to Iris last night and she said that she's going to curb her drinking. I've already gotten her to see Doctor Goldman."

Being called an alcoholic is like a huge slap in the face. I don't drink every day. If I do drink, it's just a few glasses once or twice a week. I hardly think that makes me an alcoholic. Elizabeth used to drink every day, starting in the morning.

She'd have gin and tonic throughout the day and then a bottle of wine or two in the evening. It's a miracle really that Elizabeth's liver still works normally. Before meeting Eric, I never even used to drink much, even with Magda and Arek. Magda and Arek would always drink a lot at parties. They both loved vodka especially. They would always try to get me to me drink some, but I can't stand vodka. I could never understand how Magda and Arek could drink it straight. Once they made me down a vodka shot and I felt so sick afterwards. It was a horrible experience.

Again, I feel the familiar wave of sadness fall over me. I miss Magda so much. I sent her a message but she never responded. It's clear that obviously she doesn't want to be friends. I don't even hear from Elizabeth. She must be really happy with Kevin. I feel glad for her. I've always wanted Elizabeth to be happy and less reliant on me, but now she's the one avoiding me. Perhaps this is another one of her games where she's punishing me by avoiding me. She obviously still feels abandoned and has retreated to the other side of the spectrum of completely ignoring me.

"I don't think that she'd make a very good mother. I think that you're rushing into having another baby," Genevieve says.

"I love you both, but you need to stop telling me how to live my life," Eric snaps.

"I just wish that you could have married someone like Tiffany. She was perfect for you; classy, well-educated and from a good family. I don't understand why you never wanted to marry her. Especially after the scandal that David left in his wake, you should be grateful that her father was willing to give his blessing," Eric Senior says.

I feel the bile rise in my throat again. Tiffany and Eric dated? Why did Eric not tell me?

"We just worry about you darling, especially after what happened with Juliana. Your father and I feel that you should be with someone who is from a similar background to you and who shares the same values. You always seem to go for these unstable girls from poor and broken homes."

How dare they call me "unstable"? These people don't know me at all and they make such assumptions about me. At least Eric is on my side, but I feel angry that he didn't tell me about dating Tiffany.

"Look, this is my life and I'll be with whoever I want," Eric hisses.

"Your choice and your life; we won't get involved," Eric Senior says.

"Yes, we came to see our granddaughter anyway. Your father and I were thinking of going sailing today; we'd like to bring Clara along," Genevieve says.

"Why doesn't Iris come as well? You can get to know one another a bit more," Eric suggests.

"If you really insist," Genevieve says reluctantly.

I couldn't imagine anything worse than spending the day with Eric Senior and Genevieve. They'll be happy to know that I have no intention of tagging along and allowing them to degrade me any further. I'd rather put up with Elizabeth's verbal diarrhoea any day rather than Eric Senior and Genevieve's silence. Silence so sharp that it could cut you like a knife. Sometimes silence can say a lot more than words can.

There's just such a coldness and brutality about them both that I just can't fathom. I find it hard to comprehend how they could disown their own son and banish him from the family as if he never even existed. I know that David made a lot of mistakes and did a lot of bad things, but he's still their son.

There's not even a single picture around the house of David. I wonder if they ever think about him, but I somehow doubt it. They've probably completely erased him from their memory. Eric Senior strikes me as a hard and unforgiving man. The kind of person that could destroy you if you ever set a foot wrong. I don't trust him. There's something so sinister and heinous about him. Genevieve seems like the kind of woman who goes along with anything that her husband says. I don't trust my in-laws, especially Eric Senior.

Once I get dressed, I knock on the door of Eric's study. Surprisingly, he tells me to come in. It's good to know that he's not reverted to locking his door. Eric snaps the laptop shut sharply and gives me a look of annoyance, as if I was some annoying kid interrupting him.

"Yes Iris, what is it?" It's obvious that Eric is still sulking.

"Why do you always shut your laptop?"

"Again with the paranoia Iris. I'm really fed up with this. Am I not allowed to close my laptop now?"

"No, but it feels like you're hiding something from me."

"What could I possibly be hiding from you? I just think it's rude to be on my laptop when I'm talking to somebody, so I close it. Is that a good enough answer for you?" Eric sighs indignantly.

"You didn't tell me that you dated Tiffany."

Eric's eyes are burning with fury and the vein in his temple bulges. I've never seen Eric look so angry before. It scares me a bit.

"How did you find out and what does it matter?"

"I overheard you and your parents talking."

"God Iris, you're so paranoid that you've started eavesdropping on my conversations. For your information I did date Tiffany. Many years ago. We dated for a few months, but I ended it because I didn't love her. We decided that we were better off as friends. Tiffany realised that she was still in love with Tripp and they got married. Happy now?"

"Why didn't you tell me?"

"Because I knew that you'd overreact and anyway it was such a long time ago and there's nothing between us, so I really don't know why it matters."

"Tiffany acted like she couldn't stand me. Maybe she does have feelings for you."

"You're being absolutely ridiculous and paranoid. It's all in your head."

"I just guess that I feel insecure. Tiffany is beautiful and probably more suited to you than I am."

"You have absolutely nothing to worry about. Trust me if I wanted to be with Tiffany, I'd be with her. There is nothing there, trust me. You need to stop acting so jealous and crazy. I think that I'll book another appointment for you to see Doctor Goldman today."

I nod. "You're right baby, I'm acting so jealous and insecure, but you're giving me no reason to."

"Exactly, it's all in your head."

CHAPTER TWENTY-TWO

WEDNESDAY 24TH OCTOBER

Today is my birthday. I'm twenty-four today. I wake up feeling sore all over. I took the medication for sleep last night. Doctor Goldman lowered my dose but encouraged me to keep on taking it. Whenever I take it, I fall into a heavy and drugged sort of sleep and not the restful and peaceful kind of sleep. They do nothing to help with my nightmares. The nightmares are even worse and even more vivid. I had a nightmare that someone was on top of me; suffocating me. It felt so real.

Every part of my body radiates with soreness. My head is pounding like a heavy metal concert and my mouth has this horrible metallic taste. I reach for my glass of water on the bedside and greedily gulp it. On my bedside, next to the water is a huge bouquet of flowers from Eric. There's a mixed selection of luscious and fresh roses, irises, tulips, peonies, carnations and orchids. I check my phone for birthday messages. There's a message from Elizabeth just saying:

Happy Birthday Iris. I hope you're happy with your life. You obviously don't feel the need for me to be in it and I don't need you to be in mine. I think that it's best that we don't speak anymore. All the best. Mum

This is not like Elizabeth. Firstly, Elizabeth would never refer to herself as "mum" in a million years. Even from the time that I learnt to speak, I had to call her Elizabeth. The funny thing is that Elizabeth isn't even her real name. It's actually Frances, but Elizabeth hated it and changed her name when she left home. She changed her name to Elizabeth after her favourite actress, Elizabeth Taylor.

Elizabeth had a prim and proper conservative upbringing. Her parents were strict and religious and Elizabeth never got along with them. Elizabeth would often say to me," you should be lucky that you have such a liberal and cool mother like me. I was so ashamed of my mother; she looked as though she was my grandmother. She never approved of anything; boys, rock and roll, make-up. Can you imagine?"

I only met my grandparents a couple of times in my life, but we never had a real relationship. They didn't approve that I was born out of wedlock and they never treated me like a real grandchild. They didn't want much to do with me or Elizabeth. They died a few years ago.

Secondly, it's not like Elizabeth not to ring me on her birthday and babble on about how painful labour with me was and how if she had a choice, she never would have had children. "It's so hard darling and nobody appreciates it. You certainly don't appreciate it darling. You should be thankful to me that I gave birth to you darling, all by my bloody self."

Thirdly, Elizabeth wouldn't just decide to cut contact with me, would she? It explains her lack of contact lately. When Elizabeth is angry, she rants and raves, but she'd never cut me off. A few hours later, she'll ring in a cheery mood as if nothing ever happened and will harp on about something completely irrelevant. Elizabeth's message seems too controlled and emotionless- the complete opposite of the chaotic and emotional Elizabeth I know. Then again, maybe her medication and Kevin's influence have balanced her out. As much as Elizabeth has always irritated me, I can't help but feel stung by her rejection.

I receive a birthday text from Henry simply just saying *happy birthday x.* It's not like Henry either. Usually he'd say something like: *happy birthday to the best big sister ever. Love you so much.* Both Henry and Elizabeth's messages seem so cold and impersonal, which is unlike them. I don't even get birthday wishes from Magda.

Eric brings me breakfast in bed; a green smoothie and oatmeal with berries, which is not my usual breakfast.

"Happy birthday my gorgeous wife," Eric says, planting a kiss on my lips. He hands me three neatly wrapped presents. The first gift is a pair of beautiful diamond earrings. The next gift is certainly very strange. It appears to be a pregnancy test.

"Why did you get me a pregnancy test?" I ask curiously.

"What a wonderful birthday present it would be finding out that we're parents. We've been trying for about two months so it should be positive. Anyway, before you do the test, open your next gift."

The next gift is even stranger. I open the beautiful light pink box to find some sort of leather outfit, though it's so scant that it can't even be classed as an outfit. It's just strips of leather taped together. There's a lead strapped to the collar. I've never seen anything like this before, not even in Ann Summers. In the box, there's also a pair of metal handcuffs.

"What's this?" I ask.

"I just thought that we could spice things up a bit in the bedroom baby."

"Oh," I say, not knowing what to make of this gift. It's not something that I would ever imagine wearing. It seems almost degrading. It would have been nice to at least get some pretty lingerie. I don't want to upset Eric by telling him that this is something that I'd never wear or would want to wear for that matter. Next to the pregnancy test, it's the weirdest gift that anybody has ever given me. Even Elizabeth's ex-boyfriends never gave her anything this risqué. Elizabeth's boyfriends never even gave her anything as they were either too skint or too stingy.

"Why don't you take the test baby? I can't wait for those blue lines to appear," Eric says. I feel sick. I know that the test will be negative. I've been taking my pill everyday without fail. I shut myself in the bathroom and dutifully do the test. I pee on the stick and wait five minutes. As expected, the test is negative. Part of me is secretly relieved, but part of me is scared to let Eric down. I know how badly he wants us to have a baby. I feel so bad for deceiving him.

"What does it say?" Eric says like an excited child about to open his Christmas presents.

"It's negative."

"What? That can't be right. This pregnancy test is 100% accurate; it cost me a hundred dollars. It can't be wrong. It just can't. There must be something wrong with you. At your age, you should be able to fall pregnant just like that," Eric says exasperatedly, clicking his fingers.

"It's only been two months and we haven't been intimate that many times. Give it a chance," I snap irritatedly.

Eric shakes his head. "I'm going to book an appointment with the gynaecologist to figure out what the problem is. Perhaps he can give you something to help. I've even gotten Guadalupe to make more nutritious foods to help get you pregnant."

"What's this rush to get pregnant? We've got plenty of time. It takes loads of people months anyway to conceive."

"Only if you're thirty-five and over. You're at your most fertile Iris!"

I feel the tears springing from my eyes. Why is Eric so obsessed with having a baby? He already has Clara and why the rush?

"Why do you keep putting so much pressure on me?" I cry.

"I'm sorry Iris, I just want us to have a baby so bad. I'm just so scared that it won't work out. I know couples who have struggled for years to get pregnant and they've been so unlucky. I'm just scared that we'll be one of those couples."

"We won't be. Let's just give it time and not stress about it. You still have Clara and the main thing is that we have each other."

"You're right baby, I'm sorry. Why don't you get dressed so we can enjoy the rest of your special day together?"

***

Eric and I spend a lovely afternoon together on his boat. The weather is surprisingly sunny for late October. We drink champagne and have lunch at a renowned seafood restaurant. I'm having such a good time that I forget about the whole pregnancy debacle from this morning and the strange sexual gift. Elizabeth always said that men are terrible at buying gifts.

I tell Eric about Elizabeth's message. I still can't help but feel hurt that Elizabeth doesn't want to talk to me and that Magda didn't even send me a birthday message. I sent Elizabeth a message, asking her what's going on and why don't we talk about it, but I haven't gotten any reply.

"You should just respect her wishes baby. Maybe this is a blessing in disguise. Your mother has been like a parasite, sucking the joy and life out of you and taking advantage of you. She sees that she can't take advantage of you anymore because you have me. And as for Magda, I've always been telling you that she isn't a true friend. She's jealous of what we have; I could see it," Eric says, clutching my hand supportively. "In a way, I don't blame her. What we have is pretty damn special baby. I love you so much. I'm the luckiest man to have an amazing woman like you by my side."

At that moment, all of my worries vanish. Like a drug, Eric

has the power to make me feel so euphoric and on top of the world. I have a wonderful and loving husband. I'm so stupid not to trust him. I want to slap myself for my psycho behaviour recently. Eric is right about Elizabeth and Magda. I should be glad to be free of Elizabeth and Magda was obviously never a true friend.

Right now, I feel like such a princess. I wear my special little red Prada dress and my new earrings. I feel like Julia Roberts *in Pretty Woman*. I feel like I'm floating above the clouds. I drink some white wine at the restaurant. I feel so calm and relaxed that I could float into the air. Even Eric doesn't comment on my drinking. Well it is my birthday after all. Eric has even taken the day off from working to spend my birthday with me. He obviously loves me so much. Maybe I should just come off the pill and give him a baby. Maybe it won't be so bad. After all, Eric is right. You can never be prepared for a baby. I know that I would be a better mother than Elizabeth ever was. I always promised myself that. I feel all of my worries melt away with the sun.

It's after seven by the time that we get back. There's a large cake with a pearly pink ribbon tied around it. The cake is covered in pearly white icing with pink and white iced flowers. *Happy birthday Iris* is written in pink writing. It's one of those cakes that costs a fortune and that you only see in the windows of posh bakeries in London and on Instagram. The cake is almost too beautiful to eat. Guadalupe and Clara come and sing happy birthday to me, though Clara definitely doesn't sing or even look happy to be here.

"My cake! My cake! Give it!" Clara screeches and starts wailing. Guadalupe takes her upstairs. Her screaming can drive anybody crazy. The constant screaming and tantrums are what puts me off most about having kids.

Eric tells me that he's going upstairs to do a bit of work for half

MSSELO SELO

an hour and that this evening we'll have a night of passion. I really don't want to try on Eric's gift. I don't want to hurt his feelings and tell him that I don't like it. Maybe he thinks it's something that I'd be into. Our sex life hasn't been the most amazing.

I always feel like Eric isn't very present when we make love and it's always over very quickly. I feel like sex for Eric is a very mechanical thing. There's not really any foreplay and after sex, we don't cuddle or just lie there, relishing one another. Eric just says goodnight and switches off the light. I know that he's stressed with work. Maybe that's the problem. Maybe this ridiculous outfit really will spice things up.

I take a piece of the cake. It's delicious though far too rich. I feel full after a couple of bites. Since moving here, my appetite has been up and down. Feeling homesick and lonely and the awful visit from Eric's parents have really taken their toll on me. I'm just so grateful to God that they went back last week. Their presence always made me feel on edge; like I wasn't wanted or welcome in my own home.

I spend most of my days going on long walks or reading. I've been trying to do some art, but I just can't get into it. It's like my mind and my heart are no longer in it. I've tried doing a few pieces, but I just can't get anything right. I feel like my paintings lack depth and the colours are off key and flat. I feel like the spark has gone. I've been trying to go on walks for inspiration and read books about different artists, but nothing seems to work. Before, the smallest and simplest of things gave me inspiration such as the night sky or a squirrel climbing up a tree.

Although Eric has tried so hard to make my birthday special, I still can't help but feel a tinge of sadness. I feel sad that Magda couldn't even be bothered to send me a birthday message and that even Elizabeth and Henry didn't ring me or even send a card or gift. Although Elizabeth has never been the greatest mother, she would always send me something for my birthday, even if it wasn't my cup of tea.

Once she sent me this awful smelling perfume that made me sneeze and feel sick every time that I sprayed it. She said that the lady in the shop said that it contained some sort of pheromones which would make men weak at the knees when they saw me. Not that I believe in any of that pseudoscience rubbish. It didn't work and just made other people repelled by the strong smell. The only things that the pheromones attracted were dogs. I never had so many dogs trying to sniff and hump me.

Last year, Magda got me this beautiful friendship bracelet with a heart and the word *sister* engraved on it. Last year Henry sent me this Irish joke book that made me laugh so much. Even Julio organised a card for me, which everybody including Felicity signed, and a coffee and walnut cake from M&S.

Thinking about my birthday last year makes me feel nostalgic. My life is just so completely different to how it was last year. I would have never in a million years imagined that I would be married and living in a mansion. I try to count my blessings. Eric loves me and would do anything for me. This is our last week together before he goes to New York. I wish so badly that I could go with him. I've always wanted to go to New York.

I head upstairs to the bedroom to get ready for Eric. I really can't bring myself to wear the horrible strips of leather that he bought me. I put on some of my nicer underwear. I select matching lacy mint green underwear with a matching silky robe. It's nine o'clock but Eric still isn't here so I head to the study and knock on the door. There's no reply so I call his name. There's still no reply. Surprisingly the door opens and isn't locked. Maybe Eric really took into consideration my feelings about it. After all we have nothing to hide from one another.

I walk into the room to find the laptop open. Maybe this is a test and Eric is showing me that he has nothing to hide. The rational part of my mind tells me not to do it, but the other more reckless part of my brain is telling me to do it. Just so that I can be reassured. I'll probably find nothing anyway. Before I can debate the matter in my mind, I see that the MacBook isn't locked. The password screen doesn't come up. It's not clear what the image is. It looks like a film that's been paused. I feel upset that Eric has been watching a film without me.

I tap the play button and the movie continues to play. As my eyes adjust to what's going on, I realise that it isn't a movie. The more I watch, the sicker I feel. I pause the video because I can't watch anymore. It's disgusting. What I've seen has shocked me so much that I throw up right into the bin. I jump as Eric thunders into the room. I want to get as far away as possible from him.

CHAPTER TWENTY-THREE

"Iris I thought that we spoke about your fucking paranoia. Here you are again going through my computer. I go for one minute to take a piss and you're in here like a shot!"

"Well now I have every reason not to trust you. I saw the filth that you've been watching. It's sick!"

"First of all, you're completely overreacting. What you saw is a bit of porn. Porn starring consenting adults. There's nothing wrong with that. Ask any man and they'll tell you that they watch porn. I bet even your brother watches it."

"Don't talk to me like I was born yesterday! I'm not an idiot. What you were watching isn't normal porn; it's vile and it's violent and degrading to women! How can you watch stuff like this?"

"Look, it's just fantasy. It's not real. You act as if I'm watching child porn or bestiality."

"How can you call beating and raping women a fantasy?"

"Iris you need to calm down! It's like people who play violent video games. Ninety-nine-point nine percent of them know the difference between reality and fantasy. Just because you kill people in a video game doesn't mean that you're going to kill them in real life."

"This is different. I don't understand how you can even fantasize about such abhorrent things. It's vile. Is this what you want to do? Rape me and beat me?"

"Iris baby, how could you think that I could ever hurt you? You're my precious baby girl; I could never do anything to hurt you."

"What about that outfit you got me? Give it back because there's no way that I'm going to wear such a disgusting and degrading outfit!"

"Iris please! I told you that I have certain sexual desires and needs. I told you that I don't get turned on by vanilla sex."

It suddenly clicks in my mind. That's why Eric would always spend ages in the bathroom before we had sex. He was watching those horrible videos. Those nasty videos were turning him on, not me.

"Get away from me!"

"Iris baby please wait!"

I run into the bedroom and whip out my suitcase.

"Please Iris, you're completely overreacting."

"So, this is what you've been hiding from me? You're spending all day locked in your room jerking off to some degrading porn?"

"It's not like that. Juliana was very into domination and I have to admit that it turns me on. I want to dominate you. A lot of women find being dominated very sexy. They love the whole Christian Grey thing. I promise it'll be fun and we'll take it slowly ok? The video that you saw was very tame compared to some of the other stuff you find on porn sites. In fact, that video is very popular with both men *and* women. Actually it's very common for women to have rape fantasies. I know that it certainly turned Juliana on. Please baby, I don't want to lose you. I'm not some kind of monster if that's what you're thinking."

I don't know what to think. Maybe I really am making a fuss about nothing, but what I saw on the video really shocked me.

But Eric is right, Christian Grey was into all of that and it didn't make him a bad person. Maybe Eric has had a bad experience that's made him into this stuff. Maybe I can show him that sex doesn't have to be about that.

"Why don't we do a deal. You try what I'm into and I'll try being more enthusiastic about vanilla sex. I promise you that I'm not going to hurt you," Eric says, stroking my face.

"OK but I don't want to do anything that I saw on that video."

"Of course not baby! That's hardcore and not many people in reality do that. Now why don't you put on the little present that I brought you. It'd really turn me on."

I open the box containing the awful outfit and take it out. I undress out of my tame underwear and reluctantly put on the horrible bits of leather with the lead.

"I want you to get down on all fours. I want you to call me Master, do you understand?" Eric barks. I nod.

"You are my submissive and as my submissive you will do whatever I tell you. If not, you will be punished!"

I try to play along although I'm really not liking this. It feels so degrading but I want to make Eric happy and so many people do this. Before I can even reply, Eric grabs me, covering my mouth and throws me onto the bed. He grabs my arms and pulls them over my head, locking my wrists into the handcuffs. Eric strips himself naked and enters me quickly and suddenly. It hurts, especially as I'm not turned on. Eric pounds me furiously and covers my mouth so I can't breathe. I don't like this. I feel like I'm suffocating. I feel relieved when Eric takes his hands off my mouth. He lifts me up and aggressively slaps my butt. The sharp sting brings tears to my eyes.

"Ow! That really hurt!"

"Shut up you pathetic and dirty little bitch! You deserve to be hurt," Eric snarls, gripping my arm tightly.

With my other arm, I slap Eric as hard as I can around the face. "Let me go!" I scream. Eric complies and pulls out. I spring off the bed, tearing the horrible outfit off and reaching for my silk amaranth pink pyjamas.

"You promised that you wouldn't hurt me!" I yell.

"I'm sorry baby, I took it too far. I never meant to hurt you. I was just so in the moment that I completely zoned out. It wasn't real baby; it's all just pretend. It's a role play."

"I hated it and I don't ever want to do that again! It was horrible and humiliating."

"It was completely my fault; I took it too far. Please forgive me. I hate myself for hurting you," Eric looks at me with his pleading eyes, tears forming in the corner of his eyes.

"I just don't understand how you can think that this kind of thing is arousing. It's sick!"

"I'm sorry baby, I'll change for you. I promise. I'll get help. It was Juliana that introduced me to all of this. Normal sex wasn't enough for her. Not like it is for you. She had an extremely high sex drive. She liked to dominate me and treat me like a slave and in turn she wanted me to degrade her and hurt her."

"How can any woman want to be hurt?"

"Juliana derived pleasure from pain and punishment. I felt uncomfortable hurting her but if I didn't hit her or hurt her hard enough, she would say that I wasn't a real man. I wanted to make her happy by doing things her way and I got so used to it that vanilla sex no longer turned me on anymore. Please Iris, I'm so sorry."

I can hear the sincerity in Eric's voice; he sounds so genuine and troubled. He's not a bad guy and he doesn't want to hurt me. Eric loves me. Eric obviously needs help and I want to help him.

"Please Iris baby, I want to kick myself in the balls for making you feel like this. You should just go ahead and kick me hard in the balls. I deserve it. Juliana would kick me hard in the balls. Boy did that hurt."

"I'm not going to hurt you. I don't want to hurt you. I don't want us to hurt one another. It's not healthy."

"I know baby, my relationship with Juliana messed me up, but I promise that I'll get help. I'll even talk about it to Doctor Goldman."

"OK babe, let's just go to sleep. It's been a long day."

"So, do you forgive me?"

"Yes, I forgive you."

"I'm so happy baby and I'm so lucky to have someone as wonderful, caring and as understanding as you."

I fall asleep straight away but I keep on having bad dreams. It starts off as a nice dream. It's a warm, beautiful day and I'm swimming in the calm turquoise lake. All of a sudden, the sky goes dark and the lake starts moving. I try to get out of the lake, but the strong current is pulling me away from the shore. There's a big sailboat coming towards me. A faceless man of Eric's height and build lowers himself down to the water. I reach out my arms to him, ready to be rescued, but instead he pushes my head down under the water. I'm suffocating under the water; panic spreading inside of me like an inferno.

I wake up gasping for air. After that I don't feel like going back to sleep. The events of last night are still playing on my mind. I look at Eric, who is fast asleep next to me. Last night there was something so primal, dark and uncontrollable inside of him, that it truly frightened me. It was as if the devil had gotten inside him and taken over. That's not like the Eric I know. I know that Eric loves me and would never deliberately want to hurt me. He's a good person and I truly believe that. He's just confused and messed-up, like Christian Grey. Juliana must have been really messed-up. So messed-up that she messed Eric up as well. I'm committed to Eric no matter what and I want to make this marriage work. Nobody is perfect. I'm messed-up too.

I so badly wish that I could talk to Magda or even Elizabeth for once about this. Magda and Elizabeth have always been open with me about their sex lives, though Elizabeth has been far too open at times. She's been with plenty of men and the strangest fantasy or fetish that I can recall was one ex of hers who had a foot fetish and another who was a sex addict. Would Magda and Elizabeth be horrified by something like what happened last night?

I go on my phone and Google "BDSM" and "violent sex". There's a couple of articles about Fifty Shades of Grey and another few articles about "taboo fantasies." There's one article, where an anonymous woman says she likes being dominated and has rape fantasies. I don't know how anyone could be turned on by rape. The idea of it abhors me. There's another article where another woman said that she left her boyfriend who was into re-enacting violent fantasies.

Another page leads me to a forum where this woman asks if she should leave her new boyfriend who is into hardcore BDSM and rape fantasies. The majority of the replies urge the woman to break-up with her boyfriend and that he sounds like a sicko. Another site leads me to a newspaper report about a "dangerous and deranged man who strangled and beat woman to death during sex." I feel sick.

I want to believe that deep down this stuff doesn't really turn Eric on and that Juliana brainwashed him into it. But there was something so in control and intrinsic about Eric, as though some sort of mask had come off. There was something in his eyes so dark that it frightened me. It's like there was a darkness there that I never saw before.

CHAPTER TWENTY-FOUR

TUESDAY 30TH OCTOBER

Eric is going away to New York tomorrow for two weeks, possibly longer, depending on whether or not he gets the contract. I wish that Eric didn't have to go for so long. I hate the idea of staying by myself in this big house. Well technically I won't be by myself, but Clara and Guadalupe aren't much company. Eric has been very loving this week, bestowing gifts, flowers and chocolates upon me. The events of that night still linger in my mind but at the same time I try to put it out of my mind. Eric is really sorry. Perhaps I was the one who overreacted anyway. I always try to think of a rational explanation for things. It's not like he really did anything wrong and I did consent to giving it a go.

I also read that sometimes when guys are addicted to watching porn, normal stuff stops turning them on the same way and they look for more hard-core material. After all Juliana introduced him to it all. Eric opened up and told me more about his relationship with Juliana and how abusive she really was. She would hit him and constantly put him down and make him feel like he wasn't a man. Eric also feared for Clara, especially this time when Clara couldn't stop crying and Juliana smacked her. There was another incident when Juliana got arrested for drink driving with Clara in the car.

"I'm just so glad that you came into mine and Clara's lives," Eric said lovingly.

I'm lucky to have Eric as well. Things haven't been easy but no marriage is. Eric has been trying so hard to make up for things. On Saturday, he went to all efforts to make the bedroom romantic with rose petals sprinkled all over the bed, heart shaped fairy lights and candles plus beautiful maroon lace underwear. I felt so touched by all the effort that Eric went to, but I didn't feel in the mood. I still felt a bit weary after last time, but I didn't want to disappoint Eric after all the effort that he went to. I trusted that he wouldn't hurt me, but in my mind all I could think of was how forceful and aggressive he was.

Eric was true to his word, but I still felt uneasy. Things were a bit awkward and it took ages for him to achieve an erection. It felt like a clumsy awkward teenage encounter, just purely mechanical. I tried to tell Eric what I wanted (for him to kiss me and touch me all over; to make me feel like he wanted every inch of my body), but he got a bit annoyed and told me that that it wouldn't help him get an erection. When he finally did get an erection, the sex was brief and over quickly. I felt like Eric wasn't enjoying it. He didn't make any eye contact with me and made it seem like a chore. After he came, Eric put his clothes back on and kissed me on the cheek. He said that he had a bit of work to do.

I couldn't help but feel deflated. I keep telling myself that sex isn't everything and it'll get better with time, but I can't help feeling starved. I don't want to be degraded and hurt, but neither do I want to feel like just a mannequin. With Eric sex seems like two extremes; one being violent and degrading, and the other, dull and mechanical. I want passion and fire. Maybe I'm being too demanding. I want to discuss my sex life with someone. I don't feel comfortable opening up to Doctor Goldman about it. I've got a few more sessions scheduled with him whilst Eric is away. At least it'll be someone to talk to at least. I really want a friend. I miss Magda.

Eric keeps telling me that I don't need anybody else but him, Clara and our future baby. I can't help but feel panic rise inside of me like a tidal wave whenever Eric mentions having a baby.

Eric has scheduled for me to have some fertility tests and to see a gynaecologist whilst he's away.

"It's just to check that everything is functioning as it should baby, nothing to worry about," Eric reassured me.

I really wish that Eric wouldn't keep pushing this so much. All this pressure is making me not want a baby more. My supply of the pill is also running low and I have no way to get some more. Perhaps I could ring the GP back in London to send me some more. I feel awful lying to Eric, but he wants to have a baby so bad. Maybe I should just have a baby after all. At least it would keep me occupied and take my mind off of the loneliness.

It would nice to have some friends. I'm craving friendship more than ever. I don't think that I'm going to find any friends around here though. I went to the Ladies Tennis Club yesterday and that was pretty awful. I felt like I was the outsider in high school all over again. The women there were polite enough, but it was like I didn't exist. They all knew one another and gossiped about children, their husbands, shopping, holidays and other people that they knew. Tiffany was there as well, but snubbed me the whole time. I was only invited to join in the matches because they knew that it would be rude not to.

The thought of Eric once having dated Tiffany makes me feel uneasy. I know that I shouldn't be jealous, after all Eric was the one who broke up with her, but I can't help it. The thought of them once being intimate with one another makes my skin crawl. I wonder if they had a better sex life than Eric and I have. Eric didn't tell me much about their relationship other than he felt that they were better off as friends.

I feel like there's so much about Eric that I don't know. There are so many gaps and so many closed doors. I feel like I've told Eric so much about my life and my childhood, but he barely tells me anything. I can't help feeling that maybe Eric is doing something in New York that he doesn't want me to know about. Maybe that's why he doesn't want me to come. Maybe he's got another woman in New York, but Eric wouldn't cheat on me.

Deep down, in a place where I don't want to admit it to myself, I can't help but have doubts. For the first time I find myself thinking about those women that Darlene told me about. I want to slap myself for believing her ludicrous claims. Eric would never do anything, but I find myself growing more and more intrigued. I don't know why these doubts are surfacing in my mind. The more that I try to push them away, the more insistent they become.

I log onto my laptop and type *Irving New Hampshire* into Google. Google isn't very helpful and comes up with a funeral directing firm called *Irving and Son* and a whole load of people who share the same surname; *John Irving, Michael Irving, Jennifer Irving*. I type in *Eric Irving* and a few professional pages come up about Eric and his father. Nothing incriminating. There's not as much information as I thought that there would be. The search also includes different Eric Irvings from around the world. I feel so stupid for distrusting my husband. I tell myself that I'm simply just curious.

There's very little information but as I click on the third results page there's an article titled "*A Family History of Corruption and Greed*." I click on the article and I see a picture of Eric with his parents. I read on.

The Irving family are one of the most powerful and richest families in America. Eric Irving II and his son run a multi-million-dollar art dealing company- a business that was started generations ago. Just who are the mysterious Irvings? The Irving family are known to shun publicity and keep a low profile. Little is known about the family but there have been rumours of fraud and corruption. Former clients

spoke about how they were conned out of millions, but that the Irving's wealth and influence means that they can cover up their crimes and not face the consequences. In 1998, Eric Irving II was sentenced to eighteen months in federal prison for tax evasion and fraud. Irving was given a plea bargain of six months and a fine, which his former clients say is a perversion of justice.

A former client who does not wish to be named has said that he received death threats and was followed in order to maintain his silence says, "The Irvings believe that they are above the law. They are only motivated by greed, money and power."

It seems like corruption runs in the family. Eric Irving II's grandfather, Victor Irving, was accused of stealing art and taking profits from his clients. Originally a poor immigrant from Poland escaping pogroms in the late nineteenth century, Irving (whose original surname was Iwinski) made a new life in America and quickly amassed a huge fortune. He was shrouded in mystery over how he made so much money so quickly. Rumours of theft, fraud, embezzlement and lies have followed this family for generations. There have also been allegations of sexual abuse, but none have been followed up. Like with many of the most powerful, corrupt and wealthiest figures, it seems that money can buy you a place above the law.

I can't find many other articles other than that one. That's the only negative article about the Irvings, but for all I know it's probably just rumours, though I'm not surprised that Eric's father could be capable of corruption and fraud. He appears to be a ruthless and callous man, but Eric isn't like him. Eric is very highly respected. There's no evidence to back any of these claims and there's no other articles. I type in *Eric Irving New Hampshire* into the search engine and again there isn't much information other than business profiles and business-related articles about art.

I come to the fourth page of the search and scroll for more information, about to give up as there's not much information, until I see a relevant article from a New Hampshire newspaper titled: "Woman commits suicide near Irving Estate."

August 22nd 1993

The body of a twenty-five-year-old woman named Mary Turner was found in a lake near to the Irving Estate. Mary was an employee for the Irving family. She was reported missing by the family when she failed to show up for work. The death was ruled as a suicide with no foul play involved. It is believed that Mary committed suicide by drowning and that she had a history of depression. "We are deeply saddened by Mary's death. She will be greatly missed, especially by our young sons, Eric Junior and David, whom she took care of," Eric Irving said in a statement. "We hope that despite these tragic circumstances, she has now found peace."

Reading it, it doesn't seem suspicious. It seems like it really was suicide. What am I even hoping to achieve by this? I trust Eric and this is just a sign of my own insecurity. I have no reason not to trust my husband.

CHAPTER TWENTY-FIVE

Eric being away is harder than I thought that it would be. Eric has arranged for me to see Doctor Goldman. I feel that it's probably a good idea for me to see him as I've been feeling really down. I've come to enjoy my visits with Doctor Goldman. He makes me feel so at ease. His soothing tone and his warm and understanding eyes make me feel like he truly understands me. I feel that my therapy sessions really are a safe place where I can unleash all of my fears without being judged. It's no wonder that Doctor Goldman is a top professional in his field. A series of certificates, qualifications and accolades gleam on the walls like beacons. Doctor Goldman also used to be the head of a prominent psychiatric hospital in California. His wealth of experience assures me that I'm in good hands.

I open up to Doctor Goldman about my trust issues and how guilty I felt not trusting Eric. Doctor Goldman nodded sympathetically as he made notes. I even opened up to him about what happened last week in the bedroom. I felt a bit awkward mentioning it to Doctor Goldman, but I felt that I needed to get it off my chest and he's probably used to people confiding these sorts of things to him.

He said that it's completely natural and normal that I would be apprehensive and shocked, but that sexual fantasies are just fantasies and that Eric must have a lot of trust in me to want to play out his sexual fantasies. He also said that it's very common for men to have these kinds of sexual fantasies, but the fact that Eric acknowledged my discomfort and respected my boundaries and wishes, shows that our relationship is based on mutual respect and understanding. He said it's clear that Eric loves and values me and the sanctity of our relationship.

I felt a lot better after opening up to Doctor Goldman. I felt like a weight had been lifted off my chest. I also opened up about my loneliness and how I'm finding it difficult to make friends here. I tell him how much I miss Magda and even Elizabeth in a strange way, and how hurt I feel that they've both decided to completely freeze me out of their lives. He said that it's perfectly normal to feel this way, especially when making a huge transition in life. He said that marriage and moving to a new country are huge adjustments and often can put a strain on family and friends as well, especially if they are initially not ok about the idea.

He said that I should give Magda and Elizabeth time to adjust and to heal from the shock and that not contacting me is a way of processing their emotions and hurt. Doctor Goldman also says that forging new friendships takes time and that I should focus on being happy within myself and not relying on others. He said that I should also carry on taking the medication and that the side effects will eventually pass.

When I came out of the clinic, I noticed that Dmitri, Eric's driver, was waiting outside for me instead of inside of the car, which I thought was a bit strange. Maybe he went outside for a cigarette. That's probably what it was though he's wasn't smoking. He probably wanted some air. Why am I being so paranoid?

The house feels so quiet; the stillness and emptiness of the place jars and unsettles me. I don't even hear Guadalupe or Clara. Though the house it's so vast and huge, you can't hear everything. Nevertheless, the silence disturbs me. I feel so bored and fed up. Apart from having naps and going for walks, there's not much to do around here. The boredom and inertia start to gnaw away at me like a rotting flower.

I don't even go out much anymore as it's become fiendishly cold. The autumn here is bone-chillingly harsh. The minute you step outside, the cold air hits your face like a sharp slap. The wind wails like a lost child, but exerts its powerful force like a captor. I never liked autumn or winter in London, but the liveliness of the city and the busy buzz of Christmas decorations, festivals, celebrations and markets filled me with a sense of child-like warmth and security. It's like a ghost town here with acres of land and forest stretching out towards nowhere. There's no lights or ambient sounds of life and the hustle and bustle of everyday life.

I close my eyes and reminisce about walking through *Winter Wonderland* with Magda and Arek. We drank hot mulled wine and gazed at stands consisting of beautifully decorated cookies and chocolates and handmade crafts; laughter filling the air like the cheerful chirping of birds. The wave of sentimentality overwhelms me. I miss the mad rush in London, especially Christmas shopping in Oxford Circus with Magda. I never thought I'd take it for granted. I never thought that I'd find peace and quiet so disturbing.

The hordes of trees and the fleeting sight of raccoons, rabbits and squirrels don't make up for the quietude. Even Cornwall wasn't this quiet. The hissing of the waves and the noisy chatter of seagulls gave the place a certain liveliness. Though having said that, life with Elizabeth was never quiet.

I turn on some music to liven the atmosphere, but it doesn't feel right. The music feels so incongruous in this house. I try to do some painting but the mental block in my mind stifles any desire or creativity. I try to read a book, but my mind can't focus. My mind feels so foggy, as though there's a dark cloud hanging over it. The last time that I took the medication that Doctor Goldman prescribed was two nights ago and I woke up with the same aching and groggy feeling, as though my body was being weighed down by something. I had the same horrible yet realistic dream that somebody was on top of me, strangling me.

I think that the pills are still in my system. I think I'll stop taking them as they sap all of my energy and make my inertia unbearable. I don't want to feel like a zombie all the time. The only thing that I have any desire to do is to take naps. I don't like napping during the day, but there's not much else to do. I suppress my urge to nap, knowing that I'll wake up feeling even groggier. I make myself an espresso. Although I hate coffee, I can't stand this drowsy feeling.

After I down my espresso shot, I decide to have a wonder around the house. I'm so bored that I don't know what else to do. I go to Eric's study, but the door is locked. Why does he have to lock his study? Or maybe I'm just being paranoid again. If he's locked it, it must mean that he has something to hide? Stop it, why am I so distrusting? After all it's not that unusual to lock your door.

I wander around into the different rooms that I haven't explored. Many are just empty guestrooms; uniformly decorated with ivory and gold wallpaper, plush white carpets and crisp and creaseless bedsheets. There's a selection of art pieces and ornaments. Most of the bedrooms have their own en suite bathroom with marble floors and spacious tubs. These rooms are like vacant hotel rooms in a deserted hotel.

I visit the last room at the very top of the house, which is the attic room. It's much darker than the other rooms and it looks like it hasn't been used for a very long time. The air is thick and stuffy and there's dust gathering on the surfaces. It looks like it hasn't been given a clean for a few months. It's the only bedroom without a carpet and the floorboards are creaky. It's reminds me of one of those haunted rooms that people spend the night in for a thrill on Halloween. Although I don't believe in ghosts, there's a certain eeriness about the room. Although the view from the window is incredible, it seems too high up. I can't help wondering if that's how Juliana committed suicide. Eric never actually told me how she killed herself. I wonder if the isolation contributed to her suicide.

I have a poke around the room, not expecting to find anything. My earring comes loose and drops to the floor. As I bend down to look for it, something under the bed catches my eyes. It looks like a shoebox. Its wedged quite far behind and is difficult to reach. I try to push the bed but it's incredibly heavy and makes a horrible screeching sound against the floorboards. The gap is too small for me to fit under. I'm about to give up when I notice a fire poker standing by the small black fire place. I can imagine that it must get pretty cold up here.

It works and I manage to fish the shoe box out from under the bed. In marker pen, the words *"the box of us"* and a big heart is drawn on the lid. Inside, I find a mixed tape, a small teddy holding a heart and a couple of old polaroid pictures. In the pictures are a couple; perhaps in their late teens or early twenties. The man/boy doesn't look like Eric. He's attractive, though not quite as attractive as Eric. His white polo shirt emphasizes his tan and his hair is dark blonde. He has shining hazel eyes and his smile is wide and charming. The girl next to him is gorgeous with thick and shiny blonde hair and bright blue eyes. She's wearing a bright orange top showing off her slender body. They make a beautiful couple. There's a couple of shots of them goofing around and making funny faces. They both look so in love.

I can't help but wonder who they are. Maybe they were guests that stayed before, but why would they leave a box behind and hide it underneath the bed? And the photographs? Nobody prints photographs anymore or listens to tapes. I flip to the back of one of the photographs and it's dated 07/23/2002. Then it dawns on me that these people weren't guests. It must

THE MAN THAT I MARRIED

have been David and the girl that he accidentally killed. This must have been David's old room. That's why it looks like it hasn't been used. The box must have been left behind.

Inside the box I also spot a little note written in purple gel pen. It says:

You are my everything
You are my world
Let's not keep our love a secret any longer

Christina xxx

It seems like one of those sad and tragic love stories. How awful it must be to be accidentally killed by your own boyfriend. I can't imagine the guilt that David must feel. Eric said that David felt no guilt for the accident and that he was never capable of caring about anybody other than himself. From the pictures David doesn't look like someone who doesn't give a shit about accidentally killing his girlfriend. He looks so in love with her; you can see it in his eyes. However, you can't tell what someone is really like from a picture. I wonder if Eric Senior and Genevieve disapproved of Christina, like they disapprove of me. Maybe David and Christina were keeping their romance a secret because his parents didn't approve.

I scan the pictures of David and try to spot similarities to Eric, but they're both polar opposites. There's no likeness between them. Apart from their good looks, you wouldn't know that they were brothers if nobody mentioned it. I wonder what David is like. I'm curious about him. It sounds so cruel, banishing somebody from your family no matter what they did. Maybe David has changed and matured. It must be hard growing up with someone who made your life difficult, but people change and grow up. Life is too short to hold grudges, especially when we all make mistakes.

Perhaps it's time to forgive and forget. There are some siblings who hate one another growing up, but then become a lot closer when they're older. Maybe it'll be good for Eric to have a brother around again. Maybe this time they can fix things. I go downstairs and log onto my MacBook, which Eric got me.

I feel a bit annoyed as Eric hasn't really been in touch. I know that he's only been away for two days, but surely he must know how alone I feel here. I ring Eric, but it just goes to voicemail. The last time that Eric messaged me was yesterday, letting me know that he landed safely. I can't help that feel frustrated that Eric has just left me here knowing how lonely I feel. I would have loved to have gone with him to New York. It's always been my dream to go to New York. Eric promised that he'd take me next time, but that this trip wouldn't be fun for me as it was all work.

I type in *David Irving* into the search engine. The only results that Google yields are related to an anti-Semitic Holocaust denier with the same name. I definitely don't think that's David! I try *David Irving New Hampshire* but there's not many results. I keep on scrolling until I find an article that looks promising. The article is titled: *A New Start*. There's a picture of a man that looks almost exactly like the David in the polaroid shot. He's obviously a lot older than in the polaroid, but he hasn't aged much. He has a youthful glow. He looks sun-kissed and golden. I read the article.

David Miller is a successful life coach and author living in California. David (originally born David William Irving) is the son of prestigious multi-millionaire art dealer, Eric Irving II. Disowned and disinherited by his father, David made a new life for himself and forged his own career. He inspires people to achieve their goals and manage toxic relationships in their lives.

For the rest of the article, David is interviewed about his work, which I skip. At the bottom of the page is a link to

David's website. I go to the website and find his email address. I wonder whether this is a good idea contacting David. I don't want to go behind Eric's back, but this could be a good opportunity and help Eric deal with his issues. I also feel a bitterness that I never felt before; Eric has gone behind my back so many times. I paste the email address into a new email and begin writing.

Dear David,

My name is Iris Irving. I am Eric's wife. I hope that you don't mind me reaching out to you. I was looking through the attic of your old home and I found something that I think belongs to you. Perhaps I could send it to your address.

Kind regards,

Iris

The moment I press send, my heart starts hammering like crazy. What am I doing? I haven't thought about how David might feel getting an email from me. He might not even want to hear from me. He probably doesn't want to hear from his family again. He might not even reply to this email. I wish that I had never sent it now. Maybe I shouldn't be meddling in Eric's private affairs. After all it's not really any of my business. A part of me can't help thinking that getting to know David might be one of the pieces of the puzzle to helping me to understand my husband.

CHAPTER TWENTY-SIX

I spend the rest of the evening in bed, watching rubbish TV and drinking wine. A tide of calm and relaxation spreads through my body and I'm transported into the happy bubble of alcohol. I think about asking Guadalupe to join me but she's asleep. The door to Clara's nursery is ajar and I see Guadalupe fast asleep on the rocking chair next to the crib with an open book in her lap. Her gentle snores fill the room. She must be exhausted by both looking after Clara and doing all of the cooking and cleaning. I feel bad for her. Maybe I could help with the cooking and housework; it'd give me something to do.

I creep back into the bedroom and lie beneath the silk sheets. I send a message to Magda. She didn't reply to my last message. I don't know what on earth is going on. I try ringing but she doesn't pick up. Not hearing from Elizabeth is definitely the strangest of all. I haven't heard from Henry, but he's never been the greatest at messaging. Maybe Doctor Goldman is right, Magda and Elizabeth need time to process everything and will talk when they're ready. I still can't help wanting to reach out to them. I log onto Facebook which I rarely use. Elizabeth doesn't use Facebook; she's terrible with technology, but Magda and Henry use it.

I go onto Magda's profile and am shocked to see that she has unfriended me. Next, I go on Henry's profile, but the content is limited and the last recent post is from my wedding. Henry isn't one for posting much anyway, but he usually updates his Facebook once a month at least. I send him a message and Magda as well, asking her why she's unfriended me. I feel really hurt. I know that it's only Facebook, but I can't help but feel rejected. Perhaps I need to give her time. I know that she's upset that I married Eric and moved away, but I don't understand why she has to cut me out too.

I log out of Facebook and pour myself another glass of white wine. A notification pings on my phone. My heart thumps thinking that it could be Magda or Henry, but it's an email notification notifying me that David has replied to my email. My fingers shake as I click on the icon to open the email. What if he's rude and nasty? Even if he is, it's just words on a screen. At least I tried.

Dear Iris

Thank you for your email. As you probably already know, I haven't spoken to Eric or my parents in many years nor do I have any desire to. I appreciate you thinking about me though. I did ask Eric many years ago to send me that box, but he never responded and I never wanted to go back to that house.

I am away from home and will be for a few weeks, so I don't have a permanent address at the moment. I have a contract teaching a semester at Brandeis University in Boston. My work does take me all over the place. I could get a courier to pick it up as Boston is not that far from New Hampshire. I don't really need the box as it was from so long ago, but it would be nice to have it back, especially as it holds a lot of memories.

I assume that you're living at the estate. I can't say that I miss it. Anyway, I'll sort out to have a courier pick the box up. I'll let you know about the arrangements. In the meantime, if there's anything that you need, please let me know.

Best wishes,

David

I re-read the email again. I feel even more curious about him. I don't know why I want to meet him so much. Perhaps it's the loneliness and the fact that I've got no-one to reach out to. The loneliness is becoming too much to bear. I tried ringing Eric three times in the past two hours and sending messages but he hasn't responded. He didn't even reply to the message that I sent to him this morning. I fill my glass up with wine and conduct a response to David. I know that I shouldn't write to him when I'm drunk and when my inhibitions are so low, but I just want to talk to someone and not about banal matters either.

Dear David,

Thank you for your reply. It must suck having parents like yours and Eric's. They don't think much of me either.

In all honesty, I'm not just writing to you because of the box, but because I'm curious about you and I think it's really sad that Eric hasn't spoken to you in so many years. I just feel like there's so much about Eric that I don't know.

I completely understand if you don't want to, but would you like to meet? Eric is away on business for two weeks or longer and I'm stuck in this house feeling really lonely. Eric's parents don't live here anymore; they signed the house over to Eric and moved to Florida years ago.

Iris

My heart starts pounding the moment I press send. What am I doing? It feels like I'm doing something really wrong; like I'm cheating. I shake my head. Of course I'm not cheating. I would never cheat on Eric. I just want to meet his long-lost brother; is there anything wrong with that? I know that Eric would be furious that I'm going behind his back, but David is his brother!

I sit back and wonder what Eric is doing? Is he thinking about me? Does he wish that I was lying next to him, keeping his body warm? Dark thoughts sweep through my mind like a cloud of dust and debris, threatening to choke me. Maybe

Eric is with another woman right now. Maybe she's in his bed fucking him. Intrusive thoughts of Eric with another woman creep into my mind, the way that monsters under the bed fill children's minds with fears. I can't bear the thought of him touching another woman; kissing her and holding her.

Eric would never cheat on me. He loves me and he never mentions any other women. That night at the gallery opening, he didn't even glance at any other woman despite the huge female interest in him. Even with Tiffany, he didn't flirt with her or look at her longingly that evening when her and Tripp came round for dinner. I'm imagining things.

I miss him. I feel so lonely here all by myself. I ring him once again and this time he picks up.

"What is it Iris?" He sounds irritated.

"Nothing, I just wanted to say hi and that I miss you."

"Are you drunk?"

"I've had a drink or two but I'm not drunk. Are you missing me?"

"I've only been gone two days. I've been crazy busy with work. I can see that it's already been two days and you've already started drinking."

Eric's harsh words sting and I feel tears forming in my eyes. Why does he have to be so cold?

"I just really miss you."

"I think you should discuss your neediness with Doctor Goldman," Eric says frostily. Why is he being like this? Maybe I really am being too needy, but I can't help but feel so deflated. Can't Eric understand how I feel?

"Anyway, I've got to go. I'm going out for drinks with some business partners. Don't forget your appointment with the gynaecologist tomorrow."

"I won't."

"Good night," Eric says with no emotion in his voice and hangs up.

I can't stand Eric's dark moods. Sometimes it feels like Eric is two people. There's the side of him that's romantic, caring and loving and the other side that's cold, callous and detached. I can't help but feel even lonelier. I feel my stomach churning waiting for Magda and Henry's replies. They've both read my messages but they aren't replying. I feel like screaming and shouting at the top of my lungs. I can't help but feel trapped. Suddenly, an email notification pops up on my screen. David has replied.

Dear Iris,

I'm intrigued to meet you as well. You sound like you're far too good for my brother. I can understand your loneliness. Growing up there was the loneliest thing in the world. I could drive up on Saturday as the drive isn't too long from Boston. If I'm being honest, I like long drives and I've not got anything else to do. I can meet you at the house. Will be interesting to see if much has changed.

Let me know what time suits you and if Saturday is good for you.

David

I feel an odd mixture of excitement and unease. I feel like a child doing something that they're not supposed to be doing. I'm not doing anything wrong I tell myself. But then why does it feel like I am?

CHAPTER TWENTY-SEVEN

SATURDAY 3RD NOVEMBER

I don't know why I feel so nervous about my meeting with David. It's settled that he's coming at three o'clock. I tell Guadalupe that I have a guest, but all she says is "OK Señora Iris, let me know if I make food." For a moment I panic that Guadalupe will recognise David and report it to Eric, but Guadalupe has only worked here for eleven years and Eric and his parents haven't seen David for more than fifteen years.

I tell Guadalupe not to worry and that I'll take care of everything. I even helped her out with some of the cleaning and cooking. Although Guadalupe was adamant that I don't lift a finger, in the end she relented, especially when I said that I'm bored and it'll give me something to do. Well I didn't exactly put it in those words because of the language barrier. It took a few attempts before Guadalupe understood what I was trying to say.

I even offered to look after Clara for a bit, though the moment that Guadalupe went out of the door, Clara started wailing. I tried to calm her down but it didn't work. My presence seemed to distress her even more. The idea of having a baby fills me with even more dread especially if having a baby is this hard and frustrating. I think that Guadalupe felt guilty for leaving Clara and came back after ten minutes. Clara immediately stopped crying the moment that Guadalupe scooped her up in her big fleshy arms.

I wonder how Clara could ever see me as a mother figure when she's so attached to Guadalupe. Guadalupe is her mother figure and I didn't want to come between them. I go off to my bedroom and pick out an outfit for my meeting with David. I don't know why I care so much about what I'm going to wear. I'm meeting my brother-in-law. I guess I want to make a good impression. I dress casually; dark navy Levi's jeans and a pretty but plain white top with small flowers around the borders. I put on my make-up and red lipstick. Maybe the red lipstick is too much. Why am I getting so worked up over this and acting like this is a date? I'm married! I shouldn't even be meeting David.

I think I'm excited by the idea of actually having company. Having someone to talk to. I spray my wrists and collarbone with expensive perfume and head downstairs. I sit in the salon and wait for David's arrival. I pick up a book whilst I wait. I don't know why I'm feeling nervous. This is ridiculous. Maybe David might even have changed his mind about coming. Before I can engage in my thoughts any further, the chime of the doorbell throws me off balance.

I open the door and my heart sinks. David is there, holding a bunch of flowers. He's good-looking; perhaps not quite as gorgeous as Eric, but he's still very attractive. He's shorter than Eric. Eric is around six-two, whilst David looks to be around five-ten. His hair is a mixture of sand, gold and dark bronze and his eyes are a striking blend of light sky blue and greyish teal.

"You must be Iris," he says. His voice is breezy and expressive, not hard and serious like Eric's.

"I am. It's nice to meet you too David."

We're both not quite sure how to greet one another; a peck on the cheek or a hug or a handshake. Instead I offer to take his coat. I notice that his arms are toned and brown. He's not quite as muscular and as defined as Eric, but he has a good physique. He looks like he works out, but at the same time isn't one of those guys who is super obsessed with the gym. He's wearing a baby pink polo shirt and navy slacks. There's no doubt that he's attractive, but he's my brother in law and that's all. I can find another man attractive but it doesn't have to mean anything.

I take David through to the salon and ask him what drink he wants; tea, coffee, something alcoholic though I don't think that it's a good idea, especially as he's driving. And especially not after what happened with Christina.

David says that he'll take a coffee. I make myself a coffee as well and bring out the plate of sandwiches that I made.

"I wasn't sure if you had eaten or not but please help yourself."

"That's very kind of you Iris. I had something to eat when I stopped off at the gas station, but your sandwiches look very tempting. Thank you."

David tucks in and helps himself to the selection of tuna, salmon and crème cheese and cheese and ham sandwiches. My first impressions of David are that he seems nice and charming. He seems more laid-back than Eric, but maybe life is more laidback in California. I scan his face for similarities to Eric, but I don't find any. He seems so different to Eric; they're like chalk and cheese.

We make small talk. David tells me about his work and his position in Boston. I tell him a bit about how Eric and I met and how after the wedding, Eric wanted to move here.

"That's Eric for you; he's always been intense," David says sardonically.

"Do you ever miss him?" I ask.

David laughs. "If I'm being perfectly honest, I'm glad that he's out of my life. He made my life miserable growing up."

"Eric said the same about you."

"I bet he did; he's always been good at twisting the truth."

"What do you mean by that?"

"It's a long story and I didn't really come here to talk about Eric. Gosh it feels so strange being back here. It hasn't changed much."

"Do you feel sad being back here?"

David shakes his head. "Weird, yes, but sad, no. I don't miss anything about this place. I thought it'd be interesting to see it again though. Good sandwiches by the way, did you make them?"

I nod. "Anyway, I guess that you'll be wanting your box. I'll go and get it for you."

I go upstairs and retrieve the box, which I keep stored in my bedroom. David takes it from me and opens it. He takes time looking through the contents of the box. I can see the look of sadness and regret on his face as he looks through the pictures. I have an urge to go over and hug him, but I don't. I don't want to overstep the boundaries.

"Christina must have meant a lot to you," I say.

"She did," he nods. "She was my first love."

"The accident must have been awful, but you mustn't blame yourself."

"I still do. I can't remember anything from that night; it's all a blur. The next thing I know is that I wake up in hospital and my father tells me that he never wants to see me again and that I'm never to set foot in the house ever again."

"That's awful."

"I don't remember taking any drugs or drinking any alcohol, that's the thing. We were going to spend the weekend together in Vermont. It was supposed to be a little get away. One minute

I remember being so excited to be going away with Christina and the next, I wake up in hospital." David shakes his head. The sadness in those grey blue eyes of his is evident.

"Are you married I ask?"

David shakes his head. "After Christina died, no woman really compared to her. That was a long time ago and I've had relationships since then, but I've always felt that there's been something missing. I want to know that I'm with the right woman. Maybe that's living in California. A lot of the women there are superficial and self-obsessed. It'd be nice to find someone that gets me and truly likes me for me."

We sit in silence for a while. I realise that I don't want him to go back. Maybe it's just because I'm craving company so badly. The idea of being left alone when he leaves depresses me. The endless days of nothingness, stretched beyond me; time passing slowly. Every minute exacerbating my loneliness. I feel like I've been spun into a vortex of darkness and nothingness. I feel like a princess locked away in a tower. I know that I'm free to leave, but there's nowhere to go. Maybe having a baby would be something to keep me busy and end the monotony.

I saw the gynaecologist yesterday, Doctor Kraus, a polite but patronising older man. I find something about men who decide to be gynaecologists a bit strange. Why would you choose to examine the body parts of a gender that you don't understand? Doctor Kraus said that I look like a young and healthy woman and that he's sure that I should have no trouble. He ran a few tests including an ultrasound and blood and urine test. Doctor Kraus said that everything looked fine from the scan but the blood and urine tests would need to be analysed and that I'd get the results in a few days.

"Are you happy Iris?" David asks. His question takes me completely by surprise. Maybe it's because Eric has never asked me whether or not I'm happy.

I don't feel like pretending I'm ok when I'm not. I love Eric, but I'm not happy here.

"I just don't like it here. I miss my home and I miss my friends and my family." Before I know it, tears are spilling from my eyes. David comes over to me and puts his arm around me. He gently strokes my arm. Although it's an innocent and kind gesture, at the same time it feels so intimate and wrong.

"Why don't you just tell Eric that?"

"I've tried but he tells me that I'll soon adjust. I mean it has only been two months. It takes time to settle in. I'm sure you must have felt like that when you moved to California."

"Sure, but it helped knowing that I chose to go there. It seems like Eric didn't give you much of a choice. But that's Eric for you; he always wants his own way." I can sense the anger and venom in David's tone whenever he talks about Eric. It definitely doesn't seem like a relationship that David is willing to repair.

"Did you miss New Hampshire when you moved to California?" I ask.

"Not at all. The only thing, well person that I missed was Christina. To be honest I was glad not to have to have anything to do with my family again. They're all a bunch of hypocrites, especially my father. I despise him. He's a terrible person. He always despised me right from the beginning. Eric was always the favourite; the perfect son. I might as well have not existed. I was glad to be away from all of it; from all of the toxicity.

I never wanted to go into the art dealing business anyway. I don't care about money and connections. I always wanted to help people which my father couldn't understand. My father only cares about himself. He doesn't even care about my mother or Eric. He's the kind of man that would flash his cash in front of a homeless person, but not give him a single dime. God I hate his guts."

"Eric Senior is certainly very intimidating. He doesn't think much of me."

"He doesn't think much of anyone so I wouldn't take it personally."

"Did you ever get on with your mother?" I ask.

"No. She's not much better than my father. She's just his puppet. She goes along with anything that he says. If he told her to jump off a cliff, she'd do it. She's pathetic."

"God it must have been awful for you growing up with such parents."

"It sure was. There was never any love; well it wasn't geared towards me at least. Eric was always their golden boy and I was always the black sheep of the family. If I'm being honest, I feel nothing being back here. It could be someone else's home for all I care. Anyway, I should be getting back. Thank you for the box; it means a lot to me to have it back. Also thank you for the hospitality. Eric is lucky to have you. I just hope that he appreciates you."

"Please don't go just yet; you've come such a long way."

"You're great Iris, but I wouldn't want Eric to know that I've been back here and that I've been talking to you."

"Well he's not here and he won't be back for at least two weeks or more. I think that Eric is really missing out not having you in his life."

"You're the only one who seems to think so. You know, I'm enjoying talking to you too Iris. You're very sweet and you're absolutely stunning. I know that I probably shouldn't be saying that. Eric is very very lucky."

***

We're sitting in the kitchen, drinking wine and eating some chicken and salad that I prepared. We've just been talking, like we've known one another for ages. We don't even chat about Eric or his parents. We talk about everything such as politics, music, books and America. David has so many interesting stories and a great sense of humour as well. He has me in stitches with his impressions of Donald Trump. I can't remember the last time that I laughed so hard. A sad thought crosses my mind. Eric and I never laugh together. I hadn't realised how much I crave laughter and light-heartedness.

I can't even remember Eric and I having such long and flowing conversations with so much to say. I feel like David really listens and is genuinely interested in what I have to say. Sometimes when I'm with Eric, it feels like he's a million miles away and he isn't really interested in what I have to say. Then there's times when I feel that he talks at me, making me feel stupid. I didn't realise how much it bothered me until now.

A sudden pang of guilt hits me like a bullet. Of course Eric cares about what I have to say and when we're together we can have an amazing time. I'm just still really mad at Eric for rebuffing me last night. Marriage isn't easy. I'm so lucky to have Eric; I should start appreciating him more. Maybe I need to make more effort as well. Maybe he's right; I am being too needy. I know that Eric has a lot on his plate. He's good to me and I know that he loves me. He's intelligent and dedicated. How can I even dare to compare Eric to David? I barely even know David. But then why does it feel like I've known him for ages?

I pour myself another glass of wine. I know it's probably a bad idea, but I'm feeling so relaxed and so at ease, that I want that feeling to last. I've told David that he can stay the night in one of the guest bedrooms so he won't have to worry about drinking and driving. It felt like a bold move asking David to stay the night. Stop it, I tell myself. It's not like I'm inviting him into my bed! We're enjoying one another's company that's all. Plus, he drove a long way.

I know that I'm going behind Eric's back and that David shouldn't even be here. This will probably be the last time that I see David anyway. It's obvious that there's no chance of Eric and David ever reconciling and they'll be no reason to see one another again. I feel sad at the idea of not seeing David again. Maybe I can persuade Eric to let David back into his life.

It feels so good just to drink and talk and be in good company. I even confide in David my worries and fears. I tell him about how Eric is pushing me into having a baby despite me not feeling ready and how I'm struggling to adapt to the role of being a step-mother.

"This is not how I saw my life to be. Kids are the furthest thing from my mind. I want to travel and to have a career. I just feel like Eric doesn't support that. He encourages me to do my painting, but I just can't find the motivation."

"Eric has always been a control-freak. You should do what makes you happy. You shouldn't always do what makes Eric happy Iris."

"I know that."

"It's so unfair and manipulative of him to push something onto you that you're not ready for and to just expect you to take on the role as a mother to his daughter. Talking about Clara, it'd be nice to get to know my niece, but it's not going to happen," David sighs sadly. "Even though blood isn't everything, it's still part of you and Clara hasn't done anything wrong. What happened to her mother by the way?"

"Juliana, Eric's ex-wife committed suicide. It's very sad, but she had a lot of problems."

"Are you sure that Eric didn't drive her crazy?" David says, his tone half joking and half serious.

"Eric is good to me, really he is." I feel like I've definitely overstepped the mark by confiding in David about my personal matters with Eric. I'm so stupid! Why did I say anything? Why am I even confiding my marriage secrets to a man that I don't know? A man who is my brother-in-law. What am I doing? This is improper. Maybe inviting David here was a mistake. The alcohol clouds my judgement and I can't think clearly.

"You know, I think you're far too good for Eric," David says.

"Don't say that."

"It's true. He doesn't deserve you. The way that he treats you sounds like typical Eric. He's got you under his thumb."

"It's not like that." I know that I should be annoyed; what right does David have to say that? He doesn't know anything about what Eric and I have? However, I feel annoyed with Eric. Annoyed that he acts so cold and distant and the way that he always shuts me out and keeps things from me. Sometimes he makes me feel like he doesn't care. I haven't heard from him today either. Damn Eric! I've sacrificed so much for him and he doesn't even appreciate it. I'm fed up of him always criticising me.

"Another glass?" David asks, breaking my trail of thought. I've definitely had too much already and should stop- stop before I overstep anymore boundaries that I'll later regret. However, I don't want to stop. I'm enjoying the feeling of intoxication. I feel my fears and anxieties start to float away; sailing further away from the shore of my mind. A warm glow spreads inside of me like flowers blooming; opening their buds to the world for the first time. I don't want to think about Eric, Elizabeth, Magda, Henry or anybody else. I'm fed up of thinking about everybody else. Right now, I feel free; freer than I've felt in ages.

"To you Iris," David says, lifting his glass for a toast.

"Yes, to me," I giggle, clinking my glass with him. We look one another in the eyes; our gazes firmly fixed on one another. David's eyes really are beautiful. They're so blue like cloudy ice. I don't know who makes the move, but suddenly our lips meet. I know that I should pull away, but part of me doesn't want to. The kiss is like CPR; bringing me back to life. David pulls me closer towards him and I let him. The feel of his hands around my waist sets off electric sparks inside of me. My super ego is telling me to stop; this is wrong on all levels. I've already overstepped the boundaries more than enough today, but the id inside of me doesn't care; this feels so good. It's like the alcohol has switched my super ego off.

David pulls me onto his lap and I'm straddling him. He reaches for my T-Shirt and pulls it over my head. He then unhooks my bra and starts kissing my breasts, then my stomach; savoury every inch of my flesh. My breathing gets faster and deeper and I moan with pleasure. I pull off David's top and feel his toned and tanned chest. He's not quite as well built and toned as Eric in the fitness model kind of way, but it still turns me on. He's broad like Eric and his arms are strong and muscular. David lifts me and takes me into the salon; our uneaten sandwiches and empty plates and cups still left behind.

David lays me down onto the spacious beige couch and gets on top of me. He pulls off my jeans and then reaches to undo his belt buckle. He pulls down his jeans and pants, revealing his throbbing erection. I feel excited by his erection; his huge and straining erection. Eric would never get this hard for me. David's penis is huge; a good seven inches or so. I notice like Eric, he is also circumcised.

"Are you sure that you want to do this?" David whispers. I nod. I don't realise myself how much I want this. I want this so bad. David kisses my neck, gradually working his way down. This feels so euphoric and so passionate. This is how I wish that Eric would desire me and make me feel. David can't get enough of my body; his hands caressing me all over and kissing me everywhere.

"You're so beautiful Iris," David whispers in my ear. I feel so desired and so wanted. No man that I've ever slept with has made me feel this way.

I take David's penis in my mouth and savour every inch of his glorious, thick and hard manhood. He moans with pleasure the harder I suck. I want him inside of me. I want his big and hard dick pounding me. I'm wet and ready for him. David asks if he should wear a condom. I say that he doesn't need to. I'm still taking the pill, though I'm worried how I'm going to get hold of some more as I'm running seriously low.

David wraps my legs around his waist and enters me. Ecstasy clouds my mind. I moan in pleasure with his every thrust. My mind feels like it could burst from all of this ecstasy. I feel the heat and the passion between us. There's nothing mechanical or awkward between us. Everything feels just as it should be. My mind is so full of delight and fervour that I can't even think about what I'm doing and how I'm hurting my husband.

Desire ripples through my body and that's all that I can focus on. This is everything that I've been craving. I feel so present and so alive. Endorphins rush through my brain. I wish that I could feel this way with Eric when we make love. It's like he's never present when we have sex; like I'm the last thing on his mind. It's like I'm just a vessel. David makes me feel like I'm so much more. For once I feel that I don't have to worry about getting pregnant and having to pretend that I want a baby too.

After David ejaculates, we lie in one another's arms; sweaty from all of the love-making. David strokes my hair and my breasts. He pulls my face to his and kisses me. I feel so exhilarated. We don't talk, we just cuddle together on the couch. I don't feel tired; in fact, I feel more awake and alive than ever.

"She we go upstairs?" I whisper. David nods. He picks me up and carries me upstairs to the bedroom, where we continue to fuck on the bed that I share with my husband.

CHAPTER TWENTY-EIGHT

When I wake up the next morning, my head is pounding like a drum and a tsunami wave of realisation and regret washes over me. I cheated on Eric. Fuck fuck fuck! What did I do? What the hell did I do? I don't even recognise myself. This is so out of character for me. Here I was, acting all suspicious and paranoid that Eric was cheating on me yet I was the one who ended up cheating. There's no excuse for what I did. Even with the amount of alcohol that I downed, it's no excuse. Yes, my sex life with Eric hasn't been that great, especially after everything that happened last time, but it's no excuse to jump into bed with another man. It isn't just any man, but my husband's brother.

David is asleep next to me, snoring gently. Why on earth did I invite him here? This is a huge mistake. I feel even guiltier when I check my phone and notice that there's two missed calls from Eric and a voicemail from him. I listen to it. *"Hey baby, it's me Eric. Look listen I feel bad about the other night; I was just really tired and really under pressure. Anyway, I hope you're ok. I miss you."*

Tears spill down my cheek. My husband loves me and here's how I repay his love. I know that I should tell Eric, but I can't. I don't want to destroy my marriage; the marriage that I've made so many sacrifices for. I'm not going to let one stupid mistake ruin everything. A stupid mistake that didn't mean anything. I was lonely, bored and drunk. None of that makes it ok though. Nothing will ever make what I did ok. I don't even want to look at myself. I feel like such a whore. Even Elizabeth wouldn't cheat on her boyfriends. I never thought that I'd feel lower than Elizabeth.

"Hey, good morning, did you sleep well?" David yawns. "Why don't you come back to bed?"

"Listen David, last night was a huge mistake. What we did wasn't right. I'm married- to your brother! You need to leave."

I can see the look of hurt on David's face. It's always usually the man who gives the woman the cold shoulder after a one-night stand. David doesn't seem like the kind of guy who's an asshole and sees bedding women as a hobby. David seems sensitive. It makes me feel even worse.

"This never should have happened. I'm sorry that I invited you here," I continue.

"I'm not sorry Iris."

"Well I guess now you've got your revenge on Eric; well done."

"You think that all of this was to piss Eric off? I really don't give a fuck about Eric. Believe me, it wasn't my intention to come here and sleep with you. All I wanted was to pick up the box, but you seemed so lonely and so sad. It almost sounded to me that you were in trouble and wanted to reach out to someone. I know how cruel and domineering Eric can be. I know what he's truly capable of and it's not pretty. If you knew some of the things that I knew about Eric, you'd run a mile."

"Please just leave ok."

"It's a shame as I thought that we had a connection. I'll respect your wishes though. Just be careful Iris; I don't want to see you get hurt," David says sadly.

***

I spend the whole day feeling awful and disgusted with myself. I have a long hot shower to wash away the smell of sex and all traces of David off my body. No matter how much I scrub my body, I still feel dirty. The tears keep on falling. How could I hurt the man that I love? I'm a dirty and disgusting cheater. I didn't think that I was even capable of cheating. I always thought that I had a strong moral compass, but clearly not. I'm a weak person. I'm going to do whatever I can to make it up to Eric. I'll do anything that he wants me to do; even play out his fantasies. I deserve to be shamed and hurt. I deserve it more than ever.

When I go to my room, I fish out the awful outfit that Eric got me for my birthday; the horrible strips of leather. I'll wear it for him. I hate the thought of it, but it'll be like my repentance. I feel sick looking at the unmade bed where I had sex with David. If it's bad enough that I cheated, cheating on my marital bed makes the betrayal even worse.

I strip off the sheets and the bedcovers, ready to put in the wash. Maybe I should even throw them out. No amount of washing will ever get rid of the fact that another man came all over these sheets; the stench of sweat and sex forever etched onto the fabric. Eric may not know, but those sheets and covers will always haunt me. I need to share this heavy burden with somebody; this burden that is crushing me inside. Inside I feel like a broken mirror that can never be pieced back together. I need a session with Doctor Goldman. I have his personal number so I ring that as I know that he won't be in the clinic on Sunday.

I'm so grateful when he picks up. The soothing sound of his voice immediately puts me at ease. I'm in such a panic that my voice is wobbly and hysterical. I can't stop shaking all over. Doctor Goldman tells me to calm down and that I can come to his home for a personal appointment at three o'clock. I'm relieved that Doctor Goldman can see me. I pull on some clothes and go downstairs.

The salon is spotless when I arrive. My clothes from last night aren't there and it looks like the leather couch has been cleaned. The leftover sandwiches and the plates and cups from last night aren't there either. The table gleams from the polish that can only be achieved by applying surface cleaner. I completely forgot about my clothes. It's obvious that Guadalupe has cleaned and cleared away all the evidence of last night. I wonder if she knows. Surely, she must know. I hope that she won't tell Eric, but Guadalupe doesn't seem like she would get involved in such personal affairs. I don't even think that Guadalupe would have the level of English to tell Eric.

She's in the kitchen with Clara. Guadalupe greets me as normal in her usual formal manner. She fixes me the breakfast that I usually eat and makes my tea the way that I like it. I feel a huge sense of relief. I wonder what Guadalupe really thinks of me deep down. She probably thinks I'm a harlot for cheating on my husband. I know that Guadalupe is devoutly religious. She probably never cheated on her husband or ever even thought about another man. Guadalupe wears a large necklace with the sign of the cross and once I saw her kneeled down in prayer when Clara was asleep. Guadalupe is a pure and good woman.

"Señora Iris, I find something. I no know where I put it so I give you ok?" Guadalupe says. She goes over to the kitchen and picks up a box.

It's the box that David came for. He came all this way, only to leave without it.

CHAPTER TWENTY-NINE

I lie back on the comfortable black leather couch and close my eyes. All I can see are images of David and I fucking. I would do anything to erase last night. I feel a bit better now that I'm about to have a session with Doctor Goldman. I've never been to his home before, so this is the first time. It's pretty large, though not as large as my new home. The open rooms are wide and spacious with dark mahogany floors and black leather couches. Photographs and ornaments bedeck the room.

I study the pictures. There are pictures of who I presume are Doctor Goldman's children. There's an assemblage of pictures from babyhood, school photos, bat and bar mitzvahs, graduations and weddings. Then there's recent pictures of what are obviously grandchildren; a jolly infant and sullen looking dark-haired little girl of three or four, pose with their parents in what's meant to be a professional picture.

There's a few photos of Doctor Goldman and his wife. They look well suited. His wife is smiley and slender with her white hair styled in a fashionable bob. The Goldman family look like one of those picture-perfect families. On the walls hang degree certificates from Harvard law school and medical school. One of his daughters has followed in her father's footsteps and is also a clinical psychologist and psychiatrist. The Goldman children must be very ambitious.

In the cabinets, there's a collection of ornaments; a gold shimmering menorah, candles, awards and fashionable art sculptures. This is a home that really looks like it's been lived in. A home where happy and intelligent children grew up and shared many happy memories. Doctor Goldman and his wife must be so proud of the children that they've raised.

I can imagine that they're one of those older couples who are still very much in love. I can imagine that they read and do crosswords in bed whilst chatting about their day; communicating with one another about everything. No arguments or cross words. No secrets and no lies. Their lives uncomplicated and close to retirement, where they plan many trips and holidays together. The rest of their spare time spent looking after grandchildren and taking part in activities at their local synagogue. Life so blissful and slow-paced; the stresses of work and raising a family over.

I wonder if Eric and I will ever be like that. I wonder if Eric will ever know about my dirty little secret. I wonder if Doctor Goldman and his wife have their secrets. If one of them has ever cheated on the other. It seems so unlikely. I wonder if Doctor Goldman will even understand. How can a woman who supposedly loves her husband do something like that? Of course Doctor Goldman won't judge me. Therapists don't judge people. I trust Doctor Goldman.

Doctor Goldman comes back into the room with two mugs of coffee. Two beautiful golden Labradors follow him in. They come over to me and give me a sniff. They're so adorable. I love animals. I would love to have a pet but Eric isn't keen, especially not on dogs. He says that they make too much mess, they smell and get in the way. Plus, he said that having pets around isn't a good idea for when we have a baby. Hopefully I can change his mind.

Having a pet would give me a purpose and having an animal would be some company. I remember how much I loved Snoop, the golden cocker spaniel that I had growing up as a child. He was my best friend. Although he didn't speak, I felt that he understood me far better than any human could. He would comfort me when I was sad. He had nothing but love for me.

We had a bond that went beyond words. I feel even sadder thinking about Snoop. Snoop would never have judged me.

"How are you doing Iris?" Doctor Goldman asks; his tone filled with concern.

"I did something really terrible. Please don't tell Eric."

"Iris, our sessions are strictly confidential. Nothing you say here leaves this room."

"I cheated on Eric. It was a huge mistake." I tell Doctor Goldman the whole story. He nods as he takes in my frantic rambling.

"I'm a terrible person."

"Why do you think that Iris?" Doctor Goldman asks gently.

"Because I cheated on my husband. Not only that, but I cheated with his brother!"

"Iris, you're not the first person to have been unfaithful in a relationship. Being unfaithful to someone doesn't make you a terrible person. You made a mistake and I can see that you regret it. However, there's always a reason behind infidelity. Why do you think that you did it?"

"I just felt so lonely. I don't have any friends here and I feel like Eric freezes me out. Our sex life hasn't been great either."

"Have you tried to communicate this with Eric?"

"I try, but he always seems too busy and he brushes everything away like it doesn't matter. I feel like he doesn't realise that I've sacrificed a lot for him; my friends, my family, my home and my job. Practically overnight I discovered that I'm going to be a stepmother and Eric is desperate for a baby. I just don't feel ready. I feel so trapped."

"It sounds like there's a lot of resentment. That's perfectly understandable, but sometimes we have to make sacrifices for the people that we love. Those sacrifices may seem unfair at the time, but gradually you realise that those sacrifices were worth it and that they can help to make your relationship stronger."

I wonder if Doctor Goldman's wife made any sacrifices for him. "Did you or your wife make any sacrifices?" I ask.

"I really shouldn't bring up my personal life, but yes. My wife converted to Judaism for me. At the time it wasn't something that she really wanted to do and there were a lot of arguments. She had to give up a lot for me; Christmas and eating pork, but gradually she adapted. Now she's far more observant than I am and she's on the committee of our synagogue. Change can be a good thing, even if it doesn't seem like it at the time."

Maybe Doctor Goldman is right; maybe I need to adapt to change more. Maybe it might not seem like a good thing, but maybe everything will work out for the best.

"Should I tell Eric about what I did?"

"What do you think Iris? I can't tell you what you should do."

"I don't want to ruin everything that I have with Eric."

"Relationships can and do recover from infidelity but it takes work. It's a good thing that you're filled with regret and remorse as it shows that you've recognised what you've done is wrong and that you have no intention of repeating it. May I ask if you enjoyed the sexual encounter? Many people who are unfaithful find that they didn't even enjoy the sex."

"I did enjoy the sex." It comes out of my mouth before I can even think about the answer. Although I was drunk, I wasn't completely wasted. I only had three glasses of wine. Before that would have been enough to get me completely hammered, but now my body has gotten used to having that much alcohol in my system. Yes, I was drunk, but not drunk enough to not know what was going on. The truth was that it was incredible. I feel so ashamed admitting it to myself. It was the kind of sex and connection that I was craving with Eric.

"Perhaps it's a sign that some things need to change in your relationship. I really think that communication is key. Once you get to the root of the problem and deal with it, you can move forward in a positive way."

I decide that I'm going to tell Eric. I don't want any secrets. I decide that I won't tell him about David though. I've already hurt Eric enough by cheating on him, I don't want to push the knife in further. After all it hardly matters as I'm never going to see David again and David and Eric have no contact with each other. It would be much worse if they were close.

***

My palms are sweating and I'm shaking as I dial Eric's number. I know that the second that I tell him the truth, our relationship could be over forever. I don't want to do this, but I can't bear keeping lies from Eric. I can't live with this on my conscience. Doctor Goldman is right; I need to get to the root of the issue. There's something that needs to change.

I half hope that Eric won't pick up but he does. "What's up babe, are you ok?" Eric says. He seems to be in a better mood than the last time that we spoke.

"Eric there's something I need to tell you." I'm on the verge of tears and my voice is wobbling.

"What's wrong?"

"I understand if you want a divorce after this. I cheated on you. I had sex with another man. I'm so so sorry. It meant absolutely nothing and it will never happen again. I know that it's no excuse, but I was drunk and lonely. He was just a guy who came to fix the broken door; the one that doesn't close properly. I decided to get it fixed before you came back.

Anyway, after he fixed the door, we started talking and had a few drinks. One thing led to another. It's the biggest mistake of my life and I hate myself for it!" I ramble frantically, trying to get the words out as quickly as possible before they choke me. I feel so bad lying to him about David, but I can't tell him. Cheating on somebody is a big enough shock and betrayal. Does it really make a difference who it's with? I don't know how I even thought up the repair guy story- it just came into my mind.

My heart is racing like a formula one car; I feel like I'm going to have a heart attack and I'm sweating all over. This is the moment of truth. My marriage could be over forever.

"It's ok baby; I forgive you," Eric says. Am I hearing correctly? Did Eric say that he forgives me?? I was expecting him to put the phone down or tell me to pack my bags and go back to London. I didn't expect this!

"You forgive me? Just like that? You're not going to divorce me?"

Eric laughs. "Baby everybody would be getting divorced if people decided to call it quits after making a stupid mistake."

"Aren't you hurt? I had sex with another guy."

"Of course I'm hurt and it's not going to be easy, but we'll talk about it when I get home ok?"

"Oh Eric thank you for being so forgiving. I feel so terrible about it; it will never happen again."

"Well I hope not. Anyway, I've got to go baby, we'll speak soon."

I feel a huge wave of relief. I didn't expect Eric to take it in his stride. In a way, it's almost as if he wasn't that upset. Wouldn't most people be furious and angry if their spouse cheated on them? It's almost like Eric was too cool about it. My head is spinning from all the adrenaline. Then a thought occurs to me, what if Eric is ok with this because he's cheating himself?

CHAPTER THIRTY

The next morning, when I go for a walk, I get the feeling that somebody is watching me. Maybe I'm just being paranoid. My emotions are still running high from yesterday. I feel like I need to clear my head, so I brave the freezing cold and set out on my walk. On the one hand, I can't help but feel relieved that Eric has forgiven me, but I'm also a bit taken aback with his reaction. Surely, he can't be ok with me cheating. I can't make any sense of his reaction.

Even my walk doesn't bring me any relief. I feel just as confused as I did before and I couldn't help but feel that I was being followed by someone or something. It really freaked me out. It was probably just an animal or something. It's like whenever I tried to catch a glimpse of it; at the speed of light, it vanished. It's probably all in my head and I'm being hyper sensitive to every little thing.

I try to busy myself with painting but no inspiration comes. Out of sheer frustration, I throw my paintbrush on the floor. I should feel happy that Eric still loves me and doesn't want to divorce me despite what I did, but I can't help but feel that there's something wrong. Something doesn't feel right.

I go to the gym room to try and burn off some of my anxiety. I run on the treadmill until I feel physically sick. Whilst the exercise takes my mind off everything as all I can focus on is the discomfort and my breathing, after I don't quite get the endorphin rush that I was hoping for. Red in the face and caked in sweat, I go and take a shower. As I come out of the shower, I notice the box that I was meant to give to David in the corner of the room. I put some clean clothes on and take the box back upstairs where I found it. I place it under the bed where it belongs.

Out of curiosity and boredom, I open the bedside drawers, not expecting anything to be in them. There's nothing in the first two drawers, but to my surprise there's a leather-bound red diary. It's dusty and looks like it's been there for a long time. It's probably David's diary but he didn't mention anything about a diary. Maybe he forgot about it. I open the first page. The name *Juliana* is written in bold letters on the front page. There's a yellow post-it note attached to the page. It says:

If you find this please use this diary as evidence

It's a rather strange thing to write. Evidence of what? Why would Juliana hide her diary here? It's obvious that she wanted it to be found. I wonder what it contains that is so incriminating. There must have been something that Juliana wanted to say if she left a diary behind to be found. I flip through the pages and there doesn't seem to be any rambling about depressive thoughts and crazy and dark ideas. Juliana's writing is neat and structured.

I skim through the first few pages. It's clear that Juliana was smitten with Eric. I turn to the last page; Juliana's very last entry. The words pop out at me and I can't erase them or unseen what I've just seen. My whole body is shaking and fear curses through my veins like an electric current. I need to read Juliana's story, but most of all I need to escape. There's no way that my mind is playing tricks on me. I re-read the sentence written in black and white.

I am scared that Eric is going to kill me.

PART THREE

CHAPTER THIRTY-ONE

FRIDAY 22ND NOVEMBER 2013

I think that I am in love! I have met the most perfect man! He is so gorgeous and he has money. I cannot wait to tell my mother; she will be so happy for me. All she wants for me is to have better life. After all that is why I came to the United States. Life here is not easy and I must cope alone. I make less than seven dollars an hour and work six days a week. My tiny little room in New York is so expensive, but anything is better than living with Marco. I should never have married him, but it was the only way to be able to live here.

I work as a maid in a very expensive hotel. That's how I met Eric. I knocked on his door to do cleaning. The most beautiful man I have ever seen opens the door. He is wearing nothing but a towel. I nearly drop my cleaning equipment. His body is so wow! He looks like he could be a movie star! Maybe he is a famous movie star. He smiles at me and this time I drop my bucket. He bends down and picks it up. As he gives it back to me, his hand touches mine and I feel like there is fire inside of me. I want him to take me in his arms. I never felt like this about any man, not even Marco.

Eric told me that I'm too beautiful to work here and that I should be a model. He invited me for a drink and it was the most magical night of my life. It felt like I was in a dream. Why would this man who looks like a movie star and has a lot of money want a poor girl like me from a little village in Brazil? I wanted to look so special but all I had was my red dress from Forever Twenty-One. A dress like this is a luxury where I come from but in America it shows you do not have money. Eric told me I look so beautiful. This is how a woman should be treated.

Marco never did anything special for me. He wanted me to cook and clean for him and bring him beer. I loved him at first and he was nice to me in the beginning. He said that he would take care of me. He paid for me to have English lessons and I moved into his house. Marco would get angry if I didn't have dinner ready when he came home from work or if I didn't iron his shirt properly. He told me that he should have married an Italian girl, like his mama wanted him to. I don't know why he married me when he didn't like me. Sometimes when he was angry, he would hit me.

Eric is so different. He is the man of my dreams. Tomorrow he is taking me for dinner. I cannot wait!

SUNDAY 24TH NOVEMBER 2013

Last night was the most magical evening of my life! Eric took me for drinks to a rooftop bar in Manhattan with the most incredible view of the city. He looked so handsome OMG! He is so kind to me. He buy me drinks and dinner. He told me that I look so beautiful and that he cannot take his eyes off me. He is such an incredible person and so intelligent. He knows so many things and has been to so many places. He went to Harvard, which I know is a very top university in America. Eric tells me that I am so smart and that my English is impeccable.

My English is not perfect, but I practice all the time. I am even writing this journal in English so I can get more practice writing. I was always good at English at school. I've always loved learning. I would love to go to college and study to be a lawyer, but I cannot afford it and need to take exams for my English, which I haven't got time to do.

I must go to sleep now as I must get up early for work tomorrow. I know that I will have good dreams about Eric. I cannot stop thinking about him.

MONDAY 25TH NOVEMBER 2013

Today I come home from work and find a huge bouquet of roses outside of my flat. They are from Eric!! He left a note saying: **I had an incredible evening last night. You are so beautiful and amazing that it takes my breath away.**

I am crying with joy! This is like a scene from the romantic Hollywood films!

WEDNESDAY 4TH DECEMBER 2013

Eric has asked me to move in with him!! He says that he must go back home to New Hampshire and the idea of being apart from me makes him very sad. Then he asked me if I would like to come with him!! I said yes of course!! Eric says that he is in love with me and has never feel like this about anyone! I am so so happy! I've never been happy like this in my whole life. Eric is so generous. He said that I must quit working at the hotel and that he will pay for me to study. I said that I can not allow this, that I save for my own education, but he said that he already pay for it!! He said he also pay for an English teacher to make my English even better and good enough to get into college! Eric is that man that I always dreamed of- he is so gorgeous, kind and treats me so good. I sometimes worry that I will wake up and Eric will not exist. He is too perfect!

WEDNESDAY 11TH DECEMBER 2013

I love my new home! I've never seen such a huge house in my life! It is so beautiful here in New Hampshire. I cannot believe that I am living here as a girlfriend and not as a maid! I cleaned for some houses in New York for rich people, but none of the homes were as big as this! Once I tried on some dresses in the big walk-in wardrobe of one of the homes to see what it feels like to be rich. I tried on a beautiful dark blue Valentino dress when the lady came in. She was so angry and called me a thief. She tell me never to come back again. I tell her that I did not want to steal the dress but she told me to leave or she call the police. I wonder what that lady would think if she see me now!

It is so good to be able to relax and learn English. Eric hired me a very good teacher who said my English is impressive! She says that with a bit more practice, I should be able to sit an exam for college. It is a much better use of my time rather than working twelve hours every day for nothing!

Eric is so good to me. God must be rewarding me by sending Eric into my life. I told Eric I was so sad as I would not see my family for Christmas and New Year; that I have not seen my family for two years! I miss my family so much. I send my mother a cell phone so we can talk but it is not the same. They do not have the money to come here and last time I visit it was a very expensive trip.

Eric said that he will pay for my family to spend two weeks here with us over Christmas!! This is the most beautiful gift that anybody could give me. I cried and cried with happiness.

WEDNESDAY 1ST JANUARY 2014

I AM ENGAGED!! Eric proposed when the clock struck midnight on New Years Eve! He got down on one knee and said "I have only known you a few weeks, but I am in love with you and I want to spend the rest of my life with you." It was so beautiful! There were fireworks going off. Then the words "will you marry me?" exploded into the air.

"So will you marry me Juliana Ramos?" Eric said.

Of course I said yes!! I am the happiest woman in the world! I cannot stop crying because I am so happy. My mother and my sisters cannot stop crying too. My mother say to me "Juliana, letting you go was the hardest thing a mother can do, but I knew that when you came to America you would have good life. With Eric you will have good life and that is all I have ever wanted for you."

FRIDAY 17TH JANUARY 2014

Today is the day that Eric and me are getting married! Eric planned a surprise holiday to The Dominican Republic where we will be getting married! Eric says that it will be just the two of us because it is more romantic. I said that I want my family to be here and for my mother to see me get married, but Eric said we can have another wedding in the summer where we can invite friends and family. He says he is so desperate to marry me and for me to be his wife!

I have never been anywhere so beautiful! Apart from New York and New Hampshire, I have never been anywhere! I have not even seen much of my own country. I rarely went outside of my little village near the border of Bolivia. Eric says that he will show me the world. It is my dream to see the world and to travel. I am crying because it is so beautiful here; it is like what I imagine heaven is like. The water is so blue and the sand is so white!

Eric says that he will take care of me and that is why he wants to marry me. He says that he will make sure that I will live like a princess. He says that he will look after me and that he is not like the other men I was with. I told him about Marco and he said that he could kill him; that men like that don't even deserve to be called men- they are animals! I love how protective Eric is.

He is not an animal like most men who only want to have sex all the time. Marco wanted sex all the time, even when I don't feel like it. Eric is different. He said that we don't have to rush; that we have the rest of our lives. I am happy! I am marrying the most amazing man!

CHAPTER THIRTY-TWO

FRIDAY 7TH MARCH 2014

I have not written for a long time. Everyday I have been working hard studying English. Eric has been very busy with work and we haven't spent much time together. Apart from studying English, there is not much to do here. It would be nice to make some friends. Eric introduced me to some of his friends but I think they not like me because I am an immigrant. They talk to me like I do not understand English; like you would talk to a child. Eric's parents do not like me much either.

They come to stay last week. I was excited to meet Eric's parents. I even make Feijoada, a stew with beans and meat from my country, with rice and Pão de Queijo, a very delicious bread made with cheese. I also make Brigadeiro, which are chocolate balls. Before papa died and we had a bit more money, we could buy more ingredients and cook more things. My mother taught us how to cook. I cried thinking about my mother when I make the food. Eric says that he will arrange for my sisters and their family and my mother to come to America to live. He said it may take a long time to sort it out. Having my family close to me is what I pray for.

Eric's parents did not like my food. They didn't say it, but I could see on their face that they didn't like it. After, Eric said to me that I should make American food since I am in America, not Brazil. Eric says that I do not need to cook as he has Guadalupe to do everything. But I like to cook.

I try to talk to Guadalupe as I speak some Spanish, but Eric says not to talk to the help. He says that she is here to work and if I get too friendly with her, she won't know her place. I tell him that I was once a maid and people were not nice to me, but he said that this is different. He says he pay Guadalupe well and she has free food and a room, but she is here to work. He says if I will be too friendly, she will start taking advantage.

TUESDAY 13TH MAY 2014

I am so upset! Eric and me got into a huge fight! Eric wants to have a child, but I do not want. I want children, but not now. I am 22-years-old. In America women do not have babies this young. In my village yes- my sister had her first baby when she was seventeen, but that is what women in my village do. I came to America so that I could have a life different from in my village. I came here to work so I can save money for college, so I can get a good job.

I tell Eric that it is too soon to have a baby; maybe in six or seven years when I have finished college and have a job. Eric said that I don't need to worry about having a job when he can give me everything that I need. He said he does not want to wait six or seven years because he will be too old. I said that a man can wait longer than woman, but he wants a baby.

I tell Eric that it is my dream to be a lawyer, but he say I won't make it. He said that law will be too difficult for me and only the men are successful. Eric said that he doesn't want my life to be difficult. I don't care how hard it is, I want to be a lawyer. I want to make my own money.

I cry in my room. I want to tell my mother but she will be on Eric's side. She is very traditional and think that it is woman's duty to be a good wife and mother. She will be excited for me to have a child. My sisters will not understand as they think that I should have a baby at my age. They do not understand that things in America are different and not like in our village.

FRIDAY 6TH JUNE 2014

I am feeling so lonely. Eric does not spend much time with me. He says he is busy with work. I feel that sometimes he is very cold to me, like I feel like I did something wrong. Sometimes he is so romantic and charming, but sometimes he is moody and distant. I love Eric but I feel like he does not listen to me.

I ask Eric if I can invite my family to stay for a few weeks, but he say no. He say that my family only want his money and that they will want to live here with us. I said it is not like that; I miss them so much. I ask if I can fly to Brazil for a few weeks to be with them, but he says that it is not safe there and that I am safe here. I cry because I miss my family so much. Eric agreed and said they can stay here for a few weeks and he will arrange for them to come.

WEDNESDAY 2ND JULY 2014

Eric is being very distant. He say he has another business trip planned to New York. I ask if I can come but he say no. He said he will be very busy. I am worried that he has another woman. Our sex life is not good. It's like he is not there when we have sex. There is no passion. Even when I had sex with Marco there was passion- well at the beginning. Then he used to force me to have sex when I not feel like it.

I asked Eric if he has another woman, but he get very angry. He said that I am paranoid and how dare I think that he would do something like that to me. Maybe he is right. Maybe it is me who has the problem.

FRIDAY 1ST AUGUST 2014

My family is dead! I want to die and be with them. It was painful enough when my papa die when I was fourteen, but my whole family! José from my village tell me. He say that a violent gang break into the house where my family live and shoot them. It is unbelievable. I am in shock. This cannot be real. Yes there are gangs in my area and there is crime, but they not target people like us because we are poor. Why my family? Why, why, why?

Eric has been so kind. He took me in his arms and said that everything is going to be ok; that my family are at peace. I know that they did not have easy life, but they still have good life. I came to America so that I can send them money and one day make enough money so that they can come here. I want to die! Why did God take my family? Why did those evil monsters take my family? They even kill my sister's children. My heart is broken.

SATURDAY 23RD AUGUST 2014

I have been crying every day. I have horrible dreams about my family. Dream of men in masks breaking into my family's home and shooting them with machine guns. Bang, bang, bang! Blood everywhere. I am there in the dream. I ask the men to kill me too, but they won't. I wake up screaming. Eric says that I should see a therapist and that it will help me. He also said that us having a baby will help me to recover. Maybe he is right; maybe having a baby will take away this terrible pain. This pain is too terrible.

I want to go to Brazil to the funeral, but Eric said that he won't allow it because it is not safe; that the men who killed my family are still in the area. I want to find those monsters and get justice for my family.

MONDAY 15TH SEPTEMBER 2014

The pain does not get any better; it only gets worse. I am seeing a therapist, Dr Goldman. He is very nice, but he does not know the pain that I am going through. He gave me medication to make the pain better. The medication help me to sleep. I spend my time sleeping even though it is not much better than being awake. Even when I sleep I have bad dreams, like a man is on top of me and strangles me. I can never see the man's face. Maybe it is one of the monsters that killed my family. It is very scary and sometimes I wake up and I cannot breathe.

Sometimes I dream of my family. They are lying on the floor, covering in blood, begging me to help them. I wake up screaming.

I do not have English lessons anymore as I cannot focus. I cannot eat and have lost twenty pounds. Eric says I am too thin and must eat. He said that if I am too thin, I wont be able to grow a baby. I cannot even think about a baby. All I want is my family.

FRIDAY 26TH SEPTEMBER 2014

I think Eric is getting fed up with me because all the time I am crying and sleeping. He said that of course what happened to my family is tragic, but I need to be strong and not neglect him. I do not mean to neglect him. He says that him and our future baby are now my family.

I wish Eric would comfort me more but he spends so much time in his study. It is like he blames me for being sad, but I know that that cannot be true. He is just frustrated. I know that my family, especially my mother would not want me to spend my day crying and wishing that I could be dead too.

SATURDAY 27TH SEPTEMBER 2014

Eric is so lovely! He said that he is taking me to Venice next week for a few days. He is so kind and thoughtful. Although I do not feel in the mood, it will be good to get away and take my mind off my pain. I have always wanted to go to Italy. I feel so guilty for wanting to go to Venice when not long ago my family died, but Eric said it is what my family would want and they would want me to be happy. Eric says we will go to New York for two days before we go to Venice. He say that he wants me to go shopping as it will make me feel better. Maybe I will feel better. Eric is so good to me. I am lucky to have him and lucky to have found someone now that my family is gone. I am not completely alone and that makes me feel a little bit better.

CHAPTER THIRTY-THREE

FRIDAY 3RD OCTOBER 2014

It is so beautiful here in Venice; better than in my imagination. It is so romantic. I have never seen a city on water in my life! Venice is so different from New York or the other cities that I have read about. It is like everything from the past has not changed. All I can hope is that my family are with me in spirit here. I cried a bit today, but not as much. The pain will never go away, but every day it gets a little bit easier. Maybe it is a good idea to go away. Eric says that he have a surprise for me.

We have dinner in a very elegant restaurant with an incredible view of Venice. I even manage to eat. I have hardly eaten since my family die. I am suddenly so hungry. I want pizza, but Eric says that it is not classy to eat pizza. I'm not sure what he mean, but Eric knows more than me so I should listen to him. He order lobsters, ciabatta and a plate with ham like chorizo, salami and Parma ham. It was still very tasty. Eric also order red wine, though I do not like much.

After we go to our hotel, which is like a palace. It is so luxurious! It must be very expensive to stay here. Our hotel room is huge; you cannot call it a room. It is like a huge apartment! When I lived in New York, I only had a tiny room and I had to share the toilet and the kitchen, which were also very small. This room here is ten times bigger than the apartment I shared in New York.

We have a big balcony with a view of Venice. It is so beautiful that it makes me cry. The bed is covered in rose petals and there are candles. It is so romantic. There is also a gift with a big ribbon on the bed, which Eric says is for me. Maybe it is nice underwear. For the first time since my family die, I feel in the mood for sex.

I open the box and I find something strange. I do not know what it is. I ask Eric what I do with it and he says it is to wear. I put it on but it looks weird. I do not like it. It has a lead to. I feel like a dog. Even when I go shopping in New York, I do not see anything like this, even in the ladies lingerie department.

Eric says that he does not like normal sex and that he feels it is time for him to introduce me to his world. I do not know what he means. Eric explain that he like to be in control and that he want me to be his sex slave. I tell him that I do not want to be a slave and why does he want me to be a slave? He say that many couples do it and many men like this. He say that I don't have to do it, he will not make me, but it would make him happy. My mother always said that it is important to make a man happy. If I do not make him happy, he will find another woman.

Eric tells me that I must kneel to him and do as he tells me or else I will be punished. He force my head onto his man part and pushes my head down. I feel like I cannot breathe. I want to stop but he keep pushing my head. I am so glad when it is over. Eric then ties my hands together and throws me on the bed. He turns me over so my face is in the pillow. It is hard to breathe. Eric hits me hard on my butt and then pushes his man part inside. The pain is sharp. It is horrible but I want my husband to be happy. He calls me names, "bitch", "slut," "disgusting whore." I know that these are horrible names. Why does he call me such things? Marco would call me those names.

I cry so much, my pillow is wet. I am so so glad when Eric finishes. He asks me why I'm crying. I said it was horrible and why does he call me these names? He says that it is meant to be fun and that it is not real life, just pretend. He say that many women like this and that it turn him on, like normal boring sex turns me on. He said that he only does it for me and from time to time that it will be nice if I do the things that he likes. It is true, I had to have sex with Marco even when I didn't want.

If it will make Eric happy, I will do this. He is all that I have now.

SUNDAY 5TH OCTOBER 2014

Eric has been very loving and romantic to me. I almost forget about what happened that night. Eric has been good to me and he deserves for me to make him happy, even if I do not like it. At least he does not force me like Marco. Marco would never take me anywhere nice. The only place we went was Coney Island for our honeymoon.

We went on a romantic boat ride in the gondola. There was champagne and red roses waiting on the gondola and the man who rowed our gondola is also an opera singer and sang us operatic arias. His voice was like an angel. I will never forget this marvellous moment in my life. I am in love with Venice.

Eric had to work, which I was not happy about, but he had a private guide show me Venice. I saw St Mark's Square, the Basilica and Rialto Bridge. I took photos of everything so I can look back and remember Venice forever!

WEDNESDAY 12TH NOVEMBER 2014

I am pregnant! I am expecting a baby! Before I was not sure about having a child, but after my family died, I have no one but Eric. The baby will be a reason to live. It will not take away the pain, but it gives me something to be happy about. I will finally have a family!

I tell Eric and he is so happy for me! He picked me up and kissed me! Later we are going to celebrate. I am so so happy! I just wish that I could tell my family the good news, but I know that they are with me and they are so happy for me.

FRIDAY 14TH NOVEMBER 2014

I am eight weeks pregnant. I went to the doctor today. He said that the due date is June 9. He said it is too early to know if it is a boy or a girl yet. I do not mind if it will be a boy or a girl, but it would be nice to have a little filha.

TUESDAY 23RD DECEMBER 2014

I have been feeling very sad about Christmas because my family is not alive. Last Christmas they were here and we had the best time. The house filled with laughter and joy. I look at the pictures from last year and I cry so much. Life is so unfair! Why my family?

Eric has been acting funny. He is always so busy and never has time for me. I feel so bored and alone here by myself. I have been studying English in my spare time. I want to have lessons with my old teacher, but Eric says that my English is now good enough and I do not need her. I have ordered lots of English books to help me learn and I have been watching TV shows in English.
Eric has invited his parents for Christmas. They will be coming today and will spend a few days with us. I wish that they were not coming Eric says that Guadalupe will cook Christmas dinner as his parents like everything to be traditional American.

THURSDAY 25TH DECEMBER 2014

Today was horrible. It is the worst Christmas I have ever had. It is even worse than my first Christmas alone in New York after I moved from Brazil. Worse than the Christmas with Marco and his family. His mama said I do not cook well and Marco's brother, Gino, kept touching my butt when nobody was looking, even though his wife Theresa was there. Marco got me a iron as a Christmas present. I cried and cried.

Eric got me a beautiful diamond necklace for Christmas, but somehow it did not feel special. It must have cost a lot of money, but it is not about the money or the presents. My family could not always afford to buy presents for Christmas, but being together was more important than giving presents.

I was surprised that Eric's parents got me a present. An old box with shampoo and bath salt. It did not look new. I still said thank you and tried to be nice. At dinner we tell Eric's parents that we are having a baby. They said nothing! Even on their face, you could not see any expression. It was blank.

"Congratulations," Eric's father said after a long silence, but he did not look like he mean it. He did not look happy.

Dinner was horrible and quiet. Eric's parents talked to me like I do not understand English and excluded me from the conversation. I didn't want to eat or be around these horrible people so I said I felt sick and must rest.

Later I heard Eric's parents talking about me with Eric when they thought I was upstairs. I did not understand everything so I record the conversation on my phone.

"I worry about you son," Eric's father said. "Women like that are gold-diggers and will get pregnant on purpose. They'll divorce you and take the child and your money."

"Do you think I'm stupid father? Juliana signed a pre-nup agreement and if she ever tries to leave me, I'll destroy her."

The last bit shocked me. Why would the man I love want to destroy me? Why would he think that? I am shaking and crying. I take the parcels that I ordered for myself from online as a present for myself. They are the law books that I ordered; law books for beginners. I will not give up on my dream. I will not allow Eric to take my dream from me.

CHAPTER THIRTY-FOUR

SATURDAY 3RD JANUARY 2015

Eric and I are in St Barts for a little new year holiday. It is beautiful here but I feel so sad and empty inside. We are supposed to be spending time together, but it feels like I am here alone. Eric says he is busy with work. We do not have sex much. Maybe he thinks I am fat, but my stomach is not very big even though I am nearly four months now. I talk to the baby both in English and Portuguese. People will think I am mad, but I do not have anybody to talk to. All I have is my English books and my law books. Reading and studying make me feel better. What is the point of being on this beautiful island when you have nobody to share the beauty with? With beauty there always seems to be sadness. I feel that I cannot enjoy myself here. Many people would dream to be in a paradise like this, but it's too perfect here and it does not feel right.

The private beach, the massages, the spa treatments and the personal butler who will do anything, are not enough to take my loneliness away. I am treated like a queen here, but I do not feel like one.

MONDAY 12TH JANUARY 2015

We are having a boy! The doctor tell me today! I did not care if it was a boy or a girl, but it feels good to know. The baby feels more real now! I cannot wait for him to be born!

Eric is so excited and so happy! I have not seen him so happy since I tell him that I am pregnant. Eric is so happy that it is a boy. I said that now we can choose some names, but Eric said that the name is decided; it is tradition that the baby will also be called Eric. I said that this is strange to call the baby the same name, that maybe it can be middle name. Eric said that everything will not be my way all the time and that he gives me so much and I give so little. I do not ask for these things. This is my baby too.

Eric said he had to go back to work. He went upstairs and slam the door! I fell onto the couch and cried. Why is my husband being like this? I want my family so much.

THURSDAY 22ND JANUARY 2015

I lose the baby! Why is life so cruel? First my family and now my baby! What did I do wrong? Why God do you take my baby from me? It happened on Saturday night. I go to the toilet and I see blood. I screamed! Eric took me to the hospital immediately.

"Please save my baby!" I cried to the doctors but it was too late. He was gone. The doctor said that it was not my fault and that miscarriages happen a lot to women. He said that I should have no problem having a baby in the future. I do not want another baby; I want the baby that was growing inside of me. The pain is so bad. The doctors gave me medication to calm down because I could not be calm. I wanted Eric to be with me. I asked the nurses for Eric, but they say that he already left the hospital. How can he leave me like this?

SATURDAY 24TH JANUARY 2015

Things between me and Eric are not good. He has hardly been talking to me. I know that he is sad about the baby, but why is he ignoring me? I feel so alone and so empty inside. Eric say that he is busy with work, but I think it is not true. Eric does not want to talk about it. He always lock himself in his study.

I am so bored here. I want to go out and make friends, but there is nothing to do here and not many people. I want to study for college and I want to have English classes. The only person that I can talk to is Dr Goldman. He is a very kind and understanding man, but it is not the same as having friends or family. I miss my family so much it hurts. I feel that I do not want to live.

I have been taking the medication that Dr Goldman gave me, but I have the same weird dreams. I dream that somebody is on top of me and is choking me. It feels so real. It is very scary. Sometimes I wake up with bruises. I must have hurt myself in my sleep. Eric says I move around a lot in my sleep. Sometimes we do not even sleep together. It is like he does not want to be near me.

SUNDAY 1ST FEBRUARY 2015

Eric wants to try for another baby again, but I do not feel ready. He says that he doesn't know why I'm still upset about the baby and that it wasn't even a proper baby. For me, my baby was real. I even gave him a name; Miguel, after my father. I think about Miguel every day. I do not tell Eric this. Why do I feel like I cannot even talk to my husband? Maybe this is normal. Maybe a husband and wife do not need to tell each other everything. I do not like when people hide things though. I want us to be able to talk to each other. I feel like Eric is hiding something from me.

I ask him if he is seeing another woman, but he said that I am crazy. I said that I feel so lonely and that we don't talk to each other like husband and wife, but he says that I am the one creating all of the problems in our marriage. He said that he tries to make me happy and he is fed up with trying. He say that I am always crying and unhappy or accusing him of things and how does that make him feel?

Maybe Eric is right; maybe it is all my fault. He has done so much for me, buying me nice things and taking me on beautiful holidays. I go upstairs and I put on the horrible leather outfit that Eric gave me in Venice.

"Wow baby, you're incredible and amazing. I love that you want to make me happy," Eric said when he saw me. He pulled me in his arms and kissed me. It felt so good to be kissed by my husband. I

will do anything for my husband to love me, even if I hate doing the things that he like.

THURSDAY 16TH APRIL 2015

I have not written for a long time. I have not been feeling like writing. I am feeling depressed and sad all the time. I am still seeing Dr Goldman, but it does not help much. He thinks that it is a good idea that Eric and me try for another baby. Maybe he is right. I feel so lonely. I will never forget about Miguel, but I want so badly to have a baby to love. I am so scared that I will lose the next baby. I pray to my family and baby Miguel to protect this next baby.

Everyday I am studying English and reading my law books. I find law so fascinating. I have ordered more books. It make the days go by much quicker. Sometimes I go for a walk and try to find the animals. I would love to have a dog or a cat, but Eric does not like animals and thinks that they are dirty. Even an animal would be good company for me.

I tell Eric how lonely I am, but he says that it is in my head. He says that is he not enough for me? Of course he is enough, but it would be nice to have some friends. He says that he will talk to his friend Tripp's wife, Tiffany and maybe she can see if I can join the Ladies Committee. I did not like Tiffany, but maybe the other women will not be so bad. I want to find a job too, even as a cleaner or working in a shop, but Eric said that what will people here think of his wife doing a job like this? I still want to study law so bad, but Eric says that my English is not good enough and I am not smart enough to go to college and why do I want to go when I do not have to work? Eric does not understand how lonely I am. I want to do something. Anything!

FRIDAY 19TH JUNE 2015

I am worried that Eric is hiding something from me. He always lock his door. I ask him why he need to lock his door and he said that I am being controlling and that he need space from me. Eric is annoyed that I am still not yet pregnant and he hopes that I do not have a problem. I hope I do not; I very much would like to have children. If not, I would like to adopt. Eric said that he will never adopt and he will never love a child that is not his own flesh and blood. He said if I cannot have a baby, he will get a surrogate. I really hope that I can have a baby soon.

Eric is away on business this week, so I try to unlock the door to his study. I remembered a trick that my friend José back in Brazil teach me. I find my old credit card in my purse. I am worried that it will not work, but it does.

I do not like doing this, but I am scared that my husband is hiding things from me. His computer is not there, but I look in the drawers. It is just paperwork and invoices. I scan the documents, but it looks very business-like. Suddenly the name José Santos pop out at me. José Santos from my village! Maybe it is a different José Santos, but it is the address of our favela in Brazil. Eric is paying money to José; $3,000 dollars a month! Why is Eric paying money to José?

FRIDAY 26TH JUNE 2015

Eric has found out that I have been in his study. He is so angry. He does not understand why I do not trust him. He says that I am unbalanced and crazy and that this behaviour is not normal. I ask him why he is paying José. Eric say that he wants to do something nice for the people in my village because they are so poor and that José make sure that the money goes to everyone to buy enough food and for technology and material to make the homes safer.

"How dare you not trust me! Here I am being a good person and helping your people, but you don't trust me!" Eric shouted.

I ask Eric why he did not tell me about this, but he said that he did. I do not remember him telling me. Eric said that the tablets that Dr Goldman give me must be affecting my memory. He says that

I should talk to Dr Goldman about my paranoia and my breaking into his study.

"This is the last time you break into my study. Do you understand?" Eric said; his face close to mind. He pushes me to the wall and grips my arms very hard so they hurt.

"Do you understand?" Eric repeats. Spit lands on my face. I nod my head.

"Good; now you can make it up to me," Eric says. I know how he wants me to make it up to him and I don't like it. Is it normal to be so scared of your husband?

SATURDAY 27TH JUNE 2015

I think that Eric has another woman. I take out the clothes from his suitcase ready to put into the washing. I could smell woman's perfume on his shirt and there was a stain that looked like lipstick. I asked Eric if he is seeing another woman, but he got mad at me again and said that I need serious help for my paranoia and he's fed up with my constant accusations. He says that I am crazy and it is all in my head. Maybe it is all in my head, but I feel like something is wrong. Why is my husband lying to me?

THURSDAY 9TH JULY 2015

Today is my birthday. I am 24 years old today, but I feel like I look so old. Before everyone used to say I have a beautiful and young face with model-like cheekbones, but now my face is so thin and the skin so rough, like an old woman. My cheekbones now make me look like a starved model. I have got so thin. Before I had a woman's shape; now I look like a Halloween skeleton. I do not recognise myself. I look ten years older.

Eric surprised me with flowers and presents. He buy me lots of jewellery and a beautiful red Valentino dress. He took me in his arms and tell me I look beautiful and he is so lucky to have a wife like me. He says he is sorry that he has been distant recently, but he has been very stressed with work.

"You are so beautiful; how could you ever think that I would cheat on you baby?" Eric says. I love when Eric is like this; kind, romantic and loving. Maybe he would be like this more if I was a better wife to him. He is right; I have been paranoid and crazy.

Eric says that he has a surprise planned for me tonight and I will definitely love it. I cannot wait! For the first time in a long time I am feeling so happy and so loved!

CHAPTER THIRTY-FIVE

TUESDAY 6TH OCTOBER 2015

I am pregnant again! I feel both happy and sad. I feel sad that Miguel is not here; he would be three months if he was born. I think about him every day. I am worried that I will lose this baby too. I will try so hard not to lose this baby. I pray that my family and Miguel will look after this baby. This baby is all that I have to live for. I know that Eric will be happy that I am pregnant; he has been annoyed that I am not yet pregnant. I have been worrying that there is something wrong with me.

Eric ordered that I gain weight and said no wonder I cannot get pregnant if I'm so thin. I don't have any appetite but I try to eat as much as I can. Eric has got Guadalupe to make high calorie foods for me. It is torture to eat when food make you feel sick.

This pregnancy makes me feel sick but I need to eat. I do not want to lose this baby. At night I have not been able to sleep because I am scared that I will lose this baby and Eric will leave me. If I lose Eric, I will have nobody. I will have no home and I have no friends. The worst thing is that I have no family. He is the only person that I have. Now I have the baby too. I will pray so hard to God that I will not lose this baby. I cannot lose this baby.

FRIDAY 27TH NOVEMBER 2015

My pregnancy is very good. Eric is taking good care of me. I have to take special vitamins every day and I am seeing the best gynaecologist in New Hampshire. She is a very nice lady and says that I must not worry about having another miscarriage and the baby looks very healthy. It is still too early to know if it is a boy or a girl. I want to wait until the birth but Eric wants to know if we will have a boy or a girl. The baby will be due in the middle of May. I am so overjoyed!

I have been eating a lot; I am craving peanut butter and cheese. Peanut butter and cheese together is disgusting for many people, but for me it is delicious! I feel very healthy. I have gained ten pounds, but I am happy. I was too skinny. My tummy is even showing a bit; it did not show very much with Miguel.

Eric says that I should not put on too much weight in the pregnancy because it will be hard to lose weight after the baby. I am not worried about that. I am very active and I do not usually have a big appetite; only before my period and pregnancy.

I have been resting a lot. I do not exercise much as I do not want to tire my body and lose the baby. I will do anything to make this baby stay.

MONDAY 4TH JANUARY 2016

I am having a girl! I am feeling so happy! Of course, I did not mind, but it will be so nice to have a little girl. Eric is not too happy as he wants a son, but hopefully we will have more children together. Maybe Christmas and New Year will be much happier next year when we have the baby.

Eric's parents came again for Christmas. I do not like them. They ignore me most of the time. I did not see the point of them coming as Eric was busy with work and didn't spend much time with us and his parents hardly speak to me. We just sat in silence watching television. I do not think that even Eric's father and mother speak to each other much.

I wish that Eric does not have to work all the time. He is always working. He is becoming distant again. This year for New Years, I did not do anything because Eric said that he had to go to New York for business and his parents went on holiday to St Barts for the

New Year.

I was very upset because it was New Years and Eric thinks work is more important than family. Eric said that I am being dramatic and New Years is a stupid overrated tradition. I was very upset because Eric knows how important New Years Eve is in my culture. New Years Eve was always my favourite day in the whole year. Even being poor, we would have the best time.

We would wear our best clean white clothes because wearing white is a symbol of peace and prosperity. We would have a party with our neighbours and friends. We would dance and listen to music all night; drinking Cachaca and eating lentils because lentils are good for luck.

I felt so sad sitting by myself in this big house on New Years Eve, thinking about my family and thinking about what Eric is doing and why he must go to New York. I wanted to go to New York too to celebrate the New Year. The New Years celebrations in New York are incredible. One year when I was living in New York and I was not working, I went to Times Square. I went by myself because Marco doesn't like crowds and he preferred to get drunk with his stupid friends. I went to Times Square to see the ball drop and watch the fireworks. It was not the same as being with my family in Brazil, but it was still beautiful and exciting.

This year I wish that my life could be more beautiful and exciting. Sometimes I feel like I am a princess in a tower. My prince is here, but he does not wish to save me.

THURSDAY 3RD MARCH 2016

I went to see the gynaecologist today and she said that the baby is looking very healthy and has a strong heartbeat. She said that there are no problems and I have nothing to worry about. She also said that I am a healthy weight for the pregnancy and I haven't gained too much or too little. I am so happy that my baby is healthy! That is the most important thing. My prayers have been answered.

Eric does not seem as excited as I am for the baby. He does not touch my stomach and he does not touch me much. He wanted a baby so much so I do not understand why he is not happy. We have not talked much about the baby or about names. He said that I can call the baby whatever I want as it is a girl. It would be nice to choose a name together, but Eric says that he doesn't have time for that. As long as I choose a sensible American-sounding name, it does not matter.

I have been thinking about names and I will call my baby girl Clara Isabel. Clara was always my favourite name for a girl when I was a child and Isabel was my mother's name. The name sounds so perfect. I told Eric and he agreed that it is a nice name. I am so happy that he thinks so too. Eric has hired a decorator for the nursery and he said it is up to me how I would like it to be decorated. I will choose the best and prettiest nursery for my little Clara. I really hope that our baby will make Eric and me closer. Maybe a baby will be good for our marriage.

THURSDAY 17TH MARCH 2016

I found something on Eric's computer today! It made me very scared and worried. Eric has been acting very strange. He is always in his study and he always lock the door. Yesterday he thought I was having a nap, but I watched him and waited for him to leave his study. When he left the study to go to the toilet, he did not lock the door so I go in. I need to know if he is talking to another woman.

I looked at the computer and saw Eric's email. I looked through the names on the email and I saw a woman's name. A woman called Hannah Friedman. I felt sick. Perhaps Eric is having an affair with this Hannah. I open the email.

I will make sure that you pay for what you did to my sister.

It's because of you that she's dead. I will fight for justice.

I did not get to finish the email because Eric slams the laptop shut. I did not hear him come in. He is as quiet as a cat.

"I thought that we talked about this!" Eric shouted. "This is why I don't want to be around you! How would you feel if I constantly spied on you and went through your emails? I know that you're pregnant and your hormones are all over the place but that gives you no right to spy on me!"

"Who is Hannah Friedman? And why does she think that you killed her sister?"

"Wow you really don't trust me, do you? Some crazy woman writes me a crazy email and you blame me. If you must know, Hannah Friedman is the sister of an ex-girlfriend that I dated long ago. She was crazy and had a lot of problems. Well, she committed suicide recently. When I heard, I sent my condolences, but her sister went mad and blamed me. It's obvious that she's upset and is looking for someone to blame. How can it be my fault when I haven't seen or spoken to Rivka in years? It's typical! All you women are the same! Always blaming men for everything and jumping to the wrong conclusions. No wonder men say that women are crazy!"

MONDAY 28TH MARCH 2016

I cannot stop thinking about that poor girl who killed herself. I need to believe Eric. Maybe the poor sister is angry and it makes he feel better to blame somebody. I thought about writing to the sister; I remember her name but I am heavily pregnant and do not want any stress for me or the baby. I need to believe my husband. I am having his baby. He is still angry that I looked through his emails and we hardly talk with each other. Eric does not want to be near me. It make me so sad. Maybe he is right to be upset. Marco never trusted me. He always accuse me of sleeping with other men, even though he was sleeping with other women. I know that he would cheat on me. I saw him kissing another woman in his car. When I confront him, he tell me that it wasn't what it looked like and he was just giving her a lift and it was only a friendly kiss. However, when I even said hello to another man, he would go crazy.

I do not have the strength to fight with Eric. I need to protect my baby. I am just hoping that this baby will make Eric and me close again. I miss the kind and loving man that I know Eric can be. Sometimes it feel like an angry and bad spirit has taken over Eric's body and has taken the old Eric away.

CHAPTER THIRTY-SIX

SATURDAY 21ST MAY 2016

My precious baby girl is here! I cannot believe it! She is alive and healthy! I cannot stop looking at her. She was born yesterday, on Friday 20th May at 7.26pm. I was in labour for only two hours. Eric was not at home, but told Guadalupe to be at home in case I go into labour. My waters break and Guadalupe called Eric's driver to take me to the hospital. I tried to call Eric so many times but he did not answer his phone. I did not want to give birth alone.

I kept calling Eric when I was in the hospital but he did still not answer. I was getting worried that something happen to Eric. I was worried so much that I did not notice the pain. The pain did not bother me. All the time I keep waiting for Eric to call me. I cried because I have nobody to call and nobody to be there for me. I cried so much. The nurse said that they could give me an epidural, but I wasn't crying because I was in pain. My mother says that I have always been a tough girl. When I was little she said that I did not cry like other children when I hurt myself.

All I could think about was holding my baby. When the contractions started again, all I kept thinking about was meeting Clara. I focused on my breathing and in my mind I imagined my mother and my sisters were by my side. Thinking about them and hearing their voices in my head made me feel better.

Finally the baby came and I was so happy! She looked so perfect. The nurse examined her and said she is very healthy and a good size. The moment that I held Clara in my arms, nothing else mattered- my sadness or Eric. Every part of my body felt love for Clara; such a love I've never felt before. She is so perfect and so beautiful to me. She looked at me with her big blue trusting eyes like she knows that I am her mama.

"I will love you forever my meu amorzinho and I will keep you safe," I whispered into her little ear.

MONDAY 23RD MAY 2016

I woke up this morning to find that Clara was not in her Moses basket next to me. I asked Eric where Clara is and he said that she was crying too much and he didn't want her in our room.

"Guadalupe will be looking after her," Eric said.

"But I want to have my baby next to me!" I say. "I will sleep in her room then."

"For goodness sake, children should not be allowed in our room. It will only form bad habits. I don't want Clara sleeping with us till she's ten-years-old! My parents didn't even allow me in their room on Christmas Day! This is our room and now that you've given birth we can resume with sexual activities."

"I do not feel like it," I said. All I wanted was Clara close to me. I went to her nursery but Guadalupe said that Clara was asleep. Then I went downstairs to have breakfast. I can't help but feel so lonely and sad and Eric is further away from me than ever. He was not even sorry for missing the birth.

"For goodness sake Juliana, I had an important business meeting and anyway I don't want to see you giving birth. I've heard that these things can scar a man," Eric said coldly.

For the first time in my marriage, I'm thinking about leaving Eric. I am not happy and I am sure that he does not love me. If he loved me, he would not make me feel that I am so alone all the time.

WEDNESDAY 1ST JUNE 2016

I want to leave, but I want to find the right time. I need to find a job and somewhere that Clara and me can live. I will do any job; even if it is to be cleaning dirty toilets. I have been spending my time looking for jobs. When we divorce I do not want Eric's money. I want my own money even if it is very little. Maybe Marco can help me even if he is horrible. He is the only person I know. Maybe he can let me stay for a little bit with Clara until I find somewhere. I will even pay to stay with him and let him have sex with me. Anything to get away from here. At least Marco did not keep me like a prisoner at home. He was very happy to divorce me; it was very easy. Maybe Eric will give me a divorce easily, but he will want full custody of Clara. I know that he will take her from me, even though he does not care for her. I need to run away. Maybe Marco's brothers can help me get away.

I find Marco's number in my phone and ring him. He answers right away.

"Well, well if it ain't the Brazilian broad. Long time no speak sugar."

"Hello Marco, I am sorry to bother you, but I need your help."

"I would love to help you baby, but I'm kinda busy."

"Please Marco, I will pay you! I need somewhere to stay and I need to get away!"

"I'm sorry, but my lady ain't gonna let you stay here."

"Maybe I can stay with your brothers or parents; I will even pay them. Please I am desperate. I will do anything!"

"Marco who the fuck are you twalking to? It better not be some broad!" I hear a woman's voice in the background.

"I'm sorry, I gotta go," Marco says.

"Marco, please!" I beg, but he has already hung up.

FRIDAY 10TH JUNE 2016

I think that Eric is giving me those tablet that Dr Goldman gave me and that I do not want to take. Every night, I listen out for Clara and try to go to her when she cries. She is a good baby and does not cry much. I go to her nursery and watch her sleeping. Last night I do not remember going to Clara's nursery. It was like somebody had given me a drug. It was the same deep sleep, like somebody knock me out. The same sleep where I have those strange dreams.

I had the same dream; the same dream where a man is on top of me, trying to strangle me. I cannot breathe and fear rushes through my body. Usually the man does not have a face, but this time I saw his face clearly. It was Eric. There was a brief moment when I was awake and realised that it is not a dream.

CHAPTER THIRTY-SEVEN

MONDAY 13TH JUNE 2016

I am more scared of Eric than ever! He knows that I spoke to Marco!

I was awake this morning and Eric came onto the bed and got on top of me. He started pulling off my pyjamas, like he was a wild animal. I told him that I do not feel like sex but he told me to shut up and that he is in charge of me.

Tears were running down my face as he forced himself in me. It was so painful and horrible.

"You're a dirty and disgusting whore!" he whispered in my ear. "I know that you spoke to your ex-husband. You think I'm stupid eh? You want to leave so badly do you? No man is going to want a pathetic little whore like you. No man is going to give you everything that I do. I give you so much and this is how you repay me? The only way you'll leave is in a coffin. Remember I'm a very powerful man and I can get away with anything, even murder, so you better be careful. I can kill you and make it look like an accident!"

I do not know what to do. I need to run away, but I do not know how. I want to kill myself, but I do not want to leave Clara with this monster. I cannot allow it. There must be some way to get away. Maybe I can get away when Eric next goes on business to New York. It is in two weeks. I can break into his office. Last time I saw there was a safe in his study. I do not want his money, but I have no choice. I need to plan to get away.

TUESDAY JUNE 28TH 2016

Today Eric has gone away to New York for a few days. I can plan my escape. This is perfect. First I packed a suitcase for Clara and me. Next I broke into Eric's study. I used the same trick with the card. I was scared it wouldn't work and it took a while, but when the door opened, I was very relieved. I went over to the desk and started opening all of the drawers. In the top drawer I find Eric's iPad. I switch it on, but it wants a password. I do not know what Eric's password can be.

I look through the rest of the drawers, frantically looking through the documents. I do not care if this takes me forever; I will be here all night if I need to. I look through each piece of paper until find a piece of paper at the back of one of the folders that says "passwords." It is a very long list. There are passwords and codes for everything. I find the password for the iPad and it works!

I realise that I do not even know what I am looking for or expecting to find. I am lost. An email comes onto the screen and it gives me an idea. Yes I will look at Eric's emails again! I go through the list and it locks like it is business. I don't know if it will help me. I click on the emails that are from women; Meredith, Jennifer and Elaine; but they are business emails. I do not know why I care if Eric has been with other women.

I look at the other emails, but it is all business and I do not understand what they are saying. Then I find an email from José Santos. José from my village! José does not even have a computer or a cell phone! I open the email.

Look boss, I can't keep lying like this anymore. Juliana's family want to go to the police; they haven't heard from her in two years! They want to report her missing. I needed the money, but I don't want to be a part of this anymore. I feel so terrible that I lied to Juliana about her family dying; every night I can't sleep because of what I've done. You're a fucking sick son of a bitch and I can't believe I let you pay me to do this. Juliana needs to know the truth and I will tell her. You

319

can have your fucking money back.

I am shaking! My family is alive! MY FAMILY IS ALIVE! Eric was lying about my family being dead! That evil son of a bitch! I feel anger burning in my body like a big fire. I throw the iPad against the wall. Then I take the expensive watch and stamp on it until it cracks. Next I take the framed photograph of Eric's parent and throw it hard on the ground so the glass breaks.

I take the picture and tear it up. How dare that cabrão tell me that my family is dead! I want to kill him! How can José do this to me? How can he let that monster pay him to tell me that my family is dead? I will never forgive him! Never!

I am so angry that I cannot even feel happy that my family is alive. When I see José, I will tell everybody what he did! Everybody will know! I will go back to Brazil to my family! My family! They are alive! I am crying. As terrible as everything is, this is the best news! My papa used to say that good things always come out of bad situations.

I do not care if I have a poor life in Brazil; I am going back. I never want to be away from my family. Maybe the money will be enough to buy us a nice home and Clara will have the things that I did not have. I will make sure that she never has to go hungry or not have a nice and safe home. Maybe I can go to university in Brazil or find a good job. Maybe I can try to be a model.

I am so happy! My life is about to begin. Now I need to find the code to the safe. Thank God it is listed on the paper with the passwords. It opens! Inside there are piles of money. I count one of the piles, which is held together with a rubber band. There is ten thousand dollars in one pile! There are lots of piles of money! Together there must be more than five-hundred thousand dollars! I empty all of the money into a plastic bag and put it into the suitcase. Amongst all of the money, I also find my passport in the safe! I wondered where my passport was; I thought I lost it but Eric must have taken it from me.

I will be able to have a good life in Brazil! I will even be able to get a good lawyer if Eric wants to take Clara. I can even go to the police. I take Eric's iPad. It still works. I remember the password by heart. I can show this to the police. Yes I will go to the police. They have to believe me.

I need to get away from here! Far away. I look up where I can get the next train or bus. There is no transport near here. There are only a few buses in Darton, but it will take a long time to get there. Maybe I can get a taxi. In Darton, there is a Greyhound bus to Missouri arriving at 17.20. In four hours. I order a taxi to come at 16.30 to take me to Darton.

Now is an hour until the taxi will arrive. I will take the suitcases outside and then come for Clara. I will tell Guadalupe that I am taking her for a walk. I am writing this diary while I am waiting. My heart is beating so fast. I am excited but scared.

"Juliana!" I jump! Somebody is calling my name! Eric is calling my name! Porra! He is home! It cannot be. I need to hide.

I'm in the attic. In the room that nobody uses. Maybe he will not find me here. Maybe I can hide in the bathroom or in the wardrobe! I can hear him shouting my name!

"Juliana, you're fucking dead! Do you hear me?" Eric yells. I can hear his footsteps on the floor below. Maybe he will not come here. I will leave my diary here. Maybe somebody will find it and it can be used as evidence. If he kills me maybe somebody will find this and give it to the police. I will take the post-it note that I use as a bookmark for my diary and write on it and stick it on the front so it is clear if it is ever found.

Blood is rushing through my body. I've never been so scared in my life.

I am scared that Eric is going to kill me.

END OF DIARY

CHAPTER THIRTY-EIGHT

My whole body is shaking like an earthquake and my breathing is rapid and shallow. I feel like all of the air is being sucked out of my lungs and that I'm going to pass out. My whole body is paralysed yet alert with fear. My scalp prickles with numbness and my heart is beating so hard that I'm scared that I'm going to die. I can't think clearly but all I know is that everything is a lie.

My whole world has been shattered, like glass that has been smashed into a million little pieces and can never be put back together. I want so badly for this to be a nightmare and that any minute I'll wake up and everything will be ok.

Do you ever get that feeling after a nightmare? The feeling the moment that you wake up, where the blissful realisation that it's not true washes over you like cool refreshing water on a scorching hot day? I pray that any minute now I'll wake up and realise that this was all a horrible dream. This can't be real. My head is spinning as though I'm on a fairground ride. Nothing can seem to shake me back into reality. It occurs to me that this *is* my reality. Unfortunately, nightmares aren't only reserved for the unconscious mind

How could I be so blind? Eric is a monster! The man that I married is a monster. Poor Juliana! What did he do to her? What happened to poor Rivka? Did he kill her too? My body can't stop shaking as though I had some horrible degenerative disorder that causes people to shake uncontrollably. Eric killed Juliana and he'll kill me too! I can't believe that I was so stupid and so blind? I know that things weren't right about Eric but I didn't want to see it or believe it. I always blamed Elizabeth for being so stupid and so blind when it came to men, but I'm no better. In fact, I'm even worse! I allowed myself to get so caught up in this fantasy.

I feel sick; the bile rises in my throat. I go to the en suite bathroom and throw up. My whole body keeps on shaking violently. The man that I married is a monster, misogynist and a murderer. Eric never really loved me. He wanted to trap me here, like he trapped Juliana. I have to go to the police. I have to get away as fast as possible before Eric comes back. I've never been so terrified in my life.

I run to my bedroom and rifle through my drawers looking for my passport. It's not there. Eric took my passport! I have no money either. I'll take a taxi to the nearest police station. That's what I'll do. I ring the number of the nearest taxi firm, but there's an automatic voice on the line telling me that my call can't go through. I try again, but it's the same automatic tape telling me that my call can't go through. I desperately try another cab company, but it's the same; my call can't go through. Fuck, fuck, fuck!

I have an idea. I'll call Vladimir, Eric's driver. He's always on standby. I call his number and luckily, he picks up.

"Vladimir, please pick me up as soon as possible!"

"Where would you like to go Miss Iris?"

"It doesn't matter."

"I am sorry Miss Iris, but Eric says he must know where you're going at all times."

"Please can you take me to the police station?"

"Are you in trouble Miss Iris?"

"Yes! Please help me!"

"Ok, I come as quickly as possible."

Tears are streaming down my face like Niagara Falls and every part of my body feels like it's on fire. The panic keeps on rising inside of me like a giant tidal wave. The idea of going to the police station calms me down. Maybe they will help me. They *have* to help me. I take Juliana's diary with me. They'll have to believe me.

***

"Please calm down ma'am," a stern and overweight police officer tells me. I thought that coming to the police station would make me feel better, but I feel even worse.

"Please take a seat ma'am, someone will see you as soon as they can. We're very busy at the moment," the stern, overweight police officer says in his dull and irritated tone. I feel like I'm wasting his time. How can they be busy when it's such a small police station and there isn't anybody else here? Surely there can't be much crime around here. This part of New Hampshire is known for its low crime rate.

It feels like I'm back in London, waiting in A&E. Memories flood back. I remember the time when I cut my finger badly whilst chopping vegetables and it was badly swollen the next day. Magda forced me to go to A&E despite me insisting that I was fine. We ended up waiting for four hours, but it didn't matter because ironically, it ended up being kind of fun.

Magda and I just laughed the whole time. I remember there was this drunken man who kept trying to chat Magda up. It was hilarious. There was also this couple that kept talking really loudly and the woman had the most irritating laugh. She kept laughing at everything to the point that Magda and I couldn't stop laughing ourselves. It was a good job that Magda made me go to A&E as the doctor said that if I had left it longer, I might have gotten septicaemia as the finger was very infected. He gave me antibiotics and luckily my finger healed.

I would do anything to see Magda now. I know that she's mad at me, but I hope that we can make things right. I would do anything to see her and be back in the flat in Kennington. I'm shaken from my thoughts when the miserable overweight police officer calls my name.

"Iris Irving," he says impatiently. "Please come with me." I follow him into a dimly lit room with a desk and two chairs. It reminds me of the room where they question suspects on police dramas. The stern and miserable police office introduces himself. Nerves make me forget his name which is either Chip or Chuck.

"Mrs Irving; I want you to know that there is nobody out there trying to get you," Chuck or Chip says in his monotone voice.

"But I haven't told you what happened yet."

"There's no need ma'am; your husband called and told us the whole story."

My head is spinning and I feel like I'm going to faint. Vladimir must have told Eric where I'm going and Eric must have called and bribed the police officers. I thought that I was ahead of the game, but Eric is ten steps ahead of me.

"What the fuck did he tell you?" Anger is flowing through my veins like a current.

"Please keep your voice down ma'am and if you curse again, I'll give you a police caution," Chip or Chuck says harshly.

"Are you serious? My husband murdered his ex-wife and he might murder me too!"

"Please ma'am calm down."

"How can you expect me to calm down?" I rage.

"Your husband explained to me about your mental health

problems which include paranoia and delusions. Your psychiatrist is also sending over a report which confirms that."

"I have evidence!" I say, taking Juliana's diary out of my bag. "It's Juliana, Eric's ex wife's diary. Please read it! She's dead and I think that Eric killed her!"

Chip or Chuck pays no attention to the diary; treating it like rubbish to be thrown away instead of evidence.

"Ma'am, your husband did not kill anybody. I'm afraid you'll have to leave now; your husband said that his driver will come to get you. I really suggest that you be referred to a psychiatric unit."

"I'm not crazy; there's nothing wrong with me!"

"Ma'am please calm down." I think I'll punch Chip or Chuck in the face if he tells me to calm down one more time.

"I'm not going anywhere until you at least look at this diary!"

"Ma'am, I won't tell you again. If you don't leave, I'll also put your refusal to leave down as a police caution."

Seeing as I'm not going to win, I admit defeat. I just have one more request.

"Before I go, can I use the phone to ring the driver and see how far he is? My phone is out of battery," I lie, even though I know that Vladimir is waiting right outside for me.

Chip or Chuck nods and leads me to the phone in the waiting area. I'm pleased that he doesn't stand next to me and check to see who I'm calling. Chip or Chuck tells me to take care and goes back to his bureau. I get out my phone and find David's email address, which also has his mobile phone number. I ring it; anxiety hammering away at me with each ring. The phone goes to answerphone so I leave a message.

"David, it's Iris. Please help me! I'm really scared that Eric is going to hurt me or possibly even kill me."

CHAPTER THIRTY-NINE

"Surprise baby! Aren't you happy to see me? I decided to come home early to surprise you," Eric grins; malice reflected in those cold green eyes. Before, the sight of Eric gave me butterflies, but now he makes me sick to my stomach. How could I have ever loved and believed in this monster's lies? Everything was a lie.

"I know you killed Juliana. What did you do to her?" I shriek.

"Woah baby, is that how you greet your husband who has cut short his business trip to see his beloved wife?" Eric says softly, but his tone filled with menace. His lips form a wry smile. The fact that he finds this situation amusing makes him even sicker. I want to punch his stupid smug face. Clearly this is all a big joke for him.

"Just tell me the fucking truth!" I hiss.

"Please Iris, what truth? You and I know that you're paranoid and crazy. Just like your mother."

"Don't you dare call me crazy and paranoid and don't you dare call Elizabeth that either!"

"Baby you should be happy that I want to be with you. You'd send any other man running a mile with your paranoia and craziness. Nobody wanted you. I was the only one that wanted you."

"That's not true!"

"You said so yourself that nobody wanted you. I've had to put up with so much."

The sheer irony of it makes me laugh out loud. "You've had to put up with so much? What about me? What about all the lies that you told me?"

"Don't make out that you're so perfect. I know about your little lies and your dirty little indiscretion. What husband would take back their whore wife after she cheats on him with his own brother?"

"How do you know?"

"Iris, I know everything that goes on around here."

"So you've been spying on me?"

"I like to know what my wife is up to. All I know is that you've been going behind my back."

"That's rich coming from you!"

"We're talking about you Iris; not me. I haven't done anything to be ashamed of. I've been such a good husband to you. I give you everything, but it's not enough. Like every other woman. Most women would be happy to have a baby, but there's something wrong with you Iris. You thought that you could lie to me. Lie about your contraception. Yes, I know all about that. The tests showed that there are contraceptive hormones in your body. You thought that you could lie to me."

I feel the fury erupt inside of me like a volcano. "You're sick Eric. Yes, I did lie to you, but because you kept pressuring me to have a baby and you knew I wasn't ready! How can you even compare that to what you did to Juliana? What did you do to her? And what did you do to Rivka?"

"Easy with the paranoia; I didn't kill Juliana or Rivka. I told you what happened."

"Why should I believe you? I don't believe a word that comes out of your mouth. We're through! I want a divorce."

"So you're going to believe some crazy women with severe mental health issues over your husband? Juliana was crazy; it's all lies. It was the same with Rivka. You're not going to throw away what we have because of two insane women are you? Two women who made ridiculous things up in order to get back at me. I seem to have a type; crazy psycho bitches. No one will want you. Your mother certainly doesn't want you nor your slutty and vulgar little Polish friend. They don't even want to talk to you. I'm the only one that has your back."

I don't believe a word that comes out of Eric's mouth, but in order to find out the truth, I need to play dumb. I have a plan. I need to act like everything is ok.

"You're right baby, I'm the one with the problem. I believe you and I trust you. You're right about Juliana; she sounds crazy. Let's celebrate you coming home. Why don't you meet me in the bedroom and I'll bring up some champagne? I'll even put on that outfit you like."

"Really? You'd do that for me? You know how much it turns me on?" Eric grins lasciviously. "You have a lot of making up to do. You're going to show me how sorry you are. I'm going to beat the fuck out of you, do you understand? I want to break your bones."

"Yes master. Go upstairs and like your slave, I will bring you champagne. Is there anything else I can bring you master?"

"God I'm turned on," Eric gasps. "You make the perfect slave." He kisses me on the cheek and I have to do everything in order not to throw up. I tell myself to keep it together. I'm relieved when he finally goes upstairs. I reach for my bag and take out the pills that Doctor Goldman gave me. I take two tablets and crush them into powder. I then pour it into Eric's champagne glass. In order to differentiate the glasses, I put little coloured umbrellas in the glasses; green for me and red for Eric.

M S SELO

Hopefully it'll be enough to knock him out for a few hours. I checked the dosage and two pills should be enough. Even the dosage for one pill is too much.

The plan goes better than I expected. Eric downs the glass and within ten minutes he becomes sleepy and disorientated. Another five minutes later, he falls fast asleep. I make my way over to the chair in the corner where his jacket is draped. I find the set of keys in the pocket and head to his study. I try a couple of keys until the correct one fits and unlocks the door. I don't know what I'm expecting to find, but I need to start somewhere. Why else would Eric lock his study if he didn't have anything to hide?

CHAPTER FORTY

I creep into Eric's study like a thief in the night. I just pray that the medication is enough to knock Eric out for a few hours. I switch on the light and close the door behind me. My heart is racing: fear shooting through my veins. I'm terrified of what I'll find or not find.

The study is spotless and innocuous looking. I go over to the desk and start with the drawer. Luckily it isn't locked, but there's nothing incriminating. Just stationary. I move onto the next drawer, which is just filled with files that are related to accounts and business. I need to find the list of passwords. I rifle through the drawers and through all of the papers. I hope that this won't take me all night.

I skim through the papers, but I can't find anything. I'm careful to put everything back properly in its right order; mindful not to leave any traces that I've been here. The last and final drawer is locked. I really hope that the keys to this drawer are on the chain.

I start to panic when none of the keys fit. I desperately try to think where Eric could hide his keys and then I think of the bookshelf. I rummage through the books; opening and looking through each one. When that fails, my mind ticks manically through other options. Think Iris, think! Then it occurs to me. There's a small expensive African vase on the bottom shelf. I tip it over and a small key falls out. I laugh with joy. I rush back over to the desk and turn the key in the lock. It opens! I feel so victorious that I have found the key that will unlock the truth and mystery of what goes on in Eric's warped and sick mind, however a sickening feeling of trepidation pervades through my body. I'm scared of what I will find. Nothing can be scarier than the fact that my husband is a murderer. I need to confirm it. The police will have to believe me. There must be some evidence leading to Juliana's death. I need to find it.

The first thing that I find in the drawer is the list of passwords. Perfect. Eric's MacBook Pro sits on the desk. I find the password for the MacBook Pro from the list and luckily, it works. I don't know where to start. I'm not that good with technology so I don't want to mess around too much. I go through Eric's search history but I can't find anything of relevance apart from the disgusting porn sites which I don't even want to look at. Maybe I'll find something in his emails. Luckily, I don't need to log into his email account as I'm already automatically logged in.

I scan through the email list slowly. Most of the emails I go through seem related to work and are of little relevance. I keep scanning the list until I see an email from Adam Goldman. Doctor Goldman. I click on the email and read it.

Hi Eric,

Here is the report that I've compiled for you. See the attachment for the report.

Please let me know if I can make any changes.

Best wishes,

Adam

I'm curious about the report. What report is it? Maybe it's a report from Eric's own sessions. Eric said that he sometimes has sessions with Doctor Goldman. I open the attachment and am shocked to see my name appear. It's a report about me. Reading it leaves me absolutely horrified. Goosebumps are dotted around my arms as a cold shiver runs down my whole entire body. Doctor Goldman has betrayed me.

PATIENT NAME: IRIS IRVING

DATE OF BIRTH: 10/24/1994

<u>OVERVIEW</u>

I have seen Iris on several occasions. She has presented to me psychotic symptoms and paranoia. Iris obsessively believes that her husband is hiding things from her and is being unfaithful. She also believes that she is being trapped against her own will as well as being watched and followed. Her behaviour is difficult to manage and causes problems at home. Iris admits that she has lashed out at her husband before and has threatened to hurt him and his daughter as well as herself.

Iris also has unpredictable and volatile mood swings and behaviour that include the following: drinking to excess, impulsive extramarital intercourse and violent outbursts. It is also important to note that Iris's mother has bi-polar disorder. On the occasions that I have seen Iris, she appears to be out of touch with reality. Iris strongly meets the criteria for both Schizoaffective Disorder- Manic Type and Borderline Personality Disorder.

I feel that Iris would benefit from hospitalisation but at the time being her husband does not feel it is necessary and it should be used as a last resort. I have prescribed 300mg of quetiapine for Iris to take daily. I will review any adjustments that may need to be made in terms of dosage and changing medication.

I'm shaking with rage. How could he? I trusted Doctor Goldman. What he's written is complete bullshit. I know I'm not crazy. It now comes back to me what Chip or Chuck said about the report from the psychiatrist. How could Doctor Goldman do this to me? How could Eric do this to me? It was his plan to set me up and make me look crazy. I wonder if that's what he did to Juliana and Rivka. Made them look like they had severe mental health problems so that their deaths wouldn't be suspicious. Suicide would be easily believable, especially for someone with a documented history of mental health problems.

How can I prove that this is all lies? Another terrible thought occurs to me that I didn't register before. The medication. Was I given the medication in order to knock me out so that Eric could rape me? It all comes flooding back. The realistic dreams of a man on top of me; choking me. The bruises the next morning. It wasn't a dream. It was Eric. I feel violently sick! What kind of sick person does that? I feel so violated and degraded. I wish that I had never met Eric. What I would do to turn back the clock. A chill runs down my spine. This doesn't feel real. I need to find proof that Eric is a rapist and a murderer.

I go back to the drawer where I also find my passport. Tucked inside my passport is my credit card. That monster tried to take my passport and credit card so that I couldn't get away. I tuck my passport and credit card safely into my pocket. I rummage through the drawer and find a folder titled JULIANA. Maybe this will offer some sort of clues to her death or shall I say murder. I look to see if there's a folder for Rivka too, but there isn't. I open Juliana's file and skim through the papers. My jaw drops wide open at what I see.

FAIRFIELD PSYCHIATRIC HOSPITAL, CALIFORNIA

PATIENT NAME: JULIANA IRVING

ADMISSION DATE: FRIDAY 1ST JULY 2016

CASE REPORT BY DR LARRY ANDERSON

Juliana was admitted to us due to an incident that put her young daughter's life and her own life in danger. The woman has history of mental instability. We were sent a

case report by renowned psychiatrist, Dr Adam Goldman, under whom Juliana was a patient. Dr Goldman reported that Juliana showed comorbid symptoms of schizophrenia and borderline personality disorder. According to Dr Goldman, Juliana exhibited signs of extreme paranoia, loss of touch with reality and volatile behaviour. Her husband called the police after she tried to harm her two-month old daughter and herself. With Juliana's history, she was evaluated by another psychiatrist who decided together with her husband, that she be transferred here as we are one of the leading, high-security psychiatric hospitals in the state of California and the US.

Juliana tried to drown her daughter in the bath, which was confirmed by the nanny who thankfully checked in before anything happened. Juliana was hysterical and told police that God and her deceased relatives were telling her to kill her child. This is not the first time that Juliana tried to harm her daughter. Bruises were seen on the child's body.

Juliana was given medication previously but according to her husband she refused to take it. He feels that it is best that she does not have contact with her daughter as he fears for the wellbeing of their daughter. We have also come to the conclusion that Juliana is not fit to be near her daughter or to function in society. We will treat her with a variety of drugs and monitor her progress. Juliana has also been placed on suicide watch as she tried to cut her wrists with broken glass. In the meantime, Juliana's husband has filed for divorce and requested full custody of their daughter which the court has fully approved.

This can't be right. I'm shaking all over. I re-read the report over and over again. Juliana isn't crazy and I'm not crazy. Eric has framed both of us. Why? Why is he doing this? However, this also means that Juliana is alive. I don't know whether I feel relief or fear. Fear that I'll end up where Juliana is.

CHAPTER FORTY-ONE

I pound on Guadalupe's door. I don't care that it's two o'clock in the morning. I need answers. I checked to see if Eric is still asleep and luckily, he's still dead to the world. I keep on hammering on the door until Guadalupe wakes and opens the door.

"Señora Iris, what is wrong?" Guadalupe asks; her expression betraying that she is still half asleep. She has rollers in her hair and is wearing a pink nightdress. Under any normal circumstances she seems like a nice and innocent lady, but she isn't. She's just as bad as Eric.

"What happened to Juliana?" I yell.

"I no understand," Guadalupe says innocently.

"Don't play dumb with me; she didn't hurt Clara, did she?"

"I sorry. I no understand Señora Iris."

"Cut the crap Guadalupe; you know perfectly well what I'm talking about. Maybe I should speak slower. Did Juliana hurt Clara?"

Guadalupe still looks confused. I genuinely don't think that she understands. I sigh and get my phone out. I go to Google translate and translate what I've said into Spanish.

"No, Juliana no hurt Clara."

I type into Google translate. "Then why did you tell the police that Juliana tried to drown Clara?"

"I no say to police. Señor Eric say me to say to police. I no understand but Señor Eric say I must say what he say me."

It seems to me that Guadalupe is also the victim in this situation. That's why Eric hired her; a naïve and uneducated older woman who doesn't speak much English and does what her employer tells her to do without questioning it.

"Juliana good mother. Poor niña. Eric say Juliana die," Guadalupe says, making the sign of the cross and muttering something in Spanish, which I assume to be something religious.

***

I dread being around Eric. I feel disgusted even sharing the same bed with him however I have to pretend that everything is normal until I figure out how to frame him. I barely sleep a wink all night and when he kisses me this morning, I feel physically sick. I take a long hot shower in order to wash away any traces of him off of my body. I feel so dirty even being around him. Luckily, Eric doesn't stick around and goes straight to his study as usual. I took extra care to put everything back as it was and locked the drawer and the door. I really hope that I've done a good enough job of concealing my search of his study.

I go downstairs and make myself a strong coffee. I can't even stomach any breakfast. I find the number for the Fairfield Psychiatric Hospital and dial the number. When I ring, I'm led to a pre-recorded message with options. I select the option for *other inquiries*. I'm put on hold for two-minutes, listening to some stupid upbeat and cheerful tune, which is a bit ironic considering a psychiatric hospital is hardly an upbeat and cheerful place.

I consider the possibility that I might not even be put through considering that this is such a high security place, but I'll take my chances. Finally, a dull and robotic sounding woman answers the phone.

"Fairfield Psychiatric Hospital, how can I help you?

"I'd like you to put me through to Juliana Irving," I say.

"Are you a relative?"

"Yes, I'm her sister. From Brazil. I want to know how she's doing." Oh God, why did I say that I'm from Brazil. I don't sound remotely Brazilian, but the woman doesn't seem to notice or care.

"OK, I'll find out what ward she's in for you. Please hold." I wait for what seems like ages. I almost hang up before I hear a voice speak into the receiver.

"Hello, who is this?" a shaky and frightened voice mumbles.

"Hello am I speaking to Juliana?"

"Yes, who is this?"

"I'm Iris. I'm married to Eric Irving. I know everything. I read your diary. I know that you're not crazy. I'm going to try to frame Eric."

"He is a very powerful man; nobody will believe you. He is the devil. Because of him I will never see my baby. I miss her so much that I want to die. Is Clara ok?"

"Yes, she's absolutely fine. Guadalupe takes good care of her."

"Clara will not remember me, but tell her that I love her and she is always in my heart."

"There must be a way to make the police believe us."

"Nobody will believe you as long as Eric is giving them money. Nobody can stop him; not even God. Please just promise me that you will not let him harm Clara."

***

M S SELO

"How could you?" I scream.

"Iris you can't just barge in here like this," Doctor Goldman says, trying to be as composed as possible, but I can see the fury behind his eyes. I lied and told Eric that I had an appointment with Doctor Goldman. Being the control freak that he is, he got Vladimir to drive me there. I could feel Vladimir's eyes on me the whole time; making sure that I couldn't get away.

"I have every right to barge in here after what you did! I saw the report. It's all lies and you know it! You should have your license as a psychiatrist revoked! You shouldn't be allowed to practice! How much did Eric pay you to lie?"

"I will kindly ask you to leave Iris," Doctor Goldman says coldly.

"You want me to leave because you know that I'm telling the truth!"

"I will not discuss this here. If you want to discuss anything, you know that you must book an appointment."

"You're disgusting! I trusted you! I will never book an appointment with you again. You should be reported and I'll make sure of that."

"Iris, I have an excellent reputation and am one of the leading clinical psychiatrists in the US. Now I will kindly ask you to leave now. If you do not leave, I shall call security to escort you off of the premises."

"Fine, I'm going! I don't know how you sleep at night!"

I storm out of the building. Vladimir is waiting for me outside. His presence makes me feel extremely uncomfortable. Why does he have to spy on me?

"Vladimir, I want to go to town for a few hours. You can pick me up later."

Vladimir shakes his head. "I am sorry Miss Iris, but Eric says that I must escort you everywhere outside of the house."

"Are you serious?" I can't believe this; Eric is treating me like a prisoner. I'm imprisoned in my own personal hell. I need to get out. Maybe I could make a run for it. I have my passport and my credit card in my bag; perhaps if I run, I can get away. Get a bus anywhere far away from here and contact the police. Police that haven't been bribed by Eric.

I start running, but Vladimir catches up with me. He's much faster and stronger than me. I've never exactly been very fit. Vladimir is very tall and well-built. He seems like the kind of guy that could lift the heaviest weights at the gym. He pulls me with his bulky arms and firmly places my arms behind me, as if he's arresting me. There's nobody around to witness it. I try to wriggle out of his iron grip, but it's pretty much impossible. He leads me back to the car and drives me back home or shall I say back to my prison.

I need to get away. I try calling David again, but there's a voice at the other end telling me that my call cannot be connected. I try to ring again three more times, but my call can't be connected. Fuck fuck fuck! I wonder if David got my message. Maybe he's still annoyed at me or doesn't want to help me. I try to send him an email but I get a message saying that my email could not be sent. I try again and again but the email won't send. It then occurs to me that Eric is monitoring my calls and emails and has had certain emails and numbers blocked and restricted. I feel even sicker. Eric is holding me hostage here. Why is he doing this?

All along it was Eric who cut me off from my family and from Magda. That's why they didn't call or respond to my messages; because Eric blocked their numbers. I feel a simultaneous wave of happiness that Elizabeth and Magda haven't abandoned me and cut contact with me, but crippling fear that Eric has cut everything and everyone out of my life and has reduced me to a prisoner. Even prisoners can still speak to and see their friends and family. Eric did to me almost exactly what he did to Juliana but telling her that her family was dead.

I'm trapped here; the panic inside of me is overwhelming. There's nowhere or nobody that I can go or run to. Maybe I can try to walk to Darton and take a bus. Darton is a long way by foot and I don't know the way. I go to Google Maps on my phone and look up directions on how to get to Darton town centre by foot but according to Google Maps, a route cannot be found. Damn it! Maybe I could just try and walk there. I don't care how long it will take me and if I get lost, as long as I get away from this prison. I don't even care about packing anything. All I take is my credit card and passport. That's all I need. I'll pretend that I'm going for a walk. I put on my comfortable trainers and walk towards freedom.

CHAPTER FORTY-TWO

I've been walking for about two hours and my feet are really starting to hurt. I take little breaks, but I'm starting to feel tired, hungry and thirsty. Why didn't I bring something to eat and drink with me? My stomach is rumbling with intense hunger and my mouth is dry. All of the space around me is just forests and fields. There's no gas station or shops in the vicinity. I'm in the middle of nowhere. I feel like I'm wandering in the desert. It's starting to get dark and the air is beginning to grow thick with fog and frost. I really didn't think this out very well. There's nobody around here and there's no signposts anywhere. There are no fishermen by the lake. Well I guess it's too cold for fishing.

I panic especially as it's starting to get really dark and I've been walking and walking and don't seem any closer to civilization. There's no roads or cars around here. I try Google Maps on my phone again but I don't have any connection. Fuck! My body starts trembling with panic, especially as I hear noises. Noises that sound like they come from an animal. Shit what if there are bears? I've heard that there are black blears in New Hampshire. What if I get eaten by a bear?

I'm scared and alone and it's so dark here. I'm lost and I don't know where I'm going. I sit on a log and cry. It's freezing and I'm starving. At least dying in the woods would be better than being imprisoned by Eric. That's the only comfort I take in this bleak situation. Nevertheless, I still pray for a miracle.

I think I must have dozed off as I'm awakened by a flashlight in my face. Oh good, somebody's here. As my eyes adjust to my surroundings, I see two police officers in front of me.

Thankfully Chip or Chuck isn't one of them. Maybe they're from a different police station and will believe me about Eric. Maybe my prayers have really been answered.

"We've found her!" one of the police officers calls to another in the distance.

"What do you mean that you've found me?"

"Ma'am your husband reported you missing and sent us out to look for you. I don't know what you were thinking ma'am; it's not safe out here, especially at night. If the bears catch sight of you, you'll be their dinner."

"In truth I was running away from my husband. I'm not allowed to go anywhere. I know it sounds crazy, but he's keeping me trapped. He set up a device that screens all of my calls and emails and blocks them. He has his driver follow me everywhere when I am allowed out of the house."

I immediately regret what I say because the police officers don't believe me. In their eyes, what I've said just confirms that I'm crazy.

"Ma'am, nobody is trying to trap or follow you and I'm sure that nobody is controlling your phone. You're safe."

"Please, you don't understand! I'm not crazy; Eric has set this all up!"

"Ma'am your husband made us perfectly aware of your problems and that you haven't been taking your medication. You need help ma'am. I suggested to your husband that you be sectioned, but he said he'd rather deal with things himself."
"It's all lies; you can't believe him! How much is he paying you?"

"Ma'am, please calm down. We're going to take you home OK?" one of the police officers speaks to me as though I were a small child. I decide not to say anything more as it will only fuel their conviction that I'm crazy. Why won't anybody believe me? I feel like screaming to the top of my lungs. I'm doomed and there's no way out of this miserable hell that Eric has constructed for me. I've got no way to escape and there's nobody here to save me. I've hit a dead end and I'm all out of ideas. I've never felt so defenceless and hopeless in my whole entire life. I've always been in control of my life, but now it's been taken away from me. I'm like a puppet in Eric's sick play.

I'm reminded of that film, *The Truman Show*, where Truman is trapped in an artificial world created for him. I feel like that. Eric has removed me from the rest of that world and trapped me in his own little world that he's built for me. God knows what else Eric is capable of. Maybe he'll even plant a chip in my brain and turn me into a robot like in the *Stepford Wives*. The idea sounds so ludicrous that I burst out laughing. The police officers turn and look at me, probably further convinced that I'm crazy. The paradoxical laughter only masks my fears. My fear that nobody is going to save me.

***

"Thank God you've found her!" Eric says, rushing over to pull me into his arms. I don't want him to touch me. The police officers probably think that Eric is a caring and loving husband. On the surface it seems like that. The officers say their farewells and leave; leaving me alone with the monster who is intent on destroying my life. In the police car, I prayed that somebody or something could save me. I've never been religious and I've never really prayed much before, but since this situation is out of my control, it seems that only God can help me.

"Iris, I was so worried about you. What were you thinking running away like that?" Eric says, as if he were a normal husband worried about his wife.

"Eric, I want a divorce and I want to go back to England!"

"Remember that you have nobody and nowhere to go. Your mother doesn't care about you, neither does your stupid little Polish friend!"

"I know what you did. You blocked their numbers and emails so that they couldn't contact me or that I couldn't contact them."

"I'm only doing what's best for you. I'm the only one who loves you and cares about you."

"You call this love Eric! This is not love! You're sick and you need help!"

Eric gives a deep hollow laugh as though this were all a big joke.

"I want a divorce!" I yell.

"You don't tell me what to do. Nobody tells me what to do! Even God can't tell me what to do!" Eric shouts, his tone filled with venom.

"Why are you doing this to me?"

"Because I can Iris." Again, he laughs that sickening and demonic laugh. It sends shivers down my spine.

"If only you had been a good little wife and would have done as you were told. Instead, you go snooping and fucking around like a dirty little whore. You're the one who should be on your knees begging for forgiveness for what you did to me."

"Then why don't you just divorce me?"

"That would be too easy. You deserve to be punished."

"So, you're just going to stick me inside a mental asylum like you did with Juliana?"

"No, no; I've got something else planned for you," Eric smirks;

the grin on his face wide and threatening. I feel like prey ready to be attack by a predator.

"I'll give you a choice," Eric continues. "You can stay here and have the life that every woman dreams of; luxury, money, children and a gorgeous and loving husband who loves his disgusting and ungrateful little cunt of a wife even though he deserves better, or…" Eric reaches into his trouser pocket and pulls out a gun. I almost piss myself at the sight of the gun.

Eric senses my fear. "Don't worry, you get to make that choice. If you decide to leave, this baby will blow your stupid little brains out in an instant."

"If you kill me, you'll be framed for murder."

"I won't kill you; it'll be suicide. All of the cops know that you're a mentally unstable, schizophrenic and suicidal headcase. I'll be the poor widower, devastated by his wife's suicide. The poor widower who always goes for unstable and crazy women because he wants to help them, but for them it's never enough."

"Why do you want to kill me? Why didn't you kill Juliana too?"

"I decided that killing her wouldn't do her any good. She can spend her whole life suffering because she made the wrong decision. If she just continued being a good little wife and had honoured her husband, we might still be together and she'd get to be a mother to Clara."

"You're sick! You're a psychopath! I wish I had never met you!"

"Before you met me, you were no one. I gave you everything. If it wasn't for me, you'd still be slaving away for that faggot boss of yours at the gallery, living in that disgusting little apartment and being hounded every day, all day by your unstable mother. I did you a favour. I rescued you. You should be grateful to me. Who else would have wanted you? You would only follow your mother's example and date jerks who use and abuse you. I've been so good to you. If you just obeyed me and behaved like a good wife, I would give you the world."

"My old life might not have been perfect, but I was happy!"

"So, I guess that you'd like that bullet through your head. If you leave here and you leave me, your life will be so shit that you'll wish that you were dead. So really I'm just doing you a favour."

"Please don't shoot me," I cry.

"Good girl Iris, you've made the right decision. You won't regret it. You'll be happy here," Eric says, stroking my hair. "If you obey me, I will give you everything."

"Get the fuck away from her!" a voice that isn't Eric's roars.

Both Eric and I jump. Eric releases me from his grip. He looks like he's seen a ghost; he's absolutely speechless. Relief floods through my veins. He came. He really came. My prayers have been answered and hopefully this time for good.

CHAPTER FORTY-THREE

"Well, well, well; if it isn't my little brother. Long-time no see," Eric sneers sarcastically.

"I'm not all that thrilled to see you either; especially after what you did!" David retorts.

"Get the fuck out of my house!" Eric roars.

"It's not your house; our parents gave it to you."

"And now it's my house and I'm telling you to get the fuck out! You fucked my wife once; you're not going to fuck her ever again!"

"I'm not going anywhere and I'm certainly not leaving her here with you. What kind of maniac threatens to kill his wife? I heard everything."

"I'll shoot you as well if you don't leave."

"You don't scare me anymore Eric. Plus, you didn't think that I didn't come prepared." David pulls out a gun from his pocket. I can see the wrath in Eric's face that his own brother has outsmarted him. Eric throws the gun onto the table.

"I'll call the police then," Eric threatens.

"The good old good-for-nothing Darton police that can so easily be bribed. The way that father bribed them after Mary died."

"Who's Mary?" I ask, but then I remember. Mary was the woman who was found dead in the lake near the Irving Estate; the one who apparently committed suicide. Now it comes back to me; the woman who that lady in the diner told me about.

The one who warned me about Eric. I wish I had listened to her.

"Mary used to be our nanny, but she was having an affair with our father. She was found dead in the lake or shall I say that she was murdered!" David says.

"You don't know what you're talking about," Eric hisses.

"I saw it; I saw everything that happened. Father killed her. They were having a fight. He held her head down under the water until she couldn't breathe anymore. I cried for him to stop, but he wouldn't listen. After he was done, he punched me in the face and told me that if I ever told anyone what I saw, he would drown me as well. I was terrified of father. He always hated me. I'll never forget what I saw that day. It'll stay with me for the rest of my life. I'll never forget the fear on Mary's face when he grabbed her forcefully and pushed her head down into the water. I see that scene every night before I go to sleep. I was nine years old."

"You're lying," Eric snorts. "Even if father did kill Mary, I don't blame him. She was a home-wrecking whore who got what was coming to her. She threatened that if father wouldn't give her money for her bastard child, that she'd tell everybody about their affair. Father only tried to be reasonable. He gave her money for an abortion and when she refused, she blackmailed him to accept responsibility for the baby and pay a hefty monthly allowance. My father couldn't allow his reputation to be ruined by some pathetic whore."

"You always defended our father, but you were always his favourite son. Like father like son," David says; the resentment in his voice evident.

"It's not my fault that our parents loved me more and that you were the runt of the litter," Eric says derisively.

"You made my life a living hell growing up!" David clamours.

"That's what you said about David, Eric. That he made your life a living hell," I say mockingly.

"He would say that wouldn't he? Eric, did you tell Iris about the time that you held my head down the toilet and the time that you killed our cat Whiskers? Whiskers was the only ally I had in this family and the only person who actually showed any love towards me. You knew that. Hey, remember the time when I spent ages on that school project? The one where we had to make a model city. The one that I worked so hard on? So many days and nights I worked on that project. I remember the morning that I had to hand the project in; it was destroyed. I know it was you who did it. I got a fail for that.

I would always get the blame for everything, even when I didn't do it. You would always plant your drugs in my room and I would get in trouble. Remember that girl I liked in seventh grade, Suzy? Remember when you told her that I wet the bed and slept with stuffed toys? She told the whole school and the bullying got so bad that I stopped going to school," David vents.

"Father was right; you always were oversensitive. All brothers tease one another and are mean to each other," Eric says flippantly.

"What you did went far beyond brotherly teasing and being mean! You terrorized me and our parents did nothing. Father even encouraged it! It was like you were always trying to prove that you were the better and stronger one; like the survival of the fittest. You always took sadistic pleasure from destroying people's lives, like our father."

"Please David, stop trying to act like the victim here!"

"You're a sick and twisted son of a bitch. You've never cared about anybody but yourself. You didn't even care about Christina. You had to take everything from me, including the girl I loved."

"She wasn't yours; she was mine in the first place and you took her from me."

"Christina never loved you. She said you were weird, creepy and controlling!" David protests.

"Wait so Christina was your girlfriend Eric?" I ask. I'm confused.

"Yes, Christina was my girlfriend. We dated for two years. I loved her and I would even have married her if he hadn't of stolen her from me!" Eric shouts. "I would have done anything for Christina; she was the most perfect girl. She was in the year below me at school; David's year. When I went to Harvard, I promised her that I would stay devoted to her. I even drove down almost every single weekend to see her. I treated her like a fucking princess, but that cheating whore threw it all back in my face! I came home during the summer break to catch her in bed with David! Turns out they were sleeping together for months."

"You never cared about Christina. What pissed you off the most was that you couldn't control her anymore."

"Quite the psychoanalyst aren't you doc?" Eric says disparagingly.

"You were responsible for her death! I never would have drunk before driving. You set me up! You wanted to kill us both!"

"Well done, didn't take you long to figure that out detective," Eric jeers. "It was easy really. All I had to do was put drugs and alcohol in the trunk of your car and put ketamine in your glass of water."

"You really are a sick mother fucker! Because of you Christina died! I spent years blaming myself for her death!"

"It's a shame that you both didn't die. Christina got what she deserved; she was messing with the wrong guy," Eric says unemotionally.

"You're despicable! You should be rotting in jail!" I shout.

"You should know that I'm above the law. Christina only got what was coming to her. What goes around comes around. Nothing good comes out of treating a woman like a queen; all they do is use and abuse you."

"Just because one girl hurt you doesn't mean that all women are like that!" I object.

"You see Iris, they are. All women care about is money, status and looks. I've dated enough women to know that. The only way that women respect you is if you put them in their place. When you're too nice to them, they shit all over you."

"Wow you really need serious therapy Eric!" I say. "You're so fucked up."

"Oh I'm not fucked up; I'm the exact opposite of fucked up. I'm so close to perfection that it scares me."

"Wow you really are a sadistic and narcissistic sociopath! You killed Christina and you locked Juliana in a psychiatric asylum for life! What did you do to Rivka? Did you kill her too?" I scream.

"No, I didn't kill Rivka. The stupid little bitch ran away, but actions have consequences as you'll soon find out. I made sure that no man would want her, especially when they found out how deranged and crazy she was. It was really quite fun watching her trying to convince one of the guys she was dating that she didn't write him those crazy messages or destroy his car. Even her own parents thought she was mad. Well, she died of madness in the end; swallowed some pills. Poor, mad Rivka. Such a shame she had to learn the hard way," Eric smirks.

"You're really disgusting, do you know that? You may have destroyed Christina, Rivka and Juliana's lives but I'm not going to let you destroy mine!"

"Oh I will destroy you Iris. As I've shown you, it's very easy. It was even easier with Juliana. All I had to do was tell that stupid Mexican maid to say a few words to the police, confirming that Juliana tried to kill Clara, and give Clara a few bruises to make it look like Juliana had hurt her."

"You hurt Clara?"

"Come on Iris, all I did was give her a few bruises. She hardly felt anything and it's not like she'll never fall over and hurt herself or get bruises from other kids when she's older. Being so sensitive to life does nothing for a child."

"You're an absolute monster! How on earth do you think that I'd ever want to stay with you?"

"Like we agreed Iris, I can make your death look like a suicide. I'll be able to get away with it," Eric says callously.

"You lay a finger on her and I'll point that gun you deranged bastard!" David yells.

"I'd like to see you try. If you kill me, you'll enjoy the rest of your life on death row. If I kill you, nothing happens to me," Eric says, picking up his gun from the table.

"Just stop please!" I cry. "Eric just let me go. Forcing me to stay against my own will won't make me love you! I promise if I go, I won't say a word about what's happened to anyone. I swear."

"Do you think I give up? I always win Iris and I always get my way," Eric says cruelly. "Like I said; if you two die, no one will ever suspect me for anything." Eric points his gun at David and me. My whole body is shaking with panic. I don't want to die. I want to live. I've never thought about what my last words or thoughts would be before I die. I never gave any thought to death, but now it's inevitable.

I've lost the battle. Eric has won. I just hope that there's justice in the afterlife. I close my eyes, ready for my life to be over. Will I ever know that I'm dead? I hear a gunshot. I don't feel the bullet hit me. I feel no pain. I feel nothing. I open my eyes. Eric is lying on the floor covered in a pool of blood. He's still alive. He wails in excruciating agony as blood spills from his chest. David is standing right next to me. He clutches my hand and I let him.

"You fucking bitch; you shot me!" Eric screams. "Don't just stand there! Somebody call 911!"

I didn't shoot Eric, what is he talking about? It takes me a few seconds until I realise who did. Guadalupe is standing there with a gun in her hand. She was the one who shot Eric.

CHAPTER FORTY-FOUR

BREAKING NEWS! PROMINENT MULTI-MILLIONAIRE BUSINESSMAN ERIC IRVING III FACING LIFE SENTENCE FOR DESPICABLE CRIMES

Multi-millionaire businessman Eric Irving III, 35, has been arrested for attempted murder of his wife, Iris, 24 and brother, David, 34. Irving is also being charged with coercive control and domestic abuse towards his wife as well as sex trafficking and rape charges. He is also being investigated for the death of Christina Miller in 2002. Furthermore, adding to the horrendously shocking list of crimes, Eric is also facing charges for fraud and bribery.

Police were called after a scene broke out at Irving's home in New Hampshire, which lead to Eric being shot in the chest by the maid. Apparently, the maid was awoken by shouting and went to see what was going on. She saw Eric pointing a gun at his wife and an unknown man, later confirmed to be Irving's brother. The maid was scared and shot Irving in the chest. Irving survived the shot and is being treated in hospital where after he will be transferred to one of New York's high security prisons.

Evidence has been compiled including a cell phone recording of the scene that transpired on the evening of Wednesday 7th November where Irving admitted to killing Christina Miller and threatened to kill his wife if she left him. Irving's MacBook was also taken by police which lead to the discovery of a sex trafficking business led by Irving and accomplices. Also, a diary of Irving's ex-wife was found, which clearly depicted the abuse that she suffered in

Irving's hands. Former girlfriends of Irving have also spoken out and their stories are eerily similar.

"At first, he was really charming; he treated me like a princess, but then he started becoming controlling and began to cut me off from my friends and family. My father didn't like the relationship and threatened him, so Eric broke up with me," ex-girlfriend, Jessica Marks stated.

Irving has also been accused of bribing police officers and psychiatrists. Eminent psychiatrist, Adam Goldman, has had his licensed revoked after being bribed by Irving to forge reports falsely diagnosing his ex-wife of suffering from schizophrenia and borderline personality disorder, deeming her a danger to herself and others in order to take her child from her. Top officials at Fairfield Psychiatric Hospital in California were also bribed.

"I did not think that she (Irving's ex-wife) met the criteria for either diagnosis, but when I voiced my concerns with my superiors, they threatened to have me fired," a psychologist, who does not wish to be named, working at the Fairfield Psychiatric Hospital asserts.

Irving and other associates, including Adam Goldman and Tripp Barrett III were involved in a sex trafficking ring based in New York that involved horrific and brutal attacks on women, which has been called a crime against humanity. Irving lured these naïve women, many of them foreign and knowing little English with "job offers" including a lot of money. These "job offers" included being Irving's slave.

"Men like Eric Irving think that they are above the law. They think that they can get away with the things that others wouldn't be able to. It is people like this who pose a danger to society. Their money, power and status enable them to get away with it for as long as possible. Men like Irving are narcissistic sociopaths who enjoy hurting others, especially vulnerable young women. It is men like him who pray on women who are vulnerable, financially-

disadvantaged and often have strained or distant relationships with family," criminal psychologist, Daniel Bloomstein explains.

Illicit business dealings have also been discovered. It also transpires that Irving has conned clients out of millions of dollars. His father, Eric Irving II, 67, has also been accused of fraud and embezzlement and is being investigated for the suspicious death of the former nanny of his children in 1993. Questions have been asked how police and important officials have allowed for these crimes to be overlooked. This is the one of the biggest scandals to shake America and the world. However, Irving's victims can be assured that now there will finally be justice.

It's all over the news and the papers. There are journalists camping outside of The Plaza where David and I are staying. It's been an exhausting seventy-two hours, speaking to and liaising with police, but I'm relieved. Relieved that this ordeal is over and that this time the police believe me. If it wasn't for the recording and Guadalupe's account, I'm not sure if the police would have believed me.

Whilst Eric and David were arguing, not even noticing that I was in the room, I pressed the record button on my phone and kept it on the whole time. Thanks to the state-of-the-art phone that Eric gave me; the recorder can pick up sounds even from far away, even when it's in your pocket, so Eric's confessions were very clear. The idea came to me all of a sudden. The police would have to believe me if they had the recorded evidence.

Juliana's diary also helped. Apparently one of the police officers at the station read the diary (I forgot that I had left it there) and wanted to investigate these claims, but Chip or Chuck, whose actual name is actually Chuck Harrison, who was head of the Darton police force, refused. Chuck is now being investigated for bribery, neglect and tampering with evidence. It looks like he's going to be saying goodbye to his career.

It's been exhausting recounting my story endless times, but I'm so glad that I'm being taken seriously. The police have been absolutely lovely and have paid for David, Guadalupe and I to stay in The Plaza in New York in order to co-operate with the investigation.

Every time I switch on the news, Eric dominates the headlines. My statement was filmed (with my permission) and now I'm being bombarded by journalists and the media to give interviews and go on television. I've received a lot of support and positive messages from people and women thanking me for speaking out about abuse.

At the moment I don't feel ready to give any interviews or go on television. I'm just so exhausted with everything that's been going on. Today I slept for twelve hours straight. Twelve hours of restful and dreamless sleep. I can't remember the last time that I slept so well. I feel so much better, but obviously everything that has happened has been a huge shock to the system. It's been a lot to process and get my head around. I still can't believe that I'm free. I'll never take my freedom for granted ever again. This still all feels like a dream, but it's going to take time to come to terms with everything.

The best part has been speaking to Elizabeth, Magda and Henry again. They were all in tears when they spoke to me and so was I.

"Oh darling! I can't believe it. I was so desperately worried about you! I thought at first you were ignoring my calls and messages, but I knew that something was wrong when you weren't replying to any of my messages or calls. I went to the police, but they were useless darling. I knew that something was wrong. There was something strange about Eric when I met him at the wedding, but I didn't want to say anything darling. Now I wish that I had! I could kill that bastard! Oh darling I'm so glad you're OK, I've missed you and I know that

I haven't always been the best mother, but I love you darling," Elizabeth cried emotionally. It felt so good to hear Elizabeth's voice. It turned out that she didn't write me that message on my birthday, telling me that she didn't want to have any contact with me. That was Eric. That sick bastard!

Speaking to Magda was also very emotional.

"Irenka, your mother, Henry, Arek and I were so worried about you! I knew that there was something messed up with that chuj!" I laugh. I've missed Magda's Polish curse words!

"I wish I had listened to you."

"It's normal not to listen to those closest to you when you're so loved up. We've all been there. My first boyfriend was a chuj too. My mother warned me and my friends warned me, but I found out the hard way. Sometimes that's the only way to really find out, but no one could have seen how fucked up and sick Eric was. I thank God that you're OK," Magda said.

We both ended up talking on Facetime for over three hours. I told her absolutely everything.

"So I guess you're moving back in," Magda laughs.

"If my room is still available."

"Of course it is. One of Arek's friends is staying there, but I'll kick him out. I missed you so much. It wasn't the same without you. Arek has been constantly complaining how miserable I've been. He was really worried about you too. So when are you coming home?"

"As soon as I can."

EPILOGUE

ONE YEAR LATER

"How many more pictures do you want me to take? I'm sure they all look stunning," I sigh but I'm smiling. Taking lots of pictures of Magda is part of the job description of being her best friend, but I don't mind. Magda has turned into a bit of an Instagram star. She's gotten herself thousands of followers and big brands have been in contact with her to do modelling for them.

Magda keeps saying that I should join social media, but it's not my thing. Plus being catapulted into the centre of media attention has made me want to keep a more private profile. As well as overwhelming messages of support, I've also received a lot of trolling. The comments have been very nasty. I've been called a "gold-digger", "media whore" and a "liar" amongst many insults. I'm perfectly content with my private Facebook account that only contain a handful of people.

It's been an incredibly busy year. I've travelled a lot, especially to America where I've been interviewed on television to tell my story and have been invited to give talks. It's great being a spokesperson for women's rights and abuse, but there's a lot of pressure as well. I don't enjoy being in the spotlight, but I know it's important to talk about it especially if my story will help others. When I'm not doing media work and talks, I paint. In fact, I'm even displaying my art at the Waldenburg Gallery. I was given a huge welcome from Julio!

"Dahling, everything has been so hectic without you. I've resorted to drinking three times as much coffee. God Felicity is useless! Please come back! I'll even ask that you be paid double!"

As a result of my busy schedule, I haven't been able to work full-time, so the role is split between Felicity and myself. One of the perks of the job is being able to work from home and long distances. I never thought that I'd be happy to see Felicity again. She's as nice as pie. She treats me like I'm a celebrity and boasts about me to her friends. She even invited me to go to some swanky bar in Mayfair with her and her other posh friends, but I declined. I don't really have any desire to be friends with her.

The CEO of the gallery took interest in me and wanted me to do an exhibition based on my experience. At first, I didn't know where to start, but soon enough the creativity came flooding back and my desire to paint came back stronger than ever. I've even got my own studio now. I've developed a completely new painting style. Before my paintings were tame and sweet; now they're a lot darker and more complex. My paintings depict wealth, power, control and the role of women. My most renowned painting that has received a lot of interest and acclaim, is a picture that I painted of myself from a photograph that was taken when I was with Eric at the Ritz in London. In the picture, I'm wearing a beautiful red Valentino dress and a diamond necklace, but I don't look happy. I've named the painting *Red Sorrow* and it will be the main painting at the exhibition. *Red Sorrow* has also been printed on the flyer for the exhibition.

It feels so good to have my own career again and feel in control of my life. I've earnt a lot of money through being on television, media work and the exhibition. Enough money to buy my own flat in Hampstead. Magda visits me all the time and often stays over. Elizabeth visits a lot as well.

Our relationship has gotten a lot better. I've learnt to finally let go of the past and move forward. That's what I've been working on with my therapist, Miriam. Initially I didn't want therapy after Doctor Goldman, but Miriam is a life safer! I've definitely needed therapy after everything that has happened with Eric. The whole experience undoubtedly really shook and scarred me. I kept having nightmares about Eric. In one of the nightmares, I would be locked in a room; trapped in a tower, waiting for a prince to rescue me. The prince would come on a white horse and as he came closer, I would see that it was Eric. He would laugh that wicked laugh of his. I would beg him to save me, but he would keep on laughing until he disappeared and I was left in the tower with nobody to rescue me and no way to get out.

I'd have other dreams where a faceless man would be on top of me, strangling me so that I couldn't breathe. Suddenly, I would see the face clearly. Eric's face. In another dream, Eric and I were sailing on the lake. It was a beautiful day and everything was romantic and special, until I fell off the boat. I shouted for Eric to help me. Suddenly I was underwater, trying to get back up to the surface, but something was weighing me down. I'd then realise that it was Eric pushing my head down and trying to drown me.

The nightmares have been difficult to cope with, but they're becoming less frequent now. I find talking to Miriam helps and I know that I can trust her. I even had a family therapy session with Elizabeth. It was Miriam's idea. I was apprehensive at first, especially as Elizabeth always makes everything about her, but surprisingly it really brought a lot of closure and the resentment I felt towards her started to lessen.

I know that Elizabeth will always be Elizabeth, but I know that she's making an effort and that she loves me. There are times when she drives me insane, but all families drive each other mad sometimes. Kevin has had a really positive influence on Elizabeth. I think that he makes her more balanced. Elizabeth is still needy, but nowhere near as much as she used to be. She definitely respects my boundaries more than she used to. She's in a really good place and I can see that Kevin really makes her happy. Even though he doesn't say a lot, I like him a lot. I'm a bit too old for a father figure now, but he is technically going to be my step-father.

Yes, that's right. Elizabeth and Kevin are getting married in a few months. The wedding is going to be in France. Even Seamus is coming and Magda and Arek of course. Elizabeth adores Magda; they both get on like a house on fire. Magda thinks that Elizabeth is the coolest mum ever, though I wouldn't quite go that far.

I think this whole experience has brought the family closer together. I definitely see Henry more often and I'm excited that he's going to be studying biochemistry in London! He's even going to be living with me. I can't wait! I've even added a new addition to the family. A fluffy black and white kitten called Mittens. He was from a litter of one of Elizabeth's cats. The moment I saw him, I knew that I had to have him. There's nothing better than coming home after a long day and snuggling up with my furry little bundle of joy. Having Mittens has definitely helped me to heal and I sleep better with Mittens next to me. Although the experience with Eric was a nightmare, I feel like I've also gained so much from it. I've gained an appreciation of life that I never had before as well as new opportunities and friendships.

I've become close friends with Juliana and we talk every week on FaceTime. She currently lives in New York with Clara. Juliana and I both really bonded over the terrible experience we had with Eric. She's also been in the public eye and has given a lot of interviews and has been on television. The media have really liked our friendship and we've spoken on TV together. Juliana is one of the loveliest and kindest people that I've ever met. The media really took to her plight and paid for her family to come from Brazil to live in America. She was also awarded a big compensation for being falsely diagnosed as mentally unfit and unstable and for being wrongly admitted and kept in a high-security psychiatric unit for two years. Juliana is now fulfilling her dream and has been accepted to study law at a top university in New York.

Clara has turned into the loveliest little girl. Long gone is the terror toddler. Clara is just the sweetest and calmest little girl. She absolutely adores me and always wants to talk to Auntie Iris. Whenever I see her, she doesn't want to let me go. She loves showing me her toys and her drawings. She drew me the loveliest card with what was meant to be a picture of me in a big wobbly heart. I've stuck it on my fridge. I never thought that I would warm to Clara and she to me, but maybe it's because the pressure to be her mother isn't there anymore. Since Clara has been with Juliana, she's been so happy. Maybe Clara was so difficult and avoidant before because she sensed that something wasn't right. Even though she was too young to know what was going on, I think that babies and young children can sense things.

Guadalupe lives with Juliana and Clara. Juliana didn't want to cause a big disruption to Clara's life by separating her from the only caregiver that she had known since she was a tiny baby, plus Clara only understood Spanish. Although Juliana has her family living in the US now and they help with looking after Clara, Guadalupe has become like part of their family. Guadalupe was also a victim in the situation. Eric exploited her as well. It's thanks to Guadalupe that I'm alive and free. I'll always be grateful to her.

I also reached out to Hannah, Rivka's sister. Hannah told me the whole story about what happened to Rivka. Like with Juliana and I, Eric initially swept Rivka off of her feet. Rivka was from a strict Modern Orthodox Jewish family, but rebelled and had a strained relationship with her parents. Their parents didn't approve of Rivka having a relationship with Eric because he wasn't Jewish and threatened to cut her off. Rivka's parents regretted their decision and tried to get back in touch with her, but they couldn't contact her.

Apparently, Eric found out that she was reported missing and pressured Rivka into writing her parents a letter, informing them that she did not wish to have any contact with her family. The case was dropped as the police said that Rivka was an adult and it was clear that she didn't want to be found. When Rivka returned after two years, she was in a very bad way.

She was so traumatised. Eric abused her physically, sexually and mentally and held her captive in his home. He threatened to kill her if she left. She managed to escape and wandered through the New Hampshire wilderness for two days before she managed to find a road where cars occasionally passed. She managed to hitchhike a ride back to New York. The man who picked her up said that she was in a state when he found her. She was starving, thirsty, dirty and in a bad way mentally. The kind driver took pity on her and bought her food and drink and gave her a lift back to New York to her parent's home.

The police were contacted but they didn't do much. They contacted Eric but he lied and claimed that he broke up with Rivka weeks ago but she took it badly and kept harassing and stalking him and was making up lies to get back at him. He also claimed that she purposely went missing in the wilderness as a ploy to get his attention and hope that he'd look for her. Eric also had a restraining order against Rivka forged, so the police dropped the case.

Poor Rivka not only had to deal with the trauma of Eric's abuse, but also him continuing to ruin her life for years after. From afar Eric sabotaged everything in Rivka's life including jobs, relationships and friendships. Rivka felt that she was being followed and that somebody was stalking her. She also received threatening messages, but the police didn't do anything or take is seriously especially as they couldn't trace the sender. They just kept telling her to change her number but it didn't work. Rivka's life was ruined. She was an empty shell of a person and in a constant state of anxiety and fear. Her parents tried to hire a detective but Eric managed to outsmart every move and make it look like Rivka was crazy. Eventually Rivka couldn't take it any more and took her own life.

I'm still in touch with Hannah and I've been helping her with her campaign, *Justice for Rivka*. I often feel survivor's guilt that I was able to escape and expose Eric, but Miriam is helping me to come to terms with it.

You're probably wanting to know what's going on with David and I. We took a break after things got pretty intense with our work schedules and we hardly got to see one other, however there's still strong feelings there from both sides. We're taking things slow. I definitely have no desire to rush anything after my experience with Eric and David understands that and doesn't push me. We speak on FaceTime most days and we try to fly and see each other when we can. David is looking to expand his business in the UK. He loves London and is thinking of moving here.

He's definitely got Magda and Elizabeth's approval; they both adore him. Magda thinks that he's perfect for me and Elizabeth is already planning our wedding in her mind though I'm in no hurry to get married again. When my divorce from Eric came through, I threw a big party to celebrate my freedom and this new chapter in my life.

Everything in my life is going better than ever. I'm loving life. At the moment, Magda and I are in Rome for a girl's trip together. I'm in love with Rome; it's even better than I imagined. It feels nice being chatted up by good-looking Italian men, though I think they're more taken by Magda than me. I don't really mind though. I've definitely learnt to be more confident within myself. Miriam has really helped me work on my self-esteem and has made me realise how strong I am and how far I've come. I think that the whole experience with Eric has toughened me up and made me less naïve about life. However, I still feel that I need closure after what happened. There's one last thing that I need to do. The idea makes me feel sick to my stomach, but I need to come to face with my fears. I need to say what I have to say.

ONE MONTH LATER

A wave of nausea rises in my stomach as the officers scan every inch of me, like at the airport. I'm in New York for Eric's trial, where I'll be giving evidence. It's going to be a big thing with journalists from all over the world coming for this and plus the trial will be filmed. I'm dreading it as not only is it going to be an emotionally strung week, but it also means that the media are going to hassle me.

Today I'm visiting the high-security prison where Eric is being held. The trial starts in two days. Hopefully he'll be jailed for life. There are so many things that I want to get off my chest in order to properly move forward. I need this closure. I know that this time he can't hurt me, however I can't help but feel sick to the pit of my stomach.

Two security guards; one on each side of him, bring him in. Even in the orange prison scrubs, he's still breath-takingly gorgeous. Ironically, he looks like an actor in a prison scene on television. I can understand why I fell for him and why any woman would. Now after everything that he's done, I will never look at him in the same way. I see things that I didn't see before, such as the dark coldness behind those murky green eyes and that cruel smile. I can see the hardness and sharpness in his face. I know better than anybody what lies behind the mask. The mask that had me fooled like everybody else.

I sit down on one end of the long table and Eric on the other side; the guards standing on each side.

"You've got a nerve coming here. I knew that you'd be back and that you'd regret everything that you did. I gave you everything. It's too late now," Eric says bitterly.

"Don't flatter yourself. How can you seriously think that I'd still want you after everything that you did? I hope that you rot in prison and it certainly looks likely."

"My parents have hired the best lawyer and the best defence team in the country so don't look too happy. They're pushing for a plea bargain of four years, probably less, where I'll get my own private room in jail and will be allowed day release. I've done nothing wrong and the whole country will see that I'm innocent."

"Wow you really are a deluded narcissist, aren't you?"

Eric laughs that creepy and throaty laugh of his. "People will see that I'm innocent and that you're the dirty little liar. I've got plenty of women writing to me, convinced that I'm innocent."

"You keep telling yourself that if it makes you feel better, but you're ruined. I feel sorry for you; you really are so pathetic. You're a soulless and heartless monster who will never love anybody as much as you love yourself. You have nothing to offer anyone. The whole world knows what you are. You thought that you could destroy me, but you failed. In the end, I won. I m stronger than ever. Enjoy prison for the rest of your life. Now you'll understand what lack of freedom feels like. Your life may be over, but my life started the moment I escaped your clutches. Have a nice life, though I don't think there's going to be anything nice about it."

Eric is speechless. For the first time ever, he actually looks scared. I can see raw fear in his eyes, like a frightened animal. He just stares at me, completely bewildered. I just get up and leave. After I leave the prison, I run down the street and hail a yellow taxi. Once I'm comfortably in the taxi, I look out of the window and gaze at the cityscape. I'm in awe of New York; it's one of my favourite places in the world. I smile to myself. I feel freer than I've ever felt in my whole entire life.

THE END

Printed in Great Britain
by Amazon

85472545R00214